The Man Who Wasn't There

Michael Hjorth is one of Sweden's best-known film and TV producers, and a renowned screenwriter whose work includes several screenplays of Henning Mankell's *Wallander*.

Hans Rosenfeldt has hosted both radio and television shows, and is Sweden's leading screenwriter and the creator of *The Bridge*, which is broadcast in more than 170 countries.

The Man Who Wasn't There

A Sebastian Bergman Thriller

Translated by Marlaine Delargy

Hjorth & Rosenfeldt

CENTURY

1 3 5 7 9 10 8 6 4 2

Century
20 Vauxhall Bridge Road
London SW1V 2SA

Century is part of the Penguin Random House group of companies
whose addresses can be found at global.penguinrandomhouse.com

Penguin
Random House
UK

Text copyright © Michael Hjorth and Hans Rosenfeldt 2012,
published by agreement with Salomonsson Agency

Translation copyright © Marlaine Delargy 2016

Michael Hjorth and Hans Rosenfeldt have asserted their right to be
identified as the authors of this Work in accordance with the
Copyright, Designs and Patents Act 1988

First published as *Fjällgraven* by Norstedts, Sweden in 2012

This edition first published in Great Britain by Century in 2016

www.randomhouse.co.uk

A CIP catalogue record for this book is
available from the British Library

ISBN 9781780894577 (hardback)
ISBN 9781780894584 (trade paperback)

Typeset in India by Thomson Digital Pvt Ltd, Noida, Delhi

Printed and bound in Great Britain by Clays Ltd, St Ives plc

Penguin Random House is committed to a sustainable future for our
business, our readers and our planet. This book is made from Forest
Stewardship Council® certified paper.

Introducing the National Police Homicide unit, based in Stockholm – also known as Riksmord . . .

Torkel Höglund – Chief Inspector

Ursula Andersson – police forensics expert

Vanja Lithner – investigative police officer

Billy Rosén – investigative police officer

Sebastian Bergman – psychologist and leading criminal profiler

Trolle Hermansson – former Chief Inspector, sacked for using surveillance for personal matters and planting false evidence

Other police

Jennifer Holmgren – junior police officer in the small town of Sigtuna. Temporarily seconded to Riksmord.

2003

This time her name was Patricia.

Patricia Wellton.

New places. New name.

In the beginning, a long time ago, that had been the most difficult thing: reacting when hotel receptionists or cab drivers called her name.

But that was then. Now she became the name on her new ID documentation as soon as she received it. So far only one person had used her name on this trip – the guy at the car rental desk in Östersund, when he came to tell her that the car she had booked in advance had been cleaned and was ready to go.

She had landed on time, just after five o'clock on Wednesday afternoon, and had caught the Arlanda Express into central Stockholm. It was her first visit to the Swedish capital, but she restricted herself to an early and pretty boring dinner in a nearby restaurant.

Just before nine she boarded the night train to Östersund. She had reserved a single occupancy sleeper; she didn't think that anyone would ever catch her, regardless of how many people might provide the police with her description, but she just didn't like sleeping with strangers. Never had done.

Not with the volleyball team, playing tournaments when she was young.

Not during her training, either back at base or out in the field.

Not during assignments.

Once the train had left the station she had gone to the buffet, bought a small bottle of white wine and a packet of peanuts, then settled down in her compartment to read *I Know What You're Really Thinking*, a new book with the slightly bizarre subtitle *Reading Body*

Language Like a Trial Lawyer. The woman who was temporarily known as Patricia Wellton wasn't convinced that trial lawyers were particularly adept at reading body language; she had certainly never met one who stood out in that respect, but the book was at least short and entertaining. Just after one o'clock in the morning she had slipped between the clean white sheets and turned off the light.

Five hours later she stepped off the train in Östersund, made a few enquiries and was directed to a hotel where she ate a leisurely breakfast before heading to the Avis office where she had booked a car. She had to wait, and was offered a cup of coffee while the car was cleaned and checked over.

A new grey Toyota Avensis.

After a journey of just over 100 kilometres, she reached Åre. She had stuck to the speed limit; there was no need to attract unwanted attention, even though it wouldn't change anything in practical terms. The Swedish police weren't in the habit of searching a car involved in a minor infringement of the law, as far as she was aware; perhaps they didn't actually have the authority to do so either. However, if anyone should discover that she was armed, her assignment would be jeopardised. She had no papers giving her the right to bear arms in Sweden; if they found her Beretta M9, they would start digging, and would soon discover that Patricia Wellton existed nowhere else apart from right here, right now. So she slowed down as she drove past the grassy-green ski runs and into the little village on the hill leading down to the lake.

She went for a short walk, chose somewhere to have lunch at random and ordered a panini and a Diet Coke. As she ate she looked at the map. Just over fifty kilometres to go on the E14 before she was due to turn off and leave the car, then a twenty-kilometre stretch. She looked at her watch. Three hours to get there, one to tidy up, two to get back to the car, file her report . . . She would be in Trondheim in time to catch her flight to Oslo, then home on Friday.

She took another stroll around Åre, then got back in the car and headed west. Her work had taken her to many different places, but she had never seen a landscape like this. The soft, rolling mountains, the clearly defined treeline, the sun glittering on the water in the valley down below. She could be happy here. The isolation. The silence. The clear air. She would like to rent a remote cottage here, go for long walks. Go fishing. Experience the light in the summer, sit reading by an open fire on autumn evenings.

Some other time, perhaps.

Probably never.

She left the E14 when she saw a sign with Rundhögen on it pointing to the left. Shortly after that she got out of the car, picked up her rucksack and her map of the area, and began to run.

She stopped 122 minutes later; slightly out of breath, but not tired. She hadn't run at her full capacity, not even close. She sat down and had a drink of water as her breathing quickly returned to normal. Then she took out her binoculars and focused on the log cabin about 300 metres away. She was in the right place. It looked exactly like the picture she had been given by her informant.

If she had understood correctly, the cabin dated from the Thirties: no one would be permitted to build there at the foot of the mountain these days. A company director who had a good relationship with the Royal Court had needed some kind of shelter during his hunting trips, and to be honest you couldn't really call it a house, or even a cottage. What size was it? Eighteen square metres? Twenty? Tiny windows and a small chimney poking up through a felt-covered roof. Two steps leading up to the door, and something resembling a shed about ten metres away. One half had a door, and she assumed it housed an outside toilet. The other side was open, and as there was a chopping block outside, she guessed it was a wood store.

A movement inside the green mosquito net. He was there.

She put down the binoculars, reached inside her rucksack and took out the Beretta. With rapid, practised movements she screwed on the silencer. She got to her feet, slipped the gun into the specially made pocket in her jacket, picked up her rucksack and set off. From time to time she glanced over her shoulder, but there was no sign of any movement. The cabin was a little way off the marked trail, and at this time of year, the end of October, the area wasn't exactly crawling with walkers. She had encountered only two since leaving the car.

When she had less than fifty metres to go, she took out the gun and held it against her leg. She considered the options. Knock on the door and shoot as soon as he opened it, or assume the cabin was unlocked, walk in and take him by surprise. She had just decided to knock when the door opened. The woman stiffened for a second, then immediately crouched down. A man in his forties came out onto the step. Open terrain. Nowhere to hide. The best she could do was to keep still; the least movement could attract his attention. She tightened her grip on the gun. If he saw her she would be able to stand up and shoot him before he had time to run. Forty metres. She would definitely score a hit, probably fatal, but that wasn't what she wanted. If he was injured he might be able to get back into the cabin; what if he had a gun in there? If he spotted her, things would become so much more difficult.

But he didn't give any sign of having seen her. He closed the door, walked down the steps and headed for the shed, where he grabbed the axe from the block and started chopping wood.

She straightened up slowly, edged slightly to the right so that the house would hide her if the man took a break, turned around and gazed out across the beautiful landscape.

The axe. Could it become a problem? Unlikely. If everything went according to plan, he wouldn't have the chance to register her as a threat, let alone attack her with a close combat weapon such as an axe.

She stopped by the house, exhaled, took a few seconds to focus, then walked around the corner of the building.

The man looked surprised to see her, to say the least. He started to ask a question; the woman assumed he was wondering who she was, perhaps what she was doing out there in the middle of the mountains in Jämtland, whether there was something he could help her with.

It was irrelevant.

She didn't understand Swedish, and he was never going to get an answer.

The pistol with its silencer coughed once.

The man stopped moving immediately, as if someone had pressed the pause button while watching a film. The axe slid out of his hand, his knees buckled to the left, his body fell to the right. A dull thud as his eighty kilos hit the ground. His heart punctured by the bullet, he was already dead when he landed, as if someone had simply thrown him down on his side.

The woman walked over to the body, straddled it and calmly took aim at the man's head. One shot to the temple, three centimetres from the left eye. She knew he was dead, but fired another bullet into his brain, about a centimetre from the first.

She slipped the Beretta back into her pocket, wondering whether to do anything about the blood on the ground, or to let nature take its course. Even if someone realised the dead man was missing – and someone would, she knew that – and came up to the little cabin to search for him, they would never find the body. The blood would indicate that something had happened to him, but that was all. Even if they thought the worst, no one's suspicions would ever be confirmed. The man would be gone for ever.

'Daddy?'

The woman drew her gun again as she spun around. A single thought went through her mind.

A child. There weren't supposed to be any children.

2012

He was shaking. Trembling. His head and shoulders. Strange –
he couldn't connect the movement with the dream. Was he
actually dreaming? It wasn't the usual dream, if so. No little hand
in his. No roaring, rushing sound, inexorably coming closer. No
swirling chaos. But he must be dreaming, because someone was
saying his name.

Sebastian.

Yet if he was dreaming, then he was alone in his dream. Alone in
the darkness.

He opened his eyes. Looked straight into another pair of eyes.
Blue. Beneath black hair. Short. Tousled. Above a snub nose and a
smiling mouth.

'Good morning. Sorry, but I wanted to wake you before I left.'

With some difficulty, Sebastian raised himself on his elbows.
The woman who had woken him seemed pleased with her efforts.
She walked over to a full-length mirror at the foot of the bed,
selected a pair of earrings from a nearby shelf and started to put
them on.

The sleep immediately left Sebastian's brain, to be replaced by
the memory of the previous day.

Gunilla, forty-seven, nurse. They had seen each other a few times
at Karolinska Hospital. Yesterday had been his final outpatient
appointment, and afterwards they had left together, gone out on the
town, then back to her place. Surprisingly good sex.

'You're up.'

He realised he was stating the obvious, but he wasn't entirely
comfortable with the situation: lying naked in a strange bed while
the woman with whom he had spent the night was up and dressed,
ready to meet the day. He was usually the one who got up first,

preferably without waking his temporary partner. That was how he wanted it. The less he was required to talk before he left them, the better.

'I have to go to work,' she informed him, glancing at him in the mirror.

'What, now?'

'Yes, now. I'm slightly late, actually.'

Sebastian leaned over and picked up his watch from the bedside table. Almost half past eight. Gunilla was now fastening a slender silver chain around her neck. Sebastian gazed incredulously at her. Forty-seven years old, living in inner-city Stockholm. Surely no one could be that trusting and naive.

'Are you crazy?' he said, sitting up. 'You only met me yesterday. I could take off with half the contents of your apartment.'

Gunilla met his gaze in the mirror, smiling.

'Are you intending to take off with half the contents of my apartment?'

'No. But that's what I'd say even if I was planning to do just that.'

After a final check on her appearance, Gunilla came round to his side of the bed. She sat down and placed a hand on his chest.

'I didn't meet you yesterday. I went out with you yesterday. I've got all the information I need about you at work, so if the TV is gone when I get home, I know where to find you.'

For a moment Ellinor passed through Sebastian's mind, but he quickly pushed the thought away. He would have to devote a considerable amount of time and energy to her before long, but not now. Gunilla smiled at him again. She was joking. Sebastian thought back to the previous day.

She smiled often.

Laughed easily.

It had been a pleasant evening.

Gunilla quickly leaned forward and kissed him on the mouth before he had time to react. She got to her feet, and on her way to the bedroom door she said:

'Anyway, Jocke will keep an eye on you.'

'Jocke?' Sebastian searched his memory for a link to someone called Jocke, but found nothing.

'Joakim. My son. You can have breakfast with him if you like; he's up and about.'

Sebastian simply stared at her. He couldn't think of anything to say. Was she serious? Her son? Here in the apartment? How old was he? How long had he been here? All night? As far as Sebastian recalled, they hadn't exactly been discreet.

'I really do have to go. Thanks for yesterday.'

'Thank you,' Sebastian managed to say before Gunilla left the room, closing the door behind her. Sebastian slid down onto the pillows once more. He heard her say goodbye to someone – presumably her son – then he heard another door close. The apartment was silent.

Sebastian stretched. It didn't hurt. It hadn't hurt for the last few weeks, but he was still enjoying the sensation of moving his body without pain.

He had been stabbed just over two months ago, in the calf and the stomach – by Edward Hinde, psychopath and serial killer. Sebastian had undergone surgery immediately, and things had looked good, very good in fact, but then there had been complications. A drain had been attached to his punctured lung for just over a week, and when it was removed he was told that it would only be a matter of time before he was fully recovered. However, he then developed pneumonia and a build-up of fluid on the lung, so they made another hole in him. Drained off the fluid and stitched him up. He was given instructions on what to do and what not to do, and exercises to do at home. Too many, too difficult, too boring. Anyway, he was better now; yesterday he had been officially declared fit and well.

His body might have recovered, but the Hinde case was never far from his thoughts.

This was partly because Hinde had taken his revenge by having several women killed, women with whom Sebastian had had a sexual relationship. He hadn't been able to carry out the murders himself, of course, because he had been locked up in the secure unit at Lövhaga since 1996, thanks to Sebastian, but with the help of a cleaner in the unit he had still managed to achieve some aspects of his revenge.

Four women dead.

One thing in common.

Sebastian Bergman.

The feeling that the deaths of the four women were his fault was irrational, but he still couldn't completely shake it off. When the

National Murder Squad, known as Riksmord, had picked up the cleaner, Hinde had escaped from prison and abducted Vanja Lithner.

It wasn't a random kidnapping. It wasn't because she worked with Sebastian. No, Hinde had somehow worked out that Vanja was Sebastian's daughter.

Edward Hinde was dead, but sometimes Sebastian thought that if the serial killer had been able to suss out the truth, perhaps others could do the same. He didn't want that to happen; his relationship with Vanja was good now, better than it had ever been.

He had saved Vanja's life out there in that remote house with Hinde, and of course that played its part. Sebastian didn't give a damn whether Vanja put up with him out of gratitude; she was doing it, and that was what mattered. It was more than putting up with him, in fact. She had sought his company twice over the last two months. First of all she had visited him in hospital, and then, when he was discharged but before the pneumonia laid him low, she had suggested they should meet for a coffee.

He could still recall the feeling that flooded his body when he heard her voice.

His daughter was on the phone, wanting to meet up with him.

He hardly remembered what they had talked about. He wanted to commit every detail to memory, every nuance, but the occasion was overwhelming, the situation too much for him. They had sat in a café for an hour and a half. Just the two of them. Her choice. No harsh words. No arguments. He hadn't felt so alive, so present in the moment, since Boxing Day 2004. Time after time he went back to those ninety minutes they had spent together.

It could happen again. It would happen again. He could go back to work. He wanted to go back to work. Sometimes he even found himself longing – for some kind of context, certainly, but the most important thing was to be near Vanja. He had come to terms with the realisation that he would never be her father. Any attempt to take that role from Valdemar Lithner would end with Sebastian destroying everything. He hadn't managed to build up very much so far – one hospital visit and ninety minutes over coffee, but it was something.

Acceptance.

A certain degree of thoughtfulness towards him.

Perhaps even a burgeoning friendship.

Sebastian threw back the duvet and got up. He found his under-pants on the floor and the rest of his clothes on the chair where he had thrown them nine hours earlier. He ran his fingers through his hair, and after a quick glance in the mirror he opened the bedroom door and stood there for a moment. Sounds from the kitchen. Music. A spoon clinking on china. It seemed that Jocke was having breakfast without him. Sebastian slid into the bathroom and locked the door. He really wanted a shower, but the idea of stripping off with Gunilla's son just metres away made the idea considerably less appealing. He used the toilet, then washed his hands and face.

On his way to the front door he realised he would have to walk past the kitchen and that was exactly what he intended to do. Walk past. Jocke would see nothing but Sebastian's back if he happened to look up. Sebastian headed into the hallway, found his shoes and put them on, then started looking for his jacket. No sign.

'Your jacket's in here,' a deep voice announced from the kitchen. Sebastian closed his eyes and swore quietly to himself. He had wanted to seem in a bit of a hurry last night, as if he might not be able to stay, even though they both knew that was exactly what he was going to do. He had taken off his jacket in the kitchen while Gunilla was opening a bottle of wine.

He sighed deeply and went into the kitchen. A young man aged about twenty was sitting at the table with a bowl of cereal and an iPad in front of him. He nodded at the chair opposite without taking his eyes off the tablet.

'There.'

Sebastian had no choice but to walk over and pick up the offending garment.

'Thanks.'

'No problem. Do you want anything?'

'No.'

'Got what you came for?'

The young man still hadn't taken his eyes off the iPad. Sebastian looked at him. No doubt the easiest thing for both of them would have been to let the last remark pass without comment, and for Sebastian to turn around and leave, but why go for the easy option?

'Is there any coffee going?' Sebastian asked as he put on his jacket. If Gunilla's son didn't want him there, then he would stay a while. It made no difference to him. The young man glanced up in surprise.

'Over there,' he said, nodding in Sebastian's direction. Sebastian turned around. There was no sign of a coffee machine or a percolator or a cafetière, but then he spotted a black semi-circular object that looked like a futuristic motorcycle helmet, with a grid under some kind of tap. Buttons on the sides. Metal on top. There were three small glass cups next to it, so Sebastian assumed it delivered some kind of beverage.

'Do you know how it works?' Jocke asked when Sebastian made no attempt to approach the machine.

'No.'

Jocke got to his feet. 'What do you want?'

'Something strong. It was a late night.'

Jocke glanced wearily at him, took a capsule from a rack that Sebastian hadn't even noticed, opened the lid of the machine, put the capsule inside, closed the lid, placed one of the glass cups under the tap, then pressed a button.

'So who are you then?' he said, sounding completely uninterested.

'I'm your new daddy.'

'Cool. A sense of humour. She ought to hang on to you . . .'

He went back to his seat. Sebastian suddenly had the feeling that Joakim had experienced slightly too many mornings with slightly too many strange men in his kitchen. He picked up the cup in silence. The coffee was certainly strong. And hot. He burned his tongue, but finished it off without saying a word.

Two minutes later he was out in the grey September morning.

★ ★ ★

It took him a few seconds to get his bearings and work out the shortest route home. To the apartment on Grev Magnigatan.

To Ellinor Bergkvist.

His lodger, or whatever she might be. How she had ended up living with him was still something of a mystery to Sebastian.

They had met when Hinde started murdering his former sexual partners. Sebastian had gone to see Ellinor in order to warn her, and she had moved in with him. He should have thrown her out right away, but she was still there.

He had spent a great deal of time trying to work out his relationship with Ellinor. There were some things he was absolutely sure of.

12

He definitely didn't love her.

Did he even like her? Not really. But part of him appreciated what she had done to his life. She gave it some level of normality. Against all the odds, he found himself enjoying her company. They cooked together. Lay in bed watching TV. Had sex. Often. She whistled. She giggled. When he got home she told him she had missed him. He didn't want to admit it to himself, because he didn't want it to be true, not with Ellinor, but her presence had meant that, for the first time in many years, he had started to think of his apartment as home.

A home. Dysfunctional, but still a home.

Was he using her? Absolutely. He didn't really give a shit about her. Everything she said went in one ear and out the other. She was like background music. But she had been fantastic during his convalescence. In all honesty, he couldn't imagine how he would have coped without her during the weeks when the pneumonia knocked him for six. She had taken time off from her job at Åhlén's department store, she hadn't left his side. But however grateful he might be for her efforts, it just wasn't enough.

Ellinor was an admiring, almost self-effacing, not entirely sane home help with whom he had sex. Even if his life had become easier and more comfortable in every way, it wouldn't work in the long term. The normality of everyday life that Ellinor had introduced was no more than a construct. A chimera. He had appreciated it for a while, encouraged it perhaps, but now he was certain he didn't want it to go on.

He had recovered, he had slowly begun to establish a relationship of sorts with Vanja, he assumed he had a job. The seeds of something that could become a life.

He didn't need her any more.

She had to go.

It was going to be anything but straightforward.

Shibeka Khan was waiting. As usual. She was sitting by the kitchen window on the third floor of the run-down 1960s apartment block in Rinkeby. Outside the leaves had begun to turn yellow and red. Pre-school children were shouting and screaming in the open spaces between the blocks. Shibeka couldn't remember how many years she had sat watching the children play. Same window, same apartment, different children. Time passed so quickly out there. In her kitchen it felt as if time had stopped.

She loved the hours after her sons had left and before the day got under way. She was active, she had many friends, she worked as a care assistant, she was making excellent progress in learning Swedish, and the previous year she had gained a place on a training course to become a nurse. But, for a couple of hours on those mornings when she was free, she would sit and watch the outside world. It was her other life, somehow. A time when she could show her respect and love for Hamid.

If she thought back, she knew she would be able to work out exactly how many years she had been sitting here, but right now she couldn't do it. She couldn't cope with remembering. Her boys were the clearest sign of the time that had passed. Mehran was in his final year at secondary school now, while Eyer was struggling a couple of years below him; he didn't find things as easy as his older brother. Eyer had been four when Hamid disappeared; Mehran had just turned six. Shibeka recalled his smile when his daddy gave him a new bag, black with two blue stripes, ready for starting school in the autumn. His smile, his dark eyes shining with pride because he was growing up. The warm embrace between father and son. A week later Hamid was gone, just as if the ground had opened and swallowed him up. It was a Thursday. A Thursday a very long time ago.

Oddly enough, she almost missed him more as the years went by. Not in that intense way she had felt at first, but in a more sorrowful, painful way.

Shibeka was suddenly angry with herself. She was back there again, with her memories. Those memories were exactly what she couldn't cope with, but her mind took no notice of what she wanted. It slipped past her attempts to control it, found its way into the past. Found the friends who helped in the search. The children's questions and tears. Hamid's best suit, the one she had picked up from the dry cleaner's, waiting for him in vain. A carousel of images and individual moments, driven by the hope that her mind might find something she had missed, something that would make sense of it all. But she was always disappointed. She had examined every detail thousands of times, every face was already familiar to her. It was pointless.

In order to get away from her whirling thoughts, Shibeka got up and walked to the window. It was Friday and soon he would come, she knew that. After today it would be two days before he came again. Not that she believed he would bring anything, they had stopped replying long ago, but she refused to give up. She had carried on sending them. Practised her Swedish, her handwriting, using the right words, the official language. She had become so skilled at writing to the authorities that many of her friends now asked for her help.

Then she saw him. The postman. As usual he cycled up the path, then began his round in block two, then four and six, then he would come into block eight. Her block.

She waited until she saw him emerge from number six before tiptoeing into the hallway, trying to be as quiet as possible. Not that it was necessary, but she hoped that her silence would somehow increase her chances.

It hadn't helped so far.

She positioned herself by the door, listening. After a while she heard the dull metallic click as the main door opened downstairs. She pictured him walking to the lift, pressing the call button. He always went up to the top first, then worked his way down. That was his routine. Hers was to stand in silence in the hallway.

She pressed her body against the door. Two different sounds. One from outside, far away. One very close – her own breathing and the hum of the fridge in the kitchen. Two worlds, separated by wood and a metal letter box. The steps came closer. For Shibeka, there was something religious about this moment.

Either Allah wanted it to happen, or he did not.

It was that simple.

With a noise that seemed almost deafening the letter box flicked open and a number of colourful flyers fell to the floor in front of her. Everything around her faded away as Shibeka bent down. Beneath the latest special offers from the local supermarket lay a white envelope.

From SVT, Swedish Television.

This time Allah wanted it to happen.

It wasn't her fault.

Well, it was, but it was a mistake. Anyone could make a mistake, couldn't they? Maria was being totally unreasonable. OK, she was tired, but who wasn't? And it wasn't as if Karin had deliberately taken them on a detour.

It was a mistake.

It had all been going so well until a few hours ago, in spite of the rain.

Maria had celebrated her fiftieth birthday in July, and Karin's present had been a trip to the mountains. The Jämtland triangle.

Storulvån – Blåhammaren – Sylarna.

She thought the names alone made the trip seem more exotic than it actually was. The plan was to do some fairly easy walking, nothing too adventurous. Short, manageable routes each day, then a shower, sauna, food, wine, and a proper bed when they reached the various mountain stations. Karin had done some walking in the area with Fredrik many years ago, and thought it would be just perfect. A restorative encounter with nature, with a little luxury thrown in.

Plenty of time to talk.

It was a lovely present. An expensive present. With the journey up there, and four overnight stays, including dinner for the two of them, the cost ran to five figures, but Maria was worth it. She had been Karin's best friend for many years. She had been there for Karin when others had backed away a little. Breast cancer, divorce, the death of her mother. They had gone through it all together. They had also had a lot of fun, of course, but they had never been walking. In fact, Maria had never been north of Karlstad. Now it was time.

Karin had chosen the last weekend that the mountain stations were open: the end of September. This was partly to avoid the relatively busy summer period, and to give Maria time to plan and book a few days' leave from work, but also because Karin was hoping that the autumn would have kicked in, bringing high, clear air and a colourful display provided by the natural landscape. She wanted the mountains to show themselves at their very best to her beloved friend.

She hadn't even considered the possibility that it might pour with rain almost non-stop from the minute they got off the train in Enafors.

'They say it's going to be much better at the beginning of next week,' the bus driver taking them to Storulvån mountain station assured them when they asked if he knew anything about the weather prospects.

'Is it going to rain all weekend?'

There was a certain amount of resignation in Maria's voice.

'That's what they say,' the driver said, nodding sagely.

'Things can change very quickly up here,' Karin said encouragingly. 'It'll be fine, you'll see.'

And their stay had started well. They had arrived at the mountain station, found their room to be simple but pleasant, gone for a walk in the surrounding area, taken an afternoon nap, had a sauna and bathed in a mountain spring, and in the evening they had enjoyed a delicious meal in the restaurant, treating themselves to wine and then a liqueur with their coffee.

This morning they had got up at seven. After breakfast they made a packed lunch and filled a Thermos with coffee before setting off shortly before eight thirty. The sky was clear, but they knew there were no guarantees, so they both had wet-weather gear, sturdy boots and a change of warm clothing with them.

They crossed the river and made their way along the lush valley, which, according to the map in the hotel, was known as Parken. They took their time, chatting and stopping to take photographs or simply to enjoy their surroundings. They were in no hurry. It was only twelve kilometres from Storulvån to Blåhammaren, which was their next stop. After three kilometres they left the mountain birch forest and carried on along a plateau, heading up towards the shelter at Ulvåtjärn. By the time they arrived, they had almost forgotten it was raining. They could see a long uphill climb beyond the shelter, so they took plenty of time over their lunch and coffee. They agreed that the appalling weather was something they would remember and laugh about later. Much later, probably, but one day . . . Eventually they set off again, sometimes chatting away, sometimes walking in silence.

After another hour or so they saw Blåhammaren station up on the top of the mountain. They decided that their top priority was a shower and a sauna, and marched across the barren, sodden land-scape with renewed vigour.

With only a kilometre left to go they stopped, took out their plastic cups and drank from a stream gushing down the mountain-side. Afterwards Karin couldn't remember why she had pulled out the plastic folder containing the booking confirmation. She had opened her rucksack to get a packet of nuts and raisins, and for some reason she had glanced at her documents.

She couldn't make any sense of what she was seeing. None at all. She looked again, realised what had happened and slid the folder back into her rucksack while she worked out the best way to tell Maria what she had just discovered. There was no good way. There was only the truth.

'Shit,' she said, making it clear that she too was disturbed by what she had just read.

'What's the matter?' Maria asked, her mouth full of cashew nuts. 'If you've forgotten something you can go back on your own. In my head I'm already in the sauna with a beer.'

'No, I've just looked at our booking details . . .'

'And?' Maria dipped her cup in the water, took a sip then threw the rest away.

'We've . . . we've gone a bit wrong.'

'What are you talking about? It's up there. Did we miss some-thing along the way?'

Maria attached the cup to her rucksack and got ready to move on. Karin gritted her teeth.

'Blåhammaren is up there. We're supposed to go to Sylarna today.'

Maria stopped dead and stared blankly at her.

'But you've been saying Blåhammaren all the time. From Storulvån to Blåhammaren to Sylarna. That's what you've said all along.'

'I know, that's what I thought, but we're booked into Sylarna tonight and Blåhammaren tomorrow night, according to the book-ing confirmation.'

Maria was still staring at her. Not now. Not when they were so close. Karin was joking. She had to be joking.

'I'm sorry.'

Karin met Maria's gaze, and Maria realised immediately: she wasn't joking. But maybe it wasn't the end of the world? They'd gone a bit wrong; hopefully they would only have to go back about a kilometre.

'So how far away is Sylarna?'

Karin hesitated. She could tell from Maria's tone of voice that she was about to lose her temper, but saying 'not too far' or 'just a bit further' wasn't an option. Once again, only the truth would do.

'Nineteen kilometres.'

'Nineteen kilometres! You've got to be kidding!'

'It's nineteen kilometres from Blåhammaren to Sylarna. We haven't quite reached Blåhammaren, so eighteen. Maybe seventeen.'

'That's another four fucking hours!'

'Sorry.'

'How long does it stay light?'

'I don't know.'

'For fuck's sake, Karin! We'll never get there! Can't they take us up there tonight, and we'll move on to Sylarna tomorrow? Surely we can rebook?'

For a moment Karin felt a wave of relief. Of course, that was the solution. Sensible Maria. Secure in the knowledge that everything was going to be all right, she took out her mobile phone and the booking confirmation.

No, it wasn't possible to rebook, apparently. Everywhere was full. The last weekend they were open was extremely popular. If they had an inflatable mattress or a sleeping mat they could bed down out in the shed, and they could book a table for dinner after 21.30. Karin and Maria had considered the offer, but Maria made it very clear that she wasn't going to sleep in a fucking shed. She grabbed her rucksack and strode off.

To begin with it seemed that Maria didn't want to talk, but after a while Karin came to the conclusion that she was probably beyond speech. In spite of the fact that it was raining and the headwind was biting at their cheeks, Maria's face was greyish-white, and her skin seemed loose, as if she had no facial muscles.

She looked utterly exhausted. She hardly answered when Karin spoke to her; Karin was trying to keep their spirits up, but it was becoming more and more difficult.

It wasn't her fault.

Well, it was, but it was a mistake.

'Hang on, let's have a little rest,' Karin said after they had been walking for an hour and a half.

'Don't be so fucking stupid. We might as well keep going, then at least we'll get there at some fucking point.'

'Have some nuts, they'll give us an energy boost. I need to fill up my water bottle anyway.' She nodded in the direction of the rushing water a few metres below.

'You'll never get down there.'

'Yes I will.'

Karin sounded more convinced than she felt; she was determined to keep up the positivity rather than moaning and giving in to Maria's bad mood. She hoped that dinner and a night's sleep would make her friend feel better so that the whole trip wouldn't be ruined. She walked towards the edge of the plateau. Maria was right, it was going to be difficult to get down; it was pretty steep. Difficult, but not impossible.

Karin took a step closer to the edge and the ground disappeared beneath her feet. She fell, screamed, tried to grab something to hold on to. Her left hand found a grip on the way down, but it broke off and she rolled down the slope along with earth, mud and debris. She banged her right knee and just had time to think that it wasn't going to stop her from reaching Sylarna when she landed about a metre away from the stream. A few small stones followed her down, scattering in the mud.

'Oh my God! Are you OK? What happened?'

Maria sounded worried.

Laboriously Karin hauled herself into a sitting position. Her light-coloured waterproof looked as if she had undergone ten rounds of mud wrestling, but her body seemed to have survived. Her knee was hurting a bit, but that was all.

'I'm fine.'

'What are those sticks you're holding?'

Was she holding something? Karin looked and threw it away with a horrified shriek.

21

It was a hand.

A skeletal hand.

What Maria had thought were sticks were the bones of the forearm, snapped off at the elbow. Karin looked up at the slope where she had fallen. A metre below where Maria was standing she could see the rest of the arm protruding, and next to it there was a skull embedded in the mud.

Karin had the distinct feeling that their trip was ruined anyway.

Ellinor Bergkvist.

Valdemar Lithner sighed. She had turned up for the first time just over two months ago. Called the company and booked an appointment. Insisted on seeing him, apparently. The point of her visit had been less than clear, and the subsequent meetings hadn't exactly helped. Something to do with a business she was hoping to start; she needed advice and assistance. He had done his best, but nothing had happened. Ellinor was no closer to running her own business today than she had been the first time he met her. He had asked her why she wanted to see him in particular, and she told him he had been recommended by an acquaintance of hers. Valdemar had wondered who that might be, but she had been extremely vague. It turned out that she was extremely vague on a number of issues, such as what kind of business she was thinking of and what she was going to do.

But today was to be their final meeting, and then he could forget Ellinor Bergkvist for good. On his way to the door he pressed his hands against his aching back and stretched his spine as best he could. Ellinor was waiting in the small reception area and got to her feet as soon as she saw him.

'Good afternoon, Ellinor. Welcome.'

'Thank you.'

She smiled at him as they shook hands. He showed her into his office and she took off her red coat before sitting down opposite him with her oversized handbag on her knee.

'I've brought the papers you gave me,' she began, reaching into her bag.

'Ellinor,' Valdemar interrupted, and there was something about the way he said her name that made her stop rummaging and look up. 'I don't think you should continue to be our client.'

Ellinor stiffened. Had he become suspicious? Had she made a mistake? Had he somehow worked out that she wasn't there for financial advice, but because . . . why was she there, actually? She had just wanted to see who he was. What he was. It had been exciting, sitting there opposite a criminal who was guilty of fraud, who had threatened her man and possibly been involved in murder.

When she had moved in with her beloved Sebastian, she had found a carrier bag full of papers. Sebastian had seemed stressed when she mentioned the bag, and had told her to throw it away. Destroy it.

She hadn't done that.

She had read the contents. Recognised a name – Daktea Investments – and realised that Valdemar Lithner was definitely a criminal. She was convinced that no one who had been involved in the tangled affairs of Daktea could be innocent; there had been so much about it in the papers a few years ago.

When Sebastian was at home suffering from pneumonia, she had once asked him about Valdemar. She had just wondered who he was, nothing else. Sebastian had been furious, demanded to know where she had heard the name, what she knew. She had told the truth, said she had looked in the carrier bag. Then she had lied in response to his next question. Assured him she had thrown it away.

At the same time, she had been pleased. Sebastian's strong reaction proved that she was on the right track. He seemed to be afraid of Lithner. She really was helping Sebastian by investigating Valdemar Lithner under her own steam, with the aim of eventually bringing him to justice. But now it was over.

'Why not?' Ellinor asked, shuffling towards the edge of her chair, ready to flee if Valdemar turned violent.

'Because I don't think I can help you. This is our fourth meeting, and you haven't even started your business yet.'

'A few things have got in the way . . .'

'Let me make a suggestion. You get your business up and running, then, when you've got all the paperwork in place, come back and we'll see what we can do.'

To his amazement Ellinor nodded and got to her feet.

'You're right, that's a good idea.'

Valdemar didn't move. For some reason he had expected resistance. After all, she had spent more than six hours in his office. She had paid for his time, and got nothing out of the experience. He had assumed she would try to cling on. He didn't really know why; she just seemed to be that type.

However, she was picking up her coat and heading for the door.

'Thanks anyway. I've learnt a lot,' she said.

'Thank you – I'm glad you think so.'

Ellinor smiled at him as she left the office. She stopped in reception to put on her coat, her thoughts in a whirl. Had he seen through her?

She took a deep breath. Steadied herself. Looked calmly at the situation. She was still registered at her old address, there was no link between her and Sebastian unless Lithner had followed her, which seemed unlikely. There was probably nothing to worry about; he really didn't think he could help her. She wasn't going to get any further; it was time for the professionals to take over. Sebastian would never need to know that she was responsible for Valdemar Lithner's disappearance. It would be her secret gift to him. A token of her love.

Then nothing would ever threaten their happiness.

Shibeka was pacing around the apartment. She was excited, yet at the same time she had waited so long for something like this that now it was actually happening, she was almost afraid. She sat down, picked up the letter that she had carefully placed on the kitchen table, and read it again. The text covered only the middle of the page. It seemed strange that something so important could be so short.

Dear Shibeka,

Thank you for your letter – sorry it's taken so long to reply. The production team have evaluated the information you gave us, and would very much like to get in touch with you. It would be great if we could meet, with no obligation on either side of course; this would give us the opportunity to gain a better understanding of your story and to decide how to proceed on the subject of your husband's disappearance.

Please call me.

Lennart Stridh
Reporter
Investigation Today

At the bottom of the page there was an address and a couple of telephone numbers. Shibeka put down the letter. Should she tell her sons about it? Probably not. As far as she was concerned, the spark of hope could flare up and die away, it had happened many times over the years, she was used to it. But her children had to be protected. It had been painful enough for them, growing up without a father. But she wasn't sure. Could she really do this on her own? She read the letter again, as if to see if it could provide any answers, but it led back to the same questions. What did 'with no obligation on either side' mean? Was it just a way of not taking responsibility? What would they think of her story? It was true, but would that be enough? Could she really meet this man alone? Her family and friends wouldn't approve. They would be right, in principle, but she didn't want anyone with her. They would hold her back, speak on her behalf, make her sit in silence, and then everything would have been in vain. She didn't want that. She wanted to hear her own voice this time, make it count. Her friends knew how she had struggled, refused to give up, but would they understand that this was Sweden, a country where women could meet men without a chaperone? Unlikely.

So no one else could know. She went into the hallway and sat down next to the black cordless telephone. It was on a small table, and she remembered when she and Hamid brought it home. A telephone. They had bought it in the big department store down by the area that was now known as Bromma Blocks; she had never seen so many television sets in her life, and at first she couldn't believe her eyes. An entire wall of moving images. Row upon row of boxes containing everything from headphones to DVD players. The excess. She and Hamid had looked at one another and smiled at the thought of all those people who thought they had lots of money, but in fact had so little.

They had bought a telephone and the cheapest TV they could find. Said had given them a lift home. She remembered sitting in the back of the car, eagerly turning over the white box with a picture of a telephone on it. She couldn't wait to get it open. Hold the phone in her hand.

They had spent many evenings trying to reach friends and relatives in Kandahar. It had always been difficult. Their mobiles rarely worked, and if Shibeka and Hamid did get through, the connection could be broken at any moment. However, she still remembered those times with a warm glow.

The link to home.

The cheerful voices in the background.

They had sat there, side by side, she and Hamid. She made tea, he tried the different phone numbers and together they hoped. More often than not there was no answer, but when they did get through they would shout for joy, and she would get as close as she could just to hear the words from their former home. He allowed her to do that. Allowed her to listen. Smiled at her. Stroked her hand as she sat there in silence, listening.

Hamid. Her husband.

She picked up the telephone and stared at it. She rarely used it these days. Her contact with the old country was restricted to those occasions when she was visiting friends, sitting in the kitchen with the women while the men did the talking. It wasn't the same thing, not at all. But she couldn't make the calls herself; they wanted to talk to a man. Not to her. That was just the way it was.

She dialled one of the numbers at the bottom of the letter. A mobile number. She knew that Swedes mainly used their mobiles, so she tried that one first. It rang twice, then a male voice answered.

'Lennart Stridh.'

At first she didn't dare speak. She had almost hoped he wouldn't answer so that she would have more time to think through the conversation rather than face the reality, but the man on the other end was expecting a response.

'Hello? This is Lennart Stridh.'

She felt compelled to speak, but there was no strength in her voice.

'Hello, my name is Shibeka Khan, I got a letter from you.'

'Sorry? I can't hear you very well.'

She took a deep breath. She didn't want the man to lose interest in her.

'A letter. I got a letter from you. My name is Shibeka Khan.'

'Hi, thanks for calling,' he said with renewed energy in his voice. 'As I said in the letter, we're quite interested in your husband's disappearance. I can't promise anything, but we think it's worth looking into.'

The man spoke quickly, and she couldn't follow everything he said, but she definitely recognised the word 'interested', so she tried to sound as if she understood perfectly. She felt that was important so that he didn't simply dismiss her.

'Good.'

'Can we meet up?'

'Now?'

'No, not now. But . . .' There was a silence, and Shibeka thought she could hear him leafing through a diary. 'Monday at eleven – is that OK?'

28

Suddenly she was scared.

'I don't know.'

The man on the other end was silent for a few seconds, then he went on: 'You don't know, or you can't make it?'

'I don't know. I think.' Shibeka wasn't sure how to explain herself. She wanted to meet him, but it felt wrong. 'Would it be just the two of us? At this meeting?'

'Unless you need an interpreter, but it doesn't sound as if you do. Your Swedish is very good.'

'Thank you, I do try.'

She hesitated. In Lennart Stridh's world there was nothing strange about a woman on her own meeting a man she didn't know. In this country it was perfectly acceptable, and she lived in this country now. Shibeka took a deep breath and seized her courage in both hands.

'Where?'

'There's a coffee shop outside Åhlén's at the central station. Café Bolero.'

A coffee shop. Of course. Swedes met up for coffee. Shibeka realised she should have had a pen and paper ready to write it all down, but she ought to be able to remember Café and something beginning with B.

'What was the name of the place again?'

'Café Bolero. Just by Åhlén's City.'

'Thank you.'

'Eleven o'clock?'

'Eleven o'clock, fine.' She felt a bit stupid, simply repeating everything he said, but the man didn't seem to think it was odd.

'See you there,' he said, ending the call.

Shibeka sat quietly for a moment before she put down the phone. Things had gone better than she could ever have imagined.

It was the same apartment, and yet it wasn't. Everything was in its usual place. The wooden floor still creaked just outside the kitchen when she took her breakfast outdoors. Even the plants on the windowsill were still growing, just as if nothing had happened. But Ursula no longer felt at home. It was as if she was in an unfamiliar setting, even though she knew every nook and cranny, every square centimetre. Perhaps it was the sounds she missed, the fact that his jacket was no longer tossed on the brown armchair, or that the coffee machine wasn't on when she got home. She didn't know. Feeling like a stranger in her own home annoyed her, and her logical self tried to fight back, to make the situation comprehensible by playing it down.

Things weren't so different after all.

Most of the noise in the apartment had gone when Bella moved to Uppsala and it hadn't bothered her then, she tried to tell herself. Her relationship with Mikael had been running on empty for the last few years anyway. They had drifted apart, to be honest. Couples separated, got divorced, found new partners all the time. What had happened was perfectly natural.

But all the logic in the world couldn't hold back the painful realisations whirling around inside her. It wasn't the loneliness that bothered her; she could handle that. It was the way it had happened. The fact that he had left her. It was impossible to grasp. He was supposed to fight for her.

Not just disappear.

Not Mikael.

She had always thought that if one of them was going to walk away, it would be her.

And yet it had been Mikael. Without even trying to salvage their relationship. With no regrets, apparently. Quickly and decisively in a way she hadn't known he was capable of.

He had said that he had broken off his relationship with the other woman. Broken off, not ended. Taken a break because he wanted to sort everything out with Ursula before he moved on. That hadn't actually been true. He didn't want to sort anything out, he just wanted to tell her, make the odd excuse, then leave.

He had gone to her.

To Amanda.

He had been reasonable, gentle but determined. He hadn't given her the slightest chance to find her way back into his heart; that door was closed. He had taken her hand to comfort her as he broke the news. She knew that he was avoiding details that might hurt her, but at the same time he wasn't afraid of the truth.

Ursula loved him at that moment.

At least she thought she did. It was a feeling she had never experienced before, powerful and contradictory. As if the alphabet had suddenly acquired a new letter she had never seen before.

She had wanted to scream, throw things at him. Kiss him. Plead with him. She did nothing. Love, anger and surprise formed an absurd and totally debilitating combination. She had simply sat there and nodded. Let go of his hand and said she understood, although in fact she didn't understand at all.

He had stayed on in the apartment for a while, but more and more of his things disappeared, and his visits became shorter and shorter, until one day they stopped altogether. He had moved out.

Left her.

The two of them had faced many challenges over the years. His dependent personality and her inability to cope with a close relationship had been the two biggest obstacles they had had to overcome. In the past they had always sorted things out, found their way back to one another, discovered that their differences somehow became pieces of a puzzle that fitted together.

Not this time.

He was in love, he said.

For the second time in his life. This time with someone who gave back as much as she got.

Ursula knew she would never be able to compete with that.

So she let him go.

★ ★ ★

In the days that followed her conversation with Mikael, Ursula didn't leave the apartment. She just couldn't do it. After the initial shock there were so many questions, so many things to take care of. Her main concern was how, and above all who, was going to tell Bella. The more she thought about it, the more certain she became that it ought to be her, otherwise she could easily lose not only her husband, but her daughter too. Bella had always been Daddy's girl. The two of them had built up an easy, close relationship over the years. Obviously Ursula had been there, but slightly to one side. Sometimes.

When she wasn't working.

When she and Bella didn't get into one of their frequent arguments.

When Ursula wanted to make the effort. Then and only then.

On her terms.

She had tried to avoid facing up to this final truth for as long as possible, but it came to her in the empty, alien apartment.

Ursula suddenly realised that she needed to create a new relationship with Bella, one that was more real, something of her own, not a remnant left in Mikael's wake. She couldn't lean on him any more.

She was alone now.

Perhaps being the one to tell Bella the truth would be a promising start. At least she thought it might. She called Mikael and asked if she could explain the situation to Bella. He said yes right away, thought it was a sensible idea.

So, at the age of fifty she was facing a task she had never been any good at.

Meeting her daughter as a person.

As a mother.

Properly.

It took almost twenty-four hours before she plucked up the courage to call her.

★ ★ ★

They had met at a coffee shop within walking distance of the university, at Bella's suggestion. It was one of those American-inspired places where the cookies and muffins were gigantic and the coffee was served in cardboard cups. Ursula arrived early, ordered a latte and sat down by a window. She watched the cars and the people hurrying by. It was before lunchtime, and the place was half empty. Ursula sipped her hot coffee and tried to focus, to stop her thoughts flying off in all directions. But when she succeeded, there was only one issue on her mind. Was she going to lose Bella? Was it her fault? Why couldn't she be like every other mother? Why couldn't she . . .

Suddenly Bella was standing behind her. Ursula hadn't even seen her walk in.

'Hi, Mum.'

Ursula tried to smile, but probably failed, judging by her daughter's reaction. Bella sat down, her expression serious.

'What's happened? You're very pale.'

Ursula told her. Tried to be fair, not to blame Mikael. It was a joint decision, she said. Something they had both agreed. It sounded less than convincing, but she felt it was the right thing to do. It was essential to strike a balance. She mustn't force Bella to take sides, because she knew exactly who her daughter would choose.

They walked back to the station together. Mother and daughter. Ursula couldn't remember the last time they had done that. Bella was tall now. An adult, sensible and talented, with a capacity for closeness that enveloped Ursula. The tension had left her body, and she was enjoying the moment. She felt as if they were closer than they had ever been.

The feeling was still there as they stood on the platform next to Ursula's train back to Stockholm. Bella had asked if she wanted to stay overnight; she could easily make up the spare bed in her room. For a second Ursula considered surprising Bella by saying yes, but then she decided against it. Things had gone much better than she had expected, and she didn't want to risk seeming too pushy. She said she had to work, but promised to come and see Bella again soon. Very soon.

'Will you be OK?' Ursula asked, resisting the urge to stroke her daughter's cheek.

'Of course.'

Bella leaned forward and gave her a hug. Ursula couldn't remember the last time that had happened either. A long time ago, anyway.

'I'm not as surprised as you might think,' Bella said as she moved away.

Ursula stiffened. A little voice inside her head was yelling at her, telling her just to smile in response. Smile and get on the train. Hold on to that good feeling. She didn't listen.

'What do you mean by that?'

'It's just . . . well, I talk to Dad pretty often, and . . .'

Bella looked away, clearly uncomfortable with the situation. Ursula tried to work out the significance of what Bella was saying; she could come up with only one explanation.

'You knew he was seeing someone else?'

'No, I didn't. Absolutely not.'

'But you knew he was intending to leave me?'

'No, not at all. I promise, I had no idea.'

'But you said you weren't all that surprised. So you must have been expecting it.'

'Mum—'

'I suppose you understand why he's left me, because I'm . . . what, someone it's impossible to live with?'

'Mum, this is all wrong.' Tears sprang to her daughter's eyes. Bella held out her hand, and to her astonishment Ursula saw herself take a step back, then turn and walk towards the train. 'Don't go!' Bella shouted after her. 'Catch the next train, let's talk about this!'

But she hadn't listened. Hadn't dared to stay. Somewhere deep down inside, that little voice was telling her that Bella had been absolutely right.

Ursula had carried on going to work as normal, but hadn't told anybody what was going on. What was she supposed to say? That her husband had left her? No chance. She had never been the kind of person who shared her thoughts and problems over coffee and cake. Among her colleagues she was closest to Torkel, her boss and her lover, but she couldn't tell him anything. He would misinterpret the situation, would start hoping that their on/off sexual relationship could become something more. As long as Mikael had been part of her life, Torkel himself had closed the door on anything deeper, but with Mikael out of the picture, that would change. So she didn't say a word. It was easier than she had expected simply to play along, pretend nothing had changed.

She had tried to concentrate on the job, which had proved to be more difficult than usual. The team was on standby, but she came in early every day. Sorted out her desk. Went through case material, catalogued old documents. That saw her through about a week, then she was at something of a loss.

Vanja normally shared Ursula's frustration when things were like this; she wasn't made for a quiet life either. However, she had just applied for a three-year advanced training programme in profiling offered by the FBI in the USA, and she was spending all her time preparing for the tough tests involved in the application process. Ursula hardly saw anything of her, and when she was around she had her nose stuck in a book, or was glued to her computer screen.

Billy was back at work following the fatal shooting of Edward Hinde, but he didn't spend much time in the office. There were rumours of a new girlfriend.

Salvation came in the form of Sven Dahlén, one of her ex-colleagues from SKL, the National Forensics Lab in Linköping, who had been recruited to the recently formed Cold Case Group within the National Crime Unit. A team of six investigators, including Sven, had been working in Skåne for some time, but now the plan was to reproduce their success on a national level, with a high public profile, and Sven had been asked to take charge of forensics.

His office was on the floor below Riksmord, and they shared lab space.

Ursula started to find reasons to go downstairs. Happened to walk past Sven's room. Asked if he'd like a coffee.

Chatted.

Took an interest in the details, offered advice.

Made sure she was around at regular intervals.

It wasn't long before the first question was asked.

The team was looking into a murder in Haninge, eight years ago. Could she help?

She could.

Torkel realised what she was doing, but said nothing. An Ursula who had something to do was far preferable to an Ursula pacing around like a tiger in a cage that was much too small, waiting for someone to sink her teeth into. So he said nothing when she more or less started working in Sven's department, without even running it past him.

Late nights. Early mornings. All the time.

Sven told her to go home, take care of her family. Ursula lied and said everything was fine.

It was just her and Mikael, and her husband understood. He always had done, she assured Sven with a smile.

So she kept on working, well aware that she was using her job as a shield to keep everything else at bay.

Alexander Söderling got up from his expensive, ergonomically designed desk chair and went over to the window. A few people were strolling along Drottninggatan in spite of the late hour. He glanced at his watch. The children were fast asleep, and so was Helena. He hadn't seen any of them while they were awake today.

The whole day had been nothing but a long series of meetings. Things were going well, and had been for a while. The company was growing, but so was his workload. He had got back to the office at six and thought about just ignoring the lot of it and going home. He could give Selma a lift to her riding lesson for once. Stay and watch. Spend an hour with Helena before it was time for bed. It was an appealing prospect, but he settled on a compromise. He would disregard the pile of paperwork his PA had placed on his desk before she left, but he would go through his email inbox. Half an hour. He would probably miss the riding lesson, but he would have the hour with his wife.

Forty-five minutes later he was done, and feeling very pleased with himself. He decided to skim through the latest news before he went home.

It was at the top of the very first page.

MASS GRAVE IN THE MOUNTAINS.

The article didn't provide much more detail. A couple of walkers had stumbled upon a grave. Several bodies that had been there for a long time. Alexander had checked out other sites: the same information, nothing more. Not a word about who they were, how many bodies, how long they'd been there. Alexander sat back and dropped his shoulders, which he had subconsciously drawn up to somewhere around his ears. Exhaled, tried to relax, think clearly.

They had been found.

Or had they?

It must be them, surely. How many mass graves could there be in Jämtland?

He made himself a cup of coffee. He couldn't go home now. Drank his coffee standing by the window gazing out over Drottninggatan, then went back to his computer. He spent another hour or so surfing the net, checking whether the articles had been updated, whether any further information had been released, but there was nothing. Tomorrow, presumably. The question was, what should he do now? Make a call? They probably knew already, but if he didn't make contact it might look as if he wasn't on the ball. Careless. Getting in touch might be the wrong thing to do, but failing to do so would be even worse, he concluded.

He got up and went over to the window again. It had started raining. The few people who were out and about began to hurry, hunched against the strengthening wind. Alexander picked up his mobile. Made the call. It was answered on the third ring. Music in the background.

'Yes?'

Nothing more from the woman on the other end. Alexander recognised the music: Lykke Li, 'Possibility'. They played a lot of Lykke Li in the office.

'This is Alexander Söderling,' he said, just to be on the safe side. It had been a long time since they spoke.

'I know.'

In any other conversation, Alexander would have politely enquired how the other person was, asked how things were going, but the curt responses so far suggested that this wouldn't be appreciated right now. He got straight to the point.

'Have you read the papers?'

'What am I supposed to have read?'

'They've found a mass grave in the Jämtland mountains.'

'I didn't know that.'

'It's on the Internet.'

'Right.'

Alexander stood in silence, watching the raindrops racing down the window, forming a pattern that looked like veins. He was expecting a follow-up question, what was in the reports, for example, but it didn't come.

'I think we can assume it's them,' Alexander clarified, pointlessly. As he had said to himself earlier, how many mass graves could there be in Jämtland?

'Right.'

Nothing further this time either. It was clear that the woman on the other end of the phone had no intention of driving the conversation. She didn't even seem particularly interested; Alexander was beginning to get the feeling that the call had been a mistake.

'I'll try and find out whether the police know who they are,' he went on, trying to show some initiative.

'And if they do?'

'I don't think we have much to worry about. Everything was extremely . . . professional.'

'So what do we do?' The woman paused briefly. 'Or rather you, not we.'

'Nothing at the moment.'

'Nothing?'

'I think that's the best approach.'

'So why did you call me?'

'I just wanted to . . . I thought you'd want to know that they'd found the grave.'

'I want to know if we have problems. Do we have problems?'

'No,' Alexander replied.

'Then I don't want to know.'

Silence again. Total silence. Even Lykke Li had disappeared. The conversation was over. Alexander put down his mobile and gazed blankly at the street below.

Did they have problems?

Not yet, but Alexander was fairly sure they soon would have.

The call came just after seven thirty on Monday morning. Torkel had just fetched his first coffee of the day. He moved the mouse to wake his computer from sleep mode, took a sip of the hot drink and answered.

'Torkel Höglund.'

The caller introduced herself as Superintendent Hedvig Hedman. Torkel immediately placed her in Jämtland, not because he had the names of all the local superintendents at his fingertips, but because Hedvig Hedman had just been reported to the Attorney General for something she had said about a member of her team. It was unlikely to go any further, but her name was fresh in Torkel's mind.

'How can I help you?' he asked, taking another sip of coffee and settling himself in his chair.

A few minutes later he hung up.

Six bodies.

Out on the mountain.

They had been there for quite some time, apparently.

Hedvig Hedman had begun by saying that they had found a mass grave. Torkel wasn't sure if six bodies really constituted a mass grave, but the four major newspapers had used the term, so Torkel assumed they did. Not that it mattered.

It was enough to get them up there.

He left the office. Christel, his PA, hadn't yet arrived, so he left her a note asking her to check flights to Östersund and get back to him as soon as possible.

Back in his room he sank down in his chair and finished off his coffee as he considered his next move.

He needed to gather the team, but there were two things to think about.

First of all, Vanja's application to join the FBI training programme. She had passed the first round of the selection process, and was now down to the last eight. There were three places. Torkel was 100 per cent convinced that one of those places had Vanja's name on it. He had given her the best possible reference – with mixed feelings, he had to admit. He thought the world of Vanja, she was an outstanding police officer, an important member of the team, and she really deserved the opportunity to develop and to progress in her career. But that meant he would lose her; she would be away for three years.

Three years without his best investigator.

Torkel had already started searching for her replacement, temporary or permanent, depending on whether she decided to come back to them after her time in the USA, or whether she opted for a different route. He hadn't advertised the post or made it generally known that he was looking, partly because there was a microscopic chance that Vanja wouldn't get in, and partly because he wanted to avoid a long drawn out recruitment process which, in the worst case scenario, might involve dealing with hundreds of applications. It was his intention to respectfully ignore years of service, formal qualifications and anyone who might have priority for some reason. No doubt this contravened any number of employment regulations, but he didn't give a damn.

Riksmord was a team.

His team.

He intended to choose the person he wanted. In the end, who you were mattered far more than what you'd done. He wanted an outstanding, conscientious police officer, of course, but that wasn't enough. The right candidate needed something else, something indefinable. They would have to be able to fit in. Torkel knew several experienced officers who had worked for five, ten, twenty years, all of whom would probably do an excellent job from a procedural point of view, but he couldn't really see any of them as a member of his team. In addition, most of them were men, and Torkel was fairly sure he was going to replace Vanja with another woman. Not because of any quotas or some equality ruling, but for the simple reason that, in his experience, mixed teams worked better. He knew where this was going. He kept thinking back to a letter from a young woman who had just finished her cadet training in Sigtuna.

Jennifer Holmgren.

She had written to him a few weeks ago, on a purely speculative basis, explaining why she would really like to work for Riksmord, and something about her letter had immediately appealed to Torkel. It had been full of commitment, a desire to develop, to grow, to work with the best in order to learn rather than to climb the career ladder.

When Vanja told him she had applied to Quantico, Torkel had called Jennifer in for a brief interview. He didn't seriously think she was a potential replacement, but he was curious.

She hadn't disappointed him. She was sociable, driven, committed. Torkel had the impression that she had to make a real effort to stop herself from bubbling over with enthusiasm when she talked about what she wanted police work to encompass. She reminded him of Vanja when he had first met her, and that was the best recommendation he could give. Obviously her youth and total lack of experience counted against her, and no doubt he would get plenty of criticism on that point if he decided to give her a try. However, you could also say that she wasn't stuck in any ingrained patterns of behaviour, that she would never object to new ideas on the basis that 'We've always done it this way.' She was open and malleable.

Vanja would hear in a week or so, and leave in November. It wouldn't be out of order to bring in someone who could perhaps take her place at this stage.

Torkel decided to call Sigtuna and see if they would release Jennifer.

The other issue he needed to consider was Sebastian.

Sebastian Bergman.

Hopeless, but brilliant.

During the last two investigations he had managed to worm his way into the team. None of them had really wanted him there, but he had done some good work on both occasions, there was no denying it. Particularly in the Hinde case – he had saved Vanja's life.

At the same time, his presence created conflict that the group didn't need. A murder investigation was always stressful, and there was no doubt that with Sebastian on board it became even more difficult than necessary. With his arrogance, his egotism and his total lack of interest in his surroundings, he was a constant irritant. He was like a black hole, threatening to suck the energy out of every-one in the room and destroy the group from the inside.

A brilliant source of conflict.

For and against.

Should he bring Sebastian in once more?

Decisions, decisions.

If Vanja hadn't accepted Sebastian, Torkel wouldn't even have considered it, but the last time he spoke to her she had almost seemed to be looking forward to working with him again. Billy liked him, and so did Torkel, deep down, although it sometimes drove him crazy to see how difficult his old friend made things for himself in any given situation. Ursula had the ability to focus on what was important rather than allowing her-self to be provoked. What annoyed her most was being presented with a fait accompli rather than feeling she was part of the decision-making process. If he just explained what he was thinking, Ursula wouldn't oppose him.

At first glance, six bodies in a mass grave didn't exactly cry out for Sebastian Bergman's skills.

But six bodies meant either a serial killer or a mass murderer, and there was no one in Sweden who knew more about that particular subject than Sebastian.

Decisions, decisions.

Torkel knew what he was going to do.

First Sigtuna, then he would go down and see Ursula, make her feel part of it all. Then Vanja, Billy, and, finally, Sebastian.

Decision made. He reached for the telephone.

'You have to move out.'

Sebastian pushed the butter knife back into the pack of Bregott on the table and turned to Ellinor, who was putting her coffee cup in the dishwasher. He had chosen his moment with care. Under no circumstances could he cope with forty-eight hours of tears, reproaches, hysterical discussions and fury – which he knew would end with him physically ejecting her from the apartment – so he waited until after Ellinor had had the weekend off. Right now she was about to leave for work; she was the conscientious type and there was no chance that she would stay at home with such short notice. If she even took in what he said, which was by no means certain.

'You're so funny,' she said without even glancing at him, which confirmed his suspicions.

'No, I'm serious. You have to go, otherwise I'll kick you out.'

Ellinor closed the dishwasher, straightened up and looked at him, an amused smile on her lips.

'But, sweetheart, how would you manage without me?'

'I'd manage perfectly well,' Sebastian said, keeping the irritation out of his voice. He hated being spoken to as if he were a child.

'You're so funny,' she repeated as she came over to the table and gave his cheek a quick stroke. 'You need a shave, you're all scratchy,' she said with a smile. She bent down and kissed him on the mouth. 'See you tonight.'

She left the kitchen and Sebastian heard the bathroom door close. The all-too familiar sounds told him she was brushing her teeth. He sighed. Nothing had changed. What had he expected? With Ellinor, every conversation that wasn't about the banalities of everyday life went round in circles. She never listened to him, to what he was actually saying. She interpreted everything to her own advantage. If it wasn't possible to transform what he said into something positive, she simply chose not to take it in. Like now.

You have to move out.

Those words were not open to interpretation. They were crystal clear. They were the reality.

But reality was neither a constant nor an exact science in Ellinor's world. She could turn it into whatever she wanted. He had let her get away with it far too often, but not any more. This time he was going to make her listen. He let his irritation and frustration come to the surface; he got to his feet and made for the bathroom. He opened the door – she never locked it – and stood in the doorway. Ellinor met his gaze in the mirror.

'Don't you want to know where I was on Thursday night?'

Ellinor carried on brushing, but her expression in the mirror was clear. No, she didn't want to know.

'Don't you want to know why I didn't come home?'

Ellinor spat in the hand basin, replaced her toothbrush in the plastic glass on the shelf, then wiped her mouth on one of the striped towels she had brought home from work.

'No doubt you had your reasons,' she said, pushing past Sebastian.

'Yes – her name is Gunilla, she's forty-seven and she's a nurse.'

'I don't believe you.'

'Why not?'

'Because you would never do that to me.'

'Yes, I would.'

Ellinor shook her head as she put on her coat.

'No, you wouldn't. Because that would mean you wanted to hurt me, and why would you want to do that?'

Sebastian stared at her as she bent down and pulled on her boots with rapid, jerky movements. She lost her grip on the leather. Tried again. Even more jerky this time, as if she were struggling not to lose control. Sebastian could feel the irritation dwindling and a certain level of sympathy trying to take its place. He fought back. He had to be firm with her, but to his disappointment he heard his voice take on a gentler tone.

'I don't want to hurt you, I just want you to understand that you can't live here any longer.'

'Why not?'

'It was a mistake, you should never have moved in. It's my fault, I felt some kind of, I don't know . . . guilt. For a while I thought this was what I wanted, but it isn't.'

For the first time since they came into the hallway, Ellinor looked up and met his eyes.

'Haven't things been good between us?'

'No.'

Silence. Sebastian thought he could see tears in her eyes. Was he getting through, in spite of the fact that he had been more measured than he had intended? It was about time, if so. Now he must make sure he didn't give her any opportunity to misunderstand, to re-interpret the situation. He must hammer the message home.

'You're like a home help that I have sex with. I don't care about you, and you care a little too much about me; it's sick.'

Ellinor didn't respond, but Sebastian thought he could see a slight change in her expression. Something hardened; there was a glimmer he had never seen before. He got the feeling that someone else had once called her sick. Several others, perhaps, on several occasions. It was obvious she didn't like it.

'We'll talk about this tonight.'

A harsh note in her voice that he had never heard before either. She had definitely been listening for once. He mustn't lose his grip now.

'There's nothing to talk about. It's perfectly simple. You have to move out. You should never have moved in.'

'As I said, I'll see you tonight.'

Ellinor opened the door and left. No kiss, which was something. But the battle was far from over. Sebastian knew her well enough by now to assume that she would come home with a conciliatory gift, cook a fantastic dinner, apologise for the fact that they had quarrelled, such a silly tiff. She would want to make love and forget the whole thing.

There was a chance that she would succeed. Somehow she always managed to get past his defences, so he had to make sure she didn't have the opportunity.

When Ellinor moved in, she had brought nothing more than a small cabin case. Admittedly she had been back home a few times to pick up bits and pieces, but she didn't have many possessions in Sebastian's apartment. Her black case and a carrier bag would do. He would pack for her.

Happy with his plan he headed for the bedroom, but just then his mobile rang. He quickly went through his pockets and fished it out. Looked at the display. He was afraid it might be Ellinor, but it was Torkel. Sebastian was surprised by the surge of hope that shot through his body before he answered.

He wasn't disappointed.

Six bodies. Storulvån. They were flying to Östersund in three hours.

As he packed it was as if he had been transported fifteen years back in time. Gathering up the essentials as quickly as possible, never knowing how long he was going to be away, hoping that a challenge was waiting for him. He hadn't given it a conscious thought for many, many years, but as he moved between the wardrobe and the open suitcase, it struck him: he had missed this.

He wouldn't only be using his expertise, he would be working with Vanja. And he had got rid of Ellinor.

Things just couldn't be better right now.

Shibeka had got up early, woken her beloved boys and given them breakfast. Freshly baked *roht*, the sweet bread made of flour, yoghurt and cardamom, served with chai tea and a bowl of dried apricots that she had bought down in the square. The boys also had Frosties with milk. When they were little, Shibeka had decided that there should be Swedish food on the breakfast table too, and without hesitation they had both chosen Frosties, probably because of the sweetness, but also because they loved the big tiger on the box. She had made a few attempts to introduce different, more nutritious cereals, but without success.

It was sports day for Mehran; he was going to learn orienteering, so she made him a packed lunch. Eyer looked on enviously as she placed the plastic boxes containing yesterday's korma in Mehran's bag. He immediately asked if he could take some of his favourite curry too. She smiled at him; that was just typical of Eyer. He was always the one who went for it, tried to get more out of life. Mehran was more serious, more reserved, nowhere near as talkative. She shook her head.

'There's some for you, but you can have it as a snack when you get home.'

Eyer nodded and went back to his Frosties. Shibeka gazed at them as they sat there eating. Her boys. She had spent the whole weekend wondering what to do. Should she tell them? Mehran was old enough; he really ought to know, perhaps even go with her. Speak on her behalf. Protect her. But she didn't want that. She wanted to protect them, speak to the man on her own. Nine years ago such a thought would never even have crossed her mind. The idea that a woman could act as she was doing now was not part of her world. There was something shameful about what she was planning, yet at the same time it felt liberating. She was proud of herself, in spite of the clump of guilt deep down in her belly.

The boys got ready to leave; they usually walked to school together. Shibeka kissed them on the forehead and opened the door. They ran down the stairs and she stood there listening for a little longer than usual. She really did have two wonderful boys. Respectful and polite, unlike the children of some of her friends, where the clash between the customs of the old and new countries often led to conflict. She liked to think this was down to her; she had made a real effort to encourage them to take the best from both cultures. It wasn't easy, but she did try.

She went back inside and finished off the lukewarm tea, ate a piece of the sweet, delicious *roht*, then went to get ready. She had no intention of dressing up, but she wanted him to take her seriously. She opted for a black shawl around her head to hide her hair. She was grieving, after all, even if many years had passed since Hamid's disappearance. She was going to be early, but she was too restless to stay at home any longer. She picked up her railcard and set off.

The metro station was ten minutes away. If she met anyone she knew, she would say that she was going shopping, and hope they didn't decide to accompany her. It would be a lie, but sometimes lies were necessary.

The blue line went straight to the central station, so there was no need to change. The train was half-full. Shibeka realised she had no way of contacting the man if she couldn't find the café. She didn't have a mobile phone; she had never thought she needed such a thing. The boys both had one; all the young people in Sweden seemed to have a mobile. Perhaps she should have borrowed one of theirs? But that would have seemed strange, and they would have started asking questions she didn't want to answer. Not right now, at any rate. There were a lot of things she hadn't considered. She had been so focused on getting a reaction, and now that something was happening at long last, after all this time, she wasn't really prepared for it. Shibeka decided that if the man chose to pursue her story, she would get herself a mobile. Some of her friends, and particularly their husbands, wouldn't like it, but then they wouldn't like what she was doing anyway. Not in the slightest.

'Shall I come in with you?'

Maya switched off the engine and turned to Billy. They had just pulled up outside Terminal 4 at Arlanda. Billy glanced at his watch; his flight took off in forty-five minutes.

'No, there's no need. And it's incredibly expensive to park here.'

'OK.'

Billy undid his seatbelt, leaned over and gave her a kiss.

'I'll be in touch when I know how long I'm going to be away.'

Maya nodded. Billy opened the door and got out. He was just getting his bag out of the boot when he heard the driver's door open, and Maya appeared.

'When you get back—' she began.

'I don't know.'

'What?'

'I don't know when I'll be back,' Billy clarified, slamming the boot shut. 'I'll be in touch as soon as I know.'

'That's not what I said.' Maya grabbed his open jacket and came closer. 'I said *when* you get back.'

'Yes?'

'What do you think about the two of us moving in together?'

Billy could easily have listed twenty things Maya could have said that would have surprised him less. More, perhaps. He had no idea what to say, but he was painfully aware that to say nothing at all was probably the worst possible response. He hadn't even considered the possibility of their moving in together. How long had they been together? Since midsummer, how long was that? Approximately three months. Wasn't it a bit soon? Could he say that? He definitely had to say something.

'You don't want to,' Maya stated; he had obviously remained silent for too long.

'I'm just a bit surprised.'

'Because we haven't known each other very long?'

'Well yes, partly that, and . . .' He didn't finish the sentence. He still didn't know what to say. He had nothing more sensible in his head than ten seconds ago. 'Yes, I guess so,' he admitted.

'But we like one another, and we're practically living together now, but at two different addresses.'

That was true. They had spent a lot of time with each other right from the start, but now it was just as Maya said: they were practically living together, sometimes at her place, more often at his. He hadn't been working so much. Recently there hadn't been a great deal to do, and before that he had been suspended while the internal investigation into the fatal shooting of Edward Hinde had been carried out. Any case in which a police officer fired his or her gun was investigated, particularly if there was a fatal outcome. Billy had been interviewed several times, and had had two appointments with the Police Board's psychologist, Håkan Persson Riddarstolpe, and that was the end of that.

Billy realised Maya was looking encouragingly at him. It was definitely his turn to say something.

'So would you move into my place?' he managed eventually.

'Your place, my place, somewhere new – we can talk about that later. But it has to be what you want.'

'It . . . it is,' he said. 'Honestly,' he added, hoping she was listening to the words rather than the hesitation behind them.

'Excellent, in that case we'll sort it out when you get home. Good luck.' She stood on tiptoe and kissed him. He remained standing behind the car as she got back in and drove off.

He waved. She waved back.

A taxi sounded its horn as he was crossing the road. He looked over and saw Vanja in the passenger seat.

She waved. Billy waved back and stopped to wait for her.

It was a strange thought, but he was struck by the realisation that Vanja and Maya had never been so close as just now, in different cars at the airport. They had never met. He and Maya were about to start living together, yet Vanja, his closest colleague and perhaps his best friend – or at least she had once been his best friend – had never even met her. Wasn't that a sign that things were moving a little too fast? Or was it just a sign that he was too much of a coward to introduce them to one another? Was that why he hadn't wanted

Maya to come into the terminal with him? He was pretty sure that Vanja wouldn't like Maya, and there was a distinct possibility that the feeling would be mutual.

Which was a problem.

However, it might well solve itself. Vanja was on her way to the USA. He was pretty sure she would be allocated one of the three places. He hadn't applied. He had told himself that it was because he didn't want to live overseas for three years, that it wasn't really his thing, and that he would go for something else if he ever decided to go in for advanced training. Something more technical, more his area of expertise.

That was partly true, but deep down he knew that one of the reasons why he hadn't even applied was because he wasn't sure how he would react if Vanja was successful and he wasn't.

'Hi, you look as if you're deep in thought!' Vanja said as she came over and hugged him.

'Not really . . .'

His suspension, a department on the back burner and Vanja's focus on her FBI tests meant they had hardly seen each other over the past few months. He realised he had missed her.

'How did you get here?'

'Maya gave me a lift.'

'Oh, so you're still with Maya?'

Was it his imagination, or was there a hint of disappointment in her voice?

'Yes.'

'Cool.'

She didn't ask when she was going to meet Maya.

He didn't mention it either.

They set off towards the terminal.

★ ★ ★

As Billy and Vanja walked in they saw Torkel and Ursula standing by the screens showing arrivals and departures. There was a young woman with them, perhaps around twenty-five years old. Tall, taller than Vanja. Long brown hair tied back in a simple ponytail, a slim face, alert, bright blue eyes that turned to Billy and Vanja as Torkel raised a hand in greeting. After the usual round of hugs and hellos, Torkel introduced their companion.

'This is Jennifer. She'll be travelling up with us.'

Vanja held out her hand.

'Hi. Vanja.'

'Jennifer. We've met before actually.'

'Have we?'

'Yes, at a gravel pit in Bro. I found a burnt-out car you were interested in.'

Of course. Vanja nodded. It was hardly surprising that she hadn't remembered Jennifer, who had been a uniformed officer at the time. Her report to Vanja had taken approximately thirty seconds, plus Vanja had actively tried to forget that particular day. It had been unbearably hot, she had been hung-over and furious, and she had told Billy that she was a better cop than he was, which had threatened to destroy their relationship and tear the team apart. She and Billy had talked about it later. Sorted it out. But sometimes Vanja felt as if they hadn't really found their way back to what they had had before that day at the gravel pit in Bro.

'Did you find the boy?' Billy asked when he had shaken hands with the new arrival.

'Sorry?'

'Weren't you looking for a missing boy when you came across the car?'

'That's right – Lukas Ryd. Yes, we found him. He'd set off on a little trip all by himself and got lost.'

Jennifer smiled at Billy. Unlike Vanja, he remembered her and what she had been doing when they met. He had noticed her. Billy returned her smile.

Vanja took a step back.

When Torkel had said that he was intending to bring in a potential replacement, Vanja hadn't expected her to be so young. She looked even younger when she smiled. The slightly harsh lines around her eyes were erased, and she looked more relaxed. Could someone so young and inexperienced really replace Vanja? What was Torkel thinking?

Wasn't she better than that?

Of course she was.

Vanja was off to Quantico. That was why Jennifer was here. Vanja was actually glad that Torkel had already brought someone in, because it meant he was certain she would go all the way. He needed to make sure his team was in place, and to be honest Vanja had also been young and inexperienced when she started working with him. Not that young though.

Her thoughts were interrupted by Ursula.

'So that's the end of any chance of peace and quiet.'

Vanja turned towards the doors and saw Sebastian heading towards them, wearing a satisfied and slightly smug smile. A smile that would have driven her crazy a few weeks ago, but today she merely registered it.

'I guess you're waiting for me,' he said, putting down his bag and giving Vanja a hug. 'Good to see you again.'

'You too.'

Billy watched them. He couldn't quite work out their relationship. He understood that Vanja had accepted Sebastian after he had offered to take her place as Edward Hinde's hostage; he got that. But there was something else.

Edward Hinde's targets had been women who had had a temporary sexual relationship with Sebastian. Vanja's mother had been on a list of possible victims that Billy had found, so there was little doubt that Sebastian had slept with Anna Eriksson. Billy had dug a little further while he was under investigation, but he hadn't got very far. It was virtually impossible to work out where and when it had happened, and eventually he had decided that trying to find out more about the sex life of his colleague's mother was a little seedy. If Anna Eriksson was being or had been unfaithful with Sebastian, it was really none of his business. Of course he wondered whether Vanja would be so positively inclined towards Sebastian as she was now if she knew, but Billy had no intention of being the one to tell her. He didn't want to jeopardise his slightly battered friendship with Vanja all over again.

'Sorry I'm late,' Sebastian said once he had greeted everyone. 'I was waiting for a locksmith.'

'Had you locked yourself out?' Ursula wondered, with what Sebastian interpreted as a hopeful smirk.

'No.' He turned back to Jennifer with a warm smile. 'Jennifer, was it?'

'Yes. Jennifer Holmgren.'

Sebastian nodded and repeated her name. Torkel saw Ursula roll her eyes, and he turned to Sebastian.

'A word, please.'

Without waiting for a response he put his hand under Sebastian's elbow and drew him to one side.

'You are not going to sleep with her,' he said quietly but very clearly once they were out of earshot.

Sebastian glanced over Torkel's shoulder. Jennifer was chatting to Billy; Ursula met Sebastian's gaze, distaste written all over her face. Presumably she knew exactly what Torkel was saying. Sebastian grinned at her.

'Do you think she's interested?' he said, shifting his focus back to Torkel.

'No, I don't, but you have a remarkable ability to get women into bed. This time you're not even going to try.'

'OK.'

Torkel looked Sebastian in the eye. OK? Just like that? Too easy. He suddenly got the feeling that he had made things worse. If Sebastian was told what to do, he usually did the polar opposite. Sebastian couldn't let anyone else lay down the law where he was concerned. Had Jennifer just become more interesting because Torkel had told him not to go there?

The risk was definitely there.

'I mean it,' he said, emphasising every word. 'You'll be out so fast your feet won't touch the ground.' He hoped that Sebastian's pleasure at being back would outweigh his need to defy authority.

'I realise that. Nothing is going to happen.'

'OK. Good.'

Torkel turned to rejoin the others.

'So why is she here?' Sebastian asked.

'She might be Vanja's replacement.'

Sebastian stopped dead and grabbed Torkel by the arm. A little too quickly, his grip a little too tight. He let go as soon as Torkel looked at him with raised eyebrows.

'What do you mean?' Sebastian made an effort not to sound too surprised and anxious. 'What are you talking about, Vanja's replacement?'

'Vanja has applied for a place on an FBI training programme.'

Sebastian heard the words, understood what they probably meant, but couldn't really take them in. Didn't want to take them in.

'In the USA?' was all he could get out.

'I believe that's where the FBI usually hangs out.'

'How long for? When?' Sebastian's mouth was suddenly dry. He thought his questions sounded like a dry croak, but perhaps that was because of the rushing noise in his ears. Torkel didn't seem to notice.

'The programme?'

'Yes.'

'Three years, starting in January.'

Torkel went back to the rest of the team; Sebastian stayed where he was, as if someone had nailed him to the floor.

Three years.

Three years without her.

When he had finally got closer to her.

He heard his name. Again. Sebastian saw that the others had stopped halfway to the stairs leading to the security check, wondering if he was intending to join them. He started walking. Picked up his bag. His body was on the way to Jämtland, but his mind was in an entirely different place.

Lennart Stridh jumped out of the cab at Åhlén's, directly opposite Café Bolero. He was five minutes late and ran over the crossing just as the traffic lights were about to change to green. A driver angrily sounded his horn, but Lennart didn't even glance in the direction of the car. He hurried over to the café, pulled open the heavy glass door and went inside. The air was filled with the sweet aroma of coffee and cake. He looked around the large room; the place was busier than he had expected. She must be somewhere between thirty-five and forty-five. He knew she had two teenage boys, but that was about all. A short distance away a woman with a black shawl around her head got to her feet and looked at him. Took a few cautious steps towards him. She was slender, with dark eyes and a darker skin tone than most of those around her. That must be her. She had chosen a table away from other people, in a corner, where she was almost invisible.

'Shibeka?'

She gave a slight nod. He went over and held out his hand.

'Hi, I'm Lennart.'

She nodded again. He could see that she was uncomfortable in the middle of the room. She was probably nervous. Hardly surprising – most people got nervous when they actually met him.

'Nice to meet you. Are you happy sitting here?'

She spoke for the first time.

'Yes. Fine.'

Her accent was less noticeable than it had been on the phone, and she looked slightly more relaxed, as if her anxiety had diminished when she heard the sound of her own voice.

'Can I get you a coffee?

'Tea, please.'

Even though she hardly ever looked him in the eye, she seemed stronger than he had expected. He had got the impression of a

57

much more downtrodden woman when he spoke to her on the phone. He went over to the counter and bought a cup of tea, an Americano and two cinnamon buns, watching her as he waited for his order to be filled. She seemed tense now, hands clasped on her lap, eyes fixed on the floor. He went over to the table, put down the tray and sat opposite her. He decided to get straight to the point.

'Are you nervous? There's nothing to worry about.'

'I am not used to this kind of thing.'

'I understand, but it's quite straightforward. I'll ask you some questions about your husband, and you try to answer. Anything you say is just between the two of us.'

She nodded and took a tentative sip of her tea without looking up. Lennart took out his notepad, clicked his ballpoint pen. Some of his colleagues recorded all their interviews, but he preferred pen and paper. A recorder could make people nervous. It meant they couldn't say they had been misquoted, and Lennart thought that made them more careful, made them start censoring themselves. He didn't want that. Right now the important thing was to get a mental picture of Shibeka and to assess the potential of her story, to decide whether she was trustworthy and whether her husband's disappearance was something worth pursuing, or a dead end. Lennart had come up against several of those already this year and he didn't want any more.

'Let's start with you,' he said, pen poised. 'You and your husband came to Sweden at the end of 2001?'

'Yes, and the children. They were two and four.'

'From Afghanistan?'

Shibeka looked at him. He made it sound so easy. As if they had jumped on a plane and landed in Sweden a few hours later. For a moment she let her thoughts stray to the camp in Pakistan where they had ended up when they first fled. The stench, the overcrowding, the fear, and everywhere the sound of children crying. The tents that were ice-cold at night and stifling during the day. Hamid, persuading her that they had to get out of there. Move on. The men they had paid to get them into Iran. The terrible journey in a truck through mountains and stony deserts, days and weeks blending into one long nightmare. All she could remember was sitting pressed against the cab, clutching Eyer and Mehran in her arms. The ache in her arms from clinging to her children was her only real memory of their flight; the rest was a confusion of different images, but she never forgot the pain. She stretched her arms a fraction just to be sure that the pain was gone for ever.

'Yes, but first we went to Greece.'

'So Greece was your first country of asylum?'

Asylland. What a word. One of the first she had learned in Swedish. The first member state of the EU that a refugee reaches, and the country he or she is sent back to before being sent home.

'But then you came to Sweden?' Lennart went on when she didn't reply.

Shibeka nodded. 'We had friends and family in Sweden, so Hamid wanted to come here.'

'But you weren't granted asylum?'

'Not at first. There were many problems.'

She fell silent. Lennart leaned forward a fraction. This could determine whether he said thanks but no thanks, or carried on.

'Hamid was never granted asylum, was he? And you and your children didn't get it until a few years later, after he'd disappeared – is that right?'

Shibeka sighed; she already knew where this was going. It was always the same. Back to what the Swedish authorities always said. She was so tired of it all.

'He didn't disappear because he wasn't allowed to stay. And he didn't disappear so that we could stay.' Shibeka raised her voice and looked Lennart in the eye for the first time. 'You always say that's why he disappeared, but it's not true!'

Lennart gazed at her. Gone was the wary, slightly circumspect woman. Her eyes burned with passion. Lennart could see her inner strength, and suddenly he understood the fight for her husband that had gone on for so many years. This was a woman who never gave up, whatever the odds against her.

'That's not what I'm saying, but it is what the police and the Immigration Board are saying: that Hamid went missing after a meeting with the Immigration Board where he was informed that you were probably going to be sent back.'

Shibeka knew that she had to protest. She shook her head and clenched her fists.

'They don't know Hamid. He would never leave us, never let his boys grow up without a father. Never. Something else must have happened.'

Her expression was almost pleading as she gazed at the man sitting opposite. After a brief silence he put down his pen and asked with genuine curiosity: 'So what do you think happened?'

'I don't know.'

'But you think it's something to do with the man who turned up a week or so after Hamid went missing?'

'Yes.'

'The man you thought was a police officer?'

'He sounded like a police officer, but he wasn't in uniform.'

'And he didn't give you a name?'

'No.'

'So you have no idea where he was from?'

She shook her head. 'He asked questions like a police officer.'

'What did he ask you?'

Shibeka thought back. Where to begin? There had been so many questions, all centred on Hamid and his cousin. She realised that what she said now was crucial. She had to make Lennart Stridh understand that the Swedish man in the dark jacket who came to her apartment was important. That his visit was significant. He had been after something, something she hadn't been able to give him even if she had wanted to.

'He asked mostly about Hamid,' she said slowly. 'And Said, his cousin. Had they said where they were going, had they taken anything with them, had they met up with anyone beforehand, had they been away in the last few weeks, and . . . and . . .'

She stopped in mid-sentence. Her thoughts always returned to the other man. He and the Swede in the dark jacket had something to do with Hamid's disappearance, she was sure of it.

'And about Joseph.'

Lennart wrote down the name.

'Who's Joseph?'

'I don't know. He knew Said.'

'And Said went missing at the same time as your husband.'

She nodded. 'Said saw Joseph often. Hamid didn't like him. He told me that.'

'But you've never met this Joseph, or heard anything about him since?'

'No. I tried, but I couldn't find him.'

Suddenly Lennart wasn't sure what to think. Shibeka Khan seemed reliable; he couldn't for the life of him see why she would lie. She had been trying to find out what had happened to her husband for a very long time – longer than if she actually knew, and was doing it for show. However, the fact that she didn't know didn't necessarily mean there was anything worth pursuing as far as he and the programme were concerned. There could be any number of reasons behind the disappearance, reasons that were tragic for the family, but of no interest to an investigative journalist or the TV viewers.

And yet there was something about this woman that piqued his interest. Something in her story that didn't quite fit. No, not in her story – he believed her – but in the response from the authorities. It wasn't so much what they had said, but what they hadn't said. The small amount of research he had done after receiving her letter hadn't led to anything concrete; quite the reverse. He had started by calling the Immigration Board, and as usual he had been passed on to one official after another before he was able to speak to the right person. The Board confirmed that Hamid Khan had gone missing a few days after a meeting with them, and that they suspected he was deliberately staying away. They had no current details; the latest note on his file stated that they were awaiting the results of the police investigation. The note was dated August 2003. Nothing had happened since then, except that Hamid's wife Shibeka and her two children, Eyer and Mehran, had been granted a residence permit in 2006. Then Lennart had contacted the police, and was told that the investigation had concluded that Hamid's disappearance was probably connected to an imminent deportation order, but they were unable to comment further. Lennart had wondered why. The case was classified, he was informed. That was the real reason why he was sitting here with Shibeka. He couldn't remember any other instance where a refusal to grant asylum had been classified.

Then there was the story of Said Balkhi, Hamid's cousin, who had disappeared at the same time. He had arrived in Sweden several years earlier and had been given a residence permit back in 2000. He owned and ran a shop on Fridhemsplan where Hamid sometimes worked. On the night they went missing in 2003 he had called his wife and said he was on his way home. They had closed the shop and locked up, and nobody had seen them since. Said's wife was expecting their first child just a few months later. He had no reason to disappear, none at all. Something about this whole business just didn't feel right; Lennart was becoming more and more convinced that it was worth looking into.

He decided to go with his gut. It would take time and resources, but it wouldn't do any harm to do a little more digging.

'Shibeka, we're going to take this on. I can't promise anything, but we'll make a start at least.'

Her whole face lit up, and she almost spilt her tea as she leapt to her feet.

'Thank you! Thank you so much!'

Lennart couldn't help smiling at her obvious joy.

'Just remember, I can't promise anything.'

'I know. I know, but I've waited so long for this.'

Shibeka calmed down, realised that several people were looking at her, and sat down again. However, the happiness was still bubbling away inside her, making it difficult to keep still.

'OK, we've got a lot of work to do,' Lennart went on. 'I need a list of all your friends and relatives who might know something. I need copies of all the letters you've sent, and an authorisation from you so that I can request all the relevant material from the authorities. Then we need to sit down and go through everything you remember in detail. Can you do that?'

There were a lot of words, and he spoke very fast. She couldn't follow everything, but she did understand the last question, and she knew the answer.

'I can do anything,' she said, holding his gaze, and Lennart instinctively knew that it was true.

Their flight took off on time and was expected to land ten minutes early. This information passed Sebastian by completely in his aisle seat. Nor did he listen to the safety briefing. He had no idea how long the flight time was expected to be, or what the weather was like in Östersund. He waved away the hot drink and the roast beef wrap that the cabin crew offered him.

Vanja was going to be away for three years.

He couldn't get it out of his head. It couldn't be true. It couldn't happen. What was he going to do? He knew what he wanted to do.

Go with her.

Or follow her, at least.

There was nothing to tie him to Stockholm or Sweden, apart from Vanja. He wanted to be where she was. However, he realised that the idea of following her to the USA was impossible. She would think he was crazy. It was crazy. She would start avoiding him again, with good reason. Distrust him. Hate him. He couldn't let that happen.

Vanja was coming towards him from the toilet at the front of the plane. Sebastian touched her arm as she was passing, and she stopped.

'I hear you've applied for a place on an FBI training programme.'

'That's right.'

For a moment he considered saying what he was thinking, begging her not to go. But he had no way of following up such a plea, no response to her inevitable question: 'Why?'

'How far have you got?' he asked instead, hoping that she still had a long way to go. Several difficult hurdles. Demanding tests that she might fail.

'I've done ballistics, the physical and written tests, and this weekend I saw Persson Riddarstolpe for my psych assessment.'

'He's an idiot,' Sebastian said, almost reflexively.

'I know you think so.'

'I don't think so, he *is* an idiot. It's a fact, just like the fact that the earth is round.'

Vanja smiled at him. He loved that smile.

'Anyway, I think it went well. He has to submit a report, and then I think there are just a few role plays left.'

Of course it went well. The tiny spark of hope Sebastian had allowed himself to feel faded away and died. Of course she had passed everything with flying colours. Of course she would be accepted.

She was the best.

She was his daughter.

'Torkel thinks I'll get in,' Vanja went on. 'That's why Jennifer's here.'

'Yes, he told me.'

Vanja stayed where she was; she seemed to be waiting for something more.

Congratulations, for example.

Or good luck.

It never came.

★ ★ ★

Superintendent Hedvig Hedman was waiting for them in the arrivals hall. She welcomed them and apologised for being unable to offer them better weather. When they had collected their luggage, they accompanied her to a waiting people carrier. They left Frösön and drove alongside the lake until they joined the E14.

As they headed towards Storulvån Hedvig told them what she knew. It wasn't much. A walker had stepped out onto an overhang that had presumably been eroded by the rain. The ground had fallen away, exposing a skeleton. The police then began to dig around the remains and came across another skull. By the time they had finished they had found six bodies, side by side. Hedvig had gone through every possible database and archive, but there were no reports of a group of six people going missing at any point in the last fifty years.

'Do you know how long they've been there?' Torkel asked.

'No, we've left them on the mountain. We haven't started investigating; we thought it was better to wait for you.'

Ursula nodded approvingly. Far too many local police forces wanted to show how clever they were, prove they could get somewhere before Riksmord turned up. Hedvig Hedman seemed to have a different approach – quite rightly, in Ursula's opinion. She had realised that the case was likely to prove too complex and had called for reinforcements right away rather than waiting until they were stuck.

'Do you know how they died?' she asked, meeting Hedvig's eyes in the rear-view mirror.

'Initial indications suggest that they were shot, but we can't be certain until we've examined them.'

Jennifer was sitting right at the back with Billy, revelling in the experience. She couldn't believe how lucky she'd been. She was actually sitting in a people carrier with Riksmord. Six bodies. Shot. Buried on a mountainside. This was a bit different from running speed checks and sorting out drunken brawls on a Friday night. This was why she had joined the police. Murderers. Clues. A complex investigation. The chase, the excitement. She was bubbling over inside. She wanted to tell everyone.

Jennifer Holmgren, Riksmord.

She could hardly keep still. Billy turned to her. Jennifer knew she was sitting there with a smile on her face, but she couldn't help it.

'Why are you so happy?'

She told him the truth.

'I'm just so pleased to be here.'

Vanja glanced back at her replacement. She almost expected Jennifer to add 'with you', aimed at Billy. The two of them seemed to have clicked right away. They had sat together on the plane, laughing and chatting about who they followed on Twitter, and other stuff that Vanja couldn't care less about. In just a few hours Jennifer had managed to make her feel old. She turned her attention back to the road. She had to pull herself together. She would be leaving the team, so it was a good thing if Billy hit it off with her replacement. She wasn't jealous, but . . . it was her place. Jennifer would be taking her place. Vanja had chosen to go, but even so. For the first time since she embarked on her FBI adventure, she realised that she wasn't only on the way to somewhere new, she was also leaving something behind. Something good.

★ ★ ★

They turned left in Enafors, then right before they reached Handöl. Drove along a valley where the mountains rose up on both sides of the road, their warm autumn colours glowing in the rain. The narrow road grew even narrower, then suddenly opened out into a large car park. They had arrived. A long, low building with extensions in all directions. One side ended in some kind of octagonal offshoot that looked like a silo. Grey roofs. Everywhere. At first glance 80 per cent of the place seemed to be roof. Sebastian knew nothing about architecture, but he knew when he thought something was ugly. This was ugly. Functional, perhaps, as a mountain station, but nobody could call it attractive.

They hurried inside and were welcomed in reception by a couple who introduced themselves as Mats and Klara, issued them with keys and explained the arrangements for the next few days. They could stay as long as they liked, even though the hotel had closed for the season. There would be staff on-site during the day, getting ready for the winter; a few would stay overnight in the staff lodges. A cook would come in each day to prepare lunch and dinner. They could help themselves to breakfast in the kitchen. There might be the odd workman carrying out minor repairs, but only during the day. If they needed anything or had any questions, Mats and Klara were always available.

They decided to drop their luggage in their rooms, have a quick snack then get out onto the mountain as soon as possible, while it was still light. Hedvig had two vehicles at their disposal.

★ ★ ★

Torkel put his suitcase on the bed then went over to the window. He had a view of the river; it was high water. A suspension bridge spanned the torrent, and he could see the well-trodden track that led walkers out into the mountains. Torkel was glad to be here. He couldn't pretend that he didn't have certain hopes when it came to this trip, hopes that were nothing to do with police work. Perhaps he and Ursula could find their way back to one another. Move forward, even. For a long time they had lived by the rules that Ursula had laid down.

Only at work.

Never on home ground.

No plans for the future.

They were simple rules, they had followed them for several years, and it had worked. But then things had changed. Ursula had come to his apartment. Sought him out. Wanted him. On home ground. In Stockholm. Two of the rules had been broken, in his opinion, and it was Ursula who had broken them. It seemed to Torkel that this had complicated matters. On the few occasions when they had met or talked recently, he had got the feeling that Ursula had changed. Not much, nothing major, just small signs. Details. He thought perhaps it was because she was afraid they were on the way to breaking the third rule as well. Maybe the idea of a future together frightened her. Torkel wanted nothing more, but he knew better than to take the initiative. Everything they did was on Ursula's terms. Always. He wanted to move forward, but now they had the chance to regroup.

Go back.

Follow the rules once more.

There was no doubt that everything had been simpler then; he hoped that they could find their way back to that place, then move on. A few nights in a hotel, far away from her husband. Take a step back so that they could make some kind of progress. That was what Torkel wanted, what he was hoping for.

As usual he hadn't a clue what Ursula was thinking.

After a meal consisting of goulash soup, bread, coffee and chocolate almond biscuits, they gathered outside the mountain station. The rain was coming down more heavily now. It was pouring as they made their way across the bridge to the two four-wheel-drive vehicles waiting on the other side. Sebastian hated rain. It didn't matter that he was dressed for the weather; after just a few minutes he felt as if he was soaked to the skin. Soaking wet and cold.

'There's no such thing as bad weather, only the wrong clothes.'

Only a brainwashed fucking nature fascist would say such a thing. This was bad weather. From a purely objective point of view it was bloody awful weather, however you were dressed. Sebastian thought about turning back, waiting in the hotel. He didn't really need to see the place where the bodies had been found, but by now they had reached the cars and protection from the rain. He pushed past Jennifer and jumped in.

Half an hour later they had arrived. A large white tent had been erected over the remains, and a petrol-driven generator provided power for the floodlights both inside and outside the tent in the gathering dusk. Hedvig led them over to a man in his fifties who introduced himself as Jan-Erik Kask. He shook hands with them all, then set off through the mud.

'The overhang gave way, and this is what we found . . .'

He held open the tent flap and Sebastian walked straight in, with Ursula close behind. Torkel stopped and looked around.

'Is there room for all of us?'

'Should be. Just don't go too near the edge or you could end up down there too.'

Torkel, Billy, Vanja and Jennifer stepped inside the tent. The air was stuffy and damp; the combination of the lights and the rain made it feel like a butterfly house. They all undid their jackets.

In the middle they saw a hole approximately two by five metres, less than a metre deep. Six skeletons lay more or less side by side down at the bottom; two of them were significantly shorter than the others. Two still had rotten scraps of clothing clinging to their legs. The skeleton furthest away from the entrance had one arm stretched out under the side of the tent as if it was checking whether it was still raining outside. They could hear the water rushing past down below. Jan-Erik crouched down by the grave and nodded at the remains at the far end.

'That's where the walker fell down. She grabbed a hand and a forearm on the way; they're in a box outside.'

Ursula nodded. She took off the lens cap on her camera and it immediately misted up, just as she had known it would do. She passed it to Billy and pulled on her Latex gloves before crouching down opposite Jan-Erik. Sebastian and the others remained where they were, standing in a line. This was Ursula's department. Her show. They were merely spectators.

'Six skeletons in relatively good condition. They have been neatly arranged side by side, not thrown down.'

She spoke clearly, although she was talking to herself as much as to the team and Jan-Erik.

'Is that significant?' Jennifer wondered quietly, unsure if it was OK to talk. Ursula gave Sebastian a quick glance as if to say he could respond.

'Could be. It might mean that the killer has a certain level of respect for the victims, or that he or she prefers a highly structured approach and isn't particularly affected by emotions.'

'How did you dig them out?' Ursula asked Jan-Erik.

'We used a small digger.'

'Were they damaged? By the machine?'

'No, well, yes, it might possibly have nudged the odd one . . .'

Ursula leaned forward and picked up a thigh bone without speaking. It was greyish-brown and looked almost mouldy, with earth and mud clinging to it. In among the dark matter there was a gash where pale bone shone through, almost white. The digger had done more than nudge the odd one. Admittedly it wasn't difficult to see what damage had been caused recently, but if the operator had been more careful, they wouldn't have to waste time and energy. Ursula replaced the bone, while silently taking back all the positive thoughts she had had about the Jämtland police so far.

They were a bunch of bungling idiots.

She reached for the camera. Jan-Erik straightened up and turned to Torkel.

'At first we thought they could be old. Really old,' he said, just to make himself clear. 'Lots of people have died out here on the mountain. More than three thousand Caroleans froze to death up here in the winter of 1718-19. We still find their remains sometimes. Not often, it's been a while, but it does happen.'

'Surely it must have been obvious that these weren't three hundred years old,' Ursula said as she photographed the contents of the grave from every possible angle. 'They've all got bullet holes in their heads.'

'We couldn't assume they were bullet holes.'

Ursula lowered the camera.

'What else could they be?'

'Some kind of weapon with a rounded end that was used for stabbing . . .'

'You find six bodies with two round holes in the skull, and the first thing you think of is an ancient weapon rather than a bullet?'

'The Caroleans aren't ancient.'

Ursula decided to ignore that remark, and went back to photographing the remains.

'Did many of Charles XII's soldiers wear Gore-Tex?' She nodded towards the two skeletons with greyish-yellow scraps of clothing covering part of their bodies.

'We dug those two up last. They were the furthest from the edge of the slope.' Jan-Erik's voice was suffused with suppressed rage; it was obvious that he was running out of patience. Sebastian watched with interest. Ursula had set herself against the homegrown 'experts' before, but this was harsh, even for her. Torkel always insisted that they shouldn't upset the local force; that was one of the reasons why they were so successful. Ursula knew that perfectly well, and she was still biting the head off this poor bugger.

Torkel cleared his throat. 'Let Billy carry on with the photographs and tell us what we're looking at. We need to get back.'

Ursula stopped and looked at Torkel, who took a step forward. He met her gaze calmly. He had spoken quietly and politely, as if he were asking a favour, but the slight nod in her direction left no doubt that it was an order. Sebastian couldn't help but be impressed.

A typical Torkel solution. He had stopped a negative exchange, Jan-Erik would think that Torkel had taken his side, but by referring to a non-existent shortage of time and Ursula's expertise, he did so without raising his voice or embarrassing her. She passed Billy the camera without demur.

'First impressions: four adults, two children. Looking at the pelvic areas I would guess that two of the adults were women.'

'So how long have they been here?'

'Hard to say. Damp, porous mud, with water washing through the ground on a regular basis . . . More than five years, anyway.' She stood up and walked around the grave. 'Two of them seem to have been buried with their clothes on; no sign of clothes on the other two adults or the children.'

'Could their clothes have rotted away?' Vanja wondered. 'If they were made of a different kind of fabric that decomposed more quickly?'

'It's possible, but there's no sign of anything. No buttons, no zips, nothing.'

'Do you think those four have been here longer than the other two?'

'It doesn't look that way. They're all on the same level. Same bone discolouration. Same placement of the bodies. I think we can assume they were all buried at the same time.'

'So why undress four of them and not the other two?'

Ursula didn't answer. She crouched down again and gently turned over two of the skulls that were lying slightly to one side.

'The four without clothes have no teeth either,' she said. 'That can't be explained by the suggestion that they might have been here longer.'

'What makes teeth disappear?' Jennifer wanted to know.

'In a grave? Nothing. Someone removed them before the bodies were buried.'

'Someone who didn't want them to be identified?' Jennifer felt a shiver run down her spine. She had joined the police for the action and excitement. That was all there was to it. Admittedly there was a certain satisfaction in routine work, but this was what she had dreamt of. Tracking down the perpetrator, finding the evidence, securing an arrest. She had to stop herself from grinning; it wasn't appropriate. The atmosphere in the damp tent was heavy and subdued.

'That's one hypothesis,' Ursula said with a nod.

Sebastian hadn't said much so far. He had to get out of here. It was too oppressive; he couldn't breathe. Even the rain was preferable. He went outside and found it had almost cleared up. There was a chill wind blowing from the north. He fastened his jacket and took a few deep breaths.

Six dead. Two children. More or less executed. Riksmord hadn't often worked on murdered children during his time with them, but it had happened, and it always took its toll, more than other cases. Sebastian sighed. It wasn't everyone who could shoot a child. That alone meant they were dealing with a very particular kind of perpetrator, but then to remove their teeth . . .

The six people in that grave weren't the first he had killed.

Nor the last.

Sebastian was sure of that.

Lennart was pacing around the open-plan office that formed the heart of *Investigation Today*. The programme had been based there for over ten years, and the team now comprised more than twenty people. There wasn't much room; they were crammed into a space on the second floor of the concrete-grey headquarters of Swedish Television. Their nearest neighbour was the culture section, which consisted of fewer people in a bigger area; several even had the luxury of their own office. Lennart had been in the same position until two years ago, when Sture Liljedahl became his boss and immediately had all the internal walls removed, leaving an open space where 'creativity and spontaneity would be able to flow freely'. He claimed he wanted to increase collaboration and the exchange of ideas within the team, but Lennart knew it was really about cramming as many employees as possible into the smallest space. These days they all sat in a big room with the tables facing one another. Lennart hated it. He wanted to be able to speak on the phone and work on his writing without being disturbed all the time. When he complained, Sture had informed him that he was too conservative and needed to develop his social skills. Personally, Lennart thought that wanting to be able to get on with his work in peace and quiet was perfectly normal. What was even more infuriating was that Sture still had his own office: two smaller rooms had been knocked together and refurbished. He had installed a thick glass wall and a new conference table so that he could chair meetings in private and keep an eye on the team without having to hear them. Concepts like collaboration, the exchange of ideas and social skills were clearly not meant for everyone. But then he was the boss, which meant that different rules applied.

At the moment Sture was in there chatting to his protégé Linda Andersson, a hardworking thirty-year-old who had worked for

Expressen in the past. They had been talking for ages, and Lennart couldn't understand how a meeting could possibly take this long. Eager to share Shibeka's story Lennart had asked to speak to Sture as soon as he got back from Sergels torg. He had told Sture he had important information, and wondered if Sture had time to see him.

Yes he did.

In a while.

Not right now.

First of all he had a lunch meeting, then he was seeing the director, then he was going to watch the programme that was due to go out next Wednesday.

After that he would be happy to see Lennart.

After that Linda had turned up. Waylaid Sture as soon as he got back to the office, and they were still talking.

Lennart suddenly felt desperate for a cigarette, and popped a piece of nicotine gum in his mouth. Artificial fruit flavour, 2mg nicotine. He had given up smoking over two years ago, but still he often felt that instant desire, particularly if he was stressed or bored. At the moment he was both. The initial energy after seeing Shibeka had been replaced by restlessness. He could see them laughing behind the glass wall. He would never understand Sture. When Lennart didn't need him, he was on him like a hawk, but as soon as he really did need to see him, it was always the same.

In a while.

Not right now.

He sat down wearily at his desk, picked up his tepid cup of coffee and took a sip. It didn't taste too good. Perhaps he should check his inbox, at least that would give him something to do. At that moment Sture's door opened; they seemed to have finished at last. Linda picked up her own coffee cup and Sture's, and gathered her papers. Sture stood in the doorway and waved regally in Lennart's direction. The king was prepared to grant him an audience. Lennart nodded to him, shuffled a few pieces of paper around in order to look busy, then got up and walked slowly towards him. He didn't want to seem too eager, didn't want Sture to think he'd been on pins and needles, just waiting. No, he was a busy person too. Very busy.

He spat out his gum on the way. Unfortunately he missed the bin and had to bend down and pick it up. Sture watched him every step of the way; it occurred to Lennart that his entry into Sture's kingdom could have been a little more impressive.

★ ★ ★

It started well. Sture Liljedahl sat opposite him and listened with interest. In fact, he didn't interrupt once. Lennart couldn't help feeling proud. He was on the trail of something really good here. When he had finished, Sture leaned forward with a keen expression.

'How common is it for matters relating to asylum seekers to be marked classified?'

'The police officer I spoke to had never seen it before. Not in routine cases, he said.'

'So we have two Afghan men who disappeared in August 2003,' Sture summarised. 'The police claim they deliberately went missing because their application had been refused, but at least one of the men had no reason to disappear. What was his name again?'

'Said Balkhi. He had been granted a residence permit in 2001, and his wife was pregnant.'

Sture went over to the huge whiteboard behind him; it was the first thing he had installed, after the glass wall, and he loved to make notes on it. With a red pen. Lennart assumed it made him think he was in control: his notes up on his board for all to see. He jotted down the name 'Said'.

'So what do we know about Said?'

'Next to nothing. According to Shibeka, he was Hamid's cousin; he was the joint owner of a shop, along with two of his wife's cousins. I thought I might speak to her next.'

'No criminal record?'

'Not that I can find.'

Sture nodded. 'OK. Then there's Shileka . . . was that her name?'

'Shibeka. She's my contact; she's the only one I've met.'

'But she seems reliable?'

'Absolutely. Her written and spoken Swedish is very good. I can't imagine why she would lie. She's been trying to find out what's happened to Hamid ever since 2003.'

'And she thinks something isn't right. Why?'

'She insists that Hamid would never have taken off without saying something to her, and then there's this guy who turned up twelve days after they disappeared and started asking questions about Hamid.'

'She thinks he was a police officer?'

'Or someone from the authorities.'

'But he wasn't in uniform?'

Lennart shook his head. 'He asked about Hamid's family, his friends, all kinds of stuff.'

'Can't she give a better description?'

'No. A Swedish man in his forties. She thinks all Swedes look more or less the same.'

Lennart glanced at his notes before he went on.

'The police officers Shibeka has spoken to say they didn't send anyone to see her that week, and the Solna police confirmed that yesterday.'

Sture looked sceptical.

'Maybe Hamid was mixed up in something his wife didn't know about? Some criminal activity? Some kind of . . . network? There are endless possibilities.'

'You're right, but there's something about that period at the beginning of the 2000s. You remember the rendition case in 2002?'

Sture gave him a poisonous look. He wasn't likely to forget their rival channel's major scoop, the one that won them a prestigious award.

'This could be something similar,' Lennart said. 'In 2002 two terrorism suspects were deported to Egypt with no warning, at the request of the CIA. Both the Swedish Security Police and the Foreign Office were involved.'

Sture brightened up. This was an interesting line of enquiry. Not the most likely, perhaps, but not impossible.

'So you mean they've covered something up and hidden it behind a refusal to grant asylum?'

'A classified refusal to grant asylum,' Lennart corrected him.

'This Joseph, what do we know about him?'

Lennart shook his head. 'Nothing. Shibeka remembers his name; apparently Hamid mentioned him just before he disappeared, but that's all she knows.'

Sture wrote 'Joseph?' on the board, then sat down and gazed pensively at Lennart.

'We haven't really got enough. Focus on the police report; that's the most concrete thing we have. Find out why it's classified.'

Lennart nodded and smiled, which was something he didn't do very often during a meeting with Sture.

'That's exactly what I was planning to do.'

He must have looked too pleased, because Sture leaned forward and narrowed his eyes.

'I want you to work with Linda on this.'

Lennart's smile disappeared in a second. This was exactly what he wanted to avoid: meddling.

'But hasn't she got her hands full at the moment?' he ventured. 'Anders has already helped me out a little bit; can't I ask him if I get stuck?'

'Lennart, we need to find out if this is worth pursuing or not. I'm giving you the necessary resources, and Linda is good,' Sture said firmly.

'I know, but I'd like to run with this on my own for a bit longer. You know that's how I prefer to work . . .'

Sture nodded, but he wasn't about to give up. That wasn't his style.

'May I suggest a compromise? You tell Linda what you've got so far, and she will help out with research, but you're the one out in the field. You're running the show. OK?'

Lennart stared at him. I'm not running the show, he thought. You are. But what could he say? Sture was the boss, while Lennart could soon be replaced.

'Sounds good to me,' he said, plastering on another smile.

It was dark by the time they got back to the hotel.

All except Ursula, who had stayed behind to carry out a forensic examination of the scene, and to direct the removal of the bodies. Torkel had offered to stay with her, but she had declined on the basis that there wasn't much he could do. Which was perfectly true, though there was one thing he could help her with, thanks to his political clout within the organisation. Bodies found in Jämtland were supposed to be sent to the forensics lab in Umeå; however, Ursula wanted Torkel to see if he could get them sent down to Stockholm instead.

Easier said than done, apparently. The whole thing had turned into something of a war on two fronts. The lab in Umeå perceived the request as a slur on their expertise, while their colleagues in Stockholm made it perfectly clear that they weren't exactly short of work, and that they definitely didn't need six more bodies. If Torkel did manage to facilitate the transfer, he needn't expect the case to be given top priority. His superiors also questioned the point of the relocation. After at least a dozen calls, Torkel realised the cost was going to outweigh the benefits. Umeå it was, and Ursula would just have to live with it. He would tell her when she got back. Hopefully when they were alone. In his room. Or hers.

As they crossed the bridge they could see the warm, inviting glow from the octagonal section of the hotel where the restaurant was located. Mats and Klara met them in reception, wanting to know when they would like dinner. They agreed to spend half an hour in their rooms before they met up in the restaurant.

They were staying in what Mats and Klara referred to as 'comfort rooms'. Apparently comfort meant bunk beds, a rag rug, a plain plywood wardrobe with no doors, and a shower and toilet. Personally, Torkel thought it looked like a room in just about any walkers' hostel.

After a hot shower he positioned himself in front of the mirror with a pair of nail scissors, wiped away the condensation and got to work on keeping the unwanted hair growth at bay. His right nostril needed sorting out. He hated these long hairs that, over the past few years, had started appearing in places where he most definitely didn't want them. Few things made him feel so old as when his daughters, not without a certain amount of *Schadenfreude*, pointed out that the hair in his ears needed trimming again. His phone rang, and he left the bathroom to answer it.

Axel Weber from *Expressen*. Had he heard correctly – Riksmord were up in Jämtland? Indeed he had. Torkel knew the story would be all over the media in no time. Weber was a good journalist, and the fact that Riksmord were involved automatically attracted more attention. Weber wanted to know why they were there; what had they found? Or, to be more accurate, could Torkel confirm that they had found a mass grave? Torkel replied that they had found a number of bodies, which had been buried for a long time. He had no intention of speculating on how long, because they didn't know. But a long time.

Age, gender, how many bodies, clues, possible motives – Torkel wasn't prepared to comment on any of that. When the relatively short conversation was over, Weber didn't really know any more than he had to start with.

'You do know I'm going to find all this out anyway,' he said, and Torkel swore he could hear Weber smiling on the other end of the phone.

'Not from me.'

He ended the call. Weber was probably right. Obviously someone on Hedvig Hedman's team had already talked, and no doubt would carry on doing so. Cases with media value were almost impossible to lock down these days. From now on they would have to limit the flow of information, possibly even where Hedvig was concerned. The report to the Attorney General suggested that she didn't have the most loyal colleagues around her, or perhaps that she lacked judgement in her leadership role. And of course she had called in Riksmord; there were always local officers who thought that meant they were being sidelined. This happened less and less often; mostly they were glad of the expertise and additional resources that Riksmord brought with them, but someone usually felt that

Riksmord were treading on their toes. From now on, Torkel and his team would have to assume that Police HQ in Östersund was leaking like a sieve.

He immediately called Ursula; she could tell the team up on the mountain to keep an eye open. It was unlikely that anyone would send a photographer out into the darkness to get a glimpse of the grave and the bodies, but stranger things had happened.

'How did you get on with the lab?' Ursula asked just before she rang off.

'We'll talk about it when you get back,' Torkel said evasively.

'So it's Umeå then.'

Torkel thought for a second. He could lie, say he was working on it, but there was nothing to gain by doing so. It was still going to be Umeå.

'I tried, but it was impossible. When are you coming down?' he asked, hoping to prevent her from brooding on the negative outcome.

'I'm nearly done; in an hour or so.'

'I'll ask them to keep dinner hot for you.'

'Thanks.'

Ursula ended the call. The fact that she hadn't said goodbye didn't necessarily mean that she was annoyed. It could just be that she wanted to get back to work, that the call had disturbed her. He chose to believe the latter, and returned to the bathroom.

★ ★ ★

Game casserole, potato wedges, salad and lingonberries, followed by a white chocolate mousse. They had just started dessert when Hedvig Hedman came up the stairs leading to the section of the restaurant known as the Loft. After a brief greeting she placed a folder on the table.

'I think we might have identified two of them. The ones wearing clothes,' she clarified.

Torkel opened the folder; Vanja was sitting next to him and leaned forward, while Billy and Jennifer came around to look over his shoulder. Sebastian didn't move. He assumed the superintendent would provide some kind of verbal report, and he was right.

'Two Dutch citizens were reported missing in November 2003: Jan and Framke Bakker from Rotterdam. They were supposed to have started their walking holiday in Norway on 27 October, finishing in Vålådalen the following week. They were both very experienced walkers; we searched for them until the snow came down on 18 November that year.'

'And why do we think it's them?' Torkel asked, looking up at her. 'Are they the only people who've gone missing around here?'

'No, but they're the only couple who have disappeared in the relevant area, plus the report said that their walking clothes were grey and yellow.'

Hedvig leaned over and turned to a plastic pocket at the back of the folder. It contained a picture of a man and a woman, both just under thirty, taken on a snow-covered mountaintop somewhere. In the Alps, perhaps. They were wearing sunglasses, and looked tanned and weatherbeaten. The woman had thick red hair caught up in a ponytail; the man was more or less bald. They were both smiling into the camera, their fingers forming a V-for-victory sign. They were wearing high-quality grey walking gear with yellow detail.

'Seems to fit in with the scraps of clothing in the grave,' Vanja said.

Torkel agreed. This was something Ursula would need to take a look at when she got back.

★ ★ ★

Two hours later they were sitting in one of the conference rooms in the hotel. If it hadn't been dark outside they would have had a fantastic view of the muted autumn colours of the mountain landscape, but now all they could see were their own reflections in the windows, illuminated by four powerful fluorescent lights that made them look even paler and more washed out than they actually were. The flask, the coffee cups and the bottles of mineral water on the table made the situation feel very familiar. Apart from Jennifer, they had all sat in rooms like this many, many times. Without the amazing view, this was just a place to gather, the same as all the others.

Billy had printed off the pictures from the grave and stuck them to the whiteboard with magnets.

'We'll assume that we've found Jan and Framke Bakker,' Torkel began. 'If that assumption is correct, then we have an approximate time frame for the murders, but we have to be sure. Vanja, get in touch with the Dutch police and see if we can get hold of dental records, X-rays, anything that could help us to identify them.' He passed her a folder and she nodded.

'Where did they come from?'

All eyes turned to Sebastian, who got to his feet and lumbered over to the whiteboard.

'Erm . . . Holland. Rotterdam,' Billy said.

Sebastian gave him a weary look.

'So they were Dutch and they came from Holland. Thank you, I'd never have guessed.'

Billy opened his mouth to reply, then changed his mind and slumped back in his chair.

'I mean these six people,' Sebastian said, tapping one of the photographs with his finger. 'Someone undressed four of them, removed their teeth. That takes time. Then he digs a grave almost a metre deep, with six bodies just lying there in the open?'

'Perhaps he dug the grave first.' Billy straightened up, eager for revenge. The look Sebastian gave him was even more weary this time.

'And the six of them stood there waiting for him to finish?'

'Well no . . .'

'No. The order doesn't matter. It's unlikely that they were murdered where they were found. So where did they come from?'

The team nodded in agreement. Somewhere deep down they had all known it, but no one had put it into words. The grave wasn't necessarily the scene of the crime; in fact it was highly unlikely. If they could pinpoint the scene it would increase their chances of finding a lead. Billy pushed back his chair.

'I'll go and get a map from reception.'

Sebastian returned to his seat. Directly opposite Ursula. He sat back and gazed at her; she was obviously aware of his scrutiny, because she looked up and met his eye.

'What?'

'Are you annoyed?'

'No.'

'You look annoyed.'

'Well, I'm not. Not yet.'

Sebastian chose to ignore her expression.

'You look annoyed and tired,' he went on. 'Worn out.'

'Sebastian.' There was no misunderstanding Torkel's tone of voice. Pack it in, it said. Sebastian turned to him and spread his arms wide.

'What? She does look worn out. It's the first day, and she looks like a wreck. I'm just wondering how she's feeling.'

'So why didn't you ask me that?' Ursula said. 'Why didn't you ask me how I'm feeling instead of telling me I look annoyed?'

'Sorry. How are you feeling?'

'Fine, thank you. How are you?'

Before Sebastian had time to answer, the door flew open and Billy came in with a map of the mountain terrain. He spread it out on the table and everyone leaned forward, except Sebastian. As before he assumed they would talk about what they were doing while they were doing it.

'The bodies were found here,' Billy said, making a small cross on the map. They all looked at it in silence, searching for the same thing. Failing to find it.

'No buildings. No mountain shelters. No forest. No protection anywhere nearby,' Vanja summarised, sounding disappointed.

They all sat back. Billy took the map and put it up on the wall.

'Judging by the pattern of the bullet holes, the perpetrator seems to have been a very controlled killer,' Ursula said. 'Efficient. Would he really risk being spotted?'

'It was October,' Billy pointed out. 'The mountain stations were closed, and there would have been hardly anyone around. It was probably worth taking the chance.'

'Or perhaps he was spotted,' Jennifer said quietly.

So far she had spent most of her time listening to the others, but she had been thinking things over for a while. Since dinner, in fact, when Hedvig Hedman brought the news about the Dutch couple, but she hadn't dared to speak up. If she was right, she assumed that someone else on the team would come up with the same idea, but so far no one had put forward her theory. She quickly went over it in her head one more time; it wasn't completely ridiculous. It was worth a shot.

She leaned forward, her voice stronger now. 'The two people we think we can identify, the Dutch couple. Perhaps they were walking past and saw what was going on.'

No one spoke, but Torkel could see Ursula and Vanja nodding to themselves. He looked over at Jennifer. It wasn't a bad theory.

He felt pleased, both with Jennifer and with himself. Regardless of whether the reality turned out to match the hypothesis, the suggestion showed that Jennifer was thinking along the right lines, which in turn showed that he had made the right choice.

He broke the silence. 'If we run with that idea for a while, then it means the four bodies without clothes were the original victims, so we ought to focus on them. Do we know any more about them?'

Ursula shook her head. 'Two adults, a man and a woman. Two children, impossible to determine the sex. If they were of normal height, I would guess five to eight years old.'

Sebastian rubbed his eyes. He got up and opened one of the windows. Leaned on the sill and breathed in the cold, clear night air. How was he feeling? Not great, to be honest. Not as good as he had expected, at any rate. He had been looking forward to this.

He had longed for it.

More than that – he had needed it.

Spending time with Vanja. Working again, with her. Getting closer to her, getting to know her, but now she was going away. Leaving him. Cutting the only lifeline he had that might lead him to something resembling a decent existence.

And on top of all that, they were dealing with two dead children.

This trip had been a fucking nightmare so far.

'There was visible damage to the ribs of two of the victims, which might suggest they were shot in the chest first, then in the head,' Ursula went on. 'That supports the theory that the killer is used to handling a gun. He goes for the largest target area first . . .'

Sebastian glanced at Jennifer. She was at least fifteen years too young for him, but there was no doubt that she could make his stay a little more pleasant. Then again, Torkel would kick him out if he went anywhere near her. A conversation over a beer in the bar, and the others would notice. He also suspected that Torkel would be standing guard in the corridor as if they were on a school trip.

'Are they a family?' Billy wondered.

'It seems the most likely scenario,' Ursula said with a nod, 'but we won't know until we get the DNA results.'

On the other hand, what did it matter if he got sent home? With Vanja gone, he had no reason to stay. The case was depressing and so far relatively uninteresting.

84

'We assume that all four were buried at the same time. Hedvig has checked the records: no one else was reported missing up here at any point during 2003.' Torkel looked up from his notes. 'No children have ever been reported missing around here.'

'Could you close the window please? I'm cold.'

Sebastian was jerked out of his reverie to find Vanja looking at him. He nodded, closed the window and went back to his seat. Vanja wasn't gone. Not yet. She was still here, in the same room. She would be around for another three months. He had another three months by her side, precious days that he couldn't jeopardise by hitting on a woman who probably wouldn't even consider going to bed with him anyway. He decided to feign an interest in the conversation going on around him.

'Billy, find out if anyone took off without paying their hotel bill around the time the Dutch couple disappeared,' Torkel said. 'Check if any abandoned cars have been reported or towed away, or if any camping equipment was found out on the mountain. People might just have assumed they left under their own steam, hence no missing persons report.'

Billy nodded.

'Would you like some help?' Jennifer offered.

'That would be great,' Billy replied with a smile.

Vanja stared at them. It certainly didn't take long to be replaced. Then again, that was exactly as it should be. This investigation could go on for months, and would probably be her last. Suddenly she caught herself thinking how good that felt.

The room, the coffee, the whiteboard, the photographs, the theories.

Right now she was kind of done with all that. It was time to move on. Take the next step. Grow and develop.

But at the moment this case was what mattered.

'There's no guarantee that anyone even knew they were here,' she said, waiting until she had everyone's attention. 'They might not necessarily have left any traces. They could have travelled up by train and camped on the mountain. No hotels, no car.'

'But surely they would have been reported missing somewhere,' Ursula objected. 'Someone must have noticed they weren't around.'

'Vanja, check out missing families with two children in the autumn of 2003, right across the country. Norway too.'

'OK, but we can't be sure they're one family. It could be two adults with a child each. Or mum, new partner, stepchildren. And the biological father could be the jealous kind who happens to own a gun . . .'

Sebastian saw Vanja glance almost imperceptibly at Jennifer. He smiled to himself. Jennifer had come up with the theory that the Dutch couple could have been witnesses who were in the wrong place at the wrong time. It was a good theory, but if Jennifer was good, then Vanja had to be better. The best.

Typical of Vanja.

Typical of his daughter.

'OK, let's expand the search to include missing children or adults with children,' Torkel agreed. 'There can't be that many. We'll start with autumn 2003, and assume they were all buried at the same time.'

There wasn't much more they could do at this stage. It felt like a very long time since they had left Stockholm. They were all tired and needed sleep. Torkel gathered up his papers.

'Let's say that the four of them, regardless of whether or not they were a family, were camping on the mountain. Someone walked past and shot them. While he was burying the bodies, the Dutch couple came along and he had to kill them too. Is that a theory we think we can run with?'

Everyone nodded and got ready to leave the room. It wasn't necessarily the truth, but it was something to work on. As usual they would have to adapt and reassess the situation depending on what emerged during the course of the investigation.

'Hang on a minute,' Billy said. They sank back down in their seats.

'What is it?' Torkel asked, unable to keep the weariness out of his voice.

'Why did he allow us to identify the Dutch couple, but not the other four?'

'Because the other four would tell us who the murderer was,' Sebastian said, almost over-emphasising every word. 'For God's sake, how long have you been doing this job? There is nothing whatsoever to suggest that this was an act of madness, or that the victims were chosen at random. Someone went out onto the mountain with a gun and executed those four people.' He turned to Ursula. 'Did he use a pistol or a rifle?'

'Impossible to say at the moment. We'll have to see what Umeå come up with.'

She glanced at Torkel, who thought she had put a little extra stress on 'Umeå'. He was pretty sure he wouldn't be having any company in his room tonight. Then again, they were going to be up here for a while . . .

'It doesn't matter,' Sebastian said, getting to his feet. 'Our killer knows that when those four are identified, the risk of his being caught increases significantly.'

'I know that, but the Dutch couple give us a fairly precise time frame,' Billy persisted, unwilling to give in so easily. 'And that will help us to identify the others.'

Sebastian quickly took on board Billy's argument and realised there was something in it, but he had no intention of letting the other man win. Not now. He shrugged in order to trivialise what had just been said.

'Either he made a mistake, in which case we're in luck, or the time frame won't help us at all.'

'It has to. How many families and children disappeared in October 2003?'

'None, as far as we know at the moment.'

'OK, let's leave it there,' Torkel said, getting to his feet to underline his words. 'We're not going to get any further tonight, and we've got plenty to do tomorrow.' His gaze swept over his five colleagues. 'Our top priority is to identify those four bodies. We're not going to solve this until we know who they are.'

Ellinor glanced at her watch as she pushed open the door of the apartment block on Grev Magnigatan. It was late, well after eleven. She hoped Sebastian would still be awake. The lights came on automatically as she stepped inside. She glanced at the stairs, but opted for the lift. She had done enough standing and walking today; she had worked until the store closed at nine o'clock. She often wondered about the point of staying open so late, but today they had been busy all the time; it was the week after pay day. When she had finished she had popped over to Västmannagatan, to her old apartment. That was how she thought of it: her old apartment. Home was with Sebastian.

The anxiety and anger she had more or less managed to suppress all day came flooding back. He had sounded unusually harsh this morning.

No, not harsh. Nasty.

'The home help I have sex with.'

Terrible, ugly words. And then that horrible tale of someone called Gunilla. For a while she had wondered whether to come straight home and spoil him, smooth things over, restore his good mood. She didn't like it when they quarrelled, but this time he had gone too far. It was up to him to make amends, he was the one who ought to apologise, not her. That was why she hadn't called him all day. It was unusual, and several times she had been on the point of picking up the phone, but she had gritted her teeth and stayed strong. She wanted him to know that he had hurt her; her silence was his punishment.

She closed the lift gate behind her and pressed the button for the third floor.

She had spent longer than planned in her old apartment. On the way up she had met the widow Lindell, who had naturally been curious. Where was Ellinor these days? She was never around! Ellinor had actually called in just to water her plants and to check that the carrier bag containing the documents about Valdemar Lithner was still where she had put it, but fru Lindell had insisted on inviting her in for a cup of tea. Absolutely insisted. In spite of the fact that she didn't really have time, Ellinor couldn't help thinking it would be quite nice to tell someone about the great love of her life, the renowned Sebastian Bergman. She wouldn't mention today's quarrel. What couple didn't have the occasional tiff? No relationship was a bed of roses all the time.

Forty-five minutes later Ellinor unlocked the door of her apartment. Fru Lindell had been impressed, Ellinor could see that, even though she had tried to hide it. She had even pretended that she didn't know who Sebastian was, but Ellinor didn't believe that for a moment. Typical Swede, eaten up with envy.

She went straight into the bedroom, opened the wardrobe door and saw the bag exactly where she had left it. She didn't know why, but she had had a bad feeling about everything to do with Valdemar Lithner ever since he had put an end to their professional relationship before the weekend. Most of the time she was able to tell herself that he had felt – quite rightly – that it wasn't leading anywhere, but occasionally she got the idea that she had been found out, that Valdemar or one of his criminal associates had broken into her old apartment to find out who she really was, and whether she knew anything about their shady dealings. However, there was no sign that anyone had been here, and if they had, they would hardly have left the incriminating material lying in her wardrobe. It occurred to her that she was foolish not to have made a copy of everything, but it no longer mattered. Tomorrow she was going to hand it all over to the police and let justice take its course.

She closed the wardrobe door and busied herself watering her plants. It was late, but still she didn't ring Sebastian. For a moment she considered staying the night in her old apartment. Let him worry, miss her. But if she didn't go home, he couldn't beg her forgiveness, which meant they wouldn't be able to sort out the unpleasantness between them. So now she was standing here in the lift, hoping he hadn't gone to bed.

The first thing she saw when she opened the lift door was the case. Her black cabin case. What was it doing on the landing? With a plastic carrier bag next to it. She went over and looked in the bag. Her things! He had dumped her things on the landing! Enough was enough. She took out her key.

Odd – it didn't seem to fit.

She checked; yes, it was the right key. She tried again, with the same result. She couldn't even insert it in the keyhole.

The light went out. Ellinor went over and pressed the little orange button, glowing in the darkness, and switched the light back on. Then she rang the doorbell. No response. She pressed the bell again, for longer this time. She was starting to get annoyed. There wasn't a sound from inside the apartment. She bent down and peered through the letterbox: darkness and silence. She rang again, more or less leaning on the bell. No one came.

Now she really was angry. He couldn't treat her like this! She had put up with a great deal because she loved him, but even she had her limit, and he had crossed the line with a vengeance. She took out her mobile and scrolled down to 'Darling' in her contacts list. Called him. She opened the letterbox again as she heard the tone ring out in her ear; it wasn't ringing inside the apartment. Ellinor ended the call, breathing heavily. What should she do now? Where was Sebastian, and why couldn't she get in? She glanced down and saw a white envelope stuck to the side of her case. She grabbed it and ripped it open.

The light went out again.

When she had switched it back on, she took out the single sheet of paper and unfolded it.

I meant what I said. You have to move out. I've had the lock changed. I'm not home and I will be away for some time, so there's no point in standing there ringing the bell. If you call me, I won't answer. I should never have let you move in. It was my fault, and I apologise for that.

Sebastian

Ellinor read the short message again. And again. Then she screwed up the piece of paper and threw it on the floor. Little black dots were dancing before her eyes. She let out a scream, like a wounded animal. It echoed through the stairwell, then she calmed down. Took a deep breath, regained control.

So many emotions, all at the same time. Rage, shock, fear. She had to try and think clearly.

He couldn't throw her out.

She wouldn't let him throw her out.

He hadn't thrown her out.

She tried the key one more time. It didn't fit. But it should fit. She lived here! She tried again. Pushed harder. Same result. She started stabbing at the lock. The light went out again, but she hardly noticed.

She had to get in! This was her home!

The key slipped and she gashed her thumb on a piece of metal on the door. The keys fell to the ground and she crouched down, feeling her way across the stone floor. She couldn't find them. She got on her knees, sweeping her hands from side to side. Hit the keys and sent them cannoning into the neighbour's door. She didn't have the strength to get up and fetch them. She was finished. She collapsed in a heap and burst into tears.

She didn't know how long she sat there crying in the darkness, but eventually it stopped. That was how it felt. As if it just stopped. She had finished weeping. Sitting there wasn't helping the situation. Ellinor got to her feet, her movements calm and controlled, and wiped her wet cheeks with the back of her hands. She went over and switched the light back on, sniffing to clear the snot from her nose. She bent down and retrieved her keys, put them in her pocket, went over and picked up the cabin case with one hand and the plastic carrier bag with the other. She would go back to Västmannagatan, try to work this out. Nothing had changed, she told herself. This was just temporary. A crisis. But it was a crisis that could be sorted out. There was no reason to panic or to do anything rash. She had a plan. She would stick to it.

First of all she would take care of Valdemar Lithner.

Then she would take care of Sebastian.

Sunshine.

Brilliant sunshine.

His upper body was bare and the sweat was pouring down his back. The air was damp. Sticky. The heat and the humidity made him want to sit in the shade with a book; he found it exhausting. She didn't; she was a bundle of pure energy, perched on his shoulders exhorting him to go faster. She wanted to get down to the water, to the cool waves and the games. She laughed out loud when he stumbled, and held his stubbly cheeks more tightly in her soft little hands.

'Daddy, I want one of those.'

He looked where she was pointing. A little girl was playing with an inflatable dolphin.

They reached the sea. He could feel the sun burning his shoulders as soon as he put her down. Two thoughts, almost simultaneously.

Not much water today.

He'd forgotten the sunscreen.

They ran out into the water. The splashing. The laughter. The shouts from the shore.

The roar.

The wall of water. He saw it coming. Ran towards her. Grabbed hold of her. Her little hand in his. He thought he could feel the butterfly ring he had bought her. He mustn't let go. Never let go. All his strength, all his concentration. Focused. His whole life, right there in his hand.

But then she was gone. His hand was suddenly empty. He had let her go.

Sebastian woke up tangled in the thick duvet. Hot. Sweaty. Out of breath. The cramp in his right hand spreading up to his elbow.

With wild, flailing movements he fought his way out of the bed-clothes and sat up. Painfully he straightened his fingers. Blood on his palm.

The dream.

That fucking dream.

So vivid.

Detailed. Like a film. More. He could feel it. Smell it. Like reality. The whole thing.

Sometimes it consisted of disconnected fragments, and he would wake with a manageable level of anxiety, the sticky remnants of impressions, memories and fantasies that he knew would go away. This time it was as if he had experienced the whole thing all over again. It was many years since it had affected him so badly. He felt paralysed. His heart was racing. The sweat was pouring off him. He was weeping in silent, bottomless despair.

It was the children's fault. The children in that fucking grave. He shouldn't have anything to do with dead children. He couldn't handle it any more. They had led him straight to Sabine, straight to the heart of the pain and guilt he had tried to lock away over the years, but without success; it always leaked out just a little, slowly poisoning him. Now the lock had given way, and the door was wide open, leaving him mentally bruised and battered. His body felt just the same as it had done all those years ago. Afterwards. When he came round to the Boxing Day devastation. Alone.

Eventually he managed to get up. To his surprise he discovered that his legs were capable of carrying him. Then as now.

He staggered over to the chair where he had dropped his clothes and pulled on his T-shirt. He wouldn't be able to get back to sleep. What time was it? Twenty past four. Just over four hours' sleep. When would he be able to sleep again? He was already afraid of going to bed tonight, even though it was more than twenty hours away. He didn't want to spend another night in that bed. He didn't want to be in this room.

He opened the door and went out into the corridor. The hotel was silent. It was colder out here and he wondered whether to go back and put on his trousers, but decided not to bother. He padded barefoot past reception and into the restaurant. He went over to the chill counter and took out a can of Coke.

'Are you intending to pay for that?'

Sebastian gave a start and almost dropped the can. He spun around to see Ursula sitting over by the window, with two beer bottles on the table in front of her – one empty, one half-full.

'What are you doing here?' Sebastian asked as he walked towards her.

'I couldn't sleep. How about you?'

'I had a dream . . .'

'A nightmare?'

'Yes.'

Sebastian pulled out the chair opposite her and sat down. He opened the can and took a swig. Ursula gazed searchingly at him.

'So bad you had to get up?'

'Yes.'

'What was it about?'

'Why can't you sleep?'

'I asked first.'

'Why can't you sleep?' Sebastian repeated in exactly the same tone of voice.

Ursula met his eyes as she raised the bottle to her lips. Nocturnal conversations at the kitchen table. There had been a few. Quite pleasant, as she recalled. Perhaps she needed to confide in someone. Sebastian was someone. He knew her, but he wasn't too close. Not now. Not any more. And he was capable of being objective, of keeping a welcome distance from the whole thing. He wouldn't try to console her with trite sentimentality, or try to cheer her up. It could work. On one condition.

'You can't tell anybody.'

'Keeping secrets is actually one of the things I'm really good at.'

Ursula nodded; she couldn't argue with that. He had been sleeping with her sister while they were in a relationship. With her sister and God knows how many other women. Ursula hadn't had a clue. Edward Hinde had forced them both to think back to those days, and to her surprise Ursula had discovered that the anger she had nourished for so many years had more or less disappeared, and been replaced by something that resembled sadness. The man who had betrayed her so badly no longer existed. The Sebastian who had come back to them was someone different. Still brilliant, still selfish, irritating, self-confident and impossible in every way, but it was as if he had to make more of an effort to do what had come naturally in the past. When she saw him at the chill counter, when he didn't know that anyone was watching him, barefoot in his boxer shorts and a T-shirt, he had looked lonely. That was the first word that came into her head.

Lonely.

Miserable, or at least sad.

She didn't know why. The Hinde case and Sebastian's personal links to the victims had taken their toll on him, but the old Sebastian would have got back on his feet and moved on with comparative ease. Not this Sebastian. Not now. For whatever reason. What he had just said was true: he was good at keeping secrets. His own, at least, and she hoped it would apply to others' secrets too. Hers in particular.

'Micke has left me.'

Sebastian nodded. He had suspected there was a problem at home, but thought it was probably to do with Bella. He didn't think anything involving Micke would affect Ursula so deeply. He was an intermittent alcoholic who worked too hard at a job in which Ursula had never had any interest whatsoever; they had a daughter, but very little else in common, if he had understood correctly. As far as he could tell, that had always been the case. Their marriage was a complete mystery to him.

'Are you really upset about that?'

Ursula stared at him. She didn't know quite what response she had expected, but not that.

'My husband has left me for another woman after twenty-five years. So yes, I am . . .'

'I didn't think you loved him,' Sebastian said, leaning back with the can of Coke in his hand. Ursula realised she could add 'brutally honest' to 'objective' and 'keeping a welcome distance'.

'I didn't want to be left,' she said candidly, without commenting on his remark.

'Did you want to leave him – is that it?' Sebastian eyes gleamed in the semi-darkness. 'It's not the fact that you're getting a divorce that bothers you, but the fact that he's left you. You wanted to call the shots.'

'You know what, just forget it,' Ursula said, hands palm-down on the table to indicate that the conversation was over. She decided to go back to bed, but Sebastian leaned forward and placed his hand on hers.

'I didn't mean to tease you. I can see you're upset, I just don't really understand why. You've been unfaithful to him for twenty years.'

'Twenty years ago,' Ursula corrected him.

'So the fact that you're screwing Torkel doesn't count?'

Ursula stiffened. How did he know? Or was he just guessing? She met his gaze.

'Yes, I do know, and no, he hasn't said anything,' Sebastian reassured her. 'It's obvious.'

The fight went out of Ursula and she slumped back in her chair. What he said was true. Not about Torkel – well, that was true of course, but about Micke. He wasn't the great love of her life. No one was. It could have been Sebastian once upon a time, but now she thought she was incapable of loving the way other people expected to be loved. Micke had put up with her, for a long time. Torkel was willing to try, she knew that. Accept her for what she was, on her terms. The problem was that she didn't want him. She wanted only one thing. Since Micke's departure it had emerged as the single most important element in her life, and it was the one thing she was pretty sure she could never have.

Her daughter's love.

She looked at Sebastian again. He sat in silence, giving her space.

'You're right,' she said quietly. 'It's not really Micke. It's Bella.'

'What about her?'

'She's always been Daddy's girl, but as long as we were together, at least some of her love spilled over onto me.'

Sebastian could see the tears in her eyes in the faint light. Change.

If we don't believe that everything is pre-ordained, that nothing we do has any effect, then change always means that we have to look closely at ourselves. How did I end up here? What could I have done differently? What's happening? What shall I do now? Change brings about a certain level of self-awareness, which is not always entirely painless, and doesn't necessarily show the individual concerned in a very good light.

'How many times do you think she'll come home to see me now Micke's not there?'

Sebastian remained silent; the conversation was getting uncomfortably close to home. A daughter at a distance. The yearning for closeness. The fear that it will never happen.

'Never,' Ursula said, answering her own question and shaking her head as she pictured the future. 'She'll call me on birthdays and at Christmas, then gradually she'll forget the birthdays.'

'What makes you think that?'

'We don't really know one another,' Ursula said, so quickly and with such a lack of sentimentality that Sebastian realised she must have spent a great deal of time analysing her relationship with her daughter. 'I've kept my distance. That's what I do. With everyone. I give away small parts of myself, that's all. You can't do that with children. They need you. All the time.'

'Have you told her this?'

'It's too late. She's an adult.'

'I think you're wrong,' Sebastian said, with a mixture of conviction and optimism in his voice. 'I really hope it's not too late.' He saw her reaction to his unusually sincere tone. 'For your sake,' he added, to be on the safe side.

'Thank you.'

Sebastian nodded, and they sat in silence for a little while. Sebastian had nothing more to add, and Ursula obviously had nothing else to share. She emptied the second bottle, put it to one side, and rested her elbows on the table.

'So what about you?'

'What about me?'

'What did you dream about?'

Sebastian finished off the Coke as he quickly went through the options and the current circumstances in his head. Where did he stand in the team? Vanja was OK with him, and in spite of their little performance earlier, Billy liked him too. Torkel was Torkel. Ursula was still the one he might need to win over, although she had chosen to open up – and to him, not to anyone else in the team, although it was reasonable to assume she would be closer to them. He had hurt her badly once upon a time. He had asked her to forgive him, but she had refused. Perhaps he couldn't be forgiven. For anything. Given their history, perhaps a little honesty on his part wouldn't go amiss.

And yet it went against the grain. He didn't want to tell her. It was that simple. He just didn't want to.

He could lie, of course, but that wasn't an option right now.

'Some other time,' he said with a casual shrug, hoping she would accept it.

She did.

★　★　★

As soon as it grew light, Sebastian went out for a walk. His local knowledge was non-existent, so he decided to follow the stream or the river or whatever it was called. It had stopped raining temporarily, but the mist hovered over the sodden ground, and the clouds were dense and low. He couldn't see far in among the gnarled, distorted trees when he occasionally looked up. The track was an uneven sea of mud dotted with roots, and he had to watch where he was putting his feet in order to avoid slipping and sliding.

He and Ursula had stayed in the desolate restaurant for a little while longer, then gone back to their rooms. She had reminded him that he had promised to say nothing; he had nodded and promised again.

Sebastian had sat down at the little folding table by the window in his room and switched on his mobile. Eight messages. All from Ellinor. In some she attempted to reason with him, in one she screamed and more or less threatened him, in one she begged for forgiveness and promised to fix everything if only he would get in touch. In the last one she sounded perfectly calm; she said that she understood, and would take care of everything. Sebastian switched off the phone. Perhaps he hadn't gone about the situation in the best way, but it would have to wait until he got back to Stockholm. He had other, more important, things to think about now.

He had sat there in his room, on a fairly uncomfortable wooden chair, trying to formulate a plan.

Make a decision.

He hadn't succeeded. He couldn't concentrate properly. The dream lingered like a veil over his mind. The memory took on an almost physical form; time and again he realised that his right hand was tightly clenched. He got to his feet, paced up and down, but that just made him more restless. He had to get out. Get away.

Exercise, fresh air, nature, being alone without being shut in – perhaps that would help him to focus.

So now he was walking alongside the rushing water, with his eyes on the ground. The track swung sharply to the left, leading to some kind of metal bridge with double planks of wood to walk on, and a cable handrail on either side. Sebastian walked to the middle of the bridge and stopped.

A bird he didn't know the name of was hopping around in and by the water where the river had eaten its way into the bank and was calmer, almost still. He followed the bird's jerky, almost nervous movements and let his mind wander.

From the dream to his conversation with Ursula to Vanja. Always back to Vanja.

It was all connected.

She was going to leave him. OK, he could go and visit her. But how many times before it started to look odd? Once? Twice? They could call one another, email, he could get that Skype thing if necessary. But all those were ways of maintaining a relationship that already existed, not starting a new one. It would be weird talking to her via a computer screen when they rarely spoke in real life. In five years' time it might work, when they were friends. When he was someone whose presence in her life she valued. For real, for the person he was, not because he had saved her from Edward Hinde.

That wasn't the way things were now.

Not yet.

This was his chance to get close to her, to create something that would last, something living. But only if she was here. Not thousands of miles away.

The little bird had obviously finished whatever it had been doing in the water, because it flew off among the trees above the bank and disappeared. Sebastian straightened up.

It was actually very clear.

Very simple.

It was wrong, of course. Selfish, he knew that. There was no hint of fatherly concern in what he was planning to do, but that was the way it had to be.

He turned back. By the time he stepped off the bridge, he had decided to act.

He didn't know how, but he was going to make sure Vanja didn't leave.

Make sure she stayed in Stockholm.

Stayed with him.

The morning walk was refreshing. Barnhusbron, Scheelegatan, past the Town Hall, then left along Hantverkargatan. Ellinor strode along, the plastic carrier bag clutched firmly in her left hand. She was on a mission not only to see justice done, but to save her relationship with Sebastian.

She felt surprisingly alert considering the lack of sleep. Everything had seemed utterly hopeless when she got back to her old apartment late last night. She had called Sebastian. Repeatedly. Got nothing but his brief voicemail recording. Ellinor had said something every time, she couldn't really remember what, there had been so many thoughts to deal with, so many emotions. Eventually she had slumped down on the sofa in the living room. She had no idea how long she had sat there.

However, the realisation had come to her late last night, or early this morning, to be more accurate. What was going on. How it all hung together.

Why hadn't she worked it out before? After all, she knew her Sebastian. Strength comes from being alone, that was his motto. He had problems with emotions, found it difficult to express what he really wanted.

He was too stubborn to ask for help.

Too proud to appear needy.

Too protective of her to burden her with his worries and concerns.

Just think about the way he had got her to move in with him. He had come to see her with some tale of a serial killer who might be after her, told her she had to leave her apartment instead of simply telling the truth – that he wanted her. The same thing was happening now. Clearly there was something completely different behind his actions on this occasion too. The more she thought about it, the more certain she became.

Once she had worked it out, the rest was very simple. Obvious.

What reason could he possibly have for leaving her?

He was afraid that she might come to some harm.

Someone was threatening him.

It was only natural that he didn't want her anywhere near him. She had seen that kind of thing on TV, where the detective or the prosecutor or whoever it might be sent their nearest and dearest away so that they wouldn't be in danger. That was why he had gone away. Gone to ground. That was why he wasn't answering his phone. He was ready to sacrifice their love for her safety.

But who was threatening Sebastian?

The obvious answer was Valdemar Lithner.

Anyway, she would start there and see if the situation changed when he was out of the picture. If not, she would have to make Sebastian open up to her, make him realise that they must share their troubles as well as their joys. That they could get through anything as long as they were honest, and together.

She had called Sebastian one more time and explained in a calm, convincing tone of voice that she understood, and would take care of everything.

At precisely eight o'clock she was standing outside the Economic Crime Authority on Hantverkargatan. Ellinor didn't know much about architecture, but she she thought the six-storey building in Kungsholmen had something of the Seventies about it. There was a small green area across the road behind iron railings, and down at the bottom of the street she could see the tower of the City Hall. The sun had been up for a while, and it looked as if it was going to be a glorious autumn day after last night's rain. Ellinor marched past a naked lady made of bronze, pushed open the door, looked at the information board in the foyer and took the lift to the right floor.

★ ★ ★

'How can I help you?' said the young man who had come to fetch her from reception, showing her to a chair on the opposite side of the desk.

'Well, as I told your receptionist, I've come to report a criminal.'

'Someone involved in economic crime?'

101

'That's right, economic crime.' She repeated the words with a certain amount of emphasis. It was exciting just to say them out loud. It was exciting to be here. Exciting and essential.

'OK . . .' The young man turned to his computer, brought up a form and placed his hands over the keyboard.

'Who would you like to report, and what exactly has this person done?'

'I've got everything here.'

Ellinor dumped the plastic carrier bag on the desk. The police officer regarded it with a certain amount of suspicion.

'What's that?'

'An investigation. Evidence. Everything you need.'

The man's expression suggested he was anything but convinced. He peered inside at the bundles of papers, and couldn't suppress a sigh. Ellinor realised it was time to put some weight behind her assertion.

'It's all above board – it's not something I've come up with. A police officer carried out the investigation.'

The young man's curiosity was piqued.

'A police officer?'

'Yes.'

'And who is this police officer?'

'His name is, or rather was, Trolle Hermansson. He's dead.'

The officer merely nodded politely at this information; he had clearly never heard the name before.

'What happens now?' Ellinor asked.

'We'll take a look and decide whether to carry out an investigation.'

'It *is* an investigation,' Ellinor insisted. 'As I said, everything you need is in there.'

'If we do carry out an investigation,' the young man said, ignoring the interruption, 'it will be a relatively speedy process. Our target is within fifty days in the case of less serious economic crimes.'

'I don't know how serious this is.'

'Which is why we need to take a look at it.'

Ellinor didn't move. Had she forgotten anything? She had done what she came to do. Admittedly fifty days was a hell of a long time, but no doubt they were very busy. She got to her feet. The young man did the same and held out his hand. She shook it, then hesitated. Perhaps she could get them to prioritise the case.

'The sooner this man is locked up, the better. I think he's threatening my partner.'

'You think?'

'Yes.'

'Has your partner reported a threat?'

'No, but he's thrown me out. To protect me.'

Ellinor noticed that the young man was nodding to himself in a way that might suggest he didn't believe her, but of course he must be familiar with the problem. He was a police officer, after all. She had read that witnesses being threatened was a growing problem in society.

'We'll see what we can do . . .'

'Good, but as I said, the sooner you deal with Valdemar Lithner, the better.'

Ellinor turned and left.

Peter Gornack watched her go. It had all happened very quickly. The call from reception, the meeting, the discussion. The usual. But then an ordinary report from an ordinary member of the public had turned into an 'investigation' in a plastic carrier bag, somehow involving a dead police officer and an ex-partner in danger. The second that bag had landed on Peter's desk, he had instinctively felt this was going to be a waste of his time. He would dutifully flick through some of the documents, then quickly write off the case. He had no doubt about that at all. Until she said the name.

Valdemar Lithner.

He had attended the Police Academy with Vanja Lithner; they had even hooked up for a while during their second year. She had ended the relationship after a few months: nothing dramatic, no major problems. They had carried on training together, as friends. They had never become colleagues, because they had chosen different routes once their training was finished. He knew she was working with Riksmord now, but he hadn't seen her for years. But Peter was pretty sure her father was called Valdemar, and there couldn't be that many families called Lithner, could there? Was this a complaint against Vanja's father? All the more reason to get it over and done with as soon as possible.

Peter emptied the bag on the desk, opened the top folder and stopped dead.

A copy of a police investigation.

By the Economic Crime Authority.

He closed the folder and turned to his computer. He typed in the name and the result came up immediately: a preliminary investigation from 2008. The prosecutor had decided not to take it any further due to a lack of evidence. Peter turned back to the pile on his desk. The police investigation made up only half of the documents; the rest was new material. New evidence.

He put the original folder to one side, picked up the rest, leaned back and began to read.

After less than a minute he came across Daktea Investments, a name that everyone on the team recognised only too well. He went straight to his immediate superior.

★ ★ ★

Ingrid Ericsson remembered Valdemar Lithner.

Very well, in fact. Not the biggest fish they hadn't managed to catch, but not the smallest either. A number of companies stripped just before they went bankrupt, the assets moved to Panama, a fall guy who took the rap in Sweden, and an account in Latin America where it was impossible to find out who had signed the documentation or where the money went from there. A couple of million kronor, that's what they were looking at. The summer cottage, the daughter's apartment, a new car. Valdemar hadn't been afraid of splashing the cash; he had seemed sure nothing could be traced back to him. And he had been right. Ingrid had tried, worked very hard. As head of department she had been responsible for the preliminary investigation that Peter Gornack had just brought in. According to Peter, he had got it from a woman called Ellinor Bergkvist, along with a lot of other material. The most interesting thing was the link to Daktea.

If Lithner had been involved in that particular tangled mess, then he was definitely one of the biggest economic criminals they had failed to bring to justice. Until now. If the material Ingrid had in front of her proved correct, they would bring Lithner down this time.

Daktea Investments had been a huge Ponzi scheme, ostensibly a sound financial product, but in fact a pyramid scheme where those responsible disappeared without trace when the bubble burst. Thousands of small savers and investors lost everything. The

104

Economic Crime Authority had put huge amounts of effort and resources into tracking down those behind the scheme, but they had been very adept at hiding their identity via a complex network of cross-ownership through anonymous foundations and holding companies in tax havens like Panama and the Cayman Islands. She didn't believe that Lithner was one of the major players, this was too big for him, but he had been involved in the construction, and had handled some of the money; that was very clear from the new material. It was enough for Ingrid.

It would be an over-exaggeration to say that she had taken it personally when they had had to shelve the previous investigation, but there was a certain satisfaction in the thought of bringing in someone of whose guilt she was so convinced. That was why she decided to act fast. Her department normally launched an inquiry within fifty days of being tipped off or otherwise informed of some anomaly, but this wouldn't even take five hours if Ingrid had her way.

She called the prosecutor's office and spoke to Stig Wennberg, who had been in charge of the case last time. She explained why she wanted to re-open the preliminary investigation, faxed over the new information, and after less than half an hour she had been given the green light.

Ingrid was delighted. Not only would this improve the department's clear-up rate, she would get the media on board and it would send an unmistakable message to all those who, like Valdemar Lithner, thought they had got away with something. They would discover that even if it took a few years, perhaps even several years, many years, the Economic Crime Authority could strike at any time. They would never be safe.

She gathered her team. They would go through every detail of Lithner's affairs and finances, both personal and private. This time they knew what they were looking for.

Veronica Ström didn't have time.

She really didn't have time. There was so much to do before the move to Nairobi in February. She had no desire to sit in a café pretending to enjoy a cup of coffee while she waited for Alexander Söderling. With a certain amount of irritation she flicked through the magazine on the table in front of her.

A journalist from *M Magazine* had been calling her for weeks, begging for an interview. Veronica had had such a fantastic career and she seemed to be such an inspiring woman, the journalist had chirruped. Exactly the kind of person their readers wanted to know more about.

Veronica couldn't deny that she was right. She had a degree in business administration from the School of Economics in Stockholm, and had progressed via banks and newspapers to become the editor of the press and information bureau at the Foreign Office. After three years she had been promoted to the post of adviser to the foreign secretary, and in 2002 a new post was created for her, co-ordinating security policy within the government. Since 2008 she had held a senior post in the Defence Department, and from February she would be the Swedish ambassador in Kenya.

Veronica hadn't known much about the magazine when the journalist called her, so she had checked it out online. Features, beauty, fashion, health, travel, financial tips and advice for the over-fifties, it said. Veronica didn't know whether to feel slightly insulted. She would be forty-nine in December. She had spoken to her colleagues, and they were all agreed that it was a good platform. The journalist had been overjoyed when she said yes, assuring Veronica that it would be fun. They had arranged to meet next week.

But now she had a different meeting.

Where the hell was Söderling?

She had been surprised to hear from him. She hadn't given a thought to the events in Jämtland for many years. She didn't think Söderling's call was a reason to start worrying. OK, so the bodies had been found, but the risk of anyone ever working out the whole picture was infinitesimal. The conversation with Söderling had been like a fly on a summer's day: irritating, but easily swatted away.

Then he had called again, wanting to meet. Which meant there were problems. She looked around. It was Söderling who had suggested the location: an old building on Riddargatan. The café was split over several floors, with a narrow stone staircase leading from one to the next. Small rooms designed to give the impression of familiarity, the feeling that you were in someone's home, with mismatched chairs, old sofas and wobbly tables. Veronica thought it was grubby, musty, and cluttered with too much furniture. It was like having coffee in the middle of a flea market.

He came up the stairs looking stressed and started checking out the various rooms. He didn't notice her at first, which was exactly what she wanted. There was nothing odd in their meeting, but nor was it something they needed to publicise.

Alexander came over, apologised for his late arrival and sat down. He placed his briefcase on the floor and leaned forward.

'I've given quite a lot of thought to . . . recent events,' he said quietly.

'I haven't,' Veronica said coldly. 'To be honest, I'm hoping to avoid the subject in the future too.'

Alexander shook his head.

'Unfortunately I don't think that will be possible,' he said apologetically. 'I need help.'

Veronica sighed. She didn't want to help him. She wanted to carry on getting ready for the coming move to Nairobi. She wanted to become Swedish ambassador and forget all about the autumn of 2003.

'With what?' she asked anyway, well aware that everything Alexander Söderling did to protect himself also protected her.

'You remember the refusal to grant asylum that we made sure was marked classified?'

Veronica nodded. One of the simpler elements in the operation. A word to the right person and it was done. The Solna police had enough to do without looking for refugees who had gone on the run, so they were almost grateful. No one had reacted.

'We need to remove one of the names,' Alexander went on. 'The referral.'

'Why?'

'Well, they've found the bodies,' he said, sounding surprised. He obviously thought she ought to understand. 'There's only a small risk that they'll make the connection, but if they do . . .'

He didn't finish the sentence. He didn't need to. She understood perfectly. The threads that remained were long and tangled, but it would be possible to follow them. Of course it was best to snip off as many as possible. Better late than never. She nodded.

'I'll sort it. Anything else?'

'Not that I can think of.'

'So this is the end of it.'

'Hopefully.'

'Good.'

She got up and left the little room without even looking at him. No one took any notice of her departure. She would make the call, make sure the name disappeared, and then she would put this whole sorry mess behind her.

That was the plan. It was a good plan.

Unfortunately something deep down inside told her it probably wasn't going to be that easy.

The minute hand on the clock above the door edged onto the twelve as Torkel entered the room to start the meeting. The others were already gathered.

They had said eleven o'clock.

Torkel walked in at eleven o'clock.

To the second. Vanja realised it was pure chance, but she couldn't help smiling. Torkel would have been pleased with his entrance if he had known.

'What have we got today?' he said, sitting down.

'We've checked the relevant reports from October 2003,' Billy began, pushing sets of printouts into the middle of the table. The others helped themselves; Sebastian didn't bother. Ursula caught his eye and gave him a little smile; Sebastian responded with a nod.

Torkel was just about to ask Sebastian why he hadn't taken a copy of the material, but stopped himself when he saw the nod. He watched as Ursula sat back in her chair, her smile a little wider. For a moment Torkel felt a pang of jealousy, but he quickly and efficiently pushed it aside.

Ursula and Sebastian.

It was out of the question. Unthinkable. Ursula was the member of the team who disliked Sebastian the most. They had been colleagues back in the Nineties and, if Torkel remembered rightly, they had got on very well. Then something happened. They carried on working together, but it seemed more . . . professional, more strained. The closeness, the friendship between them was gone. Then Sebastian left. Ursula had never talked about it. Torkel assumed Sebastian had hurt her in some way. That was his speciality, even back then. Whatever had happened, it hadn't gone away. On previous occasions when Sebastian had worked with Riksmord, Ursula

109

had made her displeasure very clear. She had accepted him after he had saved Vanja's life, but no more than that.

'We focused on the week when Jan and Framke Bakker went missing,' Billy went on, and Torkel turned his full attention to the matter in hand. 'There are no reports of anyone taking off without paying their bill in any hotel, guest house or hostel in the area.'

Jennifer took over: 'No abandoned cars were found or towed away, and no camping equipment was found on the mountain or handed in.'

'And, as we already know, there are no further reports of missing persons in the area at the time,' Billy finished off.

Vanja looked at them. Twenty-four hours and they were already taking it in turns to speak. Like Huey, Dewey and Louie in the Donald Duck cartoons. Or Chip 'n' Dale. Sweet, but slightly disturbing.

'I've heard from Umeå,' Ursula said. 'Nine millimetre. Probably the same gun, probably an automatic handgun, but this is only a preliminary report.'

Sebastian nodded to himself. Suddenly the case was slightly more engaging. An automatic handgun. Not nearly as common up here as a rifle. Not the kind of thing someone would usually take with them if they were out walking in the mountains. Everything suggested that the perpetrator had deliberately chosen those four, had known exactly where they were, and when. The victims knew their killer, Sebastian was sure of it. As soon as they were identified, the case would open up.

'I've been looking for reports of missing families and missing children,' Vanja began. Sebastian leaned forward; this was much more like it. 'Three families fit so far: two adults, two children. But none of them disappeared in the autumn of 2003.'

She too placed a set of printouts on the table; Sebastian took one this time. It wouldn't hurt to show an interest in Vanja's work. He hoped she would notice that he had picked up her notes, no one else's.

'As you can see, the Thorilsen family from Norway went missing during a holiday up near Trondheim in summer 2000.'

'That's close,' Billy said, more or less to himself.

'The children are the right age, if Ursula's estimate is correct,' Vanja went on. 'Six and eight. They've never been found.'

'But that means they disappeared three years before they ended up in the grave,' Torkel said. He knew everyone around the table was thinking the same thing, but no one wanted to be the one to point out the holes in a promising lead. No one apart from Sebastian, but he wasn't saying anything. Oddly enough. Instead Billy spoke up:

'Or they disappeared in 2000, but they didn't die until 2003.'

'So where were they for three years? There's nothing in the Norwegian police investigation to suggest that they were staying away deliberately,' Vanja countered. Billy didn't reply. The idea that someone would have held the family captive for three years then killed them was highly unlikely.

'Let's move on,' Torkel said, turning to the next page in Vanja's notes.

'The second family, the Hagbergs from Gävle, went missing in 2002, but their disappearance was written off as a flight to some tax haven. When they started looking into the family's affairs, it turned out that the father had embezzled large amounts of money from his employer. However, the children are the right ages: five and eight.'

No one had anything to say, so Vanja continued.

'The last family are the Cederkvists. Went missing at some point after February 2004 during a round the world sailing trip; they set off from Gothenburg in November the previous year. The father's brother got a postcard from Zanzibar in the first week of February, then nothing. Neither the family nor the boat were ever found.'

Vanja fell silent. No one had anything to say this time either, and Torkel knew why. They were disappointed. There was nothing to suggest that they had found one of the missing families. The Norwegians were the best option, but there were too many question marks for the team to feel they had actually got somewhere.

'When it comes to single individuals with children, the list is a little longer. But not much. Three men disappeared with their children in 2001, 2003 and 2004. All are believed to have kidnapped the children and taken them back to their home countries. You have all the details in my report. A woman and her daughter went missing in Örebro in 2002; the mother was deeply depressed, and the assumption is that she took her own life and that of her child. They were never found. A four-year-old disappeared in Trollhättan in 2005, he was never found either.' Vanja threw down her notes.

Silence. They had felt quite optimistic yesterday; if only they could identify the victims, it would bring them closer to the killer. Much closer. Two adults, two children. Someone somewhere must have missed them; a whole family couldn't just vanish, and yet that was exactly what they seemed to have done.

'We need to expand the search,' Torkel said with an audible sigh. 'Get in touch with Europol, go international. This is a popular tourist destination. Vanja, co-ordinate the search with Billy and Jennifer, make sure it's as wide-ranging and efficient as possible.'

Vanja nodded and gathered up her papers, a satisfied little smile on her face.

'The Dutch couple's kit,' Billy said, leaning back in his chair with his hands clasped behind his neck.

'What about it?' Ursula wondered.

'We haven't found it.'

'So?'

Billy lowered his hands, leaned forward and shrugged.

'They were still wearing their clothes, so where's the rest of their stuff?' He glanced at Sebastian as if expecting opposition from that direction. 'They were supposed to be spending a week walking in the mountains, so they must have had a fair amount with them.'

'Perhaps he took it,' Vanja suggested. 'The killer, I mean.'

'Why? That just gave him more to carry.'

'But we don't know how he got there. He might have had a four-wheel drive.'

'Billy has a point,' Ursula broke in. 'Their bags could still be up there.' She turned to Torkel. 'I'd like a wider area around the grave excavated.'

Torkel sighed again, which wasn't like him at all. He disapproved of sighs and groans in meetings; they lowered the energy level, brought an air of negativity that he preferred to avoid.

'OK, but I think there have already been protests; it's a nature conservation area.'

'And this is a murder inquiry,' Ursula snapped. 'It's a question of priorities.'

'Tell that to the tree-huggers.'

'I thought that was your job.'

She smiled at him and gathered up her papers. They weren't going to get any further; everyone began to make a move.

'There was just one thing . . .' Jennifer's voice stopped them. 'Something I found when I was looking into missing cars.'

Everyone sat back down and looked encouragingly at the newcomer.

'The dead body of a woman was found in a burnt-out car up here on 31 October 2003.'

The whole team unconsciously straightened up; this was interesting, the most interesting thing that had been said since they started.

Billy turned to Jennifer, hoping she would meet his enquiring look. Why hadn't she told him about this? He was more than a little annoyed. They had worked side by side for an hour or so after yesterday's meeting, and all morning since breakfast. He understood perfectly if she felt she needed to prove something, justify her place on the team, given that she was here for a trial period only, but surely she could have said something to him. Naturally he would have let her pass on the information to the others, let her take all the credit. She refused to meet his eye; her gaze was fixed on Torkel. A hint of doubt crept in. They had got on really well from the start, he and Jennifer. She had told him several times how pleased she was to have been given this opportunity. He was pleased too. He hadn't really admitted the reason to himself, but it was nice to have someone who was new, who was feeling their way forward. Who, to be honest, was below him in this unspoken hierarchy. But then this, out of nowhere. Important information that she had kept from him, in spite of the fact that they were supposed to be working together. Why? Had he failed to realise how ambitious she was? Did she want to be the leading investigator on the team? Did she want to be the best? Was she the new Vanja in every way?

'The woman was never identified; there were no documents in the car,' Jennifer went on, apparently oblivious to Billy's questioning looks. 'But the vehicle had been rented by a Patricia Wellton the previous day in Östersund. However, Patricia Wellton doesn't exist.'

'What do you mean, she doesn't exist?' Vanja wondered.

'She doesn't exist. Fake ID. No one knows who she is. According to the report she spoke English and had an American driver's licence.'

'But she wasn't reported missing in the USA?'

Jennifer shook her head. 'There has never been a Patricia Wellton with her ID or driver's licence number in the USA, again according to this report, which is extremely detailed.'

Jennifer handed out her notes, and Torkel quickly glanced through them.

'Double-check everything,' he said, his glance sweeping over Vanja, Jennifer and Billy. 'See if we can find out where she entered the country, get hold of everything there is on the accident – pictures, post-mortem report, the lot. When did you say she was found?'

'On the morning of 31 October.'

'Where?'

Jennifer got up and went over to the map. She circled a small area to the side of the E14 in red.

'Here. They think she lost control of the car and went into the ravine.'

'And it caught fire?' Vanja said.

'Yes.'

Vanja carried on looking through the material in silence. It was extremely unusual for a car to catch fire or explode in an accident involving only one vehicle. It happened all the time in films, of course – in reality it was very rare, which made this crash even more suspicious.

'An unidentified woman with false ID is found dead in the same week as we think six people ended up in a mass grave on the mountain.'

Torkel didn't need to say any more. There was a faint possibility that the two events weren't connected, but experience and the laws of probability made it unlikely.

Suddenly they had a new set of priorities.

★ ★ ★

'Could I have a word?'

Billy grabbed hold of Jennifer just as she was about to leave the room. He knew that what had just happened would eat away at him all day, if not longer. Best to deal with it now. Get it out of the way.

'Of course, what is it?' Jennifer was still glowing from all the praise she had been given before Torkel brought the meeting to a close. She noticed that Billy didn't look quite so happy.

'Why didn't you tell me about the burnt-out car?'

114

'Sorry?' There was genuine surprise in Jennifer's voice.

'When we were working together before the meeting,' Billy clarified. 'Why didn't you tell me about the burnt-out car?'

'I was looking for anything to do with cars during the relevant period, and it just came up.'

'And you didn't think of mentioning it to me?'

'You mean before everybody else?'

'Yes.'

'Should I have done?'

'What do you think?'

Jennifer shrugged, looking a little puzzled.

'You were busy with the hotels and hostels; if you'd found anything I wouldn't have expected you to tell me. I thought the most important thing was to inform the whole team.'

Billy didn't reply. There was something in what she said; that was why the team had such regular meetings. They all worked independently, then passed on information when they got together. Just as Jennifer had done. Why was he being so over-sensitive? He was beginning to wish he'd just let it go.

'But if I come across anything else I'm happy to run it by you first,' Jennifer said, interpreting his silence as a sign that she'd got it wrong. 'It's not a problem.'

'There's no need,' Billy said quietly. He glanced to the side, out into the corridor behind her – anything but look her in the eye.

'Are you sure? I mean, if you want to present whatever we come up with, I'm fine with that too.'

'No, really, it's OK.' Billy made eye contact and managed a faint smile, hoping it would take the sting out of his initial sourness.

'Are you sure?' Jennifer still seemed a little uneasy about the situation.

'Absolutely. I was wrong. I'm sorry.'

'So we're all good?'

'We're all good.'

'Great, because I really don't want to upset people.'

'You haven't. I promise.'

Jennifer gave him a warm smile and walked away. Billy stayed where he was, feeling more than a little troubled. What the hell had happened to him? What was he doing? Getting annoyed because Jennifer hadn't spoken to him first, which meant he felt threatened in some way. Which in turn meant that Vanja's comment about being a better cop than him had gone deeper than he thought. He was sure he'd put all that behind him; they'd sorted it out. He had gone back to the aspects of the job he was best at, realised that they had different, but equally important roles within the team. At least he thought so. But now there was this business with Jennifer. And the fact that he hadn't applied for the FBI training course. Small signals.

Did he doubt his own abilities, or was he turning into one of those bitter individuals who never climbed the ladder, and ended up believing that everyone else was working against him? He couldn't let that happen. None of it. He was too young, and he loved his job too much. Perhaps it would be better to start all over again. Leave Riksmord and apply for something new.

Valdemar Lithner rolled over onto his right side and looked at the clock on the bedside table. Time to go back to work. He had come home for lunch, eaten some cereal and a yoghurt at the kitchen island, then gone for a lie-down. He was tired these days, although he didn't really know why. He was sleeping just as well as ever, but he never felt properly rested. He had heard that could be a symptom of burnout, but it didn't seem likely in his case. He wasn't working any harder than usual, quite the reverse in fact, and he didn't feel stressed or under pressure. However, he was getting less and less done, and then there was that nagging pain in his lower back. Could he have twisted it? It didn't feel like a muscle strain though. He left the bedroom and walked through the silent, empty apartment. It would feel even more silent and empty in a few months when Vanja moved to the USA.

She hadn't lived with him and Anna for many years, but she was a frequent visitor. They had dinner together every Thursday, but she often called in, watched TV for a while, had a coffee, stayed for something to eat. If she was near his office she would call him and ask if he had time to meet up for lunch. Now all that would end. She would be far, far away, for a long time, and Valdemar would lose the thing he valued most in life: the close contact with his daughter.

Of course he wanted her to go. He was incredibly proud of her – he always had been. He had felt nothing but joy and pride when she was chosen to join Riksmord, but now those feelings were tinged with sorrow, and the sense of loss was tangible when he thought about her living in Virginia, even though there were still a couple of months to go before she actually left.

He wouldn't be alone. He wouldn't be short of love and companionship. He and Anna had a good marriage, they still loved one

117

another, and whenever he thought about his future, Anna was always there. But his relationship with Vanja was so special, they were so close. They always had been. He had had more patience with her than Anna when she was little; he had enjoyed playing games, doing things on her terms, and Anna had been grateful for the respite. When other men at work or in other contexts had complained about their teenage daughters, talked about the arguments and outbursts and saying that it was like living with an alien, Valdemar hadn't recognised their situation at all. He had always been able to reason with his daughter, to discuss things and reach a joint decision. Perhaps it was because she had always been very mature for her age, but he liked to think it was because the bond between them was so important to both of them that they weren't prepared to test the boundaries. Anna had had a more difficult time with Vanja during her teenage years, and had therefore handed over many of the decisions and rules of engagement to him. The relationship between mother and daughter was generally more complex than the one between him and Vanja. It wasn't open war, and they didn't exchange harsh words, but they just weren't as close.

Vanja had always been Daddy's girl. And now she was going to leave him.

When she told him about her plans, his initial reaction had been that she couldn't go. He would forbid it. Find a way to keep her here. For the first time he could remember, he had deliberately lied to her, said it sounded like a good idea. Over the next few weeks he had struggled to suppress the hope that she would fail. He had to keep on telling himself that this was something she really wanted. It would make her happy, and therefore it would make him happy too.

By this stage he really did want her to succeed, but sometimes the sense of loss overwhelmed him. Even before she had gone. How would he feel when it actually happened?

He shook off his gloomy thoughts, went back into the kitchen and poured himself a glass of water. He glanced at his watch; time to go. As he put the glass in the dishwasher and headed into the hallway, his mobile rang. Annika, his secretary. As soon as he answered she let fly with a lengthy and rapid harangue. He couldn't quite grasp everything she said; she seemed upset, and he hoped he had misunderstood. He fought to keep his voice steady as he asked her to calm down and repeat what she had just said. Annika took a deep breath, and unfortunately he realised that he had got it right the first time. The police were there, demanding documents dating back several years, and she thought he ought to come in right away. Valdemar told her he was leaving immediately, and ended the call.

He stood in the hallway trying to gather his thoughts.

But he'd got away with it.

He'd taken a shortcut.

The preliminary investigation had been shelved. Lack of evidence.

He'd done it for the sake of the family.

Wrong, of course. Easy, but wrong. He had put it all behind him, forgotten it, suppressed it. The police were in his office. It could hardly be about anything else. Why now? Why had they come back?

An easy way of giving them what he would otherwise have been unable to give them.

They wouldn't have come back if they didn't think they could bring him down this time. What had happened? He wasn't a criminal, it had just been so tempting. So easy.

A shortcut.

A safe shortcut.

How should he handle this?

The sound of a bell broke the silence. Valdemar gave a start. The doorbell. Who would call round at this time? Nobody was supposed to be home. He opened the door with his mind still elsewhere, but in an instant everything came together.

He recognised his visitor.

Ingrid Ericsson from the Economic Crime Authority.

She was smiling.

After the morning meeting they all had plenty to do. Billy had been tasked with finding out when and where Patricia Wellton had entered the country. They all knew it was a time-consuming and possibly futile exercise. If Patricia Wellton, whoever she was, had come in by train or car they would never find her, but they had to try. He had asked Jennifer to help him, and she was happy to oblige. He stressed that she didn't need to inform him personally if she found anything, and apologised again for his earlier comment. She waved his apology away; it was fine.

They sat down opposite one another in the empty restaurant, equipped with a laptop and mobile phone each, and started from the beginning. What did they know? Not much. Patricia Wellton had hired a car in Östersund on the morning of 30 October 2003 – that was about it. It was relatively easy to establish that there were no direct flights from overseas into Östersund at the relevant time apart from charter flights, which were very rare. No charter flight had landed on the morning of the thirtieth. The closest in terms of time was a flight from Amsterdam on the morning of 26 October. Billy and Jennifer discussed the possibility that Patricia had spent four days in Östersund, but dismissed the idea more or less right away.

That left domestic flights and trains. They decided to start with the two largest airports in Sweden; Jennifer took Arlanda, Billy Landvetter.

Before they made a start they collected a flask of coffee from the kitchen and found a packet of biscuits in one of the cupboards, jotting down what they had taken on the list by the counter. Mats and Klara had introduced the system on the first evening: 'Take whatever you want, whenever you want, but make a note of it'.

Back in the restaurant they poured themselves a cup of coffee and looked at one another across the table. Billy sighed.

120

'OK, let's do this.'

They raised their cups in a toast, then started calling every airline that had flown into Stockholm and Gothenburg on 30 October 2003 and in the preceding week, requesting access to their passenger lists. Not only would they have to plough through an enormous amount of bureaucracy, but even if they did get hold of the information they would be looking at thousands of names. There was also a significant risk that the details were no longer available.

'This is like the labour of Sisyphus,' Jennifer said, smiling at Billy over her laptop.

'Absolutely,' Billy said, smiling back. He didn't really know who or what Sisyphus was, something to do with Greek mythology perhaps, but he had no intention of asking.

★ ★ ★

Torkel's task was to see if someone in the USA could help him to identify Patricia Wellton. The driver's licence she had been using looked perfectly authentic as far as he could see from the photocopy in the car hire documentation. A good forgery; with a bit of luck it was so good that it meant she had used the alias before, in which case the US authorities might be able to trace her real identity. If she was a US citizen, of course. There was a possibility that she came from a different country, and was merely using an American ID. Still, he had to start somewhere.

It was highly unlikely that Torkel himself would be able to find the right person to speak to and get the information direct from the USA, so he contacted IPO, the department in the National Crime Unit dealing with international police co-operation. Börje Dahlberg answered. Torkel knew him well, and after a quick chat about work and life, which sadly in Torkel's case came down to the same thing, Börje said he would do his best. Torkel thanked him and hung up. There wasn't much more he could do at the moment. He left his room and wandered down the corridor. He went past Ursula's room, but didn't stop; he knew she had gone back up to the grave. Last night they had started sifting the earth they had removed; the work was continuing today, and Ursula wanted to be there. Torkel had already made the call asking for a wider area to be excavated in the hope of finding the Dutch couple's rucksacks; he had expected resistance, and had been ready to pull rank if necessary, but it had proved surprisingly easy to get a digger back out there. He had no intention of telling Ursula that, of course. The version she would hear was going to involve a whole series of officials tangled up in bureaucratic red tape, unreasonable tree-huggers, and journalists with sharpened pencils, all of whom Torkel had tirelessly battled for the sake of the investigation, but for her sake too, of course.

He went into the restaurant and saw Jennifer and Billy sitting opposite one another, both busy on the phone, both speaking English. He ambled over to the counter, picked up an empty cup, went over to their table and poured himself a coffee, then waited until one of them finished their call so that they could tell him what they needed help with.

★ ★ ★

After the meeting Vanja had decided to look into the burnt-out car. They had received all the details available from the rental firm in Östersund, and the police investigation into the accident had been very thorough. Unexpectedly thorough, Ursula would have said, Vanja thought with a smile. However, Vanja had a little more confidence in the local police, which admittedly wasn't saying much. Anyone who didn't think the local cops were hopeless amateurs with the competence of the average six-year-old had more confidence than Ursula.

Vanja decided to drive up to Åre. A report was a report, but there was always more to find out, particularly if the officers who had been working in 2003 were still there. She picked up the copy provided by Jennifer, pulled on her outdoor clothes and headed for the door.

'Where are you going?'

Vanja spun around and saw Sebastian slumped in one of the armchairs by the main entrance. He had an old copy of a magazine in his hand, and Vanja caught a glimpse of a half-finished crossword before he put it down. He seemed to be physically exuding boredom and weariness.

'Åre.'

'Why?'

'I want to see if I can find out more about that car accident.'

'Can I come with you?'

His voice full of hope. Vanja also noted that he had actually asked. 'I'm coming with you' would have been more like Sebastian's style, but after the Hinde case and everything that had happened he had changed. He was softer, somehow, she thought. Less confrontational, towards her at any rate. That was fine by her, and she really didn't mind if he came with her to Åre.

'Are you bored?' she asked with a nod at the dog-eared magazine.

'No, I can ponder over "Egyptian sun god, two letters" all day; I'd just like to get out for a while.'

Vanja nodded.

'OK. Hurry up then.'

'Two minutes,' Sebastian said, and she thought she saw a little smile of gratitude as he disappeared in the direction of his room.

Bored was an understatement. There was only one cure for the restlessness and anxiety in his body, but up here there was nobody to go to bed with. He had briefly considered Klara, but she was never more than two steps away from her beardy husband, and there was an air of the great outdoors about her that, to be honest, was something of a turn-off as far as he was concerned. A little outing with Vanja might relieve the worst of the tedium; otherwise there was nothing useful he could do up here.

Six skeletons and a car crash.

Nothing he could directly apply his knowledge to, so what should he do? In spite of the fact that it had stopped raining and turned into a fine autumn day, he had no desire to go for another walk. He had followed the river for half an hour, seen the landscape, and that was enough. He had never really understood the business of experiencing nature. Huge desolate areas were seriously overrated in Sebastian's opinion. Why was it more amazing to be able to see several kilometres in the distance rather than a couple of hundred metres? Admittedly waterfalls were impressive and mountains could be dramatic, but they did nothing for him. They didn't speak to him. During his years in the USA he had travelled around, seen the Grand Canyon, the Rocky Mountains, Niagara Falls. He had heard people ooh-ing and aah-ing, talking about how magnificent it all was, how it brought home how small we are.

As if that was a positive.

Idiots.

He grabbed his coat and headed back to the foyer. To Vanja.

★ ★ ★

They sat in silence most of the way, but that didn't bother Sebastian. There were different kinds of silence, and this was a good one. It wasn't a hostile exclusion, not an icy statement of intent, but a natural silence between two people who didn't need to fill every second with chatter. From time to time they would comment on something they saw; it was usually Vanja, and it was usually about the natural landscape all around them. She said she would like to go walking in the mountains one day, follow Kungsleden, the King's Trail, from Abisko to Hemavan. Take her time. Rucksack, tent and mosquito repellent, the whole experience. However, it was unlikely to happen any time soon if she moved to the USA.

Sebastian didn't take the bait. He didn't want to talk about the possibility of her going away. He wanted to enjoy the moment as they drove through the mountains together, enjoying each other's company. Besides which, he had decided: she wasn't going. He still hadn't worked out how to stop her; he had the beginnings of an idea, but it was far from fully formed.

'Kungsleden will still be here,' he said, looking out of the window; he was afraid that something would give away what he was thinking. Vanja was a police officer, after all, with an almost uncanny ability to tell just from their tone of voice whether people were lying or hiding something.

'Do you ski?' Vanja asked as they drew closer to Åre and began to see the wide slalom slopes and the skeleton of the ski lift on the left-hand side.

'No – how about you?'

'Not often and not particularly well, but I can get down.'

'Did your father teach you?'

Vanja quickly turned her head and gave Sebastian a questioning look. Was there something . . . strained in his tone? He kept his eyes fixed on the road ahead.

'Yes. Why do you ask?'

'No reason,' he replied with a shrug. 'It just seems like the kind of thing people teach their kids.'

Like swimming, he thought, and felt his right hand clench into a fist. He straightened his fingers and rested his elbow on the bottom of the window. He had to be careful. The dream was one thing, he had no control over that, but for it to come into his head now, in the car with Vanja . . . However much the dead children on the mountain had affected him, Sebastian Bergman was in control of his own thoughts. That was one of the reasons for his success, his greatness. He kept his intellect on a tight rein, never allowed it to run free, always made it work for him. He strove for full control, and usually achieved it.

'Have you never been married?' Vanja asked as they were passing Tegelfjäll.

Sebastian stiffened. He might be able to steer his own thoughts, but not the conversation, apparently. He quickly ran through his options. Tell her it was nothing to do with her. Not good, it would arouse suspicion and put her in a bad mood. Lie: a simple no. Could be exposed at a later stage and lead to more unnecessary questions. The truth. He decided on the truth. Up to a point, at least.

'Once, yes.'

'When?'

'Ninety-eight.'

'So when did you get divorced?'

Sebastian hesitated, but stuck to his chosen path. The truth.

'We didn't. She died.'

Vanja fell silent. Sebastian stared ahead. He had told Torkel that much when they met in Västerås, but no more. He had no intention of going any further now.

No one knew any more.

No one knew everything.

If Vanja carried on asking, he would start lying.

Or would he?

Should he tell someone for the first time? Tell her everything? About Lily and Sabine and the wave that took them both away from him. The sense of loss, the angst. How close he had been to going under. How he was still pretending to live his life, to a great extent.

It would presumably bring them closer, deepen their relationship. He couldn't see how it could be anything but beneficial, and yet it went against the grain.

He didn't want to do it.

The idea of using one daughter to get closer to the other just felt wrong, as if he were exploiting Sabine, profiting from her death for his own ends. Using her for emotional blackmail.

He didn't want to do it.

He couldn't do it.

'I'm sorry,' Vanja said quietly.

Sebastian nodded, keeping his fingers crossed that she wouldn't ask . . .

'How did she die?'

Sebastian sighed. He had to finish this. There was no point in dressing it up or trying a diversion. He couldn't leave it open to further discussion in the future. He had to finish it.

For ever.

He turned to face her.

'She died, isn't that enough? What do you want do know? Do you want to see the post-mortem report?'

Vanja glanced in his direction, then devoted her full attention to the car and the road. She had only wanted to show sympathy, but clearly this was a minefield, and whatever her intentions, she had overstepped the mark.

'I'm sorry, it's none of my business.'

'No, it isn't.'

Vanja didn't reply. What could she say? Sebastian had very efficiently put an end to any attempt at small talk. They drove on in silence.

★ ★ ★

'Are you sure this is right?' Sebastian asked as he got out of the car.

Vanja could understand his scepticism. The squat brown building in front of them looked more like a hairdresser's or a small pizzeria, but the GPS had brought them here, and the police emblem on the wall suggested they were indeed in the right place.

'They don't even occupy the whole building,' Sebastian said, pointing to the logo of an insurance company further along. 'What a dump. How many people work here?'

'I've no idea,' Vanja said, pushing open the door.

Inside they found a reception desk on the right, with a row of chairs along the opposite wall, and a table with a couple of newspapers and several police brochures scattered across its surface. Straight ahead was a door leading into some kind of office, with a staircase beside it. Vanja and Sebastian went over to the desk and Vanja explained who they were, and that they were expected. The woman behind the desk nodded, then yelled 'Kenneth!' in the direction of the stairs before turning back to the visitors with a smile. Sebastian smiled back. How old was she? Forty, forty-five perhaps? Short dark hair, high cheekbones, narrow lips, quite large breasts under the beautifully ironed uniform shirt. He leaned over the desk a fraction and noticed that she wasn't wearing a wedding ring.

'He won't be a minute,' the woman said as they heard footsteps on the floor above. A man aged about thirty-five came down and introduced himself as Kenneth Hultin.

'We've put everything out for you,' he said, showing them up the stairs. There were three desks in the room on the right at the top; Kenneth led them to the left, into something resembling a cupboard, which clearly served as the staff room. At one end there was a table covered in a yellow striped wax cloth, surrounded by four folding chairs; a small sink and a fridge had been squeezed into the other end. A microwave sat on top of the fridge, and the coffee machine was on the draining board. An unmistakable odour of fish pervaded the whole room.

'Would you like a coffee or something?' Kenneth said, nodding towards the half-full pot in the machine.

'What's something?' Sebastian asked.

'Sorry?'

'You said coffee or something – what's something?' Sebastian repeated.

'Erm . . . tea, water, some fruit maybe . . .' Kenneth waved in the direction of a bowl of apples on the table.

'We're fine, thanks,' Vanja interrupted; she looked sharply at Sebastian, who had already lost interest and was examining the large wall-hanging at the end of the table with an expression of distaste. Kenneth nodded and left them to it. Vanja sat down, opened the folder on the table and began to read.

The call had come in at 08.23 on the morning of 31 October 2003. The police had arrived at the scene at 08.57, and established that there was a dead body in the driving seat of the car, which had burnt out.

'I think I'll go for a walk.'

Vanja glanced up; Sebastian jerked his head in the direction of the door.

'I thought you came to help?'

'No, I came to get away from that depressing bloody mountain.'

He left the room and Vanja went back to her reading with a sigh.

The body in the car had been in such poor condition that it had been impossible to determine age or gender at the scene. The number plates had enabled them to identify the vehicle as a hire car that had been rented in Östersund by a Patricia Wellton from Kentucky, USA. When they tried to find her relatives, and to obtain dental records or other means to confirm the identity of the deceased, it turned out that there was no Patricia Wellton from Kentucky. Never had been. The driver's licence was a forgery, and that was as far as they'd got. They assumed that the body in the car was the woman who had called herself Patricia Wellton. No other women had been reported missing, but they could never be completely certain. The folder contained a pile of photographs; Vanja flicked through them and decided to take them with her. They would tell Ursula far more than they told her.

The car had been taken away for forensic examination. Vanja skimmed the report; there was nothing to explain why the car had left the road. The brakes and steering appeared to have been working perfectly.

Nor did the analysis of the scene provide any clue as to why the car had crashed. There was no sign of a puncture or a collision with a wild animal. The lack of skid marks or any other sign of an attempt to avert the accident led to speculation that the driver might have fallen asleep, or perhaps been taken ill.

Vanja turned back.

The post-mortem had been unable to establish whether or not the woman was alive when the car caught fire. Theoretically, she could have had a heart attack.

Vanja went back to the forensics report. At the end there was a list of the items found in the car. It was short. Very short. The boot had been empty. Vanja paused. Admittedly the woman wouldn't necessarily have had any luggage, even if that did seem rather strange bearing in mind that she had presumably travelled to Sweden, but she had provided ID when she picked up the car, and she had paid for it. She must have had a handbag, or at least a wallet or purse. But nothing like that had been found in the car or on the body. Vanja took out her notebook and wrote:

DRIVER'S LICENCE / MONEY?

Then she went back to the beginning of the folder with the notepad beside her. When she had gone through the material for a second time and jotted down the places where she had questions, she called Kenneth in the hope that he would be able to clear up at least some of them.

★ ★ ★

Twenty minutes later Vanja had the name of the person who had reported the accident, and the firm who had eventually removed the car. She thanked Kenneth, gathered up the documents she wanted to take with her, and went downstairs.

Sebastian was in reception. The woman behind the counter was laughing and jotting something down on a card. Her telephone number, Vanja assumed as she handed it to Sebastian with a little wink.

'Are you ready to leave?' Vanja asked as she passed by.

'Yes, are you?'

Vanja didn't reply; she simply pushed open the door and walked out. She took deep breaths of the fresh autumn air as she headed for the car. It was nice to escape from the fishy, increasingly stuffy air upstairs in the police station, and it also served to calm the sudden surge of irritation she had felt in reception. It was stupid, she told herself, ridiculous. Sebastian's affairs were nothing to do with her, but there was something about his compulsive need to get virtually every woman he met into bed that she found deeply offensive. Unpleasant. She realised she was slightly embarrassed on his behalf, yet at the same time there was something sad about his behaviour. Sad and desperate. What was missing from his life? What kind of empty space were these fleeting contacts supposed to fill? Besides which, Sebastian was a representative of Riksmord now, and such conduct was inappropriate. Vanja had no intention of discussing it with him; however, she would mention it to Torkel, and then it would be his problem.

Vanja could hear the woman laughing again; she called out 'See you!' as Sebastian opened the door and emerged with a smile on his face.

'So, what do we do now?' he asked as he opened the car door.

'I've got an address.'

'Whose address?'

'The guy who found the car.'

'Why do we need to talk to him?'

'Because he found the car.'

Vanja opened the driver's door and got in. Sebastian stood there for a moment replaying the conversation in his head. Vanja was annoyed. It could be that she was disappointed with Kenneth, but a more likely explanation was that he was to blame. As usual.

'Is it Bodil?' he asked as they were waiting to turn left onto the E14 when there was a gap in the cars emerging from the tunnel under the slalom slope.

'Who's Bodil?'

'The receptionist. I don't have to go to bed with her if you don't want me to.'

Vanja pulled out onto the main road and quickly accelerated to fifteen kilometres over the speed limit. He really was a mystery. It would never occur to Vanja to talk about her sex life with a colleague. She and Billy were still close, but neither of them had ever shared intimate details. Not that Vanja had much to tell these days, but even so . . . However, this was clearly yet another boundary that was present in normal people and completely lacking in Sebastian Bergman.

'What makes you think I'm interested in who you may or may not be planning to sleep with?' she asked.

'Because you seem annoyed.'

'I'm not.'

Sebastian nodded to himself. They had gone round in a circle. They weren't going to get any further. Vanja turned up the radio.

P4 Jämtland. Something about a bear.

Then Roger Pontare.

They drove on in silence.

Lennart had spent all day trying to avoid Linda Andersson, with limited success. It didn't help that they worked in the same office. Sture must have told her to contact Lennart if he didn't contact her, because just after two she came over. Lennart said he was just on his way out; he had a meeting in town. In fact he wandered around the corridors of the television centre wondering how to handle the situation. There was nothing wrong with Linda as a journalist; she was conscientious and hardworking. But she couldn't be trusted. If anything went even slightly wrong, Sture would know about it before Lennart had time to work out a defence strategy. And if it went well? Sture had suddenly seemed a little *too* interested in Shibeka's story, and that worried Lennart. Sture had a tendency to take the credit for any success, and he was equally skilled at dissociating himself from any failures. The best-case scenario was when Sture was vaguely interested – not enough to get involved, but enough to stop him blocking a project. Lennart decided to keep Linda as far away from the key material as possible. The safest thing would be to ask her to check official records: the police, the Immigration Board, the tax office. It needed to be done thoroughly, it probably wouldn't produce anything useful, but at least it would keep her busy for a few days.

Meanwhile he would focus on anything that was unofficial, hidden, and also on the people involved; that was where the breakthrough was likely to come. If it came.

Satisfied with his plan he sat down in the little café in the foyer and called Linda. She sounded pleased, but she was a little too familiar with the names – she even pronounced Shibeka correctly – and he realised that she had been fully briefed by Sture. They arranged to meet in half an hour; he was still in town at his meeting, he said.

131

He ended the call and looked around the virtually deserted café, which someone had tried to make modern and inviting, with mismatched armchairs, sofas and bold-patterned wallpaper. Unfortunately the selection of coffees tasting of tannin, sandwiches wrapped in plastic and depressing microwaveable ready meals meant that the decor was striving in vain.

Perhaps it would be best to go out for a while, Lennart thought. It would be embarrassing if Linda came down for a coffee and found him there. The sky had clouded over; he hoped it wasn't going to start raining. He realised he was in his shirt sleeves, but there was no way he could go back up to the office to fetch his jacket. He really did hate that place. Better to catch a cold.

★ ★ ★

Lennart walked down towards Filmhuset, out onto Gärdet and the extensive fields of tall yellow grass. Took out his phone. He had too few contacts that were good sources within the police. He would have liked to call Trolle Hermansson; admittedly he hadn't been a serving police officer for some years, but he must still have had contacts, because he was brilliant at digging the dirt for Lennart. But Trolle was dead. He had been found murdered in the boot of a car back in the summer. It wasn't clear how he had ended up there, but he had somehow got himself mixed up in the tangled mess of the Edward Hinde case, which had filled the front pages for weeks in July. The police couldn't or wouldn't reveal what his involvement had been, and Lennart suspected that the truth behind their vague responses was that they didn't actually know. Lennart himself had been very surprised. Trolle was a man who had had a finger in many pies. He had worked not only for Lennart but for *Cold Facts* and for *Expressen*, but Lennart couldn't work out why Trolle would be interested in someone like Hinde. The Trolle Lennart had got to know was interested in money, not in bringing killers to justice or making the world a better place. He had given all that up a long time ago.

Lennart looked at Trolle's number, stored in his phone under PC for police contact, and realised that he would never call him again. In spite of that, he didn't want to delete the number; it seemed so definitive, almost disrespectful. It was the same with his grandfather, who had passed away at Christmas the previous year; his number was still there too.

Like real memories, somehow. You wanted to hang on to them . . .

After some hesitation Lennart opted for contact number two on his PC list: Anitha Lund. To be honest, she was far too complicated to handle and often brought him more problems than solutions. She was driven not by the desire for money or adventure, but by anger, which made it more difficult to evaluate whatever she told him. She might just as easily be more interested in some private vendetta than in finding the truth, but right now he didn't have many options.

She answered almost right away. She sounded angry.

'What do you want?'

'Just a little chat,' Lennart ventured, keeping it casual.

'I'm working. I don't want to be disturbed.'

'So why answer the phone, if you're busy?'

'Because I'm well brought up.'

Lennart laughed. He had learned that there was no point in being too polite to Anitha.

'You're a lot of things, Anitha, but well brought up isn't one of them.'

'No, I'm an asshole,' Anitha said without a hint of humour in her voice. 'Ask my boss or anyone else who works here. What do you want?'

'I need to see you. There's something I'd like to talk to you about.'

'No. I don't want to work with you any more. The pay is crap and I don't get anything out of it.'

'That's not true and you know it.'

'Why not?'

'You get to know things nobody else knows. You like that, don't you?'

'No, you're the one who likes that kind of thing; you're the journalist. I'm the one you call and disturb when I'm working.'

'Listen to me, Anitha,' Lennart said, lowering his voice to stress the seriousness of the situation. 'I think you'll like this. Honestly.'

Silence. He could almost hear her weighing her curiosity against her reluctance to help him. The conversation had gone exactly the way he wanted.

'I'll see. I'll call you,' she said after a long pause.

Wrong answer. That was no good.

'No, we'll meet in an hour. If you don't like what I have to say, that's fine. Just give me the chance to explain.'

It took a little while before the answer came; Lennart was actually beginning to review his options. The problem was that he didn't have any options. He realised he needed to start working on finding a good replacement for Trolle Hermansson.

'The usual place just after three,' Anitha said eventually.

'Good.'

Lennart ended the call and looked around. He had walked almost all the way down to the Freeport. He was cold, and a light drizzle had begun to fall. The tiny drops of water were almost refreshing, but the sky was growing darker and more threatening. He turned and set off back to the office, increasing his speed. First he would have a brief chat with Linda, then he would go off to a real meeting.

With his jacket on.

Vanja turned in between two crooked gateposts and followed two churned-up, muddy tyre tracks into the yard of the isolated house. She switched off the engine and for a moment they both sat there, taking in the sight before them.

To the right, in the middle of the vast yard, stood a green two-storey house with white doors and window frames. Or at least they had been white once upon a time; now the paint was flaking off, with dark rotting wood showing through in several places. The paint on the wooden panels of the house itself had also come off in big patches, and the timber beneath looked mouldy here and there. The area surrounding the house resembled a smallish scrapyard. Vanja could see at least three snow scooters, which appeared to be in working order. A Chevy pickup, a white van and a rusty Volvo 242 were parked in a row outside a carport built of logs and a tarpaulin, which had been shredded by the wind. Between the carport and a large outbuilding, which appeared to be on the point of collapse, stood an array of machines apparently arranged at random. A log splitter, a garden shredder, a lawnmower, a snow blower and something shapeless hidden beneath a large green tarpaulin. An ice drill and a strimmer were propped against the red wall of the outbuilding. On the other side of the house was a trampoline more or less covered by last year's fallen leaves, behind a huge stack of logs. Vanja could also see a moped and a motocross bike half-covered by yet another tarp behind the trampoline, and there were garden tools and pieces of smaller mechanical equipment dotted all over the over-grown grass and protruding from the bushes. Outside the house an elkhound was tethered by a thick rope. It had leapt to its feet and started barking when they drove onto the property, and it hadn't stopped.

Vanja and Sebastian got out of the car and walked towards the house. Before they reached it the door opened and a man stepped out onto the porch. Long hair beneath a baseball cap framed his face; a thick, matted beard began just below his eyes, making it virtually impossible to make a guess at his age. He was wearing a red checked flannel shirt and wide green trousers with lots and lots of pockets, tucked into a pair of heavy boots. Vanja and Sebastian stopped. The man came down the steps and yelled at the dog to shut up, which had no effect whatsoever.

'What do you want?'

'Harald Olofsson?'

The man nodded. 'Who are you?'

Vanja introduced herself and Sebastian, holding up her police ID. Harald didn't even glance at it.

'I believe it was you who found a burnt-out Toyota up here in October 2003?'

'Might have been.'

'We'd like a word.'

'Right.'

Harald spat to the side of Vanja and shoved his hands deep in his pockets. He rocked back and forth on his heels and looked down at the ground, so that his eyes were hidden by the peak of his cap. They didn't need a degree in psychology to understand that the man in front of them felt uncomfortable with the situation.

'You found it on the morning of 31 October,' Vanja stated, taking out her notebook. 'What did you do when you found it?'

'I called the police, of course.'

'Did you go down to the car?'

Harald rubbed one hand up and down his beard a few times, hoping this would give the impression that he was giving the question careful consideration, that he realised it was important, but it was a long time ago, and he needed to think back. In fact, he was wondering when he was going to have to start lying. How much did they know? Was the question about whether he had gone down to the car a test? He had had dealings with the police before, and he usually sailed through by giving evasive, monosyllabic answers until he had worked out what they already knew and what they were trying to find out. Then it was easy to adapt his responses and his story. But these two were from Stockholm. Riksmord, no less. He had no idea why they

136

were interested in some old car accident, and he wasn't about to ask. He intended to stick to his chosen role as the taciturn, rather slow country bumpkin from Norrland. Confirm their prejudices. He would answer their questions. Be as vague as possible. Stick to his tried and tested tactics, even though he was dealing with a new opponent. No doubt he would have to stretch the truth at some point, but not yet.

'I did,' he said, nodding to himself as if he had just managed to dig the memory of that morning out of the darkest recesses of his mind. 'I went down to the car.'

'Before you called the police?'

'Yes.'

'Why?'

Harald looked up from beneath his cap and met her gaze for the first time.

'To see if anyone was hurt.'

Which was partly true, at any rate. Harald knew he was going to have to start lying quite soon.

'Did you touch anything inside the car?'

A huge leap. He was teetering on the edge.

'I shouldn't think so,' he said evasively, as if to lessen the lie, avoid crossing the line for just a little longer.

'Yes or no?'

She wasn't giving up.

'It's nine years ago,' he ventured.

'How many burnt-out cars with the dead body of a woman inside have you found since then?' asked the older man by her side, sounding distinctly irritated. 'None, I'm guessing. Am I right?'

Harald shifted his focus, looked the man in the eye. Bergman, was that his name? He hadn't said anything until now. Was that significant? And his question wasn't a question, it was a statement. Harald had the feeling that this man could see through half-truths and smokescreens. Time to make a decision: the truth or a convincing lie. He opted for the former.

'Yes.'

'The body was burnt to a crisp, so there was no point in checking for a pulse, was there?'

'No.'

'So I assume it can't be that difficult to remember whether or not you touched anything inside the car.'

'No.'

'So did you?'

Time for the lie.

'No.'

'Are you sure?'

Harald nodded several times, as if the memory had suddenly become crystal clear.

'Yes. I walked around the car to make sure no one had fallen out, so I might have touched it, I probably did, but I didn't open the doors.'

He fell silent. Sebastian thought he was probably exhausted after coming out with a long, coherent sentence. Harald spat again, focusing once more on the ground at his feet.

Vanja looked searchingly at him. The last response had been different, reasoned, explanatory. It had answered more than they had asked, in fact. Almost like an alibi. And now he was staring at the ground again. She was about to ask if he had any guns on the premises, and if so what they were, when Sebastian spoke.

'Do you have children?'

Harald glanced up, genuinely surprised.

'No.'

'So what's that doing here?' Sebastian nodded in the direction of the trampoline. 'You don't exactly strike me as the trampolining type.'

'Some neighbours of mine didn't want it any more,' Harald replied with a shrug. 'I'm going to sell it on the Internet.'

Sebastian looked around. Not a house in sight.

'You don't have any neighbours.'

'Over there,' Harald said, waving his hand vaguely somewhere behind Sebastian.

Sebastian turned to Vanja, met her gaze and realised she was thinking the same as him.

★ ★ ★

'He was lying,' Vanja said as she drove away from the isolated house and down towards the main road.

'I know. About the trampoline, anyway.'

'Do you think it's stolen?'

Sebastian shrugged.

'Maybe not by him, but I don't think he's got receipts for all the stuff lying around in his yard, if I can put it that way.'

Vanja nodded. A thief or a receiver of stolen goods. Whatever. First on the scene of the accident, and with a liberal attitude to what's mine and yours; Harald Olofsson could easily remove one of the question marks in the investigation.

'They didn't find a handbag in the car,' she said, glancing at Sebastian. 'Nor a purse or wallet.'

'They could have been destroyed by the fire.'

Possibly, but Vanja was far from convinced. As far as she could see, the investigation into the car fire had been very thorough. She was sure the technicians would have found the remains of a bag or purse if they had been there.

'The material from the Åre police is on the back seat. Check if they found any fingerprints inside the car that they weren't able to identify.'

Sebastian turned around and, with some difficulty, grabbed the folder that had slid all the way across to the opposite end of the seat.

'Billy needs to check if he has any guns,' he said as he opened the folder.

'He's bound to have – every bugger hunts up here, don't they?'

'Not with a semi-automatic pistol.'

Vanja nodded. She was glad she hadn't got round to asking Harald about his guns; he could have objected to a house search, which would have given him plenty of time to get rid of anything suspicious after they had gone, whereas now he didn't even know they were looking for a gun. It suddenly seemed as if the trip to Åre, which had seemed like a long shot, might actually prove useful. Vanja's phone rang; she picked it up and glanced at the display: 'ANNA'

For a moment she considered not answering. She wanted to carry on discussing the case with Sebastian, turning over what they knew, what they thought they knew, and what they needed to try to find out. Either her mother just wanted a chat, which Vanja couldn't cope with right now, or she was worried about something, and Vanja didn't have time for that either. She didn't want to lose focus.

'Aren't you going to answer?' Sebastian wondered, peering at the phone. 'Anna – isn't that your mother?'

'It is.'

'Why don't you want to talk to your mother?'

Vanja sighed. Typical psychologist. Tell me about your child-hood. If the alternative was to have Sebastian speculating and psychologising about her relationship with Anna all the way back, it was easier to answer.

'Hi Mum,' she said, attempting to sound as cheerful as possible.

As soon as she heard her mother's voice she knew that something had happened. Something really bad.

★ ★ ★

'You want to go back to Stockholm?'

Torkel's tone made it very clear that he hoped he had misheard. Vanja was standing just inside the door of his room, shifting from one foot to the other. She was already extremely stressed over the news that her father had been taken into custody, or arrested, Anna wasn't sure which, and she really didn't need Torkel to make her feel as if she was letting the team down, with his raised eyebrows and his obvious disapproval. He had also misunderstood her.

'I don't want to, but I have to,' she replied, stressing the fact that this was not her choice.

'Why?'

Vanja hesitated. She would tell the others eventually, however things went, but not now. She needed to find out more. She didn't even know what level of suspicion Valdemar was under, or what he was supposed to have done. If she told Torkel that her father was in custody, he would bombard her with questions.

Why?

What is he suspected of?

And perhaps the worst of all: Whatever it is, could he be guilty?

She had to find out the answers to those questions before she told anyone else.

'It's a family matter.'

Torkel's expression changed from frustration to sympathy. Vanja suddenly realised how much she would miss him when she went to the USA. She couldn't imagine finding another team leader who would be anywhere near as good as Torkel.

'What's happened?' Genuine concern in his voice.

'I'm sorry, I really can't say any more, but you know I wouldn't go unless it was important.'

Torkel looked at his best investigator. There was no doubt that she was under considerable strain. Something must have happened to her mother or father; that was all the family she had, as far as he knew. He hoped Valdemar's lung cancer hadn't come back. It wasn't long since it seemed as if he had beaten it. Surely it hadn't come back? He knew she was right; she was one of the most conscientious individuals he had ever met. Nothing came between Vanja and a case. On several occasions over the years she had put her personal and social life to one side because of the job. He would let her go, of course he would.

'Is there anything I can do to help?' he asked, and saw her visibly relax. Leaving the investigation had clearly been a difficult decision, so whatever had happened at home must be serious. Torkel wished she felt able to confide in him, but he knew better than to pressurise her.

'Not at the moment,' Vanja replied, shaking her head. 'Thanks, and I'm sorry to cause problems.'

'We'll sort it. Go and do what you need to do.'

Vanja nodded and turned away, but hesitated in the doorway.

'Could you ask someone to book my ticket while I pack?'

'No problem.'

She gave him a smile that failed to reach her eyes. Haunted. She looked haunted, Torkel thought as he picked up the phone to ring Christel and ask her to sort out a flight for Vanja. In his peripheral vision he saw a figure filling the doorway. He thought Vanja had come back; perhaps she had decided to tell him what was going on after all. But no, Sebastian was leaning on the doorframe.

'Is Vanja leaving?'

'Yes. So what happened when you were out with her?'

'It's nothing to do with me.'

Torkel was taken aback, but understood that the answer wasn't as far-fetched as it might seem. Less than two months ago, Sebastian's presence had probably been the only thing that would have made Vanja leave an ongoing investigation.

'I didn't say it was.'

'That's what it sounded like.'

'She said it was something to do with the family; I just won-dered if you knew what it might be.'

Sebastian shook his head.

'Her mother called, they spoke for a couple of minutes, then she drove back here without saying a word.'

'And you've no idea what's happened?'

Sebastian shook his head again and took a step into the room. He cleared his throat as if he knew that what he was about to say was unlikely to go down well.

'I thought I'd go with her.'

Torkel looked at Sebastian with the same expression as he had been wearing just a few minutes ago. Once again he hoped he had misheard.

'What the fuck are you saying?'

'I thought I'd go with Vanja. To Stockholm,' Sebastian clarified, just in case Torkel thought he was offering to drive her to Östersund.

'Why?'

Sebastian quickly ran through a range of possible answers. Because he didn't think he would ever be able to sleep in that room again. Because this case was affecting him in a way that made him feel he needed some distance from it. Because the hotel was boring, the environment was boring, the case was boring. He opted for the short version.

'Because I want to get away from this bloody mountain.'

'Why? Can't you find anyone to screw?'

'Exactly. All my decisions are based on the availability of possible sex partners.'

As Sebastian spoke the words aloud, he realised to his surprise how close to the truth they were. Fortunately Torkel took the com-ment as the sarcasm it was meant to be.

'Sorry,' he said. 'But the thing is, if Vanja's going, I really don't want to lose you as well.'

'Be honest, what good am I doing here? We've got six skeletons on the side of a mountain. I need a bit more than that to come up with something useful.'

Torkel knew that Sebastian was right. Losing him wouldn't make a scrap of difference at this stage. Torkel also thought they would probably move the whole case down to Stockholm in a few days unless something new came up. He sighed.

'I'll book another ticket.'

'If you really need me, I'm only a phone call away,' Sebastian said as he left the room. He felt quite excited. He had obviously wanted to get away more than he had admitted to himself. He would go and tell Vanja that he was coming with her. It wasn't completely impossible that she might be quite pleased.

This didn't feel good.

The coffee cup was still on the table, its contents cold and virtually untouched. The sausage and cheese sandwich was beside it, two bites taken. He stubbed out his fourth cigarette and exhaled the smoke with something resembling a sigh. Zeppo, who was lying by the stove, raised his head at the unusual sound. Harald Olofsson wasn't in the habit of sighing.

Harald got up, walked over the red-and-white checked cork floor to the sink, leaned over and opened the window. Four cigarettes in quick succession had more or less filled the kitchen with smoke. The dog followed him with his eyes. Harald flung the window wide and filled his lungs with the chilly fresh air, then took a glass out of one of the dark brown cupboards above the stove. He filled it with cold water and gulped it down.

This didn't feel good.

Harald had had dealings with the police in the past. Frequently. For some reason they always took a trip out to his place whenever some garage in the area had been broken into, or someone had had their snow scooter stolen. They would stroll around the place, lift the tarpaulins, search the outbuilding. They never found anything. Said they were keeping an eye on him. He usually said he was pleased to hear it, and that it was always nice to have visitors. Then they would leave.

They never found anything, but not because he wasn't involved. Most of the things they were looking for had already reached Harald before the police turned up, or were on their way. They hadn't managed to pin anything other than minor infringements on him, and that was because he was smart. Smart, consistent, and blessed with patience. When he bought this house almost twenty years ago, one of the first things he did was to rip up the outhouse floor and get in there with a small digger. Beneath the new floor there was now a storage room measuring approximately eight square metres, deep enough to stand up in. The trapdoor leading to the steep wooden staircase down into the Chamber, as he called it, was underneath the big rag rug with the snow blower standing on it, and so far no one had discovered it. Everything that found its way to Harald ended up in the Chamber. Down there he could take his time to decide what to do with each item: sell it on as it was, take it to pieces and sell the parts separately, or do it up and then sell it. There were plenty of possibilities, and Harald invariably chose the one that would bring in the most money. Snow scooters were extremely lucrative, but they also involved a lot of work, because they had to be impossible to trace. It took time, but that was just the way it was. He was good at what he did. Tools, machinery, vehicles. No art or jewellery or crap like that. Some of the Norwegian guys he worked with had brought the trampoline a year or so ago. Said it was a present for him, that he could get five thousand for it. At least. And it was impossible to trace, because they were all exactly the same. He had taken it, but when he checked the online auction site he had discovered that there were plenty on offer for less than a thousand, so he hadn't even bothered to advertise. So far, nothing he had sold on had come back to bite him on the arse. The police were a minor inconvenience, nothing more. He never even gave them a thought once they had driven away. But now it was different.

This didn't feel good.

He had watched their car disappear before he went inside and put the coffee on. He couldn't settle, and had gone out to fetch Zeppo for company. Made a sandwich. Poured himself a cup of coffee. Started smoking.

It was nine years since that car had come off the road. No one had shown any interest in him during the investigation, apart from a brief interview at the scene; he had told the truth, said he had been driving past, seen the smoke, stopped, and found the car down in the ravine. As far as Harald was aware, no one had ever suggested that it was anything other than an accident, but now Riksmord had turned up. They didn't investigate accidents. They investigated murders. Had the woman in the car been murdered? That must be it. He couldn't get mixed up in all this. He guessed the police would put a little more effort into a murder case than a stolen scooter that the insurance company would cough up for anyway. If they found something linking him to the accident – the murder, he corrected himself – they would turn the place upside down.

It would all be over.

They would discover the Chamber.

He would have nothing left.

So he had to make sure they didn't find anything. Simple.

And yet he was hesitating.

It didn't feel right to destroy something that might help the police to solve a murder. Even though Harald operated on the periphery of the law, he had morals. Receiving stolen goods was one thing; he never ordered anything, never incited anyone to commit a crime. He just earned a little money when the damage was already done. If he didn't do it, someone else would. It was just business. Killing someone was a different matter.

Then again, if they had spent all these years looking for whoever murdered the woman in the car, it seemed unlikely that they were going to catch him now. With or without the items Harald had removed from the burnt-out car.

He made a decision, put down his glass and left the kitchen. He knew exactly where the rucksacks and the handbag were. It was time for a bonfire.

Safety procedure briefing. Exactly the same as last time. Then the plane taxied over the runway, picked up speed and left the ground. Vanja was sitting by the window, gazing at the dwindling town below. Sebastian watched her out of the corner of his eye. It would be something of an exaggeration to say she was pleased when he told her she would have company on the journey to Stockholm, but at least she had accepted it. She had wanted to know why, of course. Sebastian had repeated the reason he had given Torkel: he just wanted to get away from this bloody mountain.

Billy had driven them to Östersund. Wanted to know why Vanja had chosen to leave them, but she just told him it was a family matter. Billy hadn't pushed her, but Sebastian thought he detected a certain disappointment because Vanja hadn't confided in him. He had noticed a distinct change in their relationship lately; something had definitely happened when they were working on the Hinde case, and whatever it might be, it was still affecting them.

Billy had accompanied them into the departure lounge, even though Vanja had said there was no need. Sebastian had the feeling that that was exactly why he did it. When they had checked in and Vanja went off to the loo, Billy had immediately turned to Sebastian.

'Why are you going with her?'

Sebastian was struck by the question, and Billy's suspicious tone. The choice of words suggested that Billy believed his departure was somehow linked to Vanja's, that they were travelling together rather than merely at the same time.

'I'm not,' he said. 'We're just taking the same flight.'

'Why?'

'Because it's nice to have some company.'

Billy had given him an exasperated look and sighed, as if he were talking to a small child.

'I mean why are you leaving too, if it's nothing to do with Vanja?'

Sebastian had immediately given what had become his standard response to that particular question, but he doubted whether Billy had believed him.

'Has she said anything to you about what's happened?' Billy asked.

'Vanja?'

'Yes.'

'No, nothing.'

This time there was no doubt; Billy didn't believe him. Vanja had returned and they had said goodbye. A brief, almost forced embrace, Sebastian noted. When he looked back before they went through the security check, Billy had already gone.

But now they were on their way. The seatbelt sign went out, but both Vanja and Sebastian kept theirs fastened. Vanja was still half turned away from him. He guessed she was intending to spend most of the journey ignoring him unless he did something about it.

'What's going on with you and Billy?'

Result. She immediately swung round to face him.

'What are you talking about?'

'You don't seem to be getting on so well these days.'

'You think?'

'Yes. Am I wrong?'

Vanja fell silent. She could of course brush the whole thing aside and end the conversation simply by answering yes to his question. That was probably what she would have done in the past, firstly to shut him up, and secondly because there was no way she would admit that he was right. But that was then.

'No. Things are a bit . . . strained.'

'Why?'

Vanja hesitated again, then made up her mind. She twisted her body as far as the seatbelt would allow.

'I told him I was a better cop than he was.'

Sebastian absorbed this information with a nod. Hearing something like that would undoubtedly put a professional relationship under strain.

'I know it was stupid,' Vanja went on as if she had read his mind. 'You don't need to say it.'

'It was stupid,' Sebastian said with a smile, which to his relief she returned. 'True, but stupid.'

'I know . . .'

Vanja sighed. It was clear that her damaged relationship with Billy was weighing her down. Sebastian got as comfortable as he could in his seat. This was, or at least had been, his home turf. He began by explaining that of course Billy had always known that Vanja was better than him, that Billy liked her too much to compete with her, but clearly something had changed. For some reason he had stopped being content with his position in the hierarchy; he had decided to compete with her, and now he simply didn't want to lose. Vanja asked what she could do to improve the situation. Sebastian wondered briefly whether to go for a lie that would make her feel better, or the hard truth. He opted for the latter.

'Nothing. You started this by saying you were better than him; that can't be undone. He has to deal with it, and you have to deal with him.'

Vanja nodded, her expression grim. Sebastian could see that wasn't the answer she had been hoping for. Like everyone else she wanted there to be a solution, to learn the magic words that would make everything all right. But sometimes there just weren't any. Sebastian looked at her tenderly, suppressing the urge to place a gentle hand on her arm. Softly softly. They had had a conversation. On a personal matter. Work-related, admittedly, but still. He decided to continue along the same line.

'I could have a chat with him when they get back to Stockholm,' he offered.

'Thanks, but there's no need. I feel better now we've talked about it.'

Sebastian thought fast. She had just given him an opening, an opportunity to get closer, past the job, into her personal life. He might be moving too fast, but he was definitely going to risk it.

'Perhaps you'd feel better if you talked about what's happening in your family right now.'

Vanja stiffened. Met his gaze, searching for any sign of fake concern. Was he trying to gain the upper hand, trying to find a weakness he could exploit? She looked for the old Sebastian in his eyes, but he wasn't there.

'My father has been arrested,' she said. To her surprise, saying the words out loud relieved her anxiety just a little.

'What? Why?'

'I've no idea. Anna didn't know.'

A cold shudder ran down Sebastian's spine. What if it was fraud?

They would act fast if they had got hold of the material Trolle Hermansson had dug up on Valdemar Lithner a few months ago. At Sebastian's request, when he had been hell-bent on trying to destroy the relationship between Valdemar and Vanja. The material he had told Ellinor to get rid of. She had told him she had thrown it away, but the truth was a highly subjective concept as far as Ellinor was concerned.

Could she have acted off her own bat?

Was that why Valdemar had been arrested?

Why would she have done such a thing?

Because she was Ellinor. Suddenly it seemed perfectly reasonable. She had asked about Valdemar once, he recalled, but did she know anything about Vanja? Sebastian tried to think: was there any information about her in Trolle's notes?

He couldn't remember.

In the best-case scenario, Ellinor had handed the material in anonymously. Posted it to the police. Or given it to them without leaving her name.

In the best-case scenario. But this was Ellinor. Deep down Sebastian knew that he couldn't make that assumption. It was more likely that not only had she identified herself, but that she had been very proud of what she had achieved, or would achieve when the police carried out their investigation. If that was the case, could it damage him? Would Vanja find out? Probably not. Even though she was a police officer and a colleague, it would count as gross misconduct if someone gave her the name of an informant in a case involving her father.

'You've gone very quiet.'

Vanja's voice brought Sebastian back to reality.

'Sorry . . . I was just wondering how I can help you. I do know a few people in high places, after all.'

'Thanks, but I don't want you to get involved. This is something we need to get through on our own.'

She turned away once more and stared out of the little window, out over clouds that looked like a billowing landscape made of ice.

For personal reasons.

Vanja had left the investigation for personal reasons.

Ursula wrenched the wheel to the left and turned onto the narrow asphalt track the GPS was telling her to follow for 1.2 kilometres before turning left again. Her annoyance was illogical, but that didn't make it any less real. Her husband had dumped her and her daughter was completely on his side.

Weren't those personal reasons? Didn't she have things she needed to face up to and sort out?

Of course she did, and no one would have understood better than Torkel, if he had known. But the difference between Vanja and Ursula was that Ursula hadn't told anyone, and that she wanted to carry on working. She wanted nothing more, in fact. But not on this particular aspect of the case.

Torkel had called her down from the mountain, where she had been undertaking a detailed examination of the scene with a local team. Most of the earth and gravel from the grave had been sifted and checked, but they had found nothing that would move the investigation forward. The digger had arrived, and Ursula had pointed out where she wanted the excavation to start. So far she had redirected it three times, but without success, which meant that at the moment the grave site was proving the least productive area. Torkel had quite rightly decided to prioritise by moving her temporarily, but she was still annoyed. It was Vanja's job to drive out to scrapyards and question dealers about car accidents from years ago.

Jennifer and Billy were still trying to track Patricia Wellton's journey to Sweden. Torkel was keeping in touch with Europol and Interpol. Both organisations were going through their records looking for families or various combinations of two adults and two children who had been reported missing in the autumn of 2003; so far Torkel had been given three possible cases, but had quickly been able to write off all of them.

Ursula had to admit that Torkel was also a problem, a source of further irritation. He wanted her to come to him, he wanted everything to go back to the way it used to be when they were working away from Stockholm: nights of intimacy in various hotel rooms all over Sweden. He wanted her. Physically, of course, but that wasn't all, and right now his longing for something more just felt like hard work; it was too stressful. No doubt the easiest thing would be to go to his room tonight. Have sex. Creep back to her own bed at dawn. Pretend that everything was just the same. It would be no great sacrifice.

But she couldn't do it.

Didn't want to do it.

Even though Torkel didn't know that she and Mikael had split up, the very thought of complicating life still further by adding in a boss and lover who was picturing a cosy future together was just too much for her at the moment. Ursula intended to keep him at arm's length.

And she wasn't planning on wasting much time on this visit, she thought as the GPS informed her that she had reached her destination. She turned into the scrapyard through the open metal gates and stopped in front of a grey single-storey building with a sign on the roof confirming that this was indeed Hammarén & Son Breakers Yard. She switched off the engine, picked up the folder Torkel had given her and got out of the car.

Ursula had never been to a place like this before and didn't really know what she was expecting. She hadn't given much thought to what happened to cars when they came to the end of their life, but she had probably imagined they were dismantled, everything that could be reused was recycled, and what was left was compressed into a small cube. Surely the idea of them being piled on top of one another in long rows several metres high belonged in American films? Apparently not. The vast area, surrounded by a tall corrugated iron fence topped with barbed wire, was packed with cars. Every possible model and colour. Row after row, most of them ten, twelve metres high. The cars at the bottom of each pile had been squashed down by the weight of those above. In the row nearest to her Ursula quickly counted over a hundred cars. Thousands of cars had found their final resting place with Hammarén & Son.

Her thoughts were interrupted as a door opened and closed, and she turned to see a man in his mid-fifties coming towards her from the grey building. He was wearing bright orange overalls, straining over an impressive beer gut, and an oily cap with the name of the firm on it. A few strands of grey hair poked out from beneath the cap; he had a round face with blue eyes that were quite close together, a broad nose and a dark moustache sprinkled with grey above a generous mouth. As he came closer she could see that he was chewing a plug of snuff.

'Good afternoon, how can I help you?'

Ursula introduced herself and showed her ID. The man didn't even glance at it.

'Ursula . . . wasn't that the name of the mean octopus in *The Little Mermaid*?'

'Could be,' Ursula replied, somewhat taken aback. It was a rather unexpected opening remark, and she had no idea what anyone in *The Little Mermaid* was called.

'It definitely was,' the man stated, nodding to himself. 'The kids were just the right age when it came out. We played the tape over and over again until it more or less wore out. It was VHS in those days, of course.'

Ursula was wondering whether to point out that few women, regardless of their name, would find it particularly appealing to be compared to a cephalopod mollusc, or whether she should just get down to business, when the man transferred the gloves he was carrying into his left hand and held out his right. Ursula shook it.

'Arvid Hammarén. Nice to meet you. How can I help the long arm of the law?' he said, pushing his cap back a little. Yet another remark she hadn't expected. Did anyone really use that expression to refer to the police these days? Obviously Hammarén (or was it & Son?) did; his expression was open and helpful.

'We're investigating a car accident in Storlien in the autumn of 2003. October 31.'

'Right . . .'

'No other vehicle involved. The car caught fire. One fatality.'

Ursula opened the folder and removed one of the photographs that the Åre police had taken at the scene. She held it out to Arvid.

'Oh, that one. Yes, we dealt with it; it was a hire car if I remember correctly.'

'That's right.'

'They didn't want it back,' Arvid said, returning the photograph to Ursula. 'When the police had finished with it we brought it here.'

Ursula gazed at the rows of piled-up cars and realised there was a faint possibility that the car was still here, something she hadn't even dared to consider on her way up.

'I don't suppose you've still got it?'

'Probably,' Arvid said, removing his cap and scratching his head. 'The question is where . . .'

'Could you find out?'

'I could.'

Arvid put his cap back on, turned and ambled back to his office. Ursula stayed where she was, trying not to think about how contaminated the area all around her must be. All these cars, the rain and snow passing through them, washing lead, mercury, CFCs and oil into the ground. If Hammarén & Son ever decided to shut up shop, this place would be like the aftermath of Chernobyl. Once again she was interrupted by the sound of the door opening.

'Found it!' Arvid Hammarén called out; he was so pleased with himself that Ursula couldn't help smiling.

Five minutes later they were standing in front of the remains of the grey Toyota. It was the second car from the bottom in a pile of six, on top of what had once been a pale-blue Volvo 242. Ursula walked over and looked at the flattened, burnt-out, rusty wreck.

'We used it for spare parts for a while,' Arvid informed her, 'but it's just been standing there for a long time now.'

'Spare parts?' Ursula was surprised.

'Yes, the engine was hardly damaged at all, oddly enough. Most of the fire damage was inside the car.'

Ursula peered in through the broken side window and saw that Arvid was right. In spite of all the years the car had been exposed to the worst of the weather, it was still clear that the interior was completely burnt out. She walked around the car examining it as best she could given the space available, consulting the photographs in her folder at the same time. She had only glanced at them when Torkel gave them to her, but now that she looked more closely, it was obvious. The fire had started inside the car and spread outwards. The extent of the blaze was relatively restricted; the paintwork on the bonnet was burnt away only a metre or so measuring outwards from the windscreen. The rest was intact. The boot was virtually undamaged. Which wouldn't be the case if the petrol tank had exploded, or if the contents had leaked.

Ursula edged behind the car and crouched down. Arvid was following her activities with interest. She leaned against the boot of the Volvo so that she could examine at least part of the underside of the Toyota. She saw enough. She backed out and straightened up.

'The petrol tank is smashed,' she said, mostly to herself, as she went back to the photographs.

'What does that mean?'

Ursula didn't answer immediately. She flicked through the pictures, and immediately realised that if the tank had been smashed by a rock on the way down, for example, then the petrol would have run out underneath the car and into the ravine. The fire couldn't possibly have started as a result of the accident. Someone wanted to make sure that the woman in the car couldn't be identified.

She looked through the pictures one more time; in spite of herself she was quite pleased that she had come to the scrapyard rather than Vanja. Because the car was still here, she could carry out a belated examination of the scene of the crime. The boot was open in every picture. It could of course have flown open due to the force of the collision, but Ursula was sure someone had been down to the car after it ended up in the ravine, so she decided to check it out.

She went round to the back of the Toyota again, with Arvid hot on her heels.

'Have you found something?' he asked tentatively.

'Yes.'

The boot was still open, as far as the car on top allowed. The length of time the vehicle had been exposed to the elements made it difficult to see, but Ursula thought she could make out fine scratches around the lock that couldn't be explained by the position of the car following the crash. It seemed likely that someone had forced it open. Ursula quickly ran through what Torkel had said to her, then turned to Arvid.

'Do you know a Harald Olofsson?'

'The magpie, yes.'

Ursula thought she probably knew the answer, but she asked the question anyway.

'Why do you call him that?'

Arvid looked a little uncomfortable, as if he had already said too much.

'I don't like to speak ill of anyone . . .'

'Just tell me.'

'He's never been convicted of anything,' Arvid said apologetically. 'So I'm not accusing him, but they do say he has sticky fingers.'

'He's a thief.'

'He . . .' Arvid seemed to be searching for a less judgemental description, but he failed to come up with something suitable. He shrugged and nodded. 'He's a thief. And he receives stolen goods and sells them on.'

Ursula suddenly felt the little tingle in her stomach that was always there when she discovered something that could move a case forward. All she had to do now was to find out what Harald Olofsson had taken from the boot.

'I'm taking a break.'

Jennifer glanced up from her computer; across the table Billy pushed back his chair and closed his laptop.

'OK,' she said as he strode out of the restaurant. She wouldn't have minded a break herself. She couldn't decide which was more boring: trying to get hold of the right person at the airline and persuading them to send over their passenger lists, or the monotonous task of going through the lists when they did arrive. Before Torkel asked her to come to Jämtland, before she became a part of Riksmord, Jennifer had thought someone else did this kind of work for them. But there wasn't anyone else. There was her and Billy. And now there was just her, apparently.

She glanced at her watch. Just over two hours until dinner. A little break would be good, but then there would be no one trying to find out how Patricia Wellton entered the country if Torkel happened to walk past.

★ ★ ★

Billy went to his room and put the laptop down on the table by the window. He felt slightly guilty about leaving Jennifer on her own so much; first of all he had driven Sebastian and Vanja to Östersund, and now he had left her again. The problem was that he couldn't concentrate; his mind kept going over what had happened.

Vanja had chosen to leave the investigation because of a family problem.

Billy assumed it must be something extremely serious, or she would never have walked away from the case and gone home. She wasn't prepared to say what it was, which he understood perfectly. Whatever it was, no doubt she wanted to assess the situation, find out as much as she could and let it sink in before she decided whether to confide in her colleagues, and if so, how much to tell them. Again, perfectly understandable.

It was Sebastian's behaviour that concerned him. When Vanja said she was going, he had speedily and cheerfully decided that he was going too.

Why?

Torkel clearly didn't find it strange; Sebastian didn't have much to contribute to the investigation at this stage. That was true, but why hadn't he left earlier? Why pretend that his departure had nothing whatsoever to do with Vanja? And, perhaps even more important, what did it really have to do with Vanja?

Why?

Why was Sebastian Bergman, a man who didn't care what anyone thought of him, suddenly showing such concern for a colleague? The obvious answer would have been that he wanted to get her into bed, but even Sebastian must have known that was never going to happen.

So, why?

Torkel might not think it was strange, but then he didn't know what Billy knew: the link between Vanja and Sebastian. Anna Eriksson, Vanja's mother, had been on the list of possible victims that Edward Hinde had produced.

Why?

Billy kept coming back to the same question, and after today's events he couldn't let it go any longer. He was going to have to give it some time, and hopefully find an answer to some of those 'whys'.

He sat down, opened the laptop and stared at the screen as he tried to marshal his thoughts.

What did he know?

Where should he start?

From the beginning.

All the women on Hinde's list had had a sexual relationship with Sebastian. Therefore, Sebastian and Vanja's mother must have had a sexual relationship.

When?

In Västerås Sebastian had given Billy an envelope with an address where Anna Eriksson had once lived: Vasaloppsvägen 17 in Hägersten. That was all Billy had had to go on. It had been returned to sender, and the sender had been Esther Bergman, Sebastian's mother. Sebastian had been in Västerås to clear out and sell his parents' house following the death of his mother. How old was the letter? Late Seventies – December 1979? That could fit; Anna Eriksson might have written to Esther for some reason connected to her relationship with Esther's son. Was that why Sebastian had waited over thirty years to try to find her? If they hadn't had any contact since then, Sebastian didn't know that Anna was Vanja's mother, which was why he hadn't asked her for the address.

Billy sighed. He wasn't coming up with any answers, just more questions.

Why had Sebastian wanted to get back in touch? As far as Billy could tell, Sebastian didn't need to call his old conquests if he was feeling horny – quite the reverse, if the gossip was to be believed. Sebastian went out of his way to avoid repeat performances. So why did he want to contact Anna Eriksson, over thirty years later?

And why had Sebastian's mother written to her?

Billy had seen only the envelope, not the contents, but surely there was no reason for Esther to write to one of her son's ex-girlfriends unless they had been very close? The idea of Sebastian introducing a girl to his mother and the two of them subsequently becoming good friends sounded unlikely, to say the least. Sebastian had always made it very clear that he disliked his parents; in fact he hadn't had anything to do with them since the age of nineteen. This was later, so perhaps the letter from Esther was a reply to a message Anna had sent her.

But why? Why hadn't she written to Sebastian instead?

Billy quickly googled Sebastian and clicked on the first hit: Wikipedia. Jacob Sebastian Bergman, born 1958. There was a brief introduction, then a timeline. November 1979, the University of North Carolina on a Fulbright award. Back in Sweden 1983.

Billy leaned back in his chair and went through his chain of circumstantial evidence, looking for the weak points. There weren't any.

Sebastian sleeps with Anna Eriksson in 1979 (or earlier). In 1979 Anna tries to get in touch with Sebastian, but he has moved to the USA. She writes to his mother. Esther writes back, but the letter is returned. She keeps the letter, and Sebastian finds it. The contents make him want to track down Anna Eriksson.

Why?

What was in the letter?

It must have been important for Sebastian to think it was worth searching for her after thirty years. Had they ever met? Billy couldn't remember Vanja or Sebastian ever mentioning that he knew her mother.

So why? Why does a woman write to a man with whom she has had a relationship?

To tell him she's unhappy and she wants him back?

To tell him she's happy, just to hurt him?

Would Sebastian's mother reply to something like that? Why reply at all? Why not just send Anna's letter on to Sebastian in the USA? Then again, if Sebastian had broken all contact with his parents, perhaps she didn't know where he was either.

To tell him she has an STI?

To tell him she's pregnant?

Billy stopped dead. Stared at what he had jotted down. What did he actually know, apart from his theories about the letter?

He knew that Sebastian had offered to change places with Vanja when Hinde had abducted her.

He knew that Sebastian had fought hard to rejoin Riksmord.

He knew that Sebastian had decided to go back to Stockholm with Vanja when she had a family problem.

And he knew something else: Vanja was born in July 1980.

There was a knock on the door, and Billy gave a start. Before he had time to say anything the door opened and Jennifer was standing there, looking very pleased with herself.

'I've found Patricia Wellton.'

Lennart walked into the bingo hall on Sankt Eriksgatan. They had certainly freshened the place up. Gone were the fluorescent lights and the scruffy pine tables covered in cigarette burns that had once dominated the room. The walls had been repainted, and an attractively patterned carpet toned beautifully with the modern furniture in the café area. Lots of small spotlights brought out the contrast between the round white tables and the dark green walls. It looked more like a trendy restaurant or a night club than a bingo hall, as long as you ignored the bingo machines standing in long rows in the middle of the room. With their illuminated, brightly coloured screens and the players sitting in front of them in comfortable armchairs, concentrating hard, at first glance they looked like some kind of communications centre, or the control room in a sci-fi series. Run by really old people. The hall might have had a facelift, but the clientele was exactly the same. In fact, they looked even older, even more bent, grey, still stinking of smoke. Lennart was probably the youngest person in the room. His only competition was the man in the polo shirt sitting up on the podium, calling out the numbers in his nasal voice as the machine beside him spat out the balls. It was an unusual feeling, being the youngest. These days he often felt old compared to the other customers in cafés and restaurants around Stockholm, but not here. In fact he was getting younger by the minute. He suspected that was exactly what Anitha liked about it; it made her feel young again.

Lennart sat down towards the back of the room, hidden from the street by a huge cardboard sign proclaiming bingo's magical ability to make the time fly while providing the opportunity to have fun and win big. He looked at his machine and realised that if he had inserted money and lit up the screen in front of him, he would have been able to cross off one of the numbers that had just been called out.

Two and four, twenty-four.

For a moment he toyed with the idea of actually playing, but then he saw her walk in. As usual she was wearing a brown skirt and a jumper that was far too thick. To hide the fact that she was overweight, he assumed. Her brown hair was caught up in a bun. Her face was well made up, although slightly overdone, and the colours were a little too strong. She was trying to look stylish, but it was as if she didn't really know how. Anitha Lund in a nutshell, he thought. She wanted so much, but didn't quite know how to get there.

She had been some kind of human resources officer with the National Police Board, but had fallen out with just about everybody. She had been moved several times before taking up her present post as administrator responsible for staff development. It sounded good, but meant next to nothing. She made a note of applications as they came in, then passed them on to someone who actually made the decisions. Lennart had some sympathy for her; she was bitter, and her life hadn't turned out the way she wanted. She was the archetypal misery-guts, the kind of person who took out her disappointment on everyone around her who had done better. Who thought that everything was someone else's fault. Who saw faults in every system, but none in herself.

This was often the case when it came to those who were prepared to leak information to the press. At the beginning of his career as a journalist, Lennart had thought that people revealed anomalies because they had morals and wanted to prevent wrongdoing, but unfortunately that wasn't the case. Most sources had much simpler motives: money, perceived injustices, and revenge. It wasn't pretty, but it was true.

Anitha spotted him and he smiled at her as she sat down beside him.

'Hi, Anitha.'

'Hi.'

'Can I ask if you come here in your free time too?'

She put down her pale-brown handbag on the shelf in front of the screen and looked at him.

'It has been known. This is a bit like my job, you see. Someone calls something out. I tick it off. They call out again. I tick it off. The only difference is that here I might actually win something now and again.'

She stared at the screen as if she were thinking of playing.

'Perhaps I ought to give it a try one day,' Lennart said, trying to maintain the friendly tone, but Anitha got straight to the point.

'What's so bloody important?'

'An asylum case that's been classified. Two Afghan men who disappeared. Nobody knows where they are, and nobody seems to care.'

'The Security Police obviously cared.'

Lennart turned to face her. The thought had occurred to him, but there were other agencies that could mark an investigation as classified.

'The Security Police . . . what makes you think it's Säpo?'

'Who else would it be? If they were Afghans I assume they were Muslims. You know perfectly well that Säpo are involved if it's serious. A threat to national security and so on.'

'You don't need to tell me what Säpo do,' Lennart said with a smile.

'No, but you need me, don't you?' Anitha replied with a sudden sharpness in her voice. 'In which case you can damn well listen to what I say. Or are we done here?'

She sat back in her chair, emphasising the fact that she had the upper hand.

Bloody hell, she was complicated.

'Of course I'm listening,' Lennart said. 'Sorry,' he added, in case his apologetic tone wasn't clear enough.

Anitha leaned forward again. She looked a little calmer, but Lennart knew that she could flare up at any moment.

'Have you got anything more concrete?'

Lennart nodded and handed over a sheet of paper summarising what he knew. She glanced through the brief notes while Lennart looked at the man in the polo shirt.

Four and seven, forty-seven.

Three and six, thirty-six.

'Have you got a winning line?' Anitha said, trying out a joke as she put down the piece of paper.

'That depends on you,' he quipped back.

She didn't smile. 'I don't know. Seems a bit thin to me. We've got enough immigrants, haven't we? It makes no difference to me if a few of them disappear.' She looked away.

One and seven, seventeen.

'But I do agree, there's something odd about a refusal to grant asylum being marked classified,' she said after a brief silence. 'But it's not enough.'

'What do you mean?'

'It's not enough for me to get involved.'

'Is there any way I can get you interested?' Lennart said as he felt the hope shrivel and die.

'I don't think so. The thing is, I'm the one taking the risk, while you get all the credit if I find anything.'

Lennart sighed. This wasn't going well.

Five and two, fifty-two.

A woman with grey permed hair and a blue blouse shouted 'House!' two rows away from him.

'I can't pay you much,' Lennart said, giving it one last shot. 'But maybe there's something else I can give you.'

'I doubt it.'

Anitha smiled at him for the first time. He knew why; she was enjoying the power, revelling in the knowledge that she was needed.

'You didn't even offer to buy me a coffee,' she said, getting to her feet. 'You need to work on your powers of persuasion, Mr TV Big Shot.' She picked up her bag. 'Perhaps you'll have better luck with the bingo. Bye now.'

★ ★ ★

Feeling irritated, Lennart walked towards the metro station at Fridhemsplan. With Anitha out of the picture, he would have to go down the official route. Threaten, turn up the heat, keep dragging up the principle of freedom of information, but unfortunately he would also be highly visible, which wasn't a good thing. If there was something suspect about Hamid and Said's disappearance, the message would spread like wildfire within the police, giving those involved plenty of warning, and time to prepare their counter-attack. Lennart had learnt the hard way that it was always better to apply pressure when he had concrete evidence to bring out as soon as the evasive answers started to come – incontrovertible facts that couldn't be brushed aside, information that exposed the guilty and made the excuses look sleazy. That was how to make good TV.

Right now all he had was a classified asylum refusal and some strange goings-on nine years ago. It was nowhere near enough. He had to try to get more out of Shibeka, and out of Said's wife. There might be something if he did a little digging. It wasn't much, but it was his only hope.

★ ★ ★

Shibeka was sitting at the kitchen table reading the instructions for her new mobile phone, page after page of information on how to save and synchronise contacts, download games and insert the SIM card. She didn't need a fraction of all these functions; she wanted to be reachable, and perhaps to make a call or two – to her sons and the man from the TV, Lennart Stridh. She might give a couple of her friends at school and work her number as well, but that was it. She was well aware that no one in her immediate circle would think it acceptable for a woman on her own to have a mobile phone, so she had never bought one, even though she had sometimes thought it would be useful. She pushed the boundaries of what was acceptable as it was, she knew that. It would be stupid to cause unnecessary provocation, but she carried on reading the thick booklet written in twelve languages. It was exciting to contemplate all the possibilities, even if she was never going to need them.

The landline in the hallway rang. It was Lennart, sounding tired.

'Hi, Shibeka. Everything all right?'

'Everything is all right, thank you.'

'Great. Listen, I was thinking of popping over tomorrow if that's OK.'

Shibeka stiffened in horror.

'Over here?'

'Yes – I need to see you, maybe meet your kids, and I also need to get in touch with Said's wife.'

Shibeka went cold inside. She hadn't expected this.

'That's impossible,' she answered, almost reflexively.

'What do you mean, impossible?'

Lennart sounded completely bewildered.

'I don't know how to explain, but it doesn't feel right,' she said weakly.

'Doesn't feel right?'

Shibeka hesitated. How could she make him understand? He was Swedish. Swedes could call round to see anybody, any time.

'I'm not supposed to be alone with you,' she said eventually.

She heard him sigh, and realised his day wasn't getting any better. But there were rules, even if they seemed strange to him.

'OK, I get it,' he said, much to her relief. 'Is it all right if we meet in town?'

'That's fine.'

'But I am going to have to speak to your kids and Said's wife at some point, otherwise this just won't work.'

Shibeka didn't know what to say. She hadn't really appreciated the scope of what she had started. She had thought if they just met up, it would be fine, that would be enough. The man from the TV programme would find out what had happened to her husband, and in some magical way that would solve everything. Now she understood that the journey had only just begun.

'I need to think. I'm not sure that's a good idea. It's not what I wanted.'

'That's the way it has to be, otherwise I won't be able to get any further.'

When she thought about it, it was obvious. She suddenly felt worn out. Gone was the joy she had experienced because what she had dreamt of for so long was actually happening; someone had listened to her, believed her. Now it was time for the reckoning.

'I will speak to you tomorrow,' she said eventually. 'I will call you; I've bought a mobile phone.'

'Great, can you give me the number?'

'I haven't set it up yet.'

'You don't need to set it up to get the number,' Lennart explained patiently, as if he were helping a child. 'It's on a separate piece of paper.'

'I know, but there are so many pieces of paper . . .'

Another sigh at the other end of the line.

'OK, you ring me – you've got my number, haven't you?'

'Yes, it's on the letter. I will ring you.'

'OK, tomorrow at the latest.' He sounded more tired than she felt. Then he was gone, and Shibeka was left standing there with the silent telephone in her hand.

She hung up and went back into the kitchen. Sat down at the table and stared at the new mobile and the blue packaging which had seemed like a symbol of so many opportunities just a few minutes ago. Now it was nothing more than a false prophet.

What had she imagined was going to happen? It was obvious that everything was going to collide sooner or later, and presumably that was unavoidable if she wanted answers to the questions that had been spinning around in her head for so long. She was going to have to stand up for her desire to know the truth, even if it was painful, and irrespective of what people around her thought. Personally she didn't care; many already regarded her as much too . . . Swedish, she assumed. It was her boys that concerned her. They looked up to many of the elders, regarded them as a link to the old country and to their father. She didn't want to destroy that relationship.

What should she do?

Shibeka tried to think what advice Hamid would have given her. He was always so wise, especially when she had doubts. She missed his words, his thoughts. She needed them now.

The doorbell rang, and a second later she heard a key in the lock. Mehran. He always did that – rang first, then opened the door. Eyer kept his finger on the bell until she came and let him in, but not Mehran. It was as if he were saying: Hi, I'm here, but I can manage by myself.

She went into the hallway and looked at her son. Tall, slender, glad to be home. He put down his bag and kicked off his shoes.

'How was your sports day?'

'OK. Me and Levan got lost.'

'Did it take you long to get back?'

'About an hour, but I'd left my lunch where we got changed, so I was starving.'

He kissed her on the cheek and walked past her into the kitchen.

'What's that?' he asked as he caught sight of the blue box on the table.

'A mobile phone,' Shibeka answered truthfully.

'Who's it for?'

'Me.'

Mehran gave her a look that she couldn't quite interpret as he picked up the phone and examined it. Cheap, outdated model. He immediately lost interest and put it down.

'Just be careful where you use it,' he said as he went into the living room and switched on the TV. Nickelodeon as usual. Shibeka watched him go. He had grown so tall. He was becoming a man. Time passed so quickly; sometimes it frightened her.

'I'll make you a cup of chai tea,' she called to him.

'Thanks,' he called over the sound of the television. Shibeka filled the kettle, switched it on, then stopped dead. What was she doing? She was behaving like a bad woman, keeping secrets and going behind the backs of those she loved.

It wasn't right.

It wasn't right at all.

She couldn't carry on like this. It was a dangerous road. The lies would grow, and with them the distance between her and the boys.

She made a decision. Took a deep breath and went into the living room. The words came more easily than she had dared hope.

'I've started something. Something I need to tell you about.'

Mehran looked at her with curiosity, and it struck her once again how much he had grown. He was no longer a boy, and she lowered her eyes to show respect. She sat down beside him and took his hand. He needed to know, and she would listen to what he had to say.

'It's about your father,' she said.

She felt Mehran give a start. He had never liked talking about his father. That had worried Shibeka for a long time, but after a while she realised that he was grieving in his own way. As men should.

Hamid.

The man who had disappeared, but was always present.

Shibeka began to talk. She told him everything.

The television was still on, but no one was listening.

Few things bothered Harald Olofsson. Almost everything that came his way, planned or unplanned, was dealt with steadily and systematically in a manner that most people would find impressive. Harald himself never even thought about it. He didn't have to make an effort to stay in control, or to stop himself from getting worked up. He was simply a methodical, thoughtful, calm person. Therefore, it was an unfamiliar and unwelcome sensation to feel his heart rate increasing and his breathing becoming more laboured.

He couldn't find the rucksacks.

He was very meticulous about where he put things. The yard might look like a bombsite, but Harald knew exactly where each item was and where it had come from. Organisation was a must in his line of work. Nothing that was on view could be traced back to a previous owner, and the same was true of the contents of the outbuilding. Although it was filled to bursting, with everything apparently dumped in there at random, there was a plan behind it all. Items that were at the front and clearly visible were just as safe as the stock in the yard. The further in you got, and the more difficult it became to get at a particular item, the more likely it was that you would be able to find a previous owner, with a bit of hard work. Anything that definitely mustn't be found in his possession was down in the Chamber. The two rucksacks from the car crash had spent some time in there to begin with, but over the years they had been moved upstairs. These days Harald didn't think they belonged in the category of objects that needed to be hidden, so he shouldn't have any problem finding them.

But he had.

A major problem.

He had spent a considerable amount of time in the outbuilding, gone through the whole lot at least twice. He was sure the rucksacks weren't in there. So where were they? Had he already got rid of them? They hadn't contained anything of value, as far as he recalled, but he had no recollection of having thrown them away or burned them. So where were they? Perhaps it didn't matter; if he couldn't lay his hands on them, then the police wouldn't be able to find them either, if they paid him another visit. Anyway, why would they come back? He had answered their questions, and they had seemed perfectly happy when they drove away.

He came out into the yard, squinting into the setting sun. Zeppo got up and walked towards his master as far as the rope allowed. Harald went over and patted the dog, unclipping the rope from his collar at the same time. He hadn't taken Zeppo out since this morning; a walk in the forest would do them both good. Harald went indoors to fetch the lead. He whistled and they set off along the narrow dirt track. After about a hundred metres they turned off among the trees. Within seconds Harald could feel the serenity around him doing him good. The silence. He could hear nothing but the sounds of the forest itself. He took a few deep breaths, and the last vestiges of any anxiety ebbed away. He had been getting worked up for no reason. He would forget all about the car crash and those bloody rucksacks. Harald rolled his shoulders as if to physically shake off the memory and exhaled with a contented sigh, almost expecting to see his breath. It was quite chilly in the evenings now, and the sun had lost some of its heat during the day. The weekend's rain could be the last; the next time they might well see some snow.

They carried on among the dense conifers. Zeppo stopped, sniffed, followed an interesting trail then came back. For long periods Harald neither saw nor heard the dog; they each did their own thing, and they were both happy that way. He suddenly realised that the light was beginning to fade; it was time to go home.

'Zeppo!'

The dog didn't appear. He called again, but there was still no sign of Zeppo. Harald stopped and listened, but the only sound was the faint soughing of the treetops. He swore to himself. Occasionally the dog would pick up a scent and forget everything else, out of sight and out of earshot.

'Zeppo!' he yelled again, much louder this time. Listened for some kind of response, a bark or a rustling in the undergrowth. He was about to shout for a fourth time when it struck him.

They were in the loft.

The rucksacks were in the loft.

He remembered exactly where he had stowed them, but he wasn't sure why he had moved them into the house. It wasn't something he usually did. Ever. If stolen goods were found in the outbuilding, against all expectation, there was at least a theoretical possibility that someone had put them there without Harald's knowledge. However, if something was found indoors it became more difficult, which was why none of his deliveries ever crossed the threshold. He must have decided the rucksacks were safe. Nobody had missed them, presumably nobody even knew they existed. But if Riksmord were showing an interest, it was essential to get them out of the house. If only Zeppo would come back.

'Zeppo!' he bellowed at the top of his voice. 'Get back here, for fuck's sake!' he added as if to convey the seriousness of the situation. Nothing. Harald spent another ten minutes shouting and wandering around before he heard something crashing through the undergrowth. Zeppo appeared, wagging his tail and looking as if he had had a lovely time wherever he had been, thanks for asking. Harald clipped on his lead and set off as quickly as he could.

Once they got home he tied Zeppo up in the yard and hurried indoors. He found the two slightly charred rucksacks in the attic, exactly where he had seen them in his mind's eye. He didn't really care how his brain worked, he was just glad it had come up with the answer. Time to finish this. He dropped the rucksacks through the hatch, switched off the light and clambered down. A couple of things had fallen out of one of them, including the burnt handbag. Why had he kept it? Anyway, now it could go, along with everything else. Down in the kitchen he opened what, with a little imagination, could be called the cleaning cupboard, and took out a bottle of lighter fuel and a box of matches. He went back outside; it wasn't properly dark yet, but definitely darker than twilight. Should he wait until morning? Would it look odd, lighting a fire now? He shook off the unwarranted anxiety; no one was going to see the blaze. He walked past the outbuilding towards the boundary at the back of the property. Zeppo was interested, and followed as far as the rope would allow. At the point where the drive's mud and gravel turned to grass, he threw down the bags, opened the bottle and sprinkled the maroon waterproof fabric generously with the liquid. He replaced the cap and struck a match.

Then everything seemed to happen at the same time.

The blaze flared up as Zeppo started barking. A second later Harald was caught in the powerful headlights of a car turning in through the gates. He gazed uncomprehendingly at the car, then down at the rucksacks burning at his feet, then back at the car as the engine was switched off and the lights went out. Harald blinked and saw a figure walking towards him.

'Harald Olofsson?' said a woman's voice. Suddenly someone, presumably the owner of the voice, came rushing forward and tried to put out the fire. Zeppo carried on barking and Harald backed away.

So close.

If the woman, who he assumed was a police officer, had arrived fifteen minutes later, she would have found nothing but soot and ash, and he would have got away with it.

If he hadn't remembered where the rucksacks were, he would have got away with it.

If the dog had come when he first called, he would have got away with it.

So many ifs. Too many.

He knew he wasn't going to get away with it.

'Shall we start with the car crash?'

Torkel looked at Harald Olofsson, slumped on his chair, hands clasped, head drooping, eyes fixed on the floor. He nodded.

'You need to answer my questions,' Torkel said, pointing to the mobile lying on the table between them. 'For the benefit of the recording,' he clarified when he realised that Harald hadn't seen the gesture. Harald nodded again.

When Ursula called and told Torkel what had happened, what she had found and that she was bringing Harald Olofsson in for questioning, they had decided that the simplest and closest option was to use the mountain station, which was why Harald was now sitting at the folding table in Torkel's room, opposite Ursula and Torkel. Ursula would have preferred to go through the remains of the rucksacks right away, before they were sent to the National Forensics Lab in Linköping, but Torkel had insisted that he wanted her to sit in on the interview. Under normal circumstances it would have been Vanja, but with Vanja gone he wanted . . . what did he actually want? The next best thing, presumably. Jennifer was a promising and conscientious addition to the team, but much too new to be thrown into a situation that depended on an almost instinctive ability to work together, and Billy . . . Billy was Billy. He and Vanja were a good team, but Torkel wanted Ursula, even though she clearly had no desire to be there. Torkel understood this would probably mean he could look forward to another night without company, but he had to set personal considerations aside; the investigation came first.

'Could you tell us about that morning?' Torkel said, in an interested tone which he hoped would give Harald the sense that they were just having a chat. Harald shrugged.

'I was driving along,' he said quietly, his eyes still fixed on the floor.

'Sorry,' Torkel interrupted him. 'Do you think you could speak up a bit?' Harald looked up.

'I was driving along,' he repeated.

'From where?' Ursula snapped.

Harald turned towards her. 'What?'

'Where had you been?'

'I've got a . . . friend who lives just over the border in Norway. I stay there sometimes.'

'A friend?'

'Yes.'

'A woman?'

'Yes.'

'What's her name?'

'Henny. Henny Petersen.'

Torkel extracted an address and telephone number; whatever happened, they would probably contact her, even though she was unlikely to remember whether Harald Olofsson had stayed over on the night between 30 and 31 October 2003.

'I was on my way home in the morning,' Harald went on when Torkel had finished writing. 'I saw smoke rising from down by the river, so I stopped. Then I saw the car.'

'What did you do then?' Torkel thought he knew, but it was always better if the interviewee told the story in his own words as far as possible.

'I went down to see if anyone was hurt, and I could tell that the driver was dead.'

'So what did you do then?' Ursula said, like an echo of Torkel. Harald swallowed. The woman's eyes were harder than the man's. Piercing. Merciless. She had come to his yard. She had found the rucksacks. Her question was purely rhetorical; Harald was well aware that the two police officers already knew what he had done.

'I found her handbag, or what was left of it at any rate. It was lying by the door and the window was broken so I . . . I took it.'

Ursula nodded to herself, confirming Harald's assumption that they had already worked out most of what had happened that morning.

'Go on.'

Harald hesitated, played for time by taking a sip from the glass of water Torkel had fetched from the bathroom.

'I went back up to my car to fetch a lock pick. I managed to get the boot open, and I took what was inside,' he said, carefully putting down the glass so that he wouldn't have to look them in the eye.

Ursula stared at him, contempt bubbling up inside her. After all these years she had stopped being surprised at what people were capable of doing to one another, but there was something about this scruffy individual that sickened her. He had found a woman's body in a car, and his first thought was to feather his own nest. Looting, that was what Harald Olofsson had done. On a small scale, admittedly, but it was still looting. In Ursula's book there was no excuse for profiting from someone else's misfortune in that way. None whatsoever.

'So what did you find?' Torkel asked. If he felt the same as Ursula about the man opposite, he was hiding it well.

'Two rucksacks.'

'Nothing else?'

'No.'

'No tent?' Ursula chipped in.

'No.'

Torkel understood what she was getting at. They still didn't know where the four people in the grave had been staying.

'The rucksacks sustained a certain amount of fire damage earlier today,' Torkel went on.

'Yes. Sorry.'

Harald looked at them, his expression matching the sincerity in his voice. If it hadn't been for the looting, Ursula would almost have felt sorry for him.

'Were there any address labels on them when you found them?'

'I don't know.'

'Think. Or any badges or flags, anything that might indicate who owned them?'

'I don't know.'

Ursula leaned forward, resting her arms on the table. She waited until Harald met her gaze, which took a few silent seconds.

'Let me explain,' she said once they had eye contact. 'The forensic examination suggests that the accident didn't cause the fire. That it was started deliberately, possibly to hide evidence.'

She saw Harald give a start as the implications of her words sank in. His expression shifted from apologetic to frightened in a second.

'Or perhaps to silence the woman who was driving,' Ursula went on. 'If we think she was alive when the fire started . . .'

She didn't finish the sentence; instead she allowed the image and its consequences to sink in. She could see that it was working. Harald's face lost all its colour, and when he picked up the glass of water, his hand was shaking. Ursula had no idea whether what she had just said was true; the woman probably hadn't been alive. There was nothing in the post-mortem report to suggest that she had had smoke in her lungs, but Harald Olofsson didn't know that.

'If she was alive when the fire started, we're looking at murder,' she concluded, leaning back on her chair.

'I had nothing to do with that!' Harald instinctively turned to Torkel. Even though they hadn't discussed it or even thought about it, he and Ursula seemed to have developed a good cop/bad cop strategy. Ursula seemed determined to keep it that way.

'Perhaps she was sitting there when you started taking her stuff; she came round and you realised she'd seen you, and . . . I don't know, maybe you panicked?'

'No!'

'Did you take anything else from the car?' Torkel asked calmly. Harald had been co-operative all along, but now he was scared too, so they might as well make the most of it.

'No, nothing, I swear. The handbag and the two rucksacks. Then I called the police.'

'We're going to turn your place upside down, and if you're lying to us . . .'

Torkel fell silent, but Harald knew exactly what he meant. Just as he knew it was over. It was all over. They would find the Chamber. He wasn't going to get away with it this time, but he had no intention of getting mixed up in a murder that was nothing to do with him.

'I'm not lying!' He looked from one to the other, but settled on Ursula; she seemed to be the one who needed the most convincing. 'I didn't take anything else! The handbag and the two rucksacks. And the car had already been on fire when I found it.'

Torkel and Ursula didn't say a word.

'I swear,' Harald said again.

They believed him.

It felt strange, walking into the Kronoberg custody suite as a relative. Vanja had been there so many times through work, never imagining that one day she would be here in a completely different role. She felt as if the stone walls in the reception area were closing in on her. Weighing her down. Making every step towards the duty officer more difficult than the one before. Eventually she made it. Janne Gustavsson was sitting behind the glass. He nodded in recognition.

'I didn't know Riksmord had anyone in here?'

'We don't.'

Vanja fell silent. Janne looked enquiringly at her. There was something about her voice; she didn't sound as confident as she usually did. In fact, she didn't look herself at all. Something had obviously happened.

'I want to see my father,' she went on in a weak voice. 'He's supposed to be here.'

Janne stared at her, and suddenly everything fell into place.

Lithner.

It hadn't even occurred to him, although the name should have set alarm bells ringing. Lithner.

How many people had that surname? Hardly any, apart from an attractive blonde police officer from Riksmord, and the guy in number twenty-three.

Valdemar Lithner.

He had arrived a few hours earlier, booked in by Ingrid Ericsson from the Economic Crime Authority. She was one of the few who actually knew what Janne was called, and addressed him by his first name. He wondered whether Vanja knew. Probably not.

'Is Valdemar Lithner your father?'

Vanja nodded, nervously fiddling with a strand of hair. Janne suddenly thought that she looked like a little girl. A little girl lost. He couldn't help feeling sorry for her.

'Would it be possible for me to see him?'

'Unfortunately that's a bit difficult,' Janne said as sympathetically as he could, glancing at the clock. 'The thing is, it's after five, and I'm not sure what's allowed.'

'Have any restrictions been imposed?'

Janne leafed through his papers, although he already knew what he was going to find. Ingrid Ericsson had said no to everything.

Telephone calls	[NO]
Letters	[NO]
Computer access	[NO]
Visitors	[NO]

Ericsson always said no.

Janne carried on checking for a little while longer just to be on the safe side, then looked up at Vanja.

'I'm afraid so. No access.'

'Do you really think I would compromise the investigation?'

'No, but it doesn't matter what I think,' he said, almost apologetically. 'You'll have to speak to Ingrid Ericsson or the prosecutor.'

Vanja glanced around looking vaguely confused, as if she expected Ericsson or the prosecutor to be sitting in reception. Janne might have gained a certain amount of satisfaction from the situation; Riksmord were usually so perfect, so unstoppable. They didn't have to sit behind a glass screen dealing with people the way he did. But there was something about her helplessness that was hard to resist. It didn't suit her, and it made him feel uncomfortable rather than supercilious.

'Have you got Ingrid's number?' she asked eventually.

He nodded and jotted it down on a Post-it note. 'I'll give you the prosecutor's number too – Stig Wennberg. He's usually easier to deal with than Ingrid.'

Vanja nodded gratefully as he passed her the note.

'Thanks, Janne.'

So she did know his name.

'Good luck,' he said, and meant it. She was going to need it.

As she left he saw her take out her mobile before the door had even closed behind her.

Then she was gone. He had seen most things during his ten years in the job, but this was something different.

★ ★ ★

Vanja called Ingrid Ericsson first; it was probably best to start with the person who was leading the investigation. Straight to voicemail; presumably she had switched off her phone. Vanja left a brief message asking Ingrid to ring her back as soon as possible, but gave no further details. No doubt Ingrid would realise it was to do with her father, but she couldn't make her request via an answering service. It would be hard enough in an actual conversation. Then she tried Stig Wennberg, the prosecutor. She had never come across Ingrid Ericsson's name through her work, but she was familiar with Wennberg's excellent reputation. She remembered that some of her colleagues had thought it was a shame when he moved to the Economic Crime Authority a few years earlier.

He answered almost immediately. Vanja could hear children in the background, and assumed he was at home. He sounded stressed, but relaxed slightly when she said she was a police officer. He asked how he could help her, thinking she had called about a case she was working on.

She told him how he could help her.

Any trace of relaxation disappeared.

'It's out of the question. You do realise that?'

There was a gravity in his voice that hadn't been there when he took the call. This wasn't going to be easy. It was a very tricky balancing act. Gross misconduct was just a few sentences away if she pushed too hard, which was what Vanja really wanted to do. She wanted to yell at him, tell him she had to see her father right now, rules or no rules. But she couldn't do that. She had to stay in control, word her plea very carefully.

'I know it's an unusual request,' she said tentatively, 'but I really do need to see my father.'

The response was a deep sigh.

'I'm in the middle of a case; you might have heard about the mass grave up in Jämtland,' she went on, trying a new strategy. If he

179

wasn't prepared to help a daughter, perhaps he would be willing to help a police officer. 'I need to find out what's happened to my father so that I can rejoin the team.'

'Are you with Riksmord and Torkel Höglund?'

'That's right.'

Wennberg hesitated for a second. Perhaps there was a way in after all.

'Do you know Torkel?' Vanja asked in what she hoped was a neutral tone.

'Yes, but don't imagine that will get you anywhere.'

The door closed as quickly as it had opened, but Vanja wasn't giving up. She tried to find that little gap again, gently, gently, without annoying him too much.

'I'd be happy for the visit to be supervised, of course.'

'The restrictions are imposed by the officer in charge, it's her decision.'

'Absolutely, but the restrictions are often quite sweeping. He's not a murder suspect. As prosecutor it's within your power to allow exceptions.'

Wennberg didn't say anything, but he didn't end the call either, which was something. As long as she was talking to him, she had a chance.

'I know it's a lot to ask, but I honestly can't see what harm it would do you. If something happens, I would lose my job. The only person taking a risk is me.'

For a second she thought about her FBI training; could this have a negative impact on her chances? She was ashamed of herself; why was she thinking about that now? She had more important matters to consider, the person who meant the most to her.

Her father.

He was the one she had to focus on, not herself.

At the other end of the line the children had gone quiet, or else Wennberg had moved to another room.

'If Torkel calls me and vouches for you, I'll consider it. That's the only way,' he said eventually.

'OK.' Vanja could hardly get the words out. 'He'll call you right away. I promise. He'll call you.'

'Supervised access. Ten minutes max.'

'Yes. Good. Absolutely. Thank you so much.'

'Thank Torkel if it happens.'

He ended the call, and Vanja stood there holding the phone. The first obstacle overcome. She was on the way. Now she just had to speak to Torkel. In her head she could hear herself starting a conversation she had never in her wildest dreams expected to have.

Hi, Torkel.

I need your help.

My father has been arrested.

★ ★ ★

Valdemar had wondered when the custody officer came to fetch him. He hadn't expected anything to happen before tomorrow, but then again, what did he know about the normal routine in this place? He had been sitting in the same position on the hard bed for so long that his legs felt stiff and numb, and his first steps had been unsteady. The guard had led him down the bare green corridor to the same interview room where he had been questioned earlier. Sat him in the same chair at the same table and told him to wait. The stiffness in his legs had eased, but the ache at the base of his spine had come back. He felt old and worn out and, even worse, he felt as if he wasn't quite with it, as if he were sitting in this room, yet he was somewhere else. His head was spinning. It had all happened so fast. That woman turning up on his doorstep. The first interviews. Being locked up. And now more questions, apparently.

It was probably all part of their strategy, trying to confuse him.

It was working.

He had to pull himself together, focus. Answer their questions without getting himself mixed up and losing control. He heard sounds in the corridor and sat up a little straighter. He would say as little as possible, that was the plan. It had worked last time, perhaps it would be just as effective now.

The heavy door opened and he caught a glimpse of someone behind the guard. He almost panicked. It couldn't be, it mustn't be her! The person disappeared from view for a second as the guard stood in the doorway, hiding her. Valdemar hoped it had been a figment of his imagination, that when the guard walked in there would be no one behind him. Or that it would be the self-satisfied women who had arrested him. Anything would be better than . . .

But then he saw her. She was real. She was there, just as pale and bewildered as he was. She was staring at him, her expression unreadable. He made a brave attempt at a smile, but knew it was pointless. In this room, in this situation, a smile was no use.

'Hello, Vanja,' he said as casually as he could.

She didn't reply. She walked over to the chair opposite him, but remained standing. For a second Valdemar wondered if he could refuse to see her, if he could ask the guard to take him back to his cell. Perhaps that would make things easier.

For her.

Not for him.

He was lost, he knew that now. The shortcut he had taken had led him astray, and now he was lost. She would never forgive him. She might understand, if he really tried to explain, but how could he explain when he didn't really understand it himself?

'What have you done, Dad?' she asked suddenly.

He looked down at his hands. Even they looked old, veined and wrinkled, worn. She might never want to hold them again.

The guard closed the door and came over to the table. 'You've got ten minutes,' he said officiously. 'I have to stay.'

Vanja nodded and he went and sat on a stool in the corner. He leaned against the wall and tried to look as uninterested as possible.

Valdemar looked at his daughter, who was still standing in front of him. She must have been in this room many times, but never like this.

'What have you done?' she repeated.

Valdemar felt compelled to tell her the truth.

'Something stupid, I'm afraid.'

Vanja pulled out the chair and sat down heavily. Looked at him. He seemed to have aged several years in just a few days. There was so much she wanted to say, so many questions she wanted to ask. So much she needed to know, but with the guard in the room he wouldn't be able to tell her everything. Which was perhaps just as well. Seeing him had shaken her far more than she had expected. She needed to ask a few anodyne questions so that she could pull herself together.

'Have you got a solicitor?'

'No,' he said, shaking his head. 'The office wanted to send someone, but I refused.'

'Why?'

'I don't know. I thought you might find out if I had a solicitor, and I didn't want that.'

He still couldn't look her in the eye.

'I found out anyway. Did you really think you could keep this a secret? I'm a police officer!'

Valdemar shook his head again. It was possible to keep secrets. Bury them and hope for the best. It had worked before.

'They questioned me a few years ago, but the preliminary investigation was shelved. I was hoping that's what would happen this time too,' he said, looking up at her. 'Then you'd never have to know.'

Vanja went pale. He realised that wasn't what she wanted to hear. She wanted everything to go back to normal, just as he did. She wanted this ridiculous situation to be a parenthesis in their lives, a mistake that could be explained away, that would vanish as quickly as it had appeared. Knowing that there had been a previous investigation didn't do much to preserve that illusion.

'What was the previous investigation about?' she asked, sounding unexpectedly composed.

He knew her. Whatever feelings she had had when she walked into the room, they had been pushed aside. Now she was angry.

'Same thing. Embezzlement, fraud, tax evasion, breach of trust . . .'

'But they didn't pursue it?'

'No, but now they're saying they've found new evidence.'

Valdemar stopped himself, he didn't want to say any more, but there was no escape; Vanja was bound to ask about this new evidence. She would find out anyway, sooner or later; it was probably best if she heard it from him.

'About Daktea,' he said quietly.

She leaned forward, staring at him as if he were a stranger, someone she didn't even know. She had never looked at him that way before, with such coldness.

'Were you involved in Daktea?'

'I certainly didn't know everything,' he said, shaking his head as if even he still couldn't understand what had actually happened. 'How big it was. I trusted the wrong people.'

He reached for her hand, but she didn't respond. If his hands had aged, hers had completely lost interest. He glanced at the guard, who was now looking at them with curiosity. She deserved an explanation, but he had to choose his words carefully.

'I just wanted us to have a good life, sweetheart.'

He could hear how hollow the excuse sounded.

So could she, apparently.

'We've always had a good life,' she snapped.

She was right as usual. They might have lacked material things. Stuff. Nothing that really meant anything. Nothing that could replace what he was losing now, but he had so wanted to be the daddy who never saw anything as a problem, the daddy who could give his family the life everyone else seemed to have. Someone they could be proud of.

'Yes, but your mother really wanted a summer cottage, you needed an apartment . . .'

She went up like a rocket.

'An apartment! Are you trying to drag me into all this? Are you trying to tell me you're sitting here because of me?'

'Please, Vanja, no, that's not what I meant.'

'So what did you mean?'

He shrivelled before her eyes. Collapsed. He was worthless. He was a liar, a cheat. He must make her understand how simple it had been, how tempting. Intoxicating. How he had been carried along, until in the end he didn't even consider the fact that it was illegal. He needed to explain it to her, but he couldn't find the words.

'I don't know,' he said at last. 'I don't know, Vanja.'

The whole thing was such a mess. The only words left were banalities.

'I love you. I love you so much and I wanted . . .' He stopped and wiped away a tear. 'I wanted to give you everything.'

'I never asked you for everything.'

The chill in her voice was dreadful. It twisted and turned in his breast like an ice-cold worm; he could hardly breathe. She didn't care about his love. How could that be? It used to mean the world to her, he knew that. But he had let her down, in the worst way imaginable. He had gone behind her back, turned out to be a different person from the man she thought she had known all these years, lied to her. You couldn't do that to Vanja. She was totally honest, and she demanded honesty in return. It was perfectly simple. Valdemar knew that, knew what he needed to do to win her back, but instead of telling the truth, he lied again.

'I haven't done anything illegal.'

'So what have you done?'

He knew she could see through him. He was wide open, but still he was trying to wriggle away. He couldn't do anything else.

'I might have pushed the boundaries a bit. Helped people I shouldn't have helped.'

'You did it,' she stated flatly, all emotion gone from her voice. She might just as well have been commenting on the weather. Valdemar didn't speak; he gazed at her pleadingly as she calmly pushed back her chair and got to her feet.

'Whatever they're accusing you of, you did it.'

She turned and headed for the door.

'Please, Vanja. Wait,' he begged.

The guard looked at the clock. 'You've got three minutes left.'

She turned and Valdemar hoped he would get those minutes.

One hundred and eighty seconds.

You could achieve a lot in 180 seconds.

'Thank you, but I'm done here.'

With those words she was gone. Valdemar buried his face in his hands, hoping he would never have to see reality again. The reality where his daughter was gone.

Mehran's heart was pounding with rage, and he felt hot and sweaty. He had told his mother exactly what he thought. He had slammed the door of his room so hard that one of the family photographs in the hallway had fallen down. Now he was lying on his bed, staring up at the ceiling. They had never argued like this before, not even when she had caught him smoking with Levan. But this was different. In every way. His mother had gone behind his back. Deceived both him and Eyer. She said it was for their sake, that she wanted to protect them, but he knew that wasn't true.

It was just as Memel had said.

Shibeka is confused. Hamid was her backbone. Without a backbone, we wobble and fall. You have to help her, you understand?

He had always defended his mother to the stubborn old man who thought she didn't know her place. Mehran had told Memel how hard she fought for them, how she always did everything for them. She was the best mother a son could have. She worked and studied so that they would have a better life. She had learned Swedish for their sake. But now he realised that Memel was probably right.

His mother was confused.

There was no other explanation. She had gone much too far. He hadn't said anything when she sent letter after letter to everyone from social services to the police to the press. He had stood silently by her side and allowed her to go on and on about Hamid to the police, even though he knew they didn't care. To them she was just some immigrant complaining. But he had said nothing. He had always stood by her side.

And this was how she thanked him.

By going behind his back.

Mehran turned over and picked up the mp3 player he had been given for his birthday. He liked house music, particularly Avicii. He scrolled down to 'Levels' and turned up the volume. There was something about music that made things clearer; it was as if what had happened became simpler, purer, which in turn made his anger more manageable. Through the music he saw life as an image, and it didn't hurt so much. It wasn't easy for his mother, he knew that. She did her best.

But she was confused.

That was obvious from this latest whim of hers.

It was good that she had learned Swedish; she could help him and Eyer and their friends. But there was also something bad about it; Memel was right. Because it wasn't only the language, she had acquired additional knowledge, learned things that Memel and the other men didn't approve of.

They were worried.

About their own wives.

What if they became confused too?

Mehran liked Memel. It was Memel who would put his arm around him and tell him about the old country and about Hamid. He took Mehran to the mosque and showed him how to wash, how to get ready for prayers.

Mehran had always stuck up for his mother, but now she had met up with someone from the TV. Alone. A Swedish man. After all he had done for her.

The anger was back, and not even Avicii could calm him this time. A Swedish man! The Swedes had done nothing for them until now. On the contrary, the Swedes were to blame. His father had disappeared here, in safe, secure Sweden, not in dangerous Afghanistan. Not on the way here. But in Sweden, where he and his family were supposed to feel grateful all the time. The whole thing was a lie. Sweden wasn't safe, not for most of the people he knew. They lived in a constant state of insecurity. Would they be allowed to stay or not? Would they be deported one day? Or even worse, would they simply disappear like his father? He remembered the official at the Immigration Board who had wanted to throw them out, even though Hamid had gone missing. Shibeka had been terrified that someone would come for them one day, drive them to the airport and send them away.

It was all a lie. He hated lies.

And now his mother had lied too.

Mehran took a deep breath and put 'Levels' on again. He hoped he would calm down if he left it on repeat. He hadn't even got close when there she was, standing in the doorway. She looked at him with her brown eyes, red-rimmed from crying.

'Forgive me, Mehran,' she said softly. 'May I come in?'

Mehran didn't answer. He simply looked at her as the music filled his head. She sat down beside him on the bed. He didn't stop her. He felt her warm hand on his stomach, which calmed him more than the music.

'Can't you take off your headphones?' she asked.

She was speaking Pashto. He used to love it when she did that. In their everyday lives she always insisted that they spoke Swedish, to help them get on. But today she was speaking Pashto. He knew why. She did it when it was important that they understood everything she said. Her voice sounded more familiar in Pashto. More real. More like his mother. He reluctantly removed his headphones, but the anger was still there.

'I know you're angry,' she went on. 'But I never wanted to hurt you. I just didn't know how to tell you.'

He looked at her, letting his anger show in his tone.

'Why can't we always speak Pashto?'

She looked surprised; she hadn't been expecting that question.

'I think it's good to speak Swedish. We live in Sweden.'

'But we're not Swedes, even if you seem to think we are.'

Shibeka took his hand.

'Don't be cross, Mehran. I thought he could help us.'

'How?'

'I don't know, but I have to find out what happened. We have to find out.'

'He's gone, Mum. Gone. Don't you get it?' he yelled.

Shibeka squeezed his hand. He kept on shouting, in spite of the pressure of her soft fingers.

'The fact that you won't accept it doesn't make things any better. You're confused! I'm confused!'

'But I can't just give up, because I knew your father so well. I see him in you; every day I am reminded of him. Don't you see? It's impossible. It's like asking me to stop breathing. Or to stop loving.'

Suddenly she began to weep. Mehran hadn't seen her cry for a long time. In the beginning, when Hamid went missing, she had cried all the time, but then one day she had stopped. It was as if she had run out of tears. He tried to console her; he sat up and looked into her eyes. He loved her so much, but she had to understand that she couldn't carry on like this.

'I miss him too, Mum. But everyone says you have to stop now. I've always told them you're fine, that you won't do anything stupid. Then you go and meet this man without telling me?'

'I think he can help us.'

'Stop it, Mum. No one here has helped us with anything. Why should he be different? You're making us all look like idiots.'

He paused and looked at her. 'You're not an idiot, Mum. I know that.'

Shibeka nodded and took her hand away.

'You're right, Mehran. I will listen to you from now on. You will make the decisions. I promise to listen to you, just as I would listen to your father. But you have to meet him. The man from the TV. Then you can decide.'

She was speaking to him in a completely different way: as an equal. He knew he had to respond on the same terms. His voice was gentle now.

'Tell him to come here tomorrow.'

'Shall we tell Eyer?'

Mehran shook his head. 'No. He's too young.'

'But you're not. Not any more.'

'No, Mum. No I'm not.'

Shibeka ventured a smile before she left the room. Mehran remained sitting on his bed. He didn't need the music now. He had grown up today, and he didn't need music to help him understand that. It was an amazing feeling. Was he really ready to take on the responsibility he had been given? He wanted nothing more, but there was also something frightening in the realisation that he could no longer hide behind his age, that he was no longer a child.

He went into the hallway; his mother was in the kitchen. When Eyer got home there would be a hot meal as always. Everything would be just the way it always was, but everything had changed.

She probably thought they were different, that he wanted to forget. But that wasn't true. It was just that they had different ways of dealing with their loss. She made phone calls, wrote letters, went on and on. Mehran kept quiet. She showed her pain, he carried it deep inside. That was what a man did. Pain that was locked inside made a man strong.

Women wept. Men did not.

Shibeka turned and smiled at him, and this time he smiled back.

She had secrets. So did he, but his were buried deep down in his childhood. Was he going to have to bring them out, or could he let them rest? He didn't know.

But he would never forget the man with the rasping voice. The man his father had warned him about.

Joseph.

Vanja had thrown up at Kronoberg, with no warning whatsoever. She had gone into the staff toilet and sat down, not because she wanted to use it, but just to be alone for a few moments. Suddenly her stomach turned inside out, and the contents landed on the floor between her feet. She stared at the yellow mess. There was a sour taste in her mouth, and she automatically leaned forward in case there was more to come. She couldn't leave the custody suite until the guard came to let her out, and he had had to take Valdemar back to his cell first. It would take a while, but she was in no hurry, and right now she didn't care if she threw up all over the floor.

Nothing mattered any more.

The memory of her meeting with Valdemar was at the forefront of her mind, and behind it there was nothing. There was only him, in a room where she could never have imagined seeing him. It was an impossibility, and yet it had just happened. Valdemar was not innocent. If she had had her doubts before, she was certain now. He had skirted around the truth, a tactic she knew so well. Vanja had seen it so often in her job.

He might have pushed the boundaries, he said. Valdemar, who never pushed the boundaries.

The sour taste in her mouth felt appropriate; it was the taste of a terrible day. She would have liked to empty her stomach completely, get it all up, get it all out.

But there was nothing more, however much she retched. So she stuck two fingers down her throat, over and over again until she felt totally empty. Her shoes and the lower part of her trouser legs were spattered with vomit, but she didn't care; she felt liberated, as if she had regained control of her body. Got rid of the crap she had ingested. It was a wonderful feeling. She wanted to stuff her face, consume as much as possible just to bring it back up.

It was a long time since Vanja had felt like that. An eternity. But she understood what she had liked about it back then.

Losing and regaining control.

The simultaneous experience of pleasure and shame.

She leaned forward and stared at the contents of her stomach on the floor.

She had been seventeen when she started; she was a student at high school in Östermalm. She was clever and quick; she loved reading, so the academic side was no problem. It was the rest of it. The social side.

Everyone else at the school seemed to be rich, beautiful and perfect. There were so many unwritten rules, codes that she knew nothing about. She wanted friends. She wanted a boyfriend. She wanted to be part of the gang. But she wasn't. Whatever she did, it was wrong. However hard she tried, she remained one of those who didn't fit in. So she started buying treats on the way home to cheer herself up: sweets, biscuits, crisps. More and more. Salt, sugar and fat became her friends, and she chose them with increasing frequency.

However, the thought of the rubbish she was consuming frightened her, made her feel worse among the stick-thin perfect bodies all around her. So she started making herself sick now and again to stop herself from putting on weight. At first it didn't seem like such a bad idea; she didn't do it often, and in fact it was the perfect combination: she could consume all that deliciousness, then get rid of it a little while later.

But it escalated, until in the end she was thinking only of food, and how quickly she could bring it back up. Nothing else mattered.

One day she read an article about eating disorders in *Dagens Nyheter*. It was about bulimia. She had merely glanced through the other articles in the series, but suddenly she recognised herself. She read about the side effects, the possibility that menstruation could become irregular and stop. Tooth enamel could be severely damaged. She had run to the bathroom and nervously checked the back of her front teeth, which was apparently where the erosion started. She couldn't feel anything abnormal with her tongue, but then again she didn't know how it was supposed to feel. However, she hadn't had a period for three months. She made herself a pile of sandwiches and read the article again, with an increasing sense of familiarity. Everything fitted. Then she threw up and burst into tears.

She was sick.

It wasn't just that she didn't fit in, she was sick, and very few people managed to recover from that particular illness.

She confided in Valdemar, went to his office. She still didn't know where she had got the strength from, because she was so ashamed of herself, but it was Valdemar she had chosen to tell. He had taken the rest of the day off, and they had gone for a walk. She had felt faint and dizzy, but he had got it all out of her, gently, step by step. When it really mattered he had stepped forward and been the father she had always hoped he would be. It was wonderful.

Two weeks later he arranged for her to move to a new school. It was already late in the summer term, so she started at Södra Latin in the autumn. He fixed everything. A two-week retreat during the summer for girls with bulimia, to provide her with the tools to fight it. He tracked down the best therapists, found someone new if she didn't like the person she was working with.

He had healed her, with his closeness and his honesty.

That was the picture she couldn't reconcile with the man she had just met in that dingy, cramped room. When she was seventeen she had revealed a painful secret to him; it had taken courage and absolute trust on her part. Why couldn't he do the same at fifty-five? When it came to the crunch, he had chosen to stay locked in the bathroom, as it were.

That made her very sad. This wasn't a betrayal, or a humiliation. It was much worse. She felt as if she had been completely abandoned.

From now on Vanja would have to cope on her own. For real. The security of knowing that he was always there when she needed him was gone.

Dad.

He would never again be there for her in the same way.

Never.

Vanja got to her feet, her shoes sticking to the stinking, slushy mess. She just wanted to get out of there. Everything disgusted her: the room, the smell, the taste.

She wondered whether to go and see Anna, but that felt too much like hard work. Anna would need a lot of support, and she would ask endless questions. Support that Vanja was incapable of giving right now, and questions she couldn't answer. Anna had plenty of friends, women who were closer to her than Vanja was. They would have to take care of her tonight if necessary.

She washed her face, rinsed her shoes and trousers, sluiced out her mouth. She realised now how important the FBI training was; more important than ever. It was no longer just a training programme and an opportunity; it was a journey she had to make. Now that she was alone.

It was time to grow up, for real.

Vanja would go as soon as she heard from the selection committee, before the course actually started. She would just go. Leave Riksmord. Leave everything. Stand on her own two feet.

It was time.

Torkel was the last to arrive at the meeting again. This was starting to become a habit, and this time he wasn't just late, he was tired and bad-tempered as well. First of all, Vanja's call had alarmed him, but he had done as she asked and spoken to the prosecutor. Then Axel Weber had called again. He had linked the car crash and the deceased woman to the discovery of the bodies on the mountain, and wanted to know what the connection was. Even if Torkel had known he wouldn't have told Weber, of course, but the very fact that the journalist seemed to know exactly what they were doing irritated the hell out of him. However, it didn't sound as if he knew that it was a hire car, or who was driving, or that Patricia Wellton had had a false ID. Fortunately Weber didn't know what Ursula had discovered at Harald Olofsson's place either; if he did find out, the press would explode with all kinds of speculation. Torkel had tried to get hold of Hedvig Hedman, but without success. Irrespective of what was going on with the complaint to the Attorney General, she needed to make sure that her team kept their mouths shut in future.

'Ursula,' he said as soon as he sat down. Might as well get down to business; it had been a long day.

'I went through what we found at Olofsson's as best I could before I sent it off to Linköping,' Ursula said as she opened up her laptop. 'The notes are in our shared folder, and there's a printout here if you'd prefer.' Jennifer and Torkel leaned forward and took a copy, while Billy opened up the folder on his computer.

'As you know it was the contents of the handbag that proved most interesting; I found the remains of a driving licence issued to a Liz McGo-something in an inside pocket.'

'Have you got anywhere with the name?' Torkel broke in, turning to Billy.

'Yes and no. Do you want me to report back now?'

'No. Carry on, Ursula.'

'There wasn't much else in the handbag; it was inside the car, and sustained more fire damage than the rucksacks. Anything that didn't burn was partially or entirely melted by the heat. As you can see I was able to identify ordinary items: make-up, a hairbrush, keys and a wallet containing the remains of notes, both kronor and dollars, plus a few Swedish coins. There were also parts of what appear to be plastic cards, but they are too badly damaged for me to get anything from them. It's possible the lab might have more success.'

'And what about the rucksacks?'

'They were in the boot, and were relatively undamaged. Harald Olofsson's attempt to destroy them caused only superficial damage to the exterior. They contained mainly clothes, belonging to an adult male, an adult female, and two children – a boy and a girl. Bullet holes and blood on some items, including the children's clothing.'

'The bodies on the mountain,' Jennifer said.

Ursula nodded. 'Sheets, pillowcases, toiletries, a few toys and children's books. In Swedish. That's all.'

'Fingerprints?' Billy wondered.

Ursula shook her head. 'The fatty acids have disappeared after such a long time.'

'No names or anything else that could identify them?' Torkel asked, although of course he would have known if Ursula had made a breakthrough like that. Not surprisingly, she shook her head again.

'Not that I could find. Our colleagues at the lab in Linköping have got completely different methods at their disposal when it comes to examining surfaces; let's hope they find something.'

'Is it worth publicising the clothes, see if anyone recognises them?'

'We can try, but there was nothing striking; they just seemed like perfectly ordinary clothes.'

'No names in the children's clothing?' Jennifer asked.

'No.'

'But don't people usually put names in their kids' clothes?'

Ursula thought about it. She had never put 'Bella' in a single item of clothing. She had read the notes from nursery and school asking her to do so, but she had always ignored them. Had Mikael obliged? She thought not; after all, she had washed her daughter's clothes on a number of occasions, and surely she would have noticed. Wouldn't she?

'Did you look at the labels?'

Ursula tore herself away from thoughts of her ex-husband and her daughter and turned to Jennifer. She's new, she told herself. New and ambitious, and she means well. Be nice.

'Yes, I looked at the labels,' she said patiently. 'All the labels, in fact, including those in the items belonging to the adults—'

'The sheets,' Torkel interrupted the exaggeratedly polite reply. He really must mention to Jennifer that it wasn't a good idea to question Ursula's professional expertise too overtly. 'You don't have sheets if you're camping.'

'You do at hostels,' Jennifer said.

'We've checked all the hostels,' Billy said.

'Check them again.'

'No sleeping bags, no tent, nothing to cook on. It doesn't look like a camping trip to me,' Ursula said.

Torkel sighed. Where the hell had these people come from? Where had they been? What were they doing out on the mountain? Where did they die? Who were they? He felt as if the team didn't know any more now than when they arrived in Jämtland. He nodded to Billy and Jennifer, hoping they would have something to contribute.

'When we got the new driving licence from Ursula, we split the tasks between us,' Billy began as he got up and went over to the whiteboard. He moved the pictures of the grave scene to make room for a timeline.

'Jennifer carried on with Patricia Wellton, because she had found her in the passenger lists, so it's best if we start there.'

He picked up a black marker pen, and Jennifer looked down at her notes.

'Patricia Wellton flew from Frankfurt to Stockholm on the afternoon of 29 October 2003. She landed at Arlanda just after five, and we assume she took the night train to Östersund.'

'How did she get to Frankfurt?' Torkel asked.

'We don't know, but she had also booked a ticket from Trondheim to Oslo on 31 October. She didn't catch that flight, and that's all we have on her.'

'Well done,' Torkel congratulated her. 'Börje Dahlberg hasn't managed to find anything on a Patricia Wellton yet; she isn't on any database, which suggests it's an identity she hadn't used before.'

'Which brings us to Liz McGo-something,' Billy took over. 'As the driving licence was found in Wellton's car, we assumed they were connected, and we started in Frankfurt. A Liz McGordon arrived there on 28 October.'

Torkel straightened up as he felt a surge of fresh energy. This was really good news. Another person, someone they had already traced to the same city at the same time as one of their suspects. He looked at the board and Billy's timeline.

'The day before Patricia Wellton left Frankfurt,' he said.

'Yes . . .'

Billy didn't look anywhere near as pleased as he ought to be, Torkel thought.

'I think you're going to have to call Börje again,' Billy said almost apologetically. 'Liz McGordon doesn't exist either. At least not this Liz McGordon.'

'What the fuck!' Torkel's shoulders dropped as he tried to work out what this meant. Two women. Two fake identities. He'd never known anything like it. What was going on here?

'Where did she come from?' Ursula asked.

'Washington DC,' Jennifer said, as Billy carried on writing. 'With Delta Airlines. We have no information regarding onward travel from Frankfurt, but she also had a return ticket – from Oslo on 1 November.'

'So how was she going to get there?'

'We don't know.'

Torkel pushed aside the disappointment and weariness, which he had allowed himself to feel just for a moment. He got up and started pacing around the room.

'So, Liz McGordon flies from the USA to Frankfurt on the twenty-eighth. Patricia Wellton flies from Frankfurt to Stockholm on the twenty-ninth, then travels on to Östersund where she hires a car on the thirtieth. On the thirty-first she's supposed to fly from Trondheim to Oslo, and the following day Liz McGordon has a ticket booked from Oslo back to Washington.'

He stopped dead and quickly checked what Billy had written on the whiteboard.

'Patricia Wellton and Liz McGordon are the same person.'

There was a silence as Torkel's words sank in.

'But Patricia or Liz, or whatever her name is, never reaches Trondheim, because her car crashes and someone sets fire to it,' he went on. 'In the boot are the rucksacks which probably belonged to four of the people whose bodies we found on the mountain. What does that tell us?'

'That she shot those four people,' Jennifer said.

'Or that she was involved, at any rate,' Ursula corrected her.

'We didn't find a gun in the car.'

It sounded like a statement, but Torkel glanced enquiringly at Ursula, who confirmed it with another shake of the head.

'Olofsson might have taken it,' Billy suggested.

'I think he would have told us,' Ursula said.

'Perhaps she'd already got rid of it,' Jennifer interjected. 'She seems very professional.'

To his delight, Torkel could actually feel the change in the atmosphere. Everyone was leaning forward, mentally on their toes. Everything that was said felt relevant, responses came quickly. Theories were tested, accepted or discarded. Liz McGordon might not exist, but her appearance had breathed new life into the investigation. The important thing now was to hold fast and to keep on trying to untangle the threads.

'So if we take it that Liz and Patricia are the same woman, she came to Europe from the USA, changed identity, travelled up to Jämtland and shot four people whom we assume are a family, and was planning to return to the USA. All within five days? She was spending less than twenty-four hours in this area. Those four people were out in the middle of nowhere. How did she find them?'

'She must have known exactly where they were.'

'How?'

'Maybe she knew them?' Jennifer said. 'They could have been Americans.'

'There were Swedish children's books in one of the rucksacks,' Billy pointed out.

'But no Swedes fitting the profile are missing.'

They all looked at the map Billy had put up earlier. It really was a huge area. Jennifer was struck by an idea, and had to suppress the urge to put up her hand.

'Perhaps they were camping with someone who told Patricia exactly where they were. He or she might have helped to kill them and to dig the grave.'

Silence once more. A fresh theory leading to fresh thoughts as they all considered what Jennifer had said, trying to find the strengths and weaknesses.

More than one perpetrator.

'That would explain why we can't find a tent,' Jennifer went on. 'Patricia took the rucksacks and her collaborator took the tent.'

'And did what?' Ursula asked. There was something about Jennifer's idea that didn't work. 'Took off somewhere else?'

'They could have left the mountain together, then for some reason they had an argument on the way to Trondheim. The other person killed Patricia and continued the journey alone.'

'In which case we should have found the tent in the car. Why would he or she take the tent and leave the rucksacks?'

Jennifer fell silent. Ursula had a point. Billy stepped in.

'Someone killed her, we're pretty sure of that. If it wasn't her pal from the mountain—'

'If she had one,' Ursula interjected.

'Then it must have been someone else,' Billy said, ignoring the interruption.

'A third perpetrator.' Ursula couldn't keep the scepticism out of her voice.

The energy was gone as quickly as it had arrived. It happened sometimes, when things got too diverse, too big. When all at once everything seemed possible, nothing was credible. Torkel suddenly missed Vanja. She was absolutely the best in these situations. She made sure they kept focus, picked out what was important, put everything else to once side. She could hold a line and take every-one with her. He understood afresh what an important part of the team she was. He hoped she was OK; he also hoped her father turned out to be innocent, and that she would soon be back.

'One, two, three perpetrators; a tent, no tent, no gun. Shall we get back to what we actually know?' he said in attempt to get the discussion back on track.

His suggestion was followed by a worrying silence.

'Don't we know anything for sure?'

'We know . . . what we know,' Billy said, waving at the white-board. 'Which isn't much.'

'I've had a very preliminary report from the lab in Umeå,' Ursula said, picking out the document from the pile in front of her. 'They've obtained dental records for the Dutch couple, which seem to confirm what we thought: they are Jan and Framke Bakker.'

'Good.' Torkel couldn't hide his disappointment, which Ursula clearly took personally.

'I'm sorry, I thought you wanted us to focus on what we actually know?'

'I know, it's just that . . .'

Torkel didn't finish the sentence. He realised they weren't going to get any further. Not tonight. After a brief outline of the next day's tasks, they brought the meeting to a close.

When he was alone in the room he sat down at the table, placed his palms together and rested his chin on his thumbs. His gaze fastened on the whiteboard, the photographs, the different coloured lines leading to brief key words or phrases, Billy's timeline. What they actually knew was that they had a woman with two false identities, of which at least one was good enough to enable her to fly to and from the USA after 9/11. Torkel sighed deeply. He had a horrible feeling that the case had just gone from complicated to unbelievably fucking complicated.

Sebastian was in full flow, clearing the apartment of everything that reminded him of Ellinor. He had thrown away the flowers on the table, followed by all those peculiar candles that smelled of strawberries or vanilla that she insisted on buying. Now he was in the living room, folding up the crocheted mats that adorned every flat surface. He wanted a clear space, no handcrafted crap under stupid little china figurines. Ellinor had bought most of the stuff he was getting rid of, but there were a few bits and pieces he recognised. She must have gone through every cupboard, searching for something to 'brighten up' his apartment. The familiar items reminded him of Lily. She hadn't been quite so 'modern and design-orientated' – the words Ellinor used to describe herself – but she had tried to make the place more welcoming and homely.

Sebastian pushed aside thoughts of Lily; nothing good ever came of going back to those days. He focused on Ellinor instead. He wasn't feeling quite so worried now; if Ellinor was somehow behind Valdemar's problems with the police, an awful lot of things would have to go badly wrong before anyone could make a connection with him.

The doorbell rang. Sebastian stopped in the middle of folding a large white cloth. Speak of the devil, he thought. Ellinor. No one else would call round at this time of the night. In fact, come to think of it, no one else would call round at any time.

He thought about keeping quiet until she went away. It would work, no doubt, but she would come back, over and over again. Besides which, it was a bit cowardly. Better to show her how little she meant to him, prove that he had not only removed her from his apartment, but from his life.

The doorbell rang again. He had no intention of letting her in, so she wouldn't actually see how much of her he had cleared away.

He would have to make do with annoying her from a distance, letting her know that he was in, but was determined to ignore her. He went over to the radio and switched it on. Smooth Radio 104.7. Her favourite station. Sebastian smiled to himself. It would drive her crazy to know that he was listening to 'her' station when she couldn't get in. He turned up the volume. Celine Dion's 'My Heart Will Go On'. The gods were on his side; Ellinor loved that song. He turned the volume as loud as it would go, until the music was reverberating through the whole apartment. He was sure it could be heard in the stairwell. Celine was really going for it. Sebastian sat down in the nearest armchair, leaned back and closed his eyes. He would have liked to close his ears too; he felt as if listening to this banal pap was shortening his life. He couldn't hear anything from the door, but assumed Ellinor was still there. She wouldn't give up that easily. He decided to join in the chorus to emphasise his presence in the apartment. He was a little hesitant at first; he hadn't sung since he was a teenager, and very little even then, but now he threw himself into the experience. No doubt it sounded appalling, but he didn't care; his main aim was to annoy Ellinor. He joined in at the top of his voice.

Eventually the music stopped. In the silence that followed he heard the doorbell yet again. Oh, this was wonderful! Another song came on; Sebastian didn't recognise it, but he hoped it was about lost love.

Heartbreak and lost love.

Then again, was that open to misinterpretation? Sebastian sat bolt upright. What if Ellinor thought he was sitting there all alone, playing her favourite music and singing along because he missed her? If that was the case she would never leave. She would kick the bloody door down, rush in like a knight in shining armour to save him from his lonely life. He got up so fast that he felt quite dizzy, and more or less staggered across the room to switch off the radio.

'Sebastian, what are you doing?' he heard from the other side of the door. He stiffened. Listened hard. Went cold inside. That wasn't Ellinor's voice. It was Vanja's.

'I'm coming!' he yelled. He stopped just before he opened the door, suddenly unsure; was it really Vanja? Could he have misheard? After all, Celine had abused his eardrums for a good three minutes.

'Is that you, Vanja?' he asked tentatively.

'Yes,' the answer came immediately.

It was Vanja. Outside his door. He opened it as fast as he could, but his smile faded when he saw her. It was Vanja, and yet it wasn't. She looked pale and pitiful.

'What's happened?' he asked with genuine concern in his voice. She looked like shit, to be honest.

'I need someone to talk to.'

And you chose me.

'Come in,' he said, stepping to one side. She came into the hall-way, her face shiny with perspiration.

Of all the people in the world, you chose me when you needed someone to talk to.

Sebastian had to make a real effort to stop himself from breaking into a smile. That definitely wasn't what she needed right now; certainly not a smug, self-satisfied smile at any rate. He put on his serious, concerned face instead.

'You're always welcome here. How are you feeling?'

She stared at him, her expression both curious and puzzled.

'What were you doing when I rang the bell?'

Sebastian didn't know what to say.

'I was . . . er . . . I was cleaning.'

Vanja raised her eyebrows, then she smiled. Perhaps smiles weren't forbidden after all.

'You sing when you're cleaning?'

He had to nod. What was he supposed to do – tell the truth? That he wanted to torment his ex-girlfriend, who might be responsible for putting Vanja's father in jail? That wouldn't go down too well.

'You surprise me,' she said, managing to keep her tone light. 'I thought you'd have a cleaner. And that you'd be sleeping with her.'

The small talk seemed to be working, calming her down. So he carried on – anything to make her feel better, anything to make her stay. He needed to know what had happened.

'The music helps me to relax.'

'Celine Dion?'

'Yes, she's good when you're cleaning.' He ventured a smile. 'Don't you have any little quirks?'

She nodded. 'Yes, but I don't sing quite so loudly.'

He flung his arms wide. 'You know me, always over the top. Come on in.'

He led the way into the apartment. He could see that some of her normal colour had returned as she looked around with a curiosity he recognised only too well.

'I didn't know you had such a big place,' she said, unable to hide the fact that she was impressed.

'As I said, always over the top.'

'Well, if you can afford it, why not.'

'I used to earn good money once upon a time. Come and sit down.'

He showed her into the living room. The sofa under the large window looked welcoming. Ellinor had moved it there against his will, but he suddenly realised that it made the room look more spacious; it could stay there.

'I'll make us a cup of coffee.'

Vanja shook her head. 'Water's fine.'

She sat down on the sofa. Sebastian went into the kitchen, took out a big jug and put in lots of ice, then added slices of lemon. Something else Ellinor had insisted on, which now felt right. He wanted to make as good an impression as possible. He wanted to be someone Vanja came to in the future when she needed to talk. He filled the jug, picked up two glasses and went back into the living room.

He was struck by how small she looked. Small and vulnerable, with her arms tightly folded across her chest, her expression tense and serious. The brief relaxation she seemed to have felt in the hallway had disappeared. Sebastian sat down opposite her and tried to look as supportive as possible. He poured them each a glass of water, took a sip and waited for a moment before he spoke. He knew that was the best way to go. The other person in a situation like this often interpreted silence as sincerity. It made them feel that the listener had time, and would therefore take what they wanted to say extremely seriously.

'Is this about Valdemar?' he said eventually.

Vanja gave an almost imperceptible nod.

'Have you seen him?'

She shook her head, and her eyes filled with tears.

'There's no rush. I've got all the time in the world, and there's plenty of water in the tap.'

She looked at him gratefully. 'I went to see him. In Kronoberg.'

'Has he been arrested?'

'Remanded in custody.'

Sebastian nodded sympathetically.

'What's he suspected of?'

'Embezzlement, fraud, tax evasion . . .' She gave a little shrug to show that she couldn't bring herself to go through the entire list. 'He's guilty,' she said, meeting Sebastian's gaze.

'Are you sure?'

She gave a single nod. He could see that she wished with all her heart that it wasn't so.

'I don't understand any of this. Apparently the Economic Crime Authority have investigated him before. They didn't pursue the case, but now they've managed to link him to Daktea.'

'How come?'

'I've no idea. Fresh evidence.'

The cold shiver down Sebastian's spine came back, accompanied by a slight stomach cramp.

The Economic Crime Authority.

Fresh evidence.

Daktea.

Ellinor. There was no other explanation. It didn't necessarily mean the trail would lead back to him, but he needed time to think – which he didn't have right now. He realised he hadn't said anything for a while; he hoped Vanja would think he was upset on her behalf, not that he was pondering on his own culpability.

'That doesn't sound good,' he managed to say. 'Do you know what they've found?' he went on, hoping for some detail that would exonerate him.

'No. The prosecutor is Stig Wennberg, and the investigating officer is Ingrid Ericsson. Do you know either of them?'

'I've heard of Wennberg.' Sebastian got to his feet. He felt torn. Part of him wanted to dance on the table. The other part was worried sick.

His plan to knock Valdemar Lithner off his pedestal, the task he had given Trolle Hermansson, had come to fruition, and it seemed to be working far better than he could possibly have hoped. In a way this was fantastic news. As long as nothing could be traced back to him. He would clamber up onto the pedestal, Valdemar would be brought down. Crushed. Now he had to tread carefully, make sure the dream became a reality. Sebastian started gently.

'Perhaps there's a good explanation. He's a financial adviser, isn't he?'

'Yes?'

'Maybe he's been dragged into something without really understanding it. And economic crimes are notoriously difficult to prove.'

Not with the evidence Trolle put together.

He had gone through the material himself, although it seemed like a lifetime ago. There were extracts from overseas accounts with names and dates. There was clear evidence of where the money had actually gone. Payments to the fall guys. The whole lot. Valdemar was toast.

Sebastian sat down again and leaned forward. Gave Vanja the best advice he could come up with.

'You have to help him. Whether he's guilty or not – you know that.'

She nodded, and the tears spilled over. Sebastian could feel her pain.

He was so happy.

He shouldn't be feeling like this.

'Why didn't he say anything? Why didn't he tell me?' she suddenly burst out.

'I suppose he just couldn't bring himself to do it.'

'Why not? He's my father!'

Not for much longer.

'A lot of people behave that way,' Sebastian said calmly as he got up to fetch her a tissue or something. 'He's probably terrified of losing you.'

He fell silent. Was he in danger of making Valdemar too human? Was he being too understanding? He had to get this right. He knew he mustn't be too critical of Valdemar; after all, she hadn't stopped loving her father. Quite the reverse – it was because of her love for him that she felt so let down. That was why she was sitting here, and he must never forget that. Never.

Vanja loved Valdemar.

Even though Sebastian would have liked to trample all over Valdemar, he couldn't do it too overtly. On the other hand, he couldn't be too gentle and understanding, because then Vanja might want to forgive her father. He had to strike a balance, keeping his long-term goal in mind. The key was to increase the distance between them, work on the crack that had appeared in their relationship, widening it little by little. He would need to use all his skills to win her over. Right now she was furious and disappointed, but there would be times when she just wanted Valdemar back, and that was when Sebastian had to make her choose him instead.

'I don't understand why he didn't tell me,' Vanja sobbed. 'That's what makes me so angry. He lied to me.'

Sebastian came back with a serviette that he had found in one of the drawers. Vanja dried her cheeks and noisily blew her nose. Sebastian sat down on the sofa beside her this time. He needed to depersonalise Valdemar, gradually turn him into a symbol. People found it easier to kill off symbols. That was the secret behind the political desire to generalise ethnic groups and sections of the populace. Faceless groups were easier to dislike. Gypsies, homosexuals, Jews and . . . criminals. He had to get Vanja to regard Valdemar as a criminal rather than her father. It wouldn't be easy, but if anyone could pull it off it was Sebastian Bergman. He was confident, but he had to get closer to her, become more human as Valdemar became less so. He took a deep breath.

'I used to have a daughter,' he said suddenly.

'What?' Vanja looked at him in surprise, her eyes red-rimmed from crying.

'With Lily, my wife. I haven't told anyone else.'

Vanja was staring at him.

'What happened to her?'

'She died. In the tsunami. She was four years old.'

'Oh my God.'

'I was holding her hand when the wave came, but I let go. She was torn away from me.' He gazed at her with all the warmth he could muster. 'So I know what it's like to lose someone.'

'I'm so sorry, Sebastian.'

'Thank you.'

He took her hand. She let him.

When she arrived, he was a colleague.

Now he was a grieving father.

It was a step in the right direction.

They had told Eyer they had to go out for a while, and left him watching TV. First of all he had wondered where they were going, and then he had wanted to go with them, but Mehran had been very firm with his little brother and told him he was staying at home. There was something Mum and Mehran needed to do.

Alone.

Shibeka was just as surprised as Eyer at Mehran's new tone, which brooked no disagreement. It certainly worked; Eyer curled up on the sofa without asking any more questions. Mehran looked at his mother.

'Let's go,' he said, leading the way.

She didn't even have time to answer, she simply followed him. She would really have liked to go and see Said's wife Melika on her own; this was going to be a difficult conversation. However, when she told Mehran that she needed to talk to Melika because Lennart Stridh wanted to meet her, he had been just as decisive as he had been with Eyer. From now on, they were doing this together. He was going to be involved in everything she did, at least if it concerned Hamid and that journalist. There was nothing to discuss. It was the two of them now. She was proud of the way he had suddenly stepped up and taken responsibility, but at the same time she couldn't help feeling that he no longer trusted her, which was a terrible thought. She had only ever wanted to put things right, and to find out what had happened to Hamid – for the children's sake as much as her own.

They walked in silence through the chilly autumn evening. It had grown much colder as soon as the sun went down. Winter was still a couple of months away, but it felt as if the cold would come early this year. They turned left and cut across the slopes between the huge apartment blocks. Melika and her son lived at the other end of the urban sprawl known as Rinkeby, and it would take about fifteen minutes to get there. Shibeka didn't see Melika very often these days. At the beginning, just after their husbands went missing, they used to meet up all the time, but now it was as if they reminded one another too much of what they had lost, and the mutual support that had been so important had metamorphosed into endless discussions about right and wrong. Another issue was that Melika hadn't had a visit from any Swedish official after the disappearance, apart from a uniformed police officer, and when Shibeka first mentioned it, they fell out. Melika thought that Shibeka was imagining conspiracies all over the place, while Shibeka thought that Melika was refusing to see the various possibilities they had to investigate.

They had reacted so differently to their grief. For Melika it was as if the new country was to blame, and she withdrew, leaning heavily on the values of her homeland. Shibeka, on the other hand, became very active. She learned more Swedish, got a job, started writing letters and calling the authorities. She didn't want to withdraw, she wanted answers. But perhaps they weren't all that different. They were both women who refused to give up; perhaps that was the source of the friction between them. They had made different choices, and were determined to defend those choices. Too determined, Shibeka sometimes felt.

As they approached Melika's blue-grey tower block, Shibeka felt a pain in her belly. Could this really work? Shouldn't she ask Mehran to wait outside? That would make things easier. They stopped at the door. Mehran turned and looked at her, then pointed to a few abandoned swings in the small play area to the left of the block.

'Dad brought me here just a few days before he disappeared.'

'I know.'

'That's probably why I hardly ever come here now.'

Shibeka nodded. Mehran looked up at the building; there were lights on in most of the windows.

'She's not going to like this,' he said as if he had read his mother's mind.

'I know.'

'She wants to forget. Just like the rest of us,' Mehran said tentatively.

'She doesn't want to forget. She wants everything to be the way it used to be. So do I. We just have different ways of getting there.'

Mehran took her hand. There was a sadness in his beautiful dark eyes that she hadn't seen before.

'But things can never be the way they used to be, Mum.'

Shibeka nodded. 'You are wise, Mehran. I will always listen to you. I promise.'

He suddenly gave her a hug, and it felt lovely. She had wanted to do exactly the same thing all evening, and from the way he squeezed her she knew he had wanted that too.

It was the two of them now.

Shibeka and her eldest son.

Hamid lived through him.

Billy was sitting outside. A pale yellow full moon hung in the sky beside the nearest mountain, spreading its cold light over the dark water below and the gnarled, sparse birch forest a short distance away. Apart from the rushing water, he could hear the cry of a bird of prey from time to time, but he had no idea what it was called. There was nothing else, and he was enjoying the cold and the quietness. He hadn't checked the temperature before he came out, but it couldn't be much above freezing, if at all. It didn't bother him; he was well wrapped up. He had come outside to call Maya, not because there was better network coverage, but because he liked being able to walk around without anyone hearing while they talked.

The conversation had lasted for about fifteen minutes. Billy had told her as much as he could about the case, while she had told him what she had been doing since he left Stockholm. She missed him, her life was boring and empty without him, did he know when he would be home? He didn't, but he missed her too. As they were talking about how much they missed one another, Billy had expected Maya to bring up the subject of moving in together, but she didn't say anything, and for a second he thought it might be something she had just mentioned on the spur of the moment, something she had blurted out because he was going away. Perhaps she had regretted it when she got home and was removed from the situation. He caught himself hoping this was in fact the case, and immediately felt guilty. It was as if she picked up the vibe, because he suddenly heard her say:

'Have you given any more thought to what we discussed at the airport?'

'No, I haven't really had time . . .'

'I've been thinking about it.'

Of course.

'I want us to live at your place.'

'At my place?'

'I want to live in Söder.'

'OK . . .'

Obviously pleased with his response, she changed the subject. Billy assumed that 'OK' could have been interpreted as 'Great, that's all sorted then,' but he couldn't quite bring himself to clarify that he had actually meant 'Right, thanks for telling me that, let's see how it goes.' They had carried on chatting for a few minutes longer before reiterating how much they were longing to see one another and ending the call.

Now Billy was sitting on the terrace, gazing at the moon. He had been out here for a while, letting his mind wander, but it kept coming back to the same thing. And it wasn't the prospect of Maya moving in.

He heard footsteps on the gravel and turned to see Jennifer coming towards him carrying a tray. She had two blankets tucked under one arm.

'Hi, I saw you out here. Am I disturbing you?'

'No.'

'I've got beer and tea, I wasn't sure which you'd prefer,' she said, putting the tray down on the table.

'A beer would be good.'

'Blanket?'

She held out two rough, bobbled dark-brown blankets with the Swedish Tourist Association logo in a grubby shade of yellow dotted here and there. Billy got the feeling they were older than him. Considerably older. He took one and put it around his shoulders; Jennifer did the same with hers and sat down beside him. He took a swig of his beer, she sipped her tea and let out a contented sigh, her breath visible in the cold night air.

'What are you doing out here?' she said after they had sat in silence for a little while.

'Nothing; I'm just thinking.'

'About the case?'

'No.'

'No?'

'No. When I'm not working I'm pretty good at switching off. I think you have to be able to do that . . .'

Jennifer nodded in agreement. The 'leave work at work' philosophy wasn't exactly something new, but that didn't make it any less valid. Personally she hadn't been able to think about anything but the case since they boarded the plane to Jämtland. She had tried to sleep after the evening meeting, relax, but it was impossible. She had got up to make a hot drink and seen Billy out on the terrace. So here she was. She took another sip of her tea; it would soon get cold.

'You looked as if you were concentrating on something.'

Billy nodded. He had been thinking about the one thing that kept on coming back to him, the thing that in many ways seemed more important than the case they were working on.

Could Sebastian Bergman really be Vanja's father?

He hadn't had time to go through it all again; he really wanted to go over what he knew and what he was guessing at, the arguments for and against. He wanted to check dates, places, assumptions. He really should have done it tonight, but he had come out to talk to Maya and ended up sitting here. It wasn't out of the question, Sebastian and Vanja. It was a possibility, based on a very shaky foundation, on letters he hadn't read, assumptions he couldn't verify. But the idea had taken root. The only thing he was sure of was that if Sebastian was Vanja's father, then Sebastian was the only one who knew. If Vanja had known, it would have been obvious. She adored her father. Or the man she believed to be her father . . .

'You shot Edward Hinde.'

Billy was jerked back to moonlit reality. He turned to Jennifer, but could hardly see her face; she had pulled up the hood of her jacket and was holding the mug of tea in front of her mouth as she spoke.

'What? Yes, I did.'

'I expect everyone asks you this, but how did it feel?'

It was the first thing Jennifer had thought when they met at Arlanda and she realised who Billy was. She had never even taken her own pistol out of its holster, but in her mind's eye she had often seen herself holding her gun, ready to fire.

Action. Instant decisions. The thrill of the chase.

But every time she fantasised about that aspect of her profession, hoping she would actually get to experience it one day, the bad guys always gave up. They felt they were outnumbered, defeated, beaten. Her daydreams never ended with her firing a single shot, let alone actually killing someone. She occasionally wondered if she would be able to do it if it came to the crunch.

She turned to Billy, who was unresponsive. She tried to work out if her question had annoyed him, or if he was thinking about what to say. Probably the former; she could hear what she sounded like. 'How did it feel?'

What a stupid question.

'I didn't mean that,' she explained. 'I mean how do you cope with something like that? How did you cope?'

Billy thought about it. He didn't have an immediate answer, because as far as he could recall, no one had ever asked him. No one in the team, not even Torkel. They had been concerned about his welfare, assured him that he would be back at work in no time, that he couldn't have done anything differently, that he had had no choice, but no one had asked him how he felt. Not properly, nothing more than the usual 'How are you?' and 'Are you OK?', delivered in a tone of voice that made it clear they weren't expecting a deep or possibly even honest answer. In spite of the fact that they were all trained in dealing with shocked and traumatised individuals, when one of their own was affected they all seemed to think it was best not to talk about it. That was what the psychologists were for. Maya hadn't asked him either, come to think of it. They had talked about it a great deal, but the focus had been on how he should use the experience to grow, rather than allowing it to make him question either his choice of profession or his character in a destructive way.

'He would have killed Vanja,' Billy said with a shrug. 'That's how I cope. Sebastian was injured and Hinde would have killed Vanja. I had no choice.'

'Just because it was the right thing to do, that doesn't necessarily mean it's straightforward.'

Billy turned to look at her again. He'd just said he had no choice. Most people would have settled for that answer; he had done the only thing he could possibly do. If there was no choice, you weren't really responsible, but clearly that wasn't enough for Jennifer. He could see genuine concern and interest in her eyes; she deserved better.

'I don't think about it,' he said honestly. 'I never think about it.'

'And is that a good thing?'

'I don't know. It works.'

He looked up at the moon. Jennifer seemed satisfied; she didn't ask any more questions. She finished off her tea and put the mug back on the tray. His last two responses had presumably made it clear that he didn't want to talk about it, but in fact he did. He liked Jennifer. She seemed to want to know more, to go beyond the violence and the sensationalism. She seemed to want to know about him, and not many people felt that way. Perhaps it would be stupid to pass up the opportunity.

'It felt good,' he said, so quietly that Jennifer had to lean closer to hear him. 'Killing him. It felt good. That's why I never think about it.'

He didn't look at her; he kept his eyes fixed on the moon. It almost seemed as if he was talking to himself. Jennifer didn't say a word. She didn't even move. She felt as if the slightest sound would remind him that she was there and make him stop.

'Even though he deserved it and would have killed Vanja, it shouldn't feel good. I didn't think I was that kind of person. I don't want to be that kind of person. It frightens me, and that's why I never think about it.'

Jennifer didn't know what to say; she hoped she didn't need to say anything at all. Billy was still gazing at the moon. If this had been an American movie she would have taken his hand and squeezed it reassuringly, but it wasn't a movie, so she sat perfectly still.

They were sitting in the living room. Melika had been surprised to see them standing at her door so late in the evening, but she had immediately asked them in. She had invited them to sit down on the big black leather sofa that Said had been so proud of once upon a time. She made a pot of red tea and brought it on a tray with cups and a plate of baklava.

'I haven't got much in, I'm afraid.'

'It's lovely,' Shibeka said warmly.

Melika still looked a little puzzled as she set out the cups and poured the steaming tea from the pretty pot. Shibeka was just about to explain why they were there when Mehran broke the silence.

'My mother has something to tell you.'

Shibeka gave him a grateful nod and tried to appear as relaxed as possible. She was mentally prepared for the fact that this conversation wasn't going to be easy.

'I need your help.'

'In what way?' Melika said, sitting down opposite them. She hadn't poured herself a cup of tea. It was a clear sign.

'I've spoken to a TV journalist. About Said and Hamid.'

They both saw Melika's face stiffen, as if the faint sense of unease she had felt from the start had suddenly crystallised into pure distaste. However, Shibeka chose to continue.

'He agrees with me; he thinks that what happened is very peculiar.'

She didn't get any further. Melika leapt to her feet. Her voice was shrill and she practically spat her words at Shibeka.

'Stop right there, Shibeka! I don't need some strange man telling me what is and isn't peculiar!'

'That's not what I mean.'

'Yes it is! You think you're the only person in the whole world who is grieving, and now you've gone running off to some man who's telling you you're right. I'm not interested!'

'I haven't gone running off to anyone,' Shibeka replied calmly. 'I've written letters, I've made phone calls, and he is the only one who has listened to me.'

'A man? A Swedish man? A stranger?'

Shibeka gave a faint nod. Melika was swaying back and forth, and seemed unlikely to sit down again while they were there.

'Can you hear what this sounds like, Shibeka?' She was gabbling. 'How many times have you met? Have you been alone with him?'

Shibeka lowered her eyes for a second; the conversation had turned into a nightmare, and there was no escape from disaster. She suddenly realised how stupid she had been; she should have known that Melika would react like this. The other woman's voice grew even louder.

'Have you been alone with him? Maybe that's why he's so interested!'

Her tone was nasty now, and she glared at Shibeka, who was on the point of losing her temper, even though she knew it was vital to remain calm. To resist provocation. If she fought back it would only make matters worse.

'Of course not, I was there. My mother knows how to behave.' Mehran's tone was authoritative and composed. Shibeka couldn't quite work out how to react. She had definitely not expected this; in fact she had almost forgotten he was sitting beside her. However, Mehran seemed perfectly at ease. 'He seems to be worth listening to,' he added, as if he had been lying all his life. He was using his new voice, the one he had acquired that afternoon. Perhaps it had been inside him for a long time; it was too confident to be brand new. Perhaps it had been lying there waiting for the moment when it would be needed.

Shibeka didn't move; she was both impressed by her son and stressed by the situation. She needed to say something so that Mehran's lie wouldn't be exposed, but it was hard to find her way in the unfamiliar landscape her son had suddenly introduced her to. Mehran, however, seemed to have no problem whatsoever with his new role.

'He wants to meet you too. My mother and I both hope you will be willing to co-operate.'

218

Melika was staring at both of them. Shibeka finally plucked up the courage to speak, taking the lead from her son.

'Melika, I know you think I have done wrong on many occasions, but I really do believe that this is the right thing to do.'

Melika still looked sceptical, but at least she sat down. Mehran's confident manner had obviously had a calming effect on her too.

'I can't. I could meet a woman, but not a man. I have too much respect for Said.'

'I understand,' Shibeka said. 'I'll speak to Lennart—'

'*I* will speak to Lennart,' Mehran quickly corrected her. 'I'm sure we can sort something out.'

Melika nodded, and Mehran smiled reassuringly at her.

'Thank you,' Shibeka said.

'Thank your son,' the other woman replied.

Sebastian had ordered a takeaway from the Italian restaurant on the corner. He had insisted that Vanja needed to eat, and had set the kitchen table. The plates were beautiful, ivory-coloured with a thin silver rim, the cutlery felt heavy and expensive and, combined with the tall crystal glasses and the tempting aroma of the food, the whole thing was so inviting that Vanja had agreed to stay without protesting too much. It had grown dark, and Sebastian lit several candles. They ate with relish, talking quietly. If an outsider had seen them, they would have seemed like two old friends enjoying dinner in his home, probably a frequent occurrence. Vanja found it liberating after everything that had happened. It was as if she suddenly had company inside the bubble in which she found herself. She didn't want to leave, not ever. She wanted to stay here in the kitchen on Grev Magnigatan with the man who had demonstrated qualities she had never even suspected he possessed. The searing honesty when he had told her about the terrible tragedy that had blighted his life. His hospitality. The way he listened to her.

It was as if there were two versions of Sebastian: the one with the huge ego who trampled on everyone around him without giving a damn, and this sincere man who had lost his whole family, but somehow kept on going. Vanja was slightly ashamed, partly because she had felt so sorry for herself and had wallowed in her bitterness, and partly because she had never given him the opportunity to show this side of his character. He had given her perspective. She had no idea what it was like to really lose someone; Valdemar's betrayal was manageable, when it came down to it. At least he was still alive. She would be able to move on with her life, choose whether that would be with or without him. Perhaps she wasn't completely alone after all.

Vanja looked at the food in front of her. The seafood pasta was delicious, and didn't evoke the irresistible urge. It was just food, with no psychological trigger. Just food. Good food.

Should she tell Sebastian about the bulimia?

He had been honest with her about his loss, shared his secret with her, and yet it didn't feel right. This wasn't a competition to prove who had suffered the most, and in any case her relapse was merely temporary, a flight mechanism in an extreme situation. She was already feeling much better.

Sebastian opened a bottle of white wine. He told her he didn't drink, but he poured her a glass. The wine was chilled to perfection, and tasted fruity and fresh. This was the way life ought to be. She made her decision: she would tell him. One day, but not now.

She wanted to know more about Sabine, but wasn't sure if she ought to ask; she didn't want to pry and upset him. However, she was genuinely interested; she liked the Sebastian who was sitting opposite her, and she suddenly understood why he was so success-ful with women.

He didn't look great. He was overweight and pretty scruffy, he obviously didn't bother much about his appearance, but he was very much present in the moment, and that was an attractive quality. She guessed that was probably his secret. She had never given it a thought; when it came to that aspect of his life she had always reacted with anger. She had assumed he was just using all those women, but now she was beginning to understand why so many of them went along with it. He said the right things at the right time. Made them feel he was listening to them, and presumably made them feel desirable too. No doubt he had honed his game to perfection over the years.

His technique.

Nothing more than a trick, in fact.

Suddenly she was struck by a thought. What if he was doing the same thing with her? The wine, the closeness, the personal revelations.

A trick.

Could he be so calculating? Was this just a ruse to get her into bed? Vanja put down her knife and fork; the wine gave her courage, and she got straight to the point.

'Are you being so nice to me because you want to sleep with me?'

Sebastian stopped in mid-mouthful. Was she seeing things, or was there a faint flush on his throat?

'Is that what you think?'

'I don't know. I mean, that's what you do, isn't it?'

'For God's sake . . . We work together, Vanja. Business and pleasure don't mix.'

She stared at him. There was something in those grey-blue eyes she couldn't quite interpret.

'I had to ask. I haven't seen this side of you before.'

'What do you mean?' he said, putting down his fork and leaning forward.

'Just being normal,' she replied with a shrug. 'Pleasant. This is the first time you've been nice to me.'

She raised her glass in a toast.

'It's not because I want to have sex with you.'

'Good. I don't want to go to bed with you either.'

'Good, in that case we both know where we are,' he said with a smile. Then his expression grew serious. 'But I really do want to be your friend.'

'You are. Honestly. And I wouldn't mind another glass of wine.'

Sebastian topped up her glass and she started eating again. Vanja couldn't remember when she had last enjoyed a meal so much. He sat watching her, his eyes warm, almost loving.

He could swear she hadn't given Valdemar a thought since she sat down at the table.

★ ★ ★

It was two o'clock in the morning and the wine bottle was virtually empty. They had sat and talked about everything under the sun. Sebastian had managed to steer the conversation away from their troubles and made sure they maintained the simple closeness they had discovered.

Vanja's head flopped back against the sofa. The terrible thing that had happened to her seemed fainter now; the present was stronger. Something to do with the alcohol, no doubt, but it wasn't just the booze. She had managed to keep Valdemar at arm's length with the help of laughter and friendship. She didn't want to go home. She closed her eyes. She couldn't go to sleep here.

She ought to go home.

Had to go home.

But she really didn't want to. It would almost have been simpler if he had seduced her. It definitely wasn't sexual, there was nothing about Sebastian that attracted her, but it would have saved her the trouble of choosing. Making a decision. She would have been able to stay. She knew that if anything happened it would be a total disaster in every possible way, but right now she almost didn't care.

She pushed the thought aside as quickly as it had come. It was utterly ridiculous. Disgusting. The idea of going to bed with him just so she could stay. She had drunk too much wine. She got up quickly; she was angry with herself, and it must be obvious.

'I have to go.'

Sebastian looked surprised, as if he couldn't quite keep up.

'No problem – shall I call you a cab?'

'Please.' She calmed down and went into the hallway to put on her shoes.

'Sorry, it's just that it's so late.'

'I understand.' He followed her, leaned against the doorpost. 'You're very welcome to stay over if you want.'

She glared at him, but he gave her a disarming smile.

'I've got a spare room. A guest room. It hasn't been used for years, but it's there if you want it.'

No, she was going home. She had made the decision, and there was nothing to discuss. At the same time, she knew what was waiting. Valdemar would come back to her as soon as she was alone again, she was sure of it. As she paced around her little apartment he would come to her, and he might even bring with him the compulsion to eat.

'OK, thanks,' she heard herself say.

Sebastian nodded and went off to make up the bed. Vanja stood there wondering what the hell had just happened. Was he trying to seduce her after all? Why didn't she protest? Why didn't she just leave?

'I'll find you a toothbrush,' he called.

Because she didn't want to, she realised.

She wanted to stay with Sebastian.

He wasn't feeling stressed, it was more a sense of being watched, even though he was alone in the unfamiliar room. He couldn't remember how he had got here. Through a door, presumably, but there didn't seem to be one. Not behind him, anyway. There might be one at the other end of the big room, but he couldn't see it. Two large spotlights were shining straight in his eyes. He took a couple of steps across the check-patterned floor. His footsteps echoed in the emptiness. He could smell . . . shampoo. He took a few more steps, but didn't seem to be getting any closer to the other side. If there actually was another side. The lights blinded him, and beyond them there was only darkness. A bell started ringing, somewhere far away. In the darkness. The sound was getting louder, coming closer in spite of the fact that he wasn't moving now. Then he felt a stabbing pain in his side, just below his ribs. Stabbing pain was wrong; it was more of a blow. He looked down in surprise, but couldn't see anything except the checked floor. Another blow, to his chest this time. The chiming sound was really close now. It was playing a tune he recognised, but couldn't quite place.

'Alexander . . .'

A woman's voice.

A name.

His name.

Alexander Söderling opened his eyes. He was lying next to Helena, his face buried in her long hair. Behind him his mobile was ringing as Helena elbowed him in the midriff.

'Yes, OK, I'm awake,' he muttered as he turned over and picked up the phone. The time was closer to morning than night. Number withheld. He took the call.

'Alexander,' he said, his voice thick. He cleared his throat.

'Alexander Söderling?'

The voice pronounced his surname 'Soderlang'. American. Alexander sat up straight.

'Yes.'

The man on the other end gave his surname and the name of the organisation he represented in a drawling southern accent. Alexander realised this was a conversation he didn't want to have just a metre away from Helena, even if she appeared to have gone back to sleep. He got up and left the bedroom.

'How can I help you?' he said as he closed the door behind him.

'Apparently the Swedish police are investigating Liz McGordon's death.'

Alexander cleared his throat again as he walked barefoot along the narrow landing towards the stairs.

'Who's Liz McGordon?' he asked, glancing in on Selma before closing her bedroom door too.

'The woman who died in a car accident up in northern Sweden some years ago.'

Alexander stopped on his way to his son's room. He had never even heard of Liz McGordon.

'Are we talking about Patricia Wellton?' he said.

There was a brief hesitation; he thought he could hear papers rustling, then the man came back.

'Possibly, yes.'

'Well, why didn't you say so?' Alexander could feel himself getting annoyed. He really didn't want to have this discussion in his home, on his mobile.

'As I understand it the police have found a number of bodies,' the man went on without the slightest indication that he had heard Alexander's question. Alexander closed Daniel's door without looking in.

'Right.'

'As I understand it,' the man whose name Alexander had already forgotten said again, 'they have made a connection between those bodies and Patricia Wellton.'

Had they? That was more than Alexander knew. He hadn't been online since he left the office around three o'clock the previous day. He had decided to spend the afternoon and evening with the family. He had taken the kids swimming, then he and Helena had cooked dinner together. Shared a bottle of wine. He couldn't remember the last time they had done that. After dinner he had put the children to bed, read not one but two bedtime stories, watched the news with his wife and finished off the bottle of wine. They had gone to bed at the same time and made love before falling asleep. He couldn't remember the last time that had happened either. By the time he dropped off Alexander he had almost felt like a normal dad, someone who knew nothing about mass murder in the mountains and dead Americans. But that was last night, and now reality was tapping him on the shoulder from the other side of the Atlantic, and he was on his way downstairs to get an update.

'You know more than I do,' he said truthfully as he picked up his iPad from the living-room table.

'It's all over your newspapers.'

'I'm just checking now.'

He quickly found *Expressen* and a second later he saw the reason for the early-morning phone call.

WOMAN FOUND DEAD IN BURNT-OUT CAR
LINKED TO MOUNTAIN MASS MURDER

He skimmed through the article. Nothing about the fact that she was American, nothing about anything really, except that the accident was somehow linked to the discovery of the six bodies up on the mountain. It didn't say how or why.

'Have you found it?' the man said, with more than a hint of impatience in his voice.

'Yes, I've got it here, but—'

'Firstly, it's unfortunate that this has come up at all.'

Alexander's growing irritation moved up a level and turned to anger. Calling and complaining about things he could do fuck all about, either back then or now.

'Listen to me,' he said, not even bothering to sound polite any more. 'If you didn't want them to be found, then you should have done a better job when it came to burying them, shouldn't you?'

'Secondly,' the man continued calmly as if he hadn't even heard Alexander.

It was Alexander's turn to interrupt. 'For your information, it's four o'clock in the morning here, so if you've got a long list maybe you could call back during office hours.'

'Secondly,' The voice in his ear suddenly acquired a sharpness which indicated that the man on the other end wasn't used to being interrupted or challenged. And that he didn't like it on the few occasions when it did happen. 'Secondly, we were under the impression that Patricia's death was an accident.'

'And?'

'As I understand it, the police are treating it as homicide.'

Shit! Alexander stiffened. He immediately understood what this meant if it was true. But it couldn't be true, could it?

No way.

He read the comparatively short article again, and this time he saw it: one sentence in which the journalist mentioned that the car fire probably wasn't a consequence of the accident. Fuck!

'I don't know anything about that,' he said, noticing to his disappointment that his voice wasn't quite steady. 'According to the information I received, it was an accident.'

'It seems you were misinformed.'

'Or the hack has got it wrong. It wouldn't be the first time.'

'Let's hope so.'

There was a brief silence as the American left the last sentence hanging in the air so that Alexander would grasp the implicit threat. He shuddered as he stood there in his pants, even though the house was always at a very pleasant 21 degrees. The air conditioning was just one of the things they had fallen for when they bought the place four years ago. As the children got a little bit older Helena became desperate to leave the city; she'd had enough of the traffic, and she wanted a garden. She got 3,000 square metres, with a sea view from the beautifully designed house on the hill. He had left the military and taken over Nuntius a few years earlier, and Helena was making her way up the ladder at Handelsbanken. They had a good life, he and Helena and the children. Or at least they had had, until these old ghosts came back to haunt him.

'We'll be following developments from here,' the voice went on, 'but we would really appreciate it if you could take the time to inform us if anything new comes up.'

What he meant was: find out what the fuck is going on and report back right away. An order in the form of a polite request.

Alexander promised to keep in touch, and the call was over. He put down the phone beside his iPad and stared out into the darkness.

He went into the kitchen and opened the fridge, a Sub–Zero PRO 48, which in his opinion had cost far too much. He scanned the shelves and concluded that he didn't really want anything, so he closed the door. He considered a glass of water, but decided against it. He went back into the living room, sat down in one of the Hans J. Wegner chairs and picked up his iPad again. Re-read the article, which was written by someone called Axel Weber. Should he contact this Weber? He dismissed the idea almost right away; given his past, it would probably just exacerbate the situation. He carried on surfing; *Aftonbladet* hadn't made nearly as much of the story. Perhaps they felt it belonged to their rival. The morning papers had simply reported the discovery of the bodies on the mountain; there was nothing about the car fire and the dead woman. Alexander sighed, put down his iPad and thought for a while. He soon realised that it didn't make any difference how he approached the problem, he always ended up in the same place, with the same person. He had to be told. It was time to take the bull by the horns. He reached for his phone and keyed in a number from memory. It was many years since they had been in touch; he hoped the details were still correct. Alexander heard it ringing, then a man's voice.

'Charles.'

No hint of having been woken up.

'It's Alexander. Söderling,' he added, just to be on the safe side.

'What do you want?'

Straight to the point. And why not? There was no reason for small talk. Alexander disliked the man he had been forced to call, and he had no doubt the feeling was mutual. Alexander was also . . . afraid was too strong a word, but the other man made him feel uncomfortable. There was something particularly unpleasant about him. Unpredictable.

'What actually happened up in Jämtland? To Patricia Wellton? The Yanks just called.'

'Seriously?'

'Yes – do you think I've called you at four in the morning for fun?'

'No, I mean "the Yanks". Do you really use that word? You sound like some 1940s movie.'

Alexander thought it sounded as if Charles was smiling. As if this wasn't important. As if it had nothing to do with him. He decided to get the call over with as quickly as possible.

'Was it anything to do with you?'

'Was what anything to do with me?'

'The way Patricia Wellton died.'

'Do you really want to know the answer?'

No, a little voice screamed inside Alexander's head. No, I don't. As long as I don't know, I only have to react, not act. I don't want to know. The voice was telling the truth, of course, he really didn't want to know, but he had no choice.

'Yes, I do.'

'But that might mean you'd have to lie to . . . the Yanks.'

Alexander closed his eyes. So Patricia Wellton had been murdered. Things had gone from bad to worse to total disaster in minutes.

'Because I'm assuming you're not going to tell anyone,' Charles went on. Alexander could tell that he was no longer smiling. Far from it.

'It doesn't really matter what I say, does it?' Alexander said, trying to keep the sense of resignation out of his voice. 'If the police know she was murdered, they're going to find out anyway.'

'That is a problem.'

'Yes.'

'But it's your problem, Alexander. If you make it mine, I will make sure that your problems get even bigger.'

Another threat. They were coming thick and fast this morning. Alexander didn't need to bother thinking of an answer; the man on the other end had already hung up.

He put his phone down on the table and got to his feet, even though he didn't know where to go or what to do. In fact, there was only one thing he did know: he wouldn't get any more sleep tonight.

Sebastian couldn't sleep. It was impossible. He had tried to settle, but however much he tossed and turned, it was no good. The apartment was silent, yet it felt as if it was teeming with life.

She was here.

She was sleeping in the guest room that Lily had insisted they should have just in case anyone came to stay.

His daughter.

Thank you, Lily.

His head was spinning. However hard he tried, he couldn't catch up with his thoughts; they were too numerous, too diverse, fears and possibilities flying in all directions.

It was four thirty when Sebastian finally gave up and got out of bed. The wooden floor creaked loudly, which bothered him; he didn't want her to wake up. As soon as she opened her eyes she would want to be on her way. He had noticed that Vanja had been on edge when she was going to bed, slightly anxious in case he touched her and turned out to be the man he really was, deep down. And yet she had stayed. He had managed to get close to her in a way he had never dreamt possible. If only he could spend more time with her, then her wariness would completely disappear. She would realise that he would never try anything with her and, secure in that knowledge, she would appreciate him even more. He would clamber up onto the pedestal, and she would never be able to work out why he never tried anything. Never.

He tried to tiptoe out of the room, but the old wooden floor creaked everywhere. In the end he gave up and hoped for the best. He went into the kitchen for a glass of water; he listened, but heard nothing. The previous evening was still enveloped in a kind of mist. In spite of the fact that he hadn't drunk anything, he felt almost intoxicated with the rush of possibilities. Fate had brought her here, and now it was up to him to make sure she came back. Again and again. Until it was just as natural for her to seek him out as it had once been for her to meet up with Valdemar.

He moved as quietly as he could to the room where she lay sleeping. The door was closed, and he pressed his ear to the white-painted wood. Nothing. He went back to the kitchen and filled a glass with water for her; if she was awake she was bound to be thirsty. She'd drunk quite a bit.

He opened the door slowly and stepped into the little room. It was dark; the only light came from the hallway behind him.

She seemed to be asleep. He could just make out the contours of her body under the duvet and her hair on the pillow. Her face was turned away from him. He moved forward and closed the door behind him. It was stuffy, the air redolent of sweat and alcohol, the characteristic smell of a hangover. But it also smelled of a human being. It was wonderful. It was a pleasant room, if a little narrow. Pale blue wallpaper, a stylish white Rococo-style chest and desk, and a bed with a solid metal frame. Lily had bought everything at an auction in Norrtälje, lovely pieces that went so well together. Especially with a living breathing person in the room.

Sebastian carefully picked up the desk chair and sat down next to the bed. His eyes had grown accustomed to the darkness. Her breathing was regular and even. One foot was sticking out from under the duvet; she had kept her white ankle socks on. He smiled to himself; suddenly he could see the child in her. He wanted to tuck her in; he felt like the father he had never been to her.

The father he was going to be.

He wanted to sit there until the dawn found its way in through the curtains and touched her blonde hair, he wanted to see her when she woke up and looked around. But he realised that would come across as weird and scary. He put down the glass of water on the bedside table and sat back in his chair.

Sabine suddenly came to him.

Sebastian hadn't sat by her bed very often. Back then he hadn't known how fragile life was; he had taken everything for granted. He did remember a time when Sabine had had a tummy bug, and he and Lily had argued about who should sit with her. He had been arrogant, thinking that Lily was exaggerating the risk of their daughter choking on her own vomit in her sleep, but he had eventually given in. They had divided the night between them, and he had taken the early hours of the morning.

Just like now.

He was watching over his daughter once more, but this time he wasn't annoyed. This time he understood that we have to love our children when we have them.

Not when we think we're going to have them.

The present was everything.

That was the secret.

Suddenly he had an idea. He got up carefully, leaned over and gently moved her hair to one side. Her forehead was soft and warm to his touch. He kissed it gently. Brushed it with his lips. He felt a little embarrassed, and straightened up. Perhaps he should leave? He probably ought to be a little more careful now that she had come to see him, started to like him, but it was difficult. Almost impossible. There was nothing more beautiful than a sleeping child. He walked over to the door, opened it, then turned and looked back at her. She began to move.

'Sebastian?'

'I just brought you a glass of water,' he whispered.

She obviously hadn't felt the kiss, otherwise her tone would have been significantly sharper.

'What time is it?'

'Almost five. Go back to sleep.'

'Mmm. It's an important day today.'

'Why?'

'I think I'll hear about the FBI today. Or tomorrow.'

Sebastian stiffened.

'You're still intending to go? After everything that's happened?'

'That's exactly why I'm going to go. Good night.'

He saw her face for a second before she turned over.

'Good night.'

So it had been nothing more than a dream after all. She would never sleep in his guest room again.

She was going to go away.

He was going to lose her once more.

Anitha Lund got to work early. As always. She was there before most people had sat down to breakfast. Before they got out of bed, in fact. She usually arrived at five thirty, which meant she could avoid the company of her colleagues for at least two hours. She would start her morning by enjoying a coffee with milk in the empty kitchen on the third floor. In the past, when she was in a position of authority, she had had her own office in which to drink her coffee, but now her desk was among the ordinary mortals, it was only from the kitchen that she had a decent view. She sat there looking down on Kungsholmen. For a long time Anitha had sneaked into the new boss's office to drink her morning coffee, but she had been caught one day a little while ago, and she didn't dare risk it any more.

At about six she went to her desk. She sorted through the new applications that had come in, which took around half an hour. With most of the day's work under her belt, she could get on with what she enjoyed most: surfing. Searching the net for nonsense. Checking out Flashback and writing posts about everything from immigration to celebs' love lives. That was her real job. She did what she had to do for thirty minutes in the morning and a little while in the middle of the day in order to get paid, nothing else. At first her minimal workload had felt limited and humiliating, but once she had discovered Flashback and the other gossip sites, it suddenly became a positive asset.

As she was passing Joakim's office – which he shared with Viktor, who was far too stylish to be straight – she saw that his computer was on. Careless. The new directive stated that all computers must be closed down at the end of the working day, for both security and energy-saving reasons. Typical Joakim; he always thought he was above the rules. But it could be useful. Anitha glanced around; the office was still deserted. Joakim never arrived before eight thirty, and Viktor was on a course this week. She had at least half an hour, which would give her time to see if Mr *Investigation Today* was on to something. That had been her plan all along: not to help Lennart, but to look into what he had told her, and to see if she could benefit from that information.

Anitha sat down at Joakim's desk and unfolded the sheet of paper Lennart had given her. Hamid Khan and Said Balkhi. Immigrants. New Swedes. Enriching our culture, as she put it on Flashback. Typical Swedish Television, always so fucking politically correct, always ready to expose injustice as long as the exposure carried the right values. They said they were on the side of the little man, but that was crap. They didn't want to know the truth, because the truth hurt. The truth was that Sweden was being destroyed by all these new people who were pouring in. Anitha had no doubts about that whatsoever.

She brought up the log-in box, wondered whose name to use. She had four favourites, all older bosses whose passwords and log-in details she had acquired. The question was, who would attract the least attention? She knew that three things were registered when anyone searched the database: the time, the computer's unique IP address, and the name of the person who had logged in.

She couldn't do much about the time; perhaps she ought to wait until after lunch when there would be more people in the building, but as the other two variables couldn't be traced back to her, she decided to risk it. She opted for Gunnar Bengtsson; he worked on the floor above, and usually got in early. It might seem odd that he was using Joakim's computer, but Anitha didn't care; that would be up to Gunnar to explain.

They were supposed to change passwords every ninety days, but Gunnar simply added a number to the name of his dog: Molly1, Molly2 and so on. He was up to Molly14 at the moment. The system accepted the password and she was in. There were more and more discussions about security, more and more routines, and she couldn't understand why no one checked whether passwords were dynamic and made sure they were actually changed. Not that she was about to point out the weaknesses of the system. She felt daring and full of life; this was the moment she loved. She clicked on the search function.

There were two references to Hamid Khan and Said Balkhi. The first was a report from the Solna police confirming that the two men were missing on 3 August 2003, and that according to the Immigration Board there was good reason to believe that they had disappeared of their own accord due to the risk of deportation. The report included personal details of the two men – nothing odd about that. There was no further information on the search, so Anitha couldn't tell how much effort the police had actually put in. The next note was more interesting. It had been added just over a week later, and stated that the case had been handed over to Säpo.

That was all.

Anitha tried to get into the file to see if there were any more details, but nothing came up. She stiffened and looked around. She thought she was still alone, but got up and went over to the door just to check. The office was still silent and deserted. Anitha sat down and concentrated on the screen again. Something wasn't right. According to the regulations, there should be the name of at least one responsible individual who could be contacted, even if the information itself was classified or deemed sensitive for some reason. But there was nothing, which was definitely against the rules. The whole idea was that the system should be clear and, for those with the right security classification, searchable. It should always be possible to pass on any questions that might arise, but in this particular case that couldn't be done. Anitha wasn't entirely familiar with Säpo's routines, so perhaps there was a simple explanation. Or perhaps there was an even simpler explanation, which seemed more likely to Anitha.

They were hiding something.

Perhaps it wasn't a coincidence that Mr *Investigation Today* was interested.

She went back to the main menu, searched for both men's ID numbers, both separately and together to see if there were any further notes. Nothing. The same two files came up again. She thought for a moment; she needed something more to work on. She wrote down the name of the investigating officer in Solna from the first document: Inspector Eva Gransäter. Anitha wasn't sure about the best way to approach her, and she probably wouldn't say anything, but it was important to be meticulous, particularly when there was so little to go on.

Just as she was about to log out, she remembered there was one more thing she could check: the date on the notes. That might be useful; the system was constructed so that the date and time were automatically recorded every time a file was updated or new information was added. Perhaps the same applied when something was removed; it was worth checking.

She clicked on the second file and double-clicked on the date function. A small white box containing several numbers appeared on the screen; she read them and smiled. She was good. They could treat her like shit, but when it really mattered she could find what others had tried to hide.

The file that had been created on 12 August 2003, stating that Säpo had taken over the case, had been edited yesterday.

She couldn't tell what had been removed, or who had done it. But yesterday someone had found it necessary to delete information from a file that had been untouched since 12 August 2003.

This was no ordinary case of an asylum seeker going missing because of the threat of deportation. This was something else. Something bigger.

Much bigger.

She could spend hours on this, a small task among all the other small tasks that gilded her days.

Now she had something to do. The only question was how to proceed.

Cold and clear, a beautiful day.

That was how the ever-smiling Klara had greeted him when they met in the corridor. Torkel hadn't given the weather a thought; he had other things on his mind this morning.

First of all, Yvonne had called.

'I see you're up in the mountains,' she had said. 'Will you be back at the weekend?'

Torkel immediately knew why she was asking; she and Kristoffer were off to Finland, Friday to Sunday. Just the two of them – a romantic weekend, presumably. It had been arranged since August, and the girls were coming to stay with him. Unless of course he was sitting in a godforsaken mountain hotel in Jämtland. He ran his hand wearily over his face, realised he needed a shave.

'I don't know, and even if I'm home I'm not sure how much time I'll need to spend working.'

'OK, that's what I thought. I'll sort things out with someone else.'

No accusation or disappointment in her voice, just a statement of fact. A problem that needed to be solved. She was good, Yvonne, he thought warmly. She made his life easier.

'I'm sorry.'

'I know. The girls had been looking forward to spending some time with you.'

Torkel knew that wasn't meant to make him feel guilty either, but it did.

'I'll talk to them, see if we can come up with something.'

'Good idea.'

Torkel glanced at his watch. 'Are they home now?'

'No, they've gone to school.'

'I'll call this evening.'

'Good.'

There wasn't really much more to say; the practical issue had been resolved, and yet somehow Torkel didn't want to end the call.

'So, is everything OK?' he said casually.

'Fine – busy, of course, with the two of them at different schools, and Elin's got herself a boyfriend.'

'A boyfriend?'

'Yes, his name is Erik. They've been together for a few weeks; he's in her class.'

Her class was HT12, the Hotel and Tourism course Elin had embarked on at the John Bauer High School in August. A decision she hadn't discussed with her father. When Torkel found out what her plans were, he had gone online to find out more. He wasn't impressed. 'After completing the course you will be able to work as a receptionist, an events or conference coordinator, or within the catering industry, for example,' he had read. He couldn't help feeling disappointed; he had hoped that Elin would aim higher than a receptionist or waitress. However, he hadn't said a word; he had no right to question her choice when he hadn't been party to the discussions leading up to her decision. They had a good relationship, but recently whenever he had expressed an opinion or wondered about something Elin had done, the response had been 'Well, if you were more involved you would have known.' It was painful, but the truth sometimes hurt. He decided to be entirely positive about the boyfriend when he spoke to her later.

'Have you met him?' he asked Yvonne.

'Yes, he seems really nice. He stayed over last weekend.'

'Stayed over?'

'Yes, on Friday night.'

Torkel was on the point of asking about separate rooms, but knew he would come across as hopelessly old-fashioned yet again. Most of his views these days were treated as if he had a prehistoric perspective on life in general.

'Shouldn't we have . . . rules about that kind of thing?' he said instead.

'We have. They're only allowed to stay over with one another at weekends, not when they have school the next day.'

He hadn't really been asking what the rules were, but because he thought he ought to have been consulted; however, he knew that

Elin considered that she lived with Yvonne, and therefore her rules were the ones that counted.

'OK,' he said.

'She'll be seventeen in three months, Torkel.' Yvonne had obviously worked out exactly what he was thinking from that one word.

'I know. I just feel shut out.'

'There's only one person who can change that.'

'I know.'

'The girls will tell you things if you ask.'

'I know,' he said yet again, even though he didn't necessarily think that was true. As the girls grew up he found it more and more difficult to be a natural part of their lives, to move beyond the basic questions about how they were getting on at school, how their courses were going. He wasn't sure how to deepen the conversation, ask about what really mattered. What they were thinking, what they were feeling, their plans and dreams. They no longer shared their thoughts spontaneously as they had when they were younger; back then he had sometimes been on the point of asking them to shut up because there was so much they wanted to tell him. Paradoxically, it seemed as if the more time passed, the less he knew about them. His fault, of course – that kind of communication has to be maintained in order to work.

'I've got to go,' Yvonne said, to his relief.

'Me too, I'd better get down to work . . .'

'Ring the girls tonight.'

'I will. Bye.'

He ended the call and sat with the phone in his hand for a while, then went into the bathroom to shave. It immediately rang again.

'Börje from IPO, did I wake you?' said a cheerful voice when Torkel answered.

'No, I've been up for a while.' Torkel sat down and pulled a notepad towards him. 'Any luck?'

Not much, as it turned out. Or, to be more accurate, none at all when it came to Patricia Wellton. According to the US authorities there had never been a female of that name born at that time who was a citizen of the USA or who had a US driver's licence.

Perhaps it was just an alias she used overseas, Torkel thought as Börje went on.

They had had more success with Liz McGordon. They weren't exactly drowning in information, but there were five references to her, all concerned with leaving or entering the USA. The first was in April 2001, the second the following year, and the last in 2003.

'She left the country on 28 October,' Börje said, 'but there's no record of her having returned. It seems as if she didn't exist within the USA; there's nothing anywhere apart from those trips.'

'She probably had a different name when she was in the country,' Torkel said; he decided to be honest with Börje. They had known each other a long time, and he knew the information would go no further. 'We think Patricia Wellton and Liz McGordon were the same person.'

'Really?'

'Yes, and the reason why she didn't travel back in 2003 is that she died up here on 31 October.'

'Shit. Do you want me to carry on searching for both names?'

Torkel didn't really think there was much point. Börje had found out all there was to know about Patricia and Liz; he wouldn't be able to dig up any more information unless they discovered a third identity.

'No, that won't be necessary,' he replied. 'But can I ask you something?'

'Shoot.'

'She had a fake US passport, good enough to travel in and out of the country the year after 9/11. Who produces forgeries of that quality?'

'What do you mean?'

Torkel hesitated. This was something he hadn't shared with anyone.

'Could she have been . . . some kind of government employee?'

'What do you mean, a government employee?'

'You know . . . an agent.'

'CIA?'

'Or something else, I don't know.'

'Is there anything to suggest she might have been?' Börje wondered, sounding interested.

Torkel didn't answer immediately. Yes, he thought there was. The two false identities, the well-planned and efficient travel arrangements, the involvement in the mass murder on the mountain, the professional pattern of the bullet holes. However, these were only theories, thoughts that had occurred to him. Thoughts that could have far-reaching consequences if it became known that they had come from the head of Riksmord.

'You know what, forget it,' he said breezily to his colleague. 'It was just a silly idea. A long shot. Forget it.'

'OK.'

'Thanks for your help.'

He had ended the call, realised he was really hungry, and had met Klara – who had commented on the weather – on his way down to the dining room. It was empty apart from Ursula, who was reading at a corner table with the remains of her breakfast in front of her. Her cup was still steaming, so Torkel assumed she was finishing off with coffee and the newspaper.

As he helped himself from the buffet he wondered if it might be time for them to leave Jämtland and take the investigation back to Stockholm. Ursula's relaxed morning routine told him they didn't really have enough to do up here. He didn't know where Billy and Jennifer were; still asleep, perhaps.

He picked up his tray and went to join Ursula.

'Morning. Did you sleep well?'

'I did. How about you?'

'Very well, thanks.'

Torkel sprinkled a little sugar on his cereal as he looked around, making sure that they really were alone.

'I miss you,' he said quietly.

Ursula sighed. This was what she had been afraid of when she saw Torkel walk in, and realised they were going to be alone. She knew he would get personal. Bring up their relationship. Force her to make some kind of decision. So she sighed, which Torkel assumed was because of the other man in her life.

'Is it Micke?' he asked.

Well, yes, it was. Whatever she was going to say to him, irrespective of whether she decided to tell the truth or lie to him, it was all about Micke.

'Yes,' she said truthfully. Torkel nodded sympathetically. He shovelled down several spoonfuls of his breakfast in silence, then said: 'So . . . how are things between you?' just as Ursula thought she had got away with her brief 'Yes'. She sighed again. Actually, it was very simple. Truth or lie. Separated or married. Difficult or even more difficult.

'I feel as if we're growing closer and closer all the time, finding our way back to one another,' she said in a suitably regretful tone.

'I understand,' Torkel nodded. 'That's good.'

'So it just wouldn't feel right, you and me,' Ursula went on. If she was going to lie, she might as well do it properly. 'That's why I've been a bit cool with you. I have to give this a go; it's probably our last chance.'

'Absolutely. I understand.' Torkel wiped his chin. 'Good luck,' he added.

He really meant it. He was a lovely man. He was bound to find out sooner or later that she and Micke had split up, that she had lied, but she couldn't deal with it right now. The immediate crisis was over. Torkel would leave her alone.

Her mobile rang. She took the call, asked two brief questions, and hung up.

'That was the team up at the grave site. They've found the Dutch couple's bags.'

Lennart was annoyed. Linda Andersson was ecstatic. They were on their way to Rinkeby via Bromma in one of Swedish Television's cars. Linda was driving and listening to the radio. Shibeka had called Lennart earlier and ruined his entire day. Apparently Said's wife was refusing to meet him because he was a man. However, she would consider speaking to a woman. Lennart tried his best to change her mind, but Shibeka insisted: it was that or nothing. He made out that it was a major problem which could jeopardise the entire project, but Shibeka ignored his veiled threat and eventually he had been forced to give in, and promised to bring along a female colleague. Shibeka had thanked him.

She was probably the only person who would, he thought. Linda and Sture would be delighted, but they were unlikely to say thank you, and now he was in exactly the position he had wanted to avoid. The story had been his, and now it was slipping away, becoming someone else's. A team effort. He had briefly considered taking Annika Morin with him instead; she was a reliable freelance reporter, but if Sture found out he had replaced Linda, he would go crazy. Sture was only too aware that Lennart wanted to fly solo and shine, so all Lennart could do was bite the bullet and make the best of the situation.

He had called Linda and quickly briefed her, and she had picked him up in the car thirty minutes later. She was efficient, he had to give her that. He made her promise that any information would stay between the two of them, and that any decision about what they used was down to him. Linda said all the right things. She knew it was his story, she wouldn't do anything he wasn't happy with – she would be a team player.

Yeah, right. As long as Sture wanted it that way. Lennart knew he would need to keep one step ahead from now on. Then again, maybe he could start trusting Linda. He hadn't decided yet. Part of him was tired of having to do everything himself. There were traffic jams just by the main offices of Svenska Enskilda Banken, and progress was very slow. Lennart sighed and stared out of the side window. A woman in the car alongside gave a big yawn. He hated jams; he couldn't understand how some people could cope with sitting in traffic for hours day after day. He was glad he lived in the inner city and usually travelled by taxi or underground. Feeling frustrated, he popped another piece of nicotine gum in his mouth. It had to be his tenth already, and the day had hardly started. Linda smiled at him.

'How long have you been trying to stop smoking?'

'I gave up three months ago,' he lied.

'You're not free from the addiction until you don't need the gum any more.'

I know, that's why I didn't tell you it's two years since I quit, he thought. So you don't get the idea that I'm a weak character.

'Have you ever smoked?' he asked.

'No, but I worked on a story about how nicotine gum has suddenly become a huge industry. Nicotine has become a pharmaceutical drug, and the profits they make out of smokers trying to give up are just ridiculous.'

Lennart looked at her. He really didn't want to have this conversation, but he had to be nice to her.

'Interesting,' was the best he could come up with. He couldn't even manage to sound sincere, but Linda didn't appear to notice.

'You and I are the only ones who think so; Sture didn't go for it at all.'

'Maybe you didn't have the right angle. Sture likes big exposures. Massive.'

'Like this?'

'If it comes to anything. I'm a bit concerned that we might be chasing something that won't lead anywhere,' he said honestly. 'We have to get these families on board.'

'I'll do my best. Do you know any more about Melika?'

'No. I don't really know anything about her, so you're very important to me.'

Lennart tried to look as friendly as possible, to convey how grateful he was without going over the top.

'As I said, I'll do my best.'

The lights changed to green and the car moved forward four metres. Lennart was already feeling the need for another stick of gum.

★ ★ ★

'Hi, we're here to see Shibeka. I'm Lennart and this is Linda,' Lennart said, smiling at the fifteen-year-old boy who had opened the door as soon as they rang the bell. The boy nodded, but didn't smile back. He was wearing blue jeans and a black shirt; he had short, neatly combed dark hair, and looked as if he had got dressed up for the occasion. His expression was wary, with a hint of suspicion.

'Mehran Khan. Come in.'

They stepped into the spacious hallway. The apartment was clean and tidy, and smelled of soap. The walls were adorned with family photographs – Lennart recognised Shibeka in a couple – and hangings in gold thread. The place was an intriguing mixture of Swedish straight lines spiced up with exotic colours. Mehran silently showed them where to hang their coats. Lennart could see Shibeka in the living room; she was perched on the edge of a large grey sofa, wearing a black shawl that covered her hair completely. Opposite her in an armchair was another woman in a shawl, with her face turned away from them. Melika, presumably. Lennart waved to Shibeka, who quickly looked away; instead it was Mehran who met his gaze, his expression challenging. That said it all. He was in their home now, and their rules applied. Lennart felt stupid. He was here to build a relationship based on trust; it was no good lumbering in as if he was visiting an old friend.

'You can sit in there while we talk,' the boy said, pointing to the bright kitchen next door to the living room.

He doesn't like me, Lennart thought. Not one bit.

He realised that Shibeka's meeting with him in the café hadn't gone down well, and that somehow he needed to connect with this boy.

'I was hoping you and I could have a chat,' he said tentatively, but Mehran obviously wasn't interested.

'Later, perhaps. I need to sit with the women now.' He turned to Linda. 'Wait here.'

He led the way into the kitchen. 'There's tea if you want some,' he said, pointing to the brown teapot on the table, before going back to Linda. Lennart flopped down on a chair as he watched Mehran take Linda into the living room and close the door behind them. Soon he could hear the murmur of voices; it sounded as if Melika didn't speak Swedish at all, and Shibeka was translating. Unfortunately they were talking too quietly for him to pick up what was said. He wondered whether to creep over to the door and listen; that was why he was here, after all, not to sit in the kitchen drinking tea. However, he decided against it; he wouldn't go up in Mehran's estimation if he was caught eavesdropping. Lennart felt as if he had not only been outmanoeuvred, but flattened.

He could hear Linda's voice; she sounded cheerful, energetic, engaged. He could understand that. She was where he was supposed to be.

The two rucksacks were identical: 65 litre Arc'teryx, black with red trim. Jan and Framke Bakker seemed to have been the kind of couple who liked to show their togetherness by looking identical. The grey and yellow Gore-Tex clothing, the red and black rucksacks, even their walking boots had been exactly the same brand and model, as far as Ursula recalled. She could picture them in the summer, wearing identical tracksuits and Crocs, camping by some lake. Although that was never going to happen, and it never had. Crocs weren't invented when the two of them walked straight into something on the mountain that immediately cost them their lives.

Ursula carefully turned over their kit; it was in surprisingly good condition, given how long it had been buried. Dirty and muddy, of course, and in places the dampness and mould had eaten right through the surface material, but what she had in front of her was significantly more rucksack than remains.

They had been found about a dozen or so metres from the bodies, which reinforced the theory that it didn't matter to the killer or killers if the Dutch couple were identified. In which case, it was strange that they had gone to the trouble of digging a fresh hole near the grave, but Ursula had no interest in speculating as to why they had done so. That wasn't her job.

A tent was attached with double straps to the bottom of one rucksack. Ursula carefully removed it and put it to one side, along with a dark-green plastic water scoop on a metal hook beside it. She moved the rucksack so that the top was facing her. She could see the remains of a bedroll and a sleeping bag, also secured with straps. She removed them, placed them next to the tent and turned her attention to the flap. The plastic buckles were full of earth and gravel, but opened relatively easily. When she folded back the flap she could feel that there was something in the two pockets, and pulled at the zips. For the first time since she had brought the rucksacks into the room set aside for the purpose, and which she had already used to examine the items found in Harald Olofsson's possession, the time they had spent in the ground made things difficult for her. The zips refused to budge. She picked up a small knife and sliced along the top of both zips. Inside she found metal cutlery and a pocket knife with a variety of functions; on the side it had a white cross surrounded by some kind of shield and set against a red background. A plastic bottle of mosquito repellent and the remains of a packet of tissues and some plasters. The other pocket contained something that was virtually unidentifiable, but what was left of the packaging suggested that it had once been a bag of chocolate, nuts, raisins and other energy-giving snacks.

She cut the thin string around the top of the inner bag and realised immediately that Jan and Framke Bakker were going to make her task a little easier. The contents were neatly packed in separate plastic bags, which were well sealed. Many were unaffected by dampness. Ursula removed bag after bag and placed them on the table before checking the outside pockets, where she found a water bottle, a camping stove, and a bottle of fuel. When the rucksack was empty, she started working her way through the plastic bags. As she had guessed when she saw the heavy tent, this was Jan's rucksack. Boxer shorts, T-shirts, waterproofs, a warm sweater, underwear. A toilet bag containing a razor, soap, condoms, deodorant, painkillers, a toothbrush and toothpaste. Ursula stopped and looked at the items spread out in front of her: ordinary, functional objects packed for a week's holiday, a week that Jan and Framke Bakker had no doubt planned and longed for. And then they ended up in the wrong place at the wrong time.

She sighed and pulled the other rucksack towards her. Once again she removed the bedroll and sleeping bag and opened the flap. She was about to investigate the pockets when her phone rang: a number she didn't recognise.

'Ursula.'

'Is that Ursula Andersson?' asked a female voice in a lilting Norrland accent.

'Yes,' Ursula confirmed, and surprised herself by suddenly wondering if she ought to revert to her maiden name now she was divorced. Not so much because of the name itself – there wasn't much to choose between Lindgren and Andersson – but because she was no longer an Andersson. Or was she? She had carried that name for so many years that perhaps she was, with or without a male Andersson by her side.

'Renate Grossman from the forensics lab in Umeå,' the caller interrupted Ursula's train of thought. 'It's about these six bodies from Jämtland; I understand you're the officer in charge.'

'Torkel Höglund is the senior investigating officer, but you can pass the information on to me.'

'First of all we have the cause of death.' Ursula could hear Renate tapping her keyboard to bring up the relevant pictures. 'All six were shot with a 9 millimetre gun. We have been able to establish that four were shot in the chest, but it's impossible to say whether those shots were fatal. All of them had been shot twice in the head, from close range; death would have been instantaneous as a result.'

'When you say that four had been shot in the chest, does that mean that the other two hadn't been, or that you were unable to establish that they had?'

'We were unable to establish that they had.'

'OK. What else?'

'We've got the preliminary results of DNA analysis on the four bodies, two children and two adults, that you asked us to check.'

'And?'

'The adults were the parents of the two children.'

'So they were a family.'

'Yes.'

Ursula didn't say anything. They had been working on the assumption that they were looking at a family, but the confirmation sent a shiver down her spine. Out there on the mountain, some of them must have seen the others die. Did the parents die first, or the children? Either way, it didn't bear thinking about.

'What about other injuries to the bodies?' Renate went on. 'Do you want me to go through them now, or shall I just send down the details?'

'Send them down, that'll be fine.'

Then she changed her mind.

'I don't suppose there's anything that could help with identification?'

Renate tapped away on her keyboard for a few seconds.

'No, all the teeth had been removed, and there's nothing relating to possible operations or hospital visits that could be traced. Sorry.'

'Thanks anyway.'

'Good luck.'

Ursula put down the phone, thought for a moment, then picked it up and dialled a number. Torkel answered right away.

'Forensics in Umeå called,' Ursula said without preamble. 'The preliminary DNA results confirm that it was a family.'

'OK,' Torkel said. 'At least we know for sure,' he added in case his brief response might be interpreted as a lack of interest or even truculence.

'The missing families Vanja came up with,' Ursula went on. 'One Norwegian and two Swedish?'

'Yes?'

'I'd like to get a DNA sample from a close relative of each family so that we can run a comparison.'

'Do we really think it could be any of them?' Torkel couldn't help sounding sceptical. 'I mean, none of them went missing at the relevant time.'

'I know, but I want to be able to rule them out completely.'

Torkel nodded to himself. Of course she did. Ursula left nothing to chance; that was how you became the best.

'I'll put Billy and Jennifer on it.'

'Good.'

'One more thing,' Torkel said before she ended the call. 'If you don't find anything in particular in those rucksacks, we're going back to Stockholm tonight.'

'At last.'

And she was gone.

Ursula put away her phone and went back to the grubby rucksack on the table in front of her. She sliced along the zip and slipped her hand inside the pocket. Something hard. Rectangular. Wrapped in plastic. Two plastic bags, as it turned out. Even before she had removed the second bag, she thought she knew what she had found. A small, slim digital camera. The battery had run down long ago, of course, but the cover of the memory card slot was closed, and appeared to be undamaged. Ursula had no idea what happened to pictures on a memory card if they were wrapped in plastic and buried for ten years, but she knew who to ask. This time she didn't call; she went to find Billy.

Shibeka Khan made a very good impression: she spoke clearly and strongly, and her Swedish was virtually fluent, with a wide vocabulary. Linda felt quite excited, sitting there on the sofa with the woman she had heard so much about from Lennart. On the other side of her was the boy who had let them in; apparently he was Shibeka's elder son. He hadn't spoken since he sat down, but he was following every word, every movement with his watchful brown eyes. Linda and Shibeka began with a few polite remarks; Linda thanked them all for giving her the opportunity to speak to them. Shibeka was friendly and welcoming, said how pleased she was that they had come, but the other woman, Melika, somewhat younger and plumper than Shibeka, was clearly uncomfortable with the situation. It was obvious from her rigid posture and the brief sentences she occasionally uttered in her mother tongue. Linda didn't need to understand the language to know that this interview wasn't going to be easy. The fact that Melika's Swedish was negligible, meaning that everything that was said had to be interpreted by Shibeka, made it even more difficult for Linda to get past Melika's defences and build a relationship. Pashto was a beautiful language, and Linda tried to look at Melika with interest and understanding while Shibeka was translating her questions. They chatted for a while about the weather and about how they were enjoying life in Sweden. Swedish became Pashto, then Swedish again. Melika seemed to be softening; it was impossible to be sure, but at least she nodded a few times and was no longer turning away from Linda.

It was important that this went well. She was quite sure that Lennart didn't want her here; he was one of the best journalists she knew, but he was a real lone wolf, so this was something special. She had been so proud when he asked her to come with him, and she wanted him to realise she was a valuable resource, not his enemy.

'How many children do you have, Melika?' she asked.

'She has one son, he is eight years old now,' came the answer via Shibeka.

'What's his name?'

'Ali.'

Linda nodded. 'So he never met his father?'

She understood the answer before Shibeka spoke; Melika shook her head.

'No, he was born in November that year.'

So sad. They were about the same age, she and Melika; Linda would be thirty-one in November. Her cat had died three years ago; that was the worst thing that had happened to her. Melika had lost her husband when she was pregnant, and had brought up her son alone. They might be about the same age, but their lives were as different as they could possibly be.

'That must have been very difficult,' Linda said sincerely. 'Do you mind if I ask a few more questions about your husband?'

'She doesn't understand why,' Shibeka said when Melika had finished shaking her head.

'We want to see if we can help you find out what happened. That's why we're here. To help you.'

Shibeka spoke a few words to Melika in the beautiful language; Melika's response sounded hostile. Shibeka looked slightly embarrassed.

'She wonders how you could possibly help her.'

Linda nodded; she had no intention of giving up yet. She had to find a way to reach this woman, who seemed determined not to let her in.

'We're trying to find out the truth.'

Linda reinforced her words with a little smile, but she got nothing back. Shibeka turned to her, looking disappointed.

'How would the truth help us, she asks. Would it bring them back?' Shibeka said, and added: 'I'm sorry, she's not feeling very positive about this.'

'No problem, I understand. But wouldn't it be better to know than not to know?'

'She doesn't think so.'

'Doesn't she want to know what happened?'

'No. She already knows. He came to Sweden. He worked hard. He was honourable. He was a good man. He still disappeared.'

'That's exactly why we want to find out the truth, precisely because he was a good man.'

Pashto again. Linda sat back and tried to look calm. Curiosity wasn't helpful; she had to be composed, dignified. She didn't speak Pashto, so her body language was all the more important. Something Shibeka had said seemed to be working; Melika's tone was more musical, less spiky this time.

'She says you can ask.'

Linda glanced down at her notes.

'Said had a residence permit, didn't he?'

'Yes.'

'He owned a shop?'

'He was in partnership with two of Melika's cousins. Said was supposed to close up that night, but he never came home.'

'And the cousins don't know anything?'

Shibeka shook her head.

'I asked them myself. They had left a few hours earlier.'

'Could you ask Melika, please? I'd like to hear it from her.'

The reply came straight back.

'She says the same thing.'

'No problems with money, or anything else?'

Melika smiled when she understood the question; Shibeka was smiling too.

'Things were going well for Said,' Shibeka explained. 'Very well, in fact. He was conscientious and hardworking.'

Linda smiled back, but she was beginning to feel frustrated. It was a pleasant chat, but she wasn't getting anywhere. She needed to sharpen up her questions.

'Did a man come to see her and ask about Said a week or so later? I believe someone came to see you.'

'She says no. No one came.'

Linda nodded.

But that's not all she said, Mehran thought, staring at Melika. He had sat in silence listening to the conversation with his pulse rate increasing. Melika's tone of voice altered as soon as the questions became sensitive. He thought his mother had noticed the difference too.

He was convinced that Melika was lying. Someone had come round to see her, he was sure of it. He joined in the discussion.

253

'What about Joseph? Do you recognise that name, Melika?' he asked her in Pashto. Melika turned to face him, looking scared.

'What did you say to her?' Linda wanted to know.

Mehran ignored the Swedish woman and glared at his mother.

'Do not translate! This is just between us.'

A different Melika from the one he knew was facing him now, a woman who definitely didn't want to be there. She more or less hissed at him: 'I don't know him. I've never heard that name.'

She was lying again.

'Said knew him; I already know that. Tell the truth. Not to her,' Mehran said, nodding at Linda. 'To us.'

Melika shook her head angrily.

'I've told you, I don't know any Joseph!'

They all fell silent. Linda was confused.

'Can someone please tell me what she said?'

Shibeka was about to speak, but Mehran got there first.

'She says she doesn't want to talk any more.'

Linda spread her arms wide. 'But why not?'

'That's what she says,' Mehran said, getting to his feet. 'So we're done here.'

Linda stared at him.

'But we've hardly started.'

Mehran could understand her frustration. She realised that something had happened, but she had no idea what it might be.

The truth would come. Not to the blonde woman his mother had just been talking to. Not to the man sitting in the kitchen. It would come to him.

Joseph.

Håkan Persson Riddarstolpe was sitting in his little office on the sixth floor of the National Police Board Headquarters completing the final assessments when someone tapped on the door frame. Håkan held up one hand and took his time finishing off the sentence he was writing before he turned around, wearing an expression that he hoped would indicate how busy he was. It was a waste of time.

Whatever his intentions were, his face showed nothing but complete surprise when he saw who was standing there.

Sebastian Bergman.

Håkan Persson Riddarstolpe could easily come up with a hundred people who would be more likely to drop in on him, including the king and Meg Ryan – in fact he had secretly been hoping she would knock on his door ever since he saw *When Harry Met Sally* in 1989.

'Morning, how's it going?' Sebastian said, as if he was in the habit of popping in for a chat. In fact it was several years since they had seen one another; more than ten, Håkan thought.

'What the hell do you want?'

He couldn't keep the surprise or anger out of his voice.

'Can I come in for a minute?' Sebastian said as he walked in without waiting for the 'no' that was bound to follow. He removed a pile of papers and folders from a chair and sat down.

Håkan Persson Riddarstolpe contemplated the man who had just invited himself into his office with distaste. Typical.

Sebastian Bergman wanted to come in and sit down.

Sebastian Bergman came in and sat down.

Without giving a thought to whether it was convenient, whether he was disturbing Håkan, whether Håkan wanted a visitor or not. Nothing had changed over the past ten years. The universe still revolved around Sebastian Bergman, apparently.

Back in the day they had actually spoken quite often. They were roughly the same age, had a similar educational background, and worked within the same organisation. It would have been an exaggeration to say they were friends, but they had had a professional relationship based on mutual respect, or so Håkan had thought.

In 1999 Sebastian had been at the top of his game. His two books on Edward Hinde had brought him a great deal of acclaim – well deserved, in Håkan's opinion. Sebastian had become a real authority in his field, someone who appeared on the news and on the sofa during daytime TV programmes to explain the most brutal crimes and to give an insight into the character of those behind such events. Since Sebastian had taken a step back from public appearances, that role had been taken over by Leif G. W. Persson, but it could have been Håkan Persson Riddarstolpe sitting there shedding light on terrible crimes, his voice full of confidence.

Should have been.

Would have been.

But for Sebastian Bergman.

In 1998 Sebastian moved to Germany, to Cologne as far as Håkan recalled, leaving the door wide open for a successor.

Only a month or so later the bodies of three girls were found in a mine outside Sala. The old shafts had been closed since the 1950s, and the council decided to open them up to the public. When they went down to carry out safety checks, the macabre discovery was made. Three teenage girls were sitting there surrounded by cushions, cuddly toys and burnt-out candles. Forensic tests revealed almost right away that the girls had died as a result of poison, ingested orally. A floral Thermos containing the remains of poisoned tea was found at the scene, and there was a cup by the side of each girl.

Sebastian was away, leaving a vacuum in the media that had to be filled. Håkan Persson Riddarstolpe, then as now employed by the National Police Board, saw his opportunity. It would have been foolish to ignore it. The case attracted an enormous amount of publicity, and there was a need for someone to explain what had driven three girls, admittedly fairly solitary and 'alternative' characters, to make a joint decision to end their lives in an old abandoned mine.

Håkan was the man who could meet that need.

Suddenly he wasn't just an expert in ritual and collective suicide, but also, in his capacity as a psychologist, well versed in topics such as the vulnerability of young women and the increasing demands placed upon them by society. Soon he found himself in TV studios and on the radio holding forth about the fixation with one's appearance, skewed norms, the growing pressure to achieve, and low self-esteem. He was exactly where he wanted to be, where he ought to be.

Until Sebastian Bergman decided to come back from Germany.

Afterwards Håkan tried to find a reason for his colleague's return, but there didn't seem to be one – except that Sebastian wanted to put him in his place.

Which he did, and then some.

After spending only one day in Sala he announced that the three girls had been murdered, and hours later forensics confirmed his conclusions when they carried out a second examination and found signs that external force had been used to administer the poison. Riksmord was brought in, and even though Sebastian didn't play an active part in the investigation, he still received a great deal of acclaim when they eventually tracked down the killer. Completely undeserved acclaim, in Håkan's view.

But that wasn't the worst part. People had been wrong before and come back, been given a second chance. The worst part was that Sebastian appeared on a news programme and totally destroyed him. He said that anyone who thought this was a case of collective suicide should go back to school and study something different; the person in question clearly wasn't suited to criminal psychology. He had repeated words and phrases that Håkan had used; on Sebastian's lips, under these new circumstances, they sounded ridiculous and utterly unreasonable.

Yes, people could come back after making a mistake, but not if the undisputed expert in their particular field completely trashed their credibility and consigned them to the ranks of the incompetent for all eternity. In the end Håkan was relieved to hang on to his job. He knew that his future had been discussed after Sala, but he was still here, kept well away from any publicity, well away from major cases and complex investigations. These days he was responsible for human resources issues, looking into the suitability of candidates, trauma counselling, and assessing applications for promotion and professional development. It was what it was. Thirteen years now. Doing the same things in the same office, far away from the limelight and the big money. Far away from the success the man sitting opposite him had achieved.

'What do you want?' Håkan asked again, although this time he managed to exercise some control, keep his tone more neutral.

'I want to ask you a favour,' Sebastian replied, making it sound as if he wanted to borrow a pen.

Once again, Håkan was taken aback. Of all the reasons he could have imagined for Sebastian's visit, a favour would have been at the very bottom of the list.

'Why should I do you a favour?' he said, although as he spoke it occurred to him that it might have been more sensible to ask what kind of favour.

'Because you're in a bloody good negotiating position.' Sebastian met his gaze calmly.

'What do you mean by that?' Håkan was still on his guard; as far as he recalled, very few people had managed a positive outcome from their dealings with Sebastian Bergman. If any.

'I mean that I need your help with something, and you can more or less dictate what you want in return.'

Still that open, honest expression. Håkan thought fast. Sebastian didn't like him either. Hadn't been anywhere near him in years. Their dislike was mutual.

And yet he was here.

'What is it you want?' he said eventually, and Sebastian leaned forward.

Anitha had spent the day at her desk, buried in the manuals relating to the computer system: three thick files that normally lived on a shelf above the departmental photocopier. The first file was well-thumbed. It contained the user's guide for laymen, and was supposed to answer the most common questions. After a brief, fruitless search Anitha decided to concentrate on the second and third files. She wanted to know how the backup system worked, and how files were recovered after a crash. A couple of hours later she had discovered that their main system had two backups. If she had understood correctly, a mirror server copied all the information from the main server every three minutes. This was the main backup, and the primary line of defence. It was completely automated, and designed to minimise the loss of data. The manual didn't say where this mirror server was located, but it was clear that I-tech, the company that had originally installed their system, was responsible for both the server and regular updates.

The second backup system was definitely old school, and consisted of tapes that copied the information each day. These tapes had to be changed and stored; the manuals didn't say whose job that was, but Anitha suspected it was down to the internal IT department, partly because keeping simpler tasks in-house meant saving money, and partly because the IT department hadn't cut staff numbers after the National Police Board bought in I-tech's system, which they should have done if that aspect of their work had disappeared. The more Anitha thought about it, the more she was convinced, and if there was a weak link in the chain, then it was the IT department. She could forget about anything to do with I-tech; they were real professionals. The program was originally Israeli, even though I-tech was a Swedish company. The software had been developed for use by Mossad, the Israeli intelligence service, and the Israeli military; only at a later stage had it become a commercial product. Anitha had no doubt that I-tech was still under the control of the Israelis. Jews were experts when it came to business, everyone knew that, and there was no way they would let some Swedish computer geeks rake in all the big money, in her opinion.

She had checked out the company while negotiations were ongoing, and she had even written an anonymous letter to the National Police Board pointing out the inadvisability of going with I-tech due to the link with the Zionist state. Obviously it hadn't cut any ice with those making the decision; her anonymous letters never did. I-tech got the job, and she had to admit it was an excellent system. It was stable, the search variables and filter functions were extremely efficient. Which was hardly surprising; after all, they were surrounded by enemies, so they had to deliver top quality. Unlike here in Sweden, where hardly anyone delivered anything other than political correctness and weakness. She assumed the Jews had to be that way, stuck in between Muslims and other terrorists.

She carried on ploughing through the files, just to make sure she hadn't missed anything. She even spent some time on the error list to see if it might help, and that was where she found the final clue that she needed.

It was known as Error 237.

The explanation was long, with the heading 'Soft write error with backup-exec.' She read on, and right at the bottom of the lengthy, incomprehensible text, full of technical terms and abbreviations, it said: 'Please contact NPB computer support.' Seek and ye shall find, she thought. It had taken time, but at least now she had a possible opening. It seemed likely that the tape backup was in the building. The amendment to the file on the two Afghan men had been carried out four days ago, which meant there was a possibility that the original unaltered file was still around.

But how long were the backups saved? She knew the tapes were reused; it would be impossible to keep them all, they just didn't have the storage capacity down there. But she guessed they would retain them for at least a month, so there was a strong chance that the original was still somewhere among all those ones and zeros.

Whether she could gain access to it was another matter, of course. She didn't have the authorisation or the technical expertise, so she needed help – and she thought she knew exactly where to find it.

★ ★ ★

He looked surprised when she knocked on his door. Morgan Hansson was wearing a white shirt stretched taut over his belly, and horn-rimmed glasses; he had medium-length curly hair and a beard. A big beard. The beard was the first thing you noticed; half his face seemed to consist of an overgrown shrubbery. The second thing you noticed was the brown sandals he always wore. He looked like a caricature of the computer geek he was. His office was a tip; there were papers everywhere, and the shelves were crammed with broken monitors and system units piled on top of one another. The small amount of space that remained was cluttered with grey leads, printers, hard drives and other discarded equipment. Anything faulty that was related to computers seemed to have drifted ashore in his office. Morgan quickly dropped the cables he was holding; his hand was warm and damp as he greeted her. It could only be sweat.

'Hi, do you need some help?' he asked.

Anitha looked around at the chaos and felt uncomfortable. She had no idea how to explain her problem to him.

'No, I was just taking a walk.'

'Down here?'

'Yes, I just needed to clear my mind, you know? Get away from the boss.'

Morgan laughed conspiratorially. She smiled at him and realised that he almost seemed embarrassed by her visit as he removed a pile of boxes from the chair opposite his desk.

'Please, have a seat.'

Anitha shook her head.

'No thanks – I was just wondering if you'd like to join me for lunch?'

The idea of stealing him away for a little while had just occurred to her. For quite some time now Anitha had suspected that Morgan fancied her; he was always the one who called her back when she contacted the IT department to complain, and he always gave her a nod when they met in the corridor. It looked as if she was right. Morgan blushed and he couldn't quite look her in the eye. He was quite sweet, in a way. Much too fat and hairy, but sweet, like a furry pet.

'If you've got time, of course,' she said, still smiling.

He seemed genuinely surprised at the question.

'Absolutely.'

Morgan grabbed his beige jacket, which was far too short. She wondered if it was the only one he owned. She'd never seen him in anything other than that pale, inappropriately sporty, Ralph Lauren-inspired jacket with the brown leather lapels. It didn't suit him at all. It might have worked on a golfer or an accountant who was trying to look youthful, but it did nothing for a man who resembled a troll.

'In the canteen, or in town?'

'Let's go into town,' Anitha said quickly.

Best to get away; besides, someone might see them together in the staff canteen. She didn't want that.

★ ★ ★

They set off along Kungsholmsgatan. At least it had stopped raining; the sun was trying to fight its way through the clouds. Morgan stopped, looking slightly lost.

'Where shall we go?'

Anitha quickly ran through the places she knew; she wanted to avoid anything too close to Police HQ.

'There's an Italian on Sankt Göransgatan that's pretty good, if that's OK with you?'

'Sounds great. I usually eat in the canteen.'

Or at McDonald's, by the look of you, she thought.

'Well, in that case a change will do you good,' she said as she patted his arm and headed for Kronoberg Park. He nodded and they strolled up the steep hill that led into the park. It was a fine autumn day, even though the grass was still wet. They met several women with buggies. The further they got from the police station, the lighter their steps became. It was as if they felt a sense of liberation from the walls of the colossus behind them, and the conversation flowed more freely than Anitha had expected. She tried to keep the focus on him, which wasn't difficult at all. She asked questions, and he answered. To her surprise she discovered that he was actually quite nice.

When they reached Fridhemsplan she suggested they should take a longer walk, perhaps go down to the pavilion by Lake Mälaren on Norr Mälarstrand. It was still open, and she hadn't been there in years. Morgan had never been, but would be very happy to try it. Anitha could probably have suggested McDonald's out in Västberga and he would have trotted along beside her.

As they turned down towards the water, Anitha wondered if it was time to broach the real reason for her invitation to lunch. Should she wait until they were sitting down, until they were having coffee, until they were walking back? She was afraid it would become more difficult to raise the matter in a natural way the longer she left it. At the same time, she needed him to feel that she was asking for his help because they were enjoying themselves, and because she trusted him. It was tricky. Best to wait until coffee, perhaps.

She had fallen silent and must have looked worried, because Morgan stopped and gazed searchingly at her.

'Has something happened? You seem a bit upset.'

She glanced up and decided that he had given her the opening she needed. If he thought she looked upset, she just had to continue along that path.

'I've got a confession.'

Her voice was serious, direct. Completely different from the way she had been speaking until now. She was very happy with the tone.

'What?'

'I've really messed up. You might as well know – it's to do with the IT system. At work.'

He went pale and immediately looked worried. It was as if a rain cloud had suddenly appeared above his head and disgorged its contents.

'What's happened?'

Anitha turned away and gazed at the lake. His reaction was a little too strong. If he was worried before she'd even told him what she had allegedly done, what was he going to be like when it came to the crunch? However, it was too late to stop now.

'Let's eat first. I didn't invite you to lunch so that you could solve my problems.' She tried to sound brave, while at the same time sending out a signal that she needed someone. Him. 'Then at least you'll have something in your stomach before you come to the conclusion that I'm a complete idiot,' she went on, looking down at the ground.

'I don't think you're an idiot.'

'You don't know what I've done.'

'So tell me.'

A deep breath, an embarrassed flicker of the eyes. She had to convey weakness now.

'I was supposed to be helping a colleague find something in the system, but I pressed the wrong button. It just disappeared, and now I can't find it.'

Morgan laughed and relaxed. He couldn't see the problem. Obviously. She hadn't got to it yet.

'That's nothing, you just have to retrieve it. I'll help you after lunch.'

She nodded, trying to find the right amount of pressure for the question she had to ask next. She walked away, hoping that a little solitary anxiety would prove most effective at this point.

'That's not all . . .'

He followed her and stood directly behind her.

'Go on.'

Anitha didn't turn around. She allowed her head to droop, stared at a cigarette stub on the ground. To think that people still smoked. She just couldn't understand it. Hitler never smoked. He hated smokers. She could see why.

'It was a classified file.'

She kept her eyes fixed on the flattened yellow filter, the dirty paper disintegrating in the dampness and the sunshine. Her tactic seemed to be working; he hadn't run away yet. She decided to turn and engage with him at the last possible moment; she felt as if he was getting closer with every second, both physically and emotionally.

'Calm down, I'm sure it'll be fine,' he said. 'If you don't have authorisation you can't delete anything on a permanent basis; it must be there somewhere.'

His voice was softer, she could tell that he really wanted to help her. He gently touched her shoulder. Perhaps it was time to turn around and reel him in. She decided to give it a little longer; she would get only one chance, and she wanted to make it even more critical, a matter of life and death. He had to feel that she was placing her life in his hands, then he couldn't possibly say no. She whispered to the cigarette stub: 'I'm going to lose my job.'

'Don't be silly.'

She felt the grip on her shoulder tighten. A hand that said: I'm here for you. She turned, despair written all over her face. She cursed the fact that she couldn't cry on demand; that would have helped enormously.

'Yes, I am. I logged in as the boss. I shouldn't even have been carrying out the search. They're going to fire me.'

The colour drained from his face as the full import of what she had said hit home. She could hear the sounds of the city and the rustle of the leaves above them as a soft breeze passed through the trees. A car horn far away. Morgan took a step back. Anitha could feel things slipping out of control. She adopted the most pleading expression she could muster; she had to make this into a moral dilemma where she was a good person, not someone who wanted to snoop because she'd found out something from *Investigation Today*.

'I just wanted to help a colleague in Solna. Eva Gransäter – do you know her?'

Fortunately Morgan shook his head and Anitha went on, congratulating herself on having remembered the name of the investigating officer.

'I was supposed to be helping her find the right person to contact in Säpo, but then I pressed the wrong button and the whole thing just disappeared.'

He seemed to be thinking things over, wondering whether to walk away or stay and listen.

Perhaps she had been too quick after all. They should have had a decent lunch first, bonded a little more, perhaps got together a few times over the next week or so. But it was easy to be wise after the event. She looked away again, ignoring the cigarette stub now. This was serious. Only one more chance left. He had to choose her.

'I'm sorry, I never meant to drag you into my mess. Let's not talk about it any more. I understand. I really am sorry.'

She began to walk away from him. She had to give him an escape route, the chance to say no by not following her. Just when she thought she had lost, he finally spoke. It was a very ordinary word, nowhere near as dramatic as she would have liked, deep down, but it was enough.

'Wait.'

He had made his choice.

Vanja was fifteen minutes late by the time she pushed open the door of Roppongi and walked in. She didn't really feel like sushi; she was still slightly hung-over and her body was craving grease, but Peter had suggested this place and she hadn't had the energy to come up with an alternative.

She had drunk too much wine last night. In Sebastian Bergman's apartment. That was something she had never expected to do, but then she had never expected her father to be sitting in a cell suspected of shady financial dealings either. It had been a very strange day. The world turned upside down. Her father had let her down, and she had seen a completely different side of Sebastian. The combination of wine and his concern had enabled her to push aside thoughts of Valdemar for a little while, but after a quick breakfast with Sebastian this morning, they had inexorably come rushing back.

She had to find out more.

Find out everything there was to know.

Vanja had gone through everyone she knew well enough to ask for help, preferably in the Economic Crimes Authority. Was there anyone? Yes, Peter Gornack. Fellow student back in the day, ex-boyfriend, but no hard feelings if Vanja remembered rightly. He had definitely been working in the unit a few years ago; was he still there? She called the exchange and was put through to him.

He wasn't an idiot; he realised what she wanted. They hadn't seen each other for years, and now she was wondering if he'd like to meet up for lunch, just when his department was investigating her father, but he had said yes. He was waiting for her when she got there, at a table by one of the huge windows looking out onto Hantverkargatan. The spot suited Vanja perfectly; the tables in the main dining area were too close together, and she didn't want any-one to overhear their conversation.

Peter stood up to greet her, and seemed unsure whether to give her a hug or not. 'Hi, it's been a while!' She made it easy by hugging him instead.

'It certainly has,' she said, taking off her jacket and sliding onto the barstool next to his.

'How are you?'

'I've been better.'

'I can understand that . . .'

They fell silent and Vanja glanced through the menu. The dish of the day was tori katsu with chilli mayonnaise. She didn't know if it was the after-effects of the alcohol or the previous day's episode in the toilets, but suddenly the chilli mayo made the tori katsu the obvious choice. She also ordered a mineral water when the waitress came, while Peter went for a large sushi.

'Thanks for coming,' Vanja said once their order had been taken.

'No problem, but we can't talk about the investigations into your father,' Peter said, his expression grave.

'I heard there was a previous investigation that didn't go anywhere,' Vanja went on as if she hadn't heard a word he said. 'Why has it been picked up again? What's changed?'

Peter sighed. Somewhere deep down he had known when he agreed to meet her that it would be all about his work. He had only himself to blame, and there were some things he could tell her without compromising his position. He just had to choose his words with care.

'Supplementary information has come to light with regard to the previous investigation,' he said, taking a sip of the low-alcohol beer he had ordered while he was waiting for her.

'What kind of supplementary information?'

Perhaps he had been expecting her to sugar the pill a little, start with an update on what they had been doing over the years, how things were going at work for both of them, revisit a few old memories; apparently that wasn't going to happen. He wasn't really surprised. The Vanja he had known had never given up until she had found out everything she possibly could – and she was impatient.

'Surely you can tell me that,' she persisted. 'If he's charged and the case goes to court, I'll be able to read the preliminary investigation anyway.'

Peter sighed again. He watched Vanja as the waitress arrived with her bottle of water and a glass. There was something in what she said, of course. He was pretty sure that Valdemar would be charged, and that he would end up in court. One step at a time, he decided. Think before you speak. Everything would be fine.

'A woman came in and handed over a bag full of material about your father,' he said slowly. 'The original case notes, plus new information about his involvement in the Daktea affair, among other things,' he went on.

'How had she got hold of the original case notes?' Vanja demanded as she poured her water.

'We don't know.' Peter shrugged to emphasise the point. 'According to this woman, it was something to do with Trolle Hermansson.'

Vanja gave such a start that water splashed onto the table.

'Do you know who he is?' Peter asked when he saw her reaction.

'He's an ex-cop.'

'Apparently he's dead.'

'I know. I found his body in the boot of a car.'

Vanja got up and fetched a handful of serviettes from the counter. This didn't make sense. Trolle Hermansson, an ex-cop she had never met and never even heard of, had turned up in her life on two occasions over the course of just a few months. What was his connection to Valdemar?

'Was this Hermansson involved in the initial investigation?' she asked as she wiped the table.

'Not as far as I know, but according to the woman who came in, he was responsible for the new material.'

Vanja hardly heard a word he said. To be honest she hadn't expected much from this lunch; she hadn't thought Peter would be either willing or able to help her. But now Trolle Hermansson had popped up again, along with some mystery woman who seemed determined to ruin her father. She had to start digging. Hermansson was dead, so that left the woman.

'Do you know who she is? The woman who brought in the material,' she clarified.

'No, but we have no reason to look into her background; the investigation into Hermansson's death is closed.'

'What's her name?' Vanja leaned forward so that she wouldn't miss a single syllable.

Peter sighed again, audibly this time. He didn't even need to think about this one. Giving Vanja the name was out of the question. Revealing the name of an informant to a relative of the suspect went against every rule in the book, even if said relative was a police officer and, he had to admit, still extremely attractive.

'Come on, Vanja. You know I can't tell you that.'

Vanja nodded. Of course she did. But she also knew that she had no intention of leaving the restaurant without a name. She quickly ran through the various options that might enable her to get it, and immediately discarded the most obvious; she didn't even know if he was single or not. Instead she decided to appeal to Peter Gornack the police officer, make it a mutual case.

'I know my father isn't innocent,' Vanja began, looking Peter in the eye. 'I might make sure he gets good legal representation, but I won't be doing anything else to help him.' She moved closer, glanced around to make sure no one was listening, and lowered her voice. Peter also had to lean forward to hear what she was saying.

'I found Trolle dead in a car, murdered by a man who killed on the orders of Edward Hinde. Hinde then escaped from Lövhaga prison, abducted me and threatened to kill me.'

Peter merely nodded; he knew part of the story, but not all of it, and he couldn't deny that he was curious. Edward Hinde's escape and subsequent death were still a hot topic of conversation among colleagues, whichever unit or department they worked in.

'If Trolle was involved in investigating my father, perhaps it's all connected. It's too much of a coincidence if some old ex-cop turns up twice in cases with me as the common denominator, wouldn't you say?'

'I don't—'

'I only want to check her out, I promise.'

Vanja gazed at Peter with big eyes and the most sincere expression she could manage. For a moment she thought of Puss in Boots in the *Shrek* films and realised she mustn't overdo it, so instead she looked away, as if to make sure once again that no one was taking an interest in their discussion.

'I won't go anywhere near her, I won't speak to her, and if I come up with anything I'll pass it on to you so that you can decide if it's worth pursuing.'

Peter leaned back. She could see that he was thinking about what she had said. He wasn't trying to work out how to say no; he was wavering. Going through the possible pitfalls. Trying to find anything that could cause him problems later. There was nothing. She'd got him, and she knew it.

'If Edward Hinde and the murders of those women in the summer are somehow linked to my father, then surely you want to know about that too?' she said in order to remove any lingering doubts.

'Ellinor,' he said quietly. 'Her name is Ellinor Bergkvist.'

'Thank you.'

Her hand brushed against his. The waitress arrived with their food, and as Vanja eagerly dipped her fried chicken in her chilli mayonnaise and asked him how things were these days, Peter Gornack got the feeling that he would spend the rest of their lunch worrying that he had said far too much.

The enormous Rottweiler wanted to get going. It was sitting at the feet of the man on the bench, staring pleadingly at him with its brown eyes. Charles could feel its scrutiny; he was well aware that the walk hadn't delivered much in the way of exercise. He had hoped to be able to come to terms with the events of the past few hours while taking the dog around the ten-kilometre track in the nearby forest, but it hadn't worked. The air was cold and clear, even the deciduous trees that had resisted the autumn so far had been forced to give in and withdraw the supply of chlorophyll, and there was no one in sight apart from him and the dog. Ideal conditions to process the consequences of those early morning phone calls, but it was as if his thoughts disintegrated with each step he took. Everything was up in the air.

This was unusual, almost frightening. Charles had always been able to process information and make rapid decisions on the hoof. In his profession it wasn't always possible to sit down and consider the options – sometimes it was, but not always. His training taught him to think fast when the situation demanded it. However, those cases almost always involved a heightened level of adrenaline, brain and body operating at top speed. Alexander Söderling's call, however, had almost evoked a sense of resignation, a deep-seated weariness; events he had put behind him and come to terms with were unlikely to remain in the past.

After only a kilometre he had sat down on one of the benches by the little lake.

What did they know, what might they discover, what would they never be able to work out?

The fact that they had linked the car fire and the bodies on the mountain was unfortunate, but no more. And before that? The two men. Four, really. A simple surveillance job. Learn from the best. Hard, implacable. But the times required that approach.

He had tried it himself.

When you think they can't take any more, you carry on for another twenty seconds, and then another ten, that's what those implacable figures had said.

Over and over again.

And in between, the questions.

Where? When? Who else?

Over and over again.

Where? When? Who else?

The mistakes right there. The mistake later on. When Charles thought he would get help, when he hoped that the person who had always been there would once again prove loyal and reliable.

The betrayal.

The difficult decision.

Patricia Wellton. He remembered waiting for her. She had been several hours late, and she was furious when she finally turned up. She had yelled at him, complaining about poor information, how the hell was she expected to do her job when the details about the target were incorrect? Charles didn't know what she was talking about. She explained. From then on, things rapidly got worse. He hit her. Fast and hard. She was completely unprepared and he was particularly well trained in that type of attack, so she had gone down. Unconscious. Into the car, down towards the ravine; put her in the driver's seat, push the car off the road. Follow it down, empty the tank, start the fire.

A regrettable accident. Until now.

Was that why he was finding it so difficult to concentrate? Was it because anxiety had evoked the memories and the suppressed grief? Because the accident had turned out to be murder. He had murdered Patricia Wellton, and the organisation she worked for was not known for its capacity to forgive and forget. So far nothing was definite. So far it was just speculation in the tabloid press, but Charles knew they were watching him. If there was official confirmation of that speculation, he was in no doubt that they would hunt him down. It might be a good idea to plan for that eventuality. There were those who could protect him; he had access to the very best resource if you wanted to motivate men and women to come to your rescue.

Information.

He got up from the bench. The dog was on its feet in a second, but the walk was over. Charles thought his threat to Alexander Söderling had hit home, but it was time to make sure. Time to act, to put his house in order. He had sacrificed far too much during those weeks and months almost ten years ago; if his actions back then were going to have consequences now, then he was going to make sure that at least he wouldn't be the only one who fell.

Flight SK071 landed at 20.35, ten minutes late. After another fifteen minutes, Torkel, Ursula, Billy and Jennifer were waiting by the baggage carousel. No one was talking; they hadn't said much on the plane down from Östersund either. Even though it remained unspoken, they were all disappointed over how little they had actually achieved during their stay. They had identified the Dutch couple and linked the death of Patricia Wellton/Liz McGordon to the victims on the mountain, but that was all. They still had no idea who the family in the grave was, nor did they know the real identity of Patricia Wellton/Liz McGordon.

Their only hope was the camera Ursula had found in the rucksack. Billy had quickly ascertained that he didn't have the right cable or charger, which meant he was unable to charge the battery. The next blow came when he opened the cover of the memory card slot. Even though the camera had been wrapped in plastic, the air and possibly dampness had got in. The metal parts of the memory card had oxidised, and the card was firmly stuck. With no proper tools at his disposal, Billy hadn't dared to try and remove it, so right now the camera was in his bag in exactly the same state as when Ursula had brought it to him.

'Hi, welcome home!'

Billy turned and just had time to catch a glimpse of Maya before she was up on her toes giving him a kiss. She placed her hands on his cheeks, pressed her body against his, and seemed to want to freeze the moment. After what felt like at least a minute, Billy broke away by taking a small step backwards, slightly embarrassed by the emotional reception.

'You haven't met my colleagues,' he said; everyone was smiling at him, just as he had expected. He introduced them one by one, and Maya appeared to give a little curtsey each time she shook someone's hand. He'd never seen her do that before, but then he'd never seen her shake hands with someone new before, come to think of it. It was quite sweet, but at the same time it was a bit odd for a grown woman to do that kind of thing. Maya turned to Jennifer, who introduced herself.

'Oh, I thought you were Vanja,' Maya said with a smile.

'No, she had to come back early,' Jennifer explained. Maya nodded, slipped her arm through Billy's and started chatting to the others as if she were a part of him, of his life. It felt good. He realised he had missed her; he was really pleased to see her. If he missed her after only a few days, didn't that mean he wanted to see her more often? All the time? Perhaps moving in together wasn't such a bad idea after all.

Their baggage arrived and they moved towards the exit.

'Where do you live?' Maya asked Jennifer.

'Sollentuna.'

'That's on our way – would you like a lift?'

'That would be great.'

Billy and Jennifer waved goodbye to Torkel and Ursula as they left.

'Shall we share a cab?' Ursula asked as she peeled the airline tag off her case. She could cope with that. She would be dropped off first, and Torkel wouldn't expect to be invited in. In his world, she was still married, with a husband waiting for her in their apartment. Ursula caught herself wishing she lived in his world.

'My car is in the long stay car park,' Torkel said, waving vaguely in the direction of the windows. 'I was planning on calling at Yvonne's to see the girls, otherwise I could have offered you a lift.'

'No problem, I'll get a cab.'

'See you tomorrow.'

'See you.'

Torkel headed for the bus that would take him out to the car park, and Ursula watched him walk away. There goes a disappointed man, she thought. In spite of the time they had spent together up in Storulvån, nothing had happened. It wasn't just that they hadn't had sex – they hadn't even gone for a walk or sat and had a chat after dinner. They hadn't spent any time together outside work, apart from one brief breakfast. Perhaps she didn't need to be quite so dismissive. She would be a little more forthcoming tomorrow. Ursula picked up her bag and went to join the taxi queue.

★ ★ ★

Forty-five minutes later she arrived home and keyed in the door code. She opened her mail box, which still bore a label declaring that it belonged to M. U. & B. Andersson. Ursula assumed it was up to her to change it. It occurred to her that perhaps the new label ought to say U. Lindgren, but she didn't pursue the idea; she certainly wasn't going to do anything about it this evening. The apartment seemed emptier than she remembered. She put down her bag in the hallway; everything was just as she had left it. Of course this had been the case each time she came home since Mikael had moved out, but now that she had been away for a few days, it was even clearer that she lived alone. That she was alone. The place felt stuffy; she opened one of the living-room windows, then went back into the hallway and took off her outdoor clothes. She left her shoes where they landed and dropped her jacket on the small knee-high bench under the mirror, upholstered in red corduroy. She went into the kitchen and opened the fridge; they had been given coffee and a sandwich on the plane, but she still felt peckish. Unfortunately her fridge was unable to help. There was cheese and a tube of fish roe, but she realised she had no bread. She picked up a pot of yoghurt from the door: the best before date was three days ago. Same with the milk. She stuck her nose in both, but by now she had lost her appetite. It was quite sad, really; her fridge was a cliché encapsulating the life of a recently divorced woman. Then again, it would have looked like this all the time if Mikael hadn't made sure there was food in the house. Shopping and feeding Bella had been his job. Among other things.

She closed the fridge door, picked up her post, sat down on the sofa and started to go through it. Nothing that interested her or made her feel remotely better. TV? She checked the time. She could watch the news on TV4, but she didn't really feel like it. She took out her phone; should she call Bella? It was a perfectly normal thing to do, to let her daughter know she was home. She'd never done it before, but decided she would be the kind of parent who did exactly that from now on. They had spoken twice since Uppsala, and on both occasions they had stuck to safe topics such as Ursula's work and Bella's studies, and had successfully avoided mentioning what had happened at the station. But it was always there, another brick in the already high wall that had been built up between them. Ursula knew it was up to her to lower the wall.

Bella answered on the third ring.

'Hi, it's me,' Ursula said; she couldn't help sitting up a little straighter. 'Am I disturbing you?'

'Kind of – I'm out with some friends.'

Ursula became aware of the unmistakable sounds of a pub or club in the background: music, laughter, life.

'I just wanted to let you know I'm home.'

'Have you been away?'

Ursula told herself not to be disappointed. How was Bella supposed to know where she had been? If she'd wanted her daughter to know, she should have called and told her. She decided that was something else she would do in future.

'Yes, up in Jämtland.'

'The mass grave?'

'Yes.'

'So how did it go?'

'We haven't finished yet; we've moved the investigation to Stockholm.'

There was silence for a few seconds, then Bella said: 'Did you want something?'

Ursula didn't answer right away. What did she want? She wanted to say how empty the apartment felt when she walked in, she wanted to invite herself to Uppsala, ask if Bella fancied going away with her in a month or so, somewhere hot and sunny. Escape the horrible November weather. Just the two of them. That was what she wanted to say.

What she actually said was: 'No, is everything OK with you?'

'Fine – I've got a lot of work on, but otherwise everything's good.'

Was that a gentle hint that she didn't have time for visitors, or to come down and see her divorced mother, or was Ursula over-thinking things?

'Great, I just thought I'd give you a call.'

'OK, maybe we could have a chat at the weekend?'

'Absolutely. I'll let you get back to your friends.'

'Speak soon. Bye, Mum.'

'Bye . . .'

Bella had already hung up. Ursula sat there with the phone in her hand. She wouldn't be able to settle tonight, all alone in the apartment. She got up, went into the hallway and put on her outdoor clothes. This was far from her dream scenario, but he was someone, and she needed someone right now.

★ ★ ★

She ran a hand through her hair and tugged nervously at her jacket before she rang the bell.

'Who is it?' came from behind the closed door after a few seconds.

'It's me. Ursula.'

She heard the lock turn. 'What are you doing here?'

'Do you fancy dinner?'

He looked at his watch.

'It's quarter to eleven.'

'A late dinner.'

He looked at her; she realised he couldn't work out what she wanted. It was too late for dinner, of course. Did she just want his company? She had made it very clear that she wasn't interested in the past. Ursula could tell that she was the last person he had expected to see, but now she was here, and he seemed genuinely pleased.

'I'm just a bit surprised,' he said, confirming her thoughts.

'I can understand that. To be honest, so am I.'

'Do you want to go out, or shall I fix us something?'

'You can fix us something,' she said, stepping inside. With one last amused glance, Sebastian closed the door behind her.

They arrived early in the morning, with old Memel leading the delegation of silent men who walked into their hallway and their lives with the authority of age. Mehran knew all five; they stood there staring at him and his mother. Shibeka seemed shocked, but Memel's focus was on Mehran, his expression stern and implacable. Gone was the lively, almost youthful twinkle in his eye that Mehran liked so much; it gave Memel an air of charm and kindliness. Now he looked as if he had a bad smell under his nose.

'We need to speak to you,' he said. 'Do you have time?'

It wasn't really a question; saying no wasn't an option. Mehran knew exactly what had happened: Melika had talked, probably as soon as she had left them yesterday. Mehran was furious; not only was Melika hiding something, but now she had chosen to involve other people.

'Of course,' he said politely, and showed Memel into the living room where Eyer was watching TV. Mehran switched it off and told Eyer, who was still in his pyjamas, to go to his room. Eyer's early morning dopiness immediately disappeared as he leapt up, gazing at the men with big eyes. He had the good sense to nod respectfully at each one as he passed them, which pleased Mehran. It was good to see that his brother knew how to behave when it mattered. He turned to Shibeka, who was still standing in the hallway, and asked her to bring their guests something to eat and drink, but Memel shook his head. They were not here to eat and drink.

The men settled down on the sofa, while Memel chose an armchair opposite the others in his role as spokesman. Mehran sat down too, and waited for Shibeka. Even though he had butterflies in his tummy, he also felt good. He was the one Memel had turned to, he was the one who spoke for his family now. In the past he too would have been sent to his room when the grown-ups were discussing important matters. He sat up a little straighter to show that he was ready to take on the role.

Shibeka joined him. She had made sure that her head was fully covered, and the black fabric emphasised the pallor of her face. It was a long time since she had gone to such trouble, Mehran thought; like him, she understood the gravity of the situation.

There was a brief silence. Memel looked at each person in turn before he began.

'We have heard what Shibeka is doing. We want to discuss it with you. Give you the chance to tell us about it.'

Shibeka lowered her eyes, and Mehran understood that it was up to him to speak. He was a little disappointed in his voice at first; it didn't sound quite as mature as he would have wished.

'We're just trying to find out what happened to my father and Said.'

'We understand that,' Memel replied after a pause. 'But we are concerned. People are coming to us, asking whether your mother really understands what she is doing.'

'I'm sorry that this is affecting others, but there's nothing to worry about. We know what we're doing.'

Memel sighed; he didn't like Mehran's answer. Did this boy think he was going to get away that easily? He leaned forward.

'Mehran, a Swedish man has been here. Is he married, unmarried? How many women is he seeing? What does he want?'

'He just wants to know what happened. He's a journalist. I am present at every meeting with him.'

'Really? That's not what we have heard.'

Memel's expression was icy. Shibeka straightened up, the lines around her mouth tightening as they always did when she got angry. Mehran could see that she was making an enormous effort to remain calm; he nodded to her and turned his attention back to Memel and the men on the sofa. His voice was steadier now; it was as if it was becoming used to its new role with every word, every sentence.

'My mother has the greatest respect for me and my father. She would never do anything without telling me. If you are angry with anyone, it should be me.'

Another silence. He could still see the doubt in Memel's eyes.

'I don't like it, Mehran. This is not our way, and you know it.'

'So what is our way?' Shibeka snapped. The fountain of emotions she had been trying to suppress burst through the surface. 'To sit in silence? To do nothing? To keep quiet?'

Memel was angry now.

'You of all people don't need to ask that question – you know the answer!'

Mehran could feel the situation slipping from his grasp. If there was one thing he knew for sure, it was that challenging Memel was not a good idea. He wasn't the kind of man anyone would want as an enemy. Mehran realised that he needed to demonstrate his position within the family to restore order. He turned to his mother and hissed: 'Quiet! You will remain silent!'

For a second he thought that Shibeka might explode. Her eyes flashed, and she was a heartbeat away from flying at him, but somehow she regained control of herself. She let out a long breath and lowered her eyes once more. Mehran both loved and hated the feeling it gave him when she submitted. He faced Memel, trying to look as apologetic as he could.

'My mother doesn't mean any harm. It's just that she's grieving. The past years have been difficult for her. I apologise.'

Memel hesitated, but then he appeared to accept the apology.

'It has been a difficult time for many people, but we must stick together. Do what is right. That's what we are saying. Do you understand, Mehran?'

Mehran nodded.

'I understand.'

'If that is really the case, then stop this right now. Melika doesn't want to get dragged in, and nor do the rest of us. You cannot think only of yourselves; you have to think of us all.'

With that he got to his feet, and the other men immediately followed suit. Mehran stood up too. Memel stepped forward and looked him deep in the eye, his gaze containing both love and a clear warning.

'Mehran, you have your father in you. I saw that today. Show me who you are. Do the right thing,' he said, patting the boy on the shoulder in a way that was almost friendly.

'I promise, Memel. You won't be disappointed.'

Memel smiled at him.

'Good. Then there is no need for us to speak of this again. Thank you for your time.'

They disappeared as quickly as they had arrived. None of them even looked at Shibeka, who was still sitting on the stool in the living room, her eyes fixed on the floor. It was as if she no longer existed.

But Mehran existed. He placed a hand on his mother's shoulder.

'It'll be fine, Mum. Eventually.'

He wasn't even sure if he believed that himself any more.

Lennart had been intending to work from home all day. He needed peace and quiet to gather his thoughts and lick his wounds. He had had such high hopes for this story, and it was all falling apart. Linda Andersson hadn't managed to get anything out of Said's wife. Quite the reverse – it had been a disaster, and they had both been asked to leave Shibeka's apartment only seconds after Melika had stormed out, slamming the door behind her. Even Shibeka had refused to meet his eye.

Presumably it was all down to the son, the boy with the truculent expression. He didn't seem to share his mother's enthusiasm at the idea of *Investigation Today* helping to reveal the truth about his father's disappearance. Perhaps it was a cultural thing. Perhaps he felt threatened because his mother had acted independently. It could be that he didn't want to revisit the pain of the past, and that he was grieving for his father in his own way. Whatever the reason, it was devastating as far as Lennart was concerned. Without the co-operation of the missing men's wives and families, he didn't even have the beginnings of a programme. However, it went against the grain to give up. He tried to cheer himself up: things weren't so bad. It wasn't the first time he had lost a story; suggestions came and went all the time, and only a few made it through. That was just the way it was. It could be much worse; he might have spent months on the project, and still have had to give up in the end. That was the reality; when you started digging, sometimes you found nothing, or at least not enough to make good TV.

But Lennart found it hard to let go. He had always been the same. It was actually a useful quality in his profession; stubbornness helped, but it took its toll. He was proud of what he did. He didn't want the simple way out; he would dig and dig until he came up with something, and Shibeka's story had moved him. It had all the ingredients for a perfect exposé: a missing husband, an attractive wife who refused to give up in spite of all the years that had passed, plus links to the security police. Lennart had been searching for a scoop like this for a long time; it was liberating to be dealing with something that wasn't about money or sleazy politicians for once. It reminded him of why he had wanted to become a journalist in the first place, and it wasn't to reveal how tycoons got even richer or how greedy managing directors avoided paying tax.

When he told stories like that, it wasn't his own voice he heard, it was the voice of the times. The voice of today.

What had happened to Shibeka suited him much better. He wanted to tell the viewers about real people, grab hold of them and wake them up. Move them. Look what's going on in Sweden right now! We don't treat people equally. His friends sometimes teased him, said he was the last idealist who still believed it was possible to change the world armed with a camera.

He needed to see Shibeka again, just the two of them this time. It was his only chance. He had called her mobile several times, but there was no reply. He decided to go for a walk, clear his head. Maybe ring his mates, make plans for the match on Sunday: Hammarby versus Brage. As he was putting on his jacket and heading for the door, his mobile rang. Shibeka. He almost dropped the phone in his eagerness to answer; he hardly heard what she was saying at first.

When he finally understood, it was a disaster. He tried to persuade her, convince her that he could help. That she would find out the truth. That he didn't give up at the first setback.

It didn't make any difference.

She was the one who was giving up.

It was over.

Mehran sat in the kitchen listening to the conversation in the hallway. It wasn't that he didn't trust her, but he wanted to be sure that she was doing what she had promised to do, that this was the end of it. It was a strange feeling, eavesdropping on his own mother, but if she was uncomfortable with the decision, she was hiding it well. Her voice remained firm, even though he could almost hear the Swede complaining, pleading with her. He was wasting his time. She kept the call short; there was nothing more to discuss. It was only when she hung up and sank down on the little stool next to the phone that he thought he understood. He saw into her heart as the dream died and a part of her life ended. He went over to her, determined to be as gentle as he could. He was proud of her, although she probably didn't realise it.

'He was disappointed,' she said without looking at him.

'And so were you.'

Shibeka nodded sadly. 'I won't lie to you. I will keep my promise. But I've fought for this for so long . . .'

Mehran sat down beside her. He could feel her pain, and he wanted to show her that he was suffering too. She had never set out to hurt him or anyone else; it was just that events had taken the wrong turn and led them to this point.

'It was necessary. You do understand that, don't you?'

He took her hand, keen to underline the fact that everything was fine now.

'To be honest, Mehran, I don't. I don't really see why it was wrong. People like you and me need someone like Lennart to fight for us, otherwise no one listens to us.'

'But if we carry on, we will be completely alone. We can't allow that to happen. We don't want that.'

'We are alone, Mehran. Who do you think is going to help us? Memel?'

Shibeka more or less spat out the name as she got to her feet. It seemed as if she needed to get away from the sorrow and disappointment, and it seemed to work; she looked stronger when she stood up. She turned to her son, holding out the mobile.

'What am I supposed to do with that?'

'I've no idea. Keep it, give it to Eyer. I don't need it any more.'

Mehran took the phone. It felt heavy in his hand, much heavier than it was. Full of broken dreams and crushed hopes.

'Promise me one thing, Mehran,' Shibeka said gravely. 'Don't just listen to everyone else. Listen to yourself. Perhaps I went too far, but you have to listen to your own voice.'

She went into her room and closed the door.

She managed to leave the sorrow and disappointment behind; she left them with Mehran.

There were twenty-three Ellinor Bergkvists in Sweden, and three of them lived in Stockholm. Vanja printed out all the details, but decided to concentrate on the three in the capital. Same name, different women.

Twenty-two of them were living their lives completely separate from Vanja's. Their paths might cross at some point in the future, but probably not. One of them, however, was directly involved in the events that had placed her father in a cell; she might even have something to do with Trolle Hermansson's death.

Vanja leaned back on the sofa as the printer hummed into life in the room next door. The problem was that she couldn't contact any of the Ellinors on the list, not because she had made a promise to Peter Gornack, but because such an act would be evidence of extremely poor judgement on her part — trying to influence an informant in an investigation into her father. It would definitely put an end to any hopes of training with the FBI, and yet she had to know more.

For a moment she considered calling Billy, but for one thing he was probably still up in Jämtland, and for another their relationship hadn't recovered sufficiently for her to ask him to carry out a personal enquiry on her behalf. It would also cause trouble for both of them if it ever came to light; she would be putting Billy in an impossible situation, and it was almost as bad as doing it herself. But she needed help.

Sebastian.

Weird. His name was the first that came into her mind. In the past she had always thought of Valdemar first, or Billy under certain circumstances. But now it was Sebastian.

A few months ago she would never have considered him as an option; Sebastian Bergman didn't do anything unless there was something in it for him, that was common knowledge. However, after the events of the past twenty-four hours she thought he might make an exception, do her a favour. Just to be kind. It was worth a try. Plus he was only loosely connected to Riksmord, he had a very liberal conscience, and would have no problems whatsoever in coming up with a cover story if he was caught.

Then again, what did she actually want him to do? Contact these women and ask if they had helped to implicate Valdemar Lithner in dodgy financial dealings? All except one of them would have no idea what he was talking about, and the one who did understand would lie. Perhaps Ellinor Bergkvist was a waste of time; the only lead she had might turn out to be a dead end. Was it even worth trying? Valdemar was guilty, she was sure of it.

What he had said to her during their brief meeting.

The way he had said it.

The look on his face.

He was in the right place; did it matter how he had ended up there? Did it matter who had informed her colleagues in the Economic Crime Authority, and why? She was off to the USA, leaving it all behind. Couldn't she just let it go?

Vanja got up and went into the bedroom, collected the sheets of paper from the printer and glanced through them on her way back to the living room.

Twenty-three names and addresses. One of them was the right one.

She went over to the coffee table; her phone started ringing before she got there.

'Vanja Lithner,' she said without bothering to check the display.

'Hi, it's Harriet from HR.'

'Hi!'

'Am I disturbing you?'

'Not at all.'

Vanja couldn't help smiling. She felt a tingle of anticipation; Harriet was responsible for staff development and the international exchange programme with the National Police Board, and she was the person who would open the door and allow Vanja to fly away. Leave the country. Look forward, not back. Vanja needed breathing space, time to focus only on herself. She would follow the trial, of course, but from a distance. The physical distance would allow her the luxury of standing outside. She had been the good girl doing everything that was expected of her for far too long. Eventually she would have to face up to her relationship with her father, eventually they would find their way back to one another, she was sure of it, but in order to do that she had to have the strength, and right now it just wasn't there. She was tired. Thirty-two years old, and tired. Of most things. The FBI and the USA would give her back her spark. Right now she just wanted to leave everything and race through the door that Harriet was about to open for her.

'I really am very sorry,' she heard Harriet say; at first she didn't understand at all.

Did Harriet know about Valdemar? Possibly: Police HQ was a workplace like any other, and gossip spread through its corridors in no time.

'Thanks, but it is what it is; there's not much I can do about it right now,' Vanja said, putting down the printouts on the coffee table. She walked over to the window and looked out beyond the increasingly sparse foliage towards Gärdet.

There was a silence on the other end of the line: a surprised silence. The kind of silence that arises when someone has completely lost the thread of a conversation.

'I don't quite understand . . .' Harriet said.

'My father,' Vanja clarified, hoping that her tone of voice would show that she wasn't too bothered, and that there was no need to discuss the matter any further.

'What about him?'

'He's been . . .' Vanja began, but broke off. Harriet didn't know, yet she had started the conversation by saying she was sorry about something. A little ball of anxiety began to roll around Vanja's belly.

'It's nothing,' she went on. 'What were you talking about?'

Silence once more. Different this time: not surprised, more troubled, the kind of silence that arises when someone is gathering the courage to deliver bad news. The ball was growing fast.

'You haven't been accepted on the FBI training programme.'

The ball grew to the size of a football in a second. Forced the air out of her lungs, made it hard to breathe. It couldn't be true. It just couldn't. In some weird way, this wasn't reality.

'Are you sure?'

Stupid question. Harriet carried the final responsibility. There weren't many candidates left. Of course she was sure.

'Yes. I'm very sorry.'

'But why?' It had to be a mistake. If she could just find out the reason, she could put it right. 'I mean . . . it was all going so well.'

'Håkan Persson Riddarstolpe,' Harriet said, and paused as if to give Vanja the chance to work out who she was talking about. Not that it was necessary with a name like that; the image of the man with the little moustache and the narrowed eyes in his messy office came into her mind right away, but it didn't provide any clues. Her interview with Håkan Persson Riddarstolpe had gone well. Really well. He had even said so himself when he shook her hand as she left.

What had happened? Had he been lying? If so, why? She needed more information.

'Right . . .' she said, to confirm that she knew who Harriet was talking about.

'He makes it very clear in his assessment that you're not suitable, and he advises against your inclusion on the programme.'

'Why?'

It was the only question she could come out with, because it was the only word in her head. Everything else had disappeared.

'He does include reasons, but it's the recommendation that's important.'

'But it's only one person's recommendation.'

'The FBI won't take you if the psychologist responsible for the assessment says you're not suitable,' Harriet said in a tone of voice that was meant to sugar the pill.

'But I am suitable,' Vanja almost shouted. 'Ask anybody. Nobody's more fucking suitable than me!'

'Vanja, I'm sorry.'

'That's not enough.' Vanja almost spat out the words. This wasn't happening. She wouldn't allow it. She never gave up, that was what made her tick. That was why she was the best.

'I can get another assessment, from someone else. He's wrong. There must be an appeal process.'

'Håkan is the psychologist who carries out our assessments for this kind of application. His decision is final.'

Vanja didn't know what to say. The door through which she had been going to make her escape had been slammed so hard and so definitively in her face that she could almost feel it, as if someone had delivered a hard blow.

'There will be other opportunities,' Harriet tried to console her. 'Not this year and probably not next year, the way things look at the moment, but in the future.'

'Right. Thanks.'

Vanja ended the call. She remained standing by the window, watching people in the distance walking, jogging, cycling. On their way to somewhere to carry on with their lives for a while, a few hours, longer. What was she going to do? How could she carry on?

She turned away. Wanted to cry but couldn't. She just felt empty. It was as if the FBI course had been a fragile foundation on which everything else had rested, enabling her to function in spite of what was going on, and now that it had disappeared, the whole edifice had come crashing down.

She ended up on the sofa. She had no idea how long she sat there, staring into space, before her gaze fell on the printouts lying on the table. She looked at them as if she didn't know what they were or how they had got there, then she leaned forward, picked them up and began to read.

Same name, different spellings, different addresses.

A conscious thought.

The first since the phone call.

Now she could track down the right Ellinor. Vanja realised that it was the risk of losing her place on the programme that had been holding her back. She wouldn't lose her job, not for something like this. She had no intention of threatening or frightening the woman; she just wanted the facts. She might possibly mark her card, but nothing more.

Every cloud has a silver lining, she thought to her surprise as she got up. The trite phrase just came into her mind, possibly because every other thought and emotion was still blocked and paralysed.

Ridiculous.

There would be no silver linings today, she was sure of it.

Morgan Hansson had the taste of blood in his mouth. It wasn't blood, of course, he knew that. It was stress, anxiety and fear. But it still had that metallic taste. Interesting that certain feelings actually have a taste, he thought. It is possible to have a concrete perception of something so abstract. Love ought to taste of chocolate, he thought. But it didn't.

It tasted like this.

He stopped and leaned against the grey, uneven wall. Tried to calm himself. He just wanted it to be over. He hadn't eaten since yesterday evening; his stomach had hurt too much for him to feel hungry. Instead he had drunk vast quantities of sparkling water; he had his own carbonating machine in the kitchen. That's what he usually did when he needed to relax. Drank carbonated water. That was probably why his stomach was bubbling, sending frequent bursts of acidity up into his throat and mouth. Morgan tried to tell himself that it was just nerves. Nothing else. He was just an IT technician on his way down to the IT room beneath the car park. He had the right security clearance, he had followed this route many times in the past, and he was even carrying two 10 TB hard drives so that it would look as if he had legitimate business down there. It wasn't as if he had a sign around his neck that declared: 'This man is about to break the law.'

Intentions were not visible, even if it felt that way. Intentions remained invisible until they were translated into action. And what he intended to do would be impossible to discover. He wasn't going to take anything away, print anything out. He was just going to check whether a file and a reference that had apparently been deleted by mistake were still there. Find a name. That wasn't illegal. It was a borderline case. Perhaps.

He was suddenly angry with himself. Of course it was wrong – who was he trying to kid? The file was classified.

He wanted to go back to his office with all those broken bits and pieces, the cables, the hard drives, the printers, all the things that made him feel comfortable. Anitha would just have to be disappointed. He didn't care if she was angry with him; he didn't have the balls for this kind of thing. Or, even better, he could lie to her, tell her the file wasn't there any more. That the backup tape had been erased for some reason. It was a nice idea, liberating and simple. All it would take was a little lie; she would never be able to check up on him. But he couldn't do it. He had made a promise. She needed help. It was important to help friends, especially if there was a chance they might become something more.

He kept on walking. He reached the last security door and took out his pass card. Held it up to the reader and waited for the click. It only took a second. He opened the door. This corridor was narrower and noticeably warmer. The server room behind the first door was air-conditioned, and some of the heat generated by the system leaked out into the corridor. He would probably start sweating any minute now. The room where the backup tapes were stored was just past the server room. Personally he thought the entire backup procedure was practically prehistoric. Surely no other modern institution used tapes these days? The system had been installed in the Sixties, when hard drives hadn't been invented and everything was stored on magnetic tape. This had made financial sense until a few years ago when the cost of really large hard disks had begun to fall, but the National Police Board had decided to stick with tapes. Morgan wasn't sure whether this was out of habit, laziness, or sheer insanity. There was a greater risk of the tapes being damaged, while the process itself was far more labour-intensive; someone had to physically change them over at regular intervals. They had to be handled and stored correctly, then demagnetised and reused. Then again, perhaps that was the real reason for the decision: to hang onto jobs within the police authority. Morgan presumed he wasn't privy to the whole picture. At any rate, he was glad he didn't have to deal with the tapes all the time. He had been trained just in case Göransson was off sick or unavailable; he was the backup to the backup who handled the backup, so to speak. He was probably the only person in the whole world who could see the humour in that.

He opened the door and walked into the room. In front of him stood the machine that was linked to the server room via fibre cables: it was an IBM TS2250 LTO generation 5, purchased in 2011. He was grateful for that; with earlier models it was necessary to bring up the information in sequence, which took time. The new model made it possible to use the tape like a hard disk, accessing everything directly via the file system, which would save him a lot of time.

Göransson ran an orderly ship. The tapes were neatly labelled in date order. Morgan knew they were kept for at least three months before they were reused. According to Anitha, she had accidentally deleted the file two days ago. Perhaps he should begin a few days before that, see what the file looked like then. Carefully he picked out the tape and held it in his hand. It was heavier than he remembered, but perhaps it was the same as the taste in his mouth; the weight came from something else.

He took a deep breath.

Intention was about to turn into action.

Mehran was walking down to the town centre. He just had to get out of the apartment, feel like a teenager again, like the person he had been before all this started, when his biggest problem had been whether they would get into the party on Lövgatan next weekend, and whether Miriam would be there. He had texted Levan to ask if the party was still on, but hadn't yet had a reply.

He should have been pleased about the way things had gone, but somehow he couldn't find that sense of satisfaction. A while ago he had thought that he would feel calm once he and the other men had got their way, but over the past few hours his mind had been in turmoil. It was weird, as if the present he had wanted for so long had turned out to be nothing special after all. Melika had lied. His mother had been right all along, but that wouldn't help her now. Quite the reverse; the others would look at Shibeka differently, even though she had listened, folded, given up. Her contact with the others would dwindle; that was how it worked. It wasn't enough just to do the right thing; you must never do wrong. It was that simple. She would be one of those who was talked about less and less, someone who slowly metamorphosed into more of a memory than a living person. That was the way it was.

Shibeka, who had always looked after him. Who never gave up. The new country had given her fresh opportunities to fight; in Sweden she didn't have to accept her situation, to fade into silence as a widow, to sit quietly. It had made her strong. Special. That was what the journalist and the Swedes liked: a woman who was prepared to fight for what she wanted. And that was exactly what Memel and the others hated and feared, Mehran presumed.

He, on the other hand, would be rewarded, drawn deeper into the community. Unlike Shibeka, he had shown that he could be trusted, that while he stood up for his family, he would do the right thing when it really mattered. It was as if he had cadged a free ride on the back of his mother's struggle – stolen her power, used it to move forward and left her behind, so that from now on they would be moving in different directions. He would be forging ahead, while she would be slipping backwards.

And in the middle of it all, Melika's lie was still there. Who would look into it now? Who would find out the truth?

No one.

That didn't feel right. Not at all.

When Mehran reached the shopping centre he saw a few of the older boys from school standing outside the dry cleaner's. They raised a hand in greeting, but he had no desire to hang out with them. He nodded back, but kept on walking. He couldn't see Levan, but realised he didn't want to hang out with him either. He carried on to Melika's apartment block and stopped by the little play area outside. He went and sat on the swing his father had never allowed him to use. He had nagged and nagged and cried and cried, but Hamid had refused to budge. It was for the older children, he always said. It almost became a kind of ritual. Mehran asked if he could go on the swing. Hamid said no, not until you're older. Mehran went on and on, but Hamid never gave in. Ever. Mehran cautiously sat down on the swing. Today it looked anything but special; it was just a big rubber tyre suspended from two chains. Hamid had let him use the other swing, which had an extra small tyre fixed underneath the big one so that you couldn't fall through. The chains were cold against his fingers, just like when he was little. He started to swing. The frame creaked rhythmically as he picked up speed.

Back and forth. Back and forth.

Every time his body moved forward, another question popped into his head.

Why had Melika lied when she was in their apartment?

Back.

What did she know about the man called Joseph?

Back.

What made her so nervous that she felt the need to turn to Memel?

Back.

He had to put this right. He couldn't just go up and see Melika; that wouldn't work. He couldn't risk her running off to Memel and the others again.

Perhaps he should visit Said's shop. He had been there several times with his father; Hamid had helped out sometimes, just for something to do. Said had owned the place jointly with two of Melika's cousins, Rafi and . . . Turyalai, that was it. Rafi was the one he remembered best; he had always joked with Mehran and given him lollipops. He hadn't thought about the cousins for a long time. They didn't live in Rinkeby, but in Vällingby, according to Shibeka. At least they used to. They had called to see Melika a few times at the beginning, and he knew they had given Shibeka a little money to help her out. However, that was years ago; he had seen less and less of them as Melika and Shibeka grew apart. They might know something, though. Said had spent most of his time with them.

He stopped the swing and slid off. Looked up at Melika's apartment once more before heading for the underground.

They had silenced his mother with his help; now he was the only one who could find out the truth.

The first Ellinor Bergkvist lived at Grönviksvägen 107 in Nockeby. Vanja entered the address into her sat nav; she didn't think she had ever been to Nockeby. In the heavy traffic en route she wondered how to approach the various women. She definitely wasn't going to say she was a police officer, but what should she say? As little as possible, she had decided by the time she pulled into the semi-circular parking area in front of the dirty grey V-shaped block. Vanja approached number 107 along the wide tarmac path between the buildings; she could see a strip of cold grey water up ahead. It looked like a canal, but she assumed it must be part of Lake Mälaren. The door was made of metal and glass; locked. She checked the entry phone on the wall: Bergkvist, second floor. Vanja pressed Levin on the third floor, said she was delivering flowers to Bergkvist but no one was home, could she possibly come in and leave them by the door? Once inside the chilly stairwell she decided to avoid the lift. Bergkvist lived in the apartment immediately on the left when she reached the second floor. She rang the bell and a woman aged about thirty-five answered the door. In the background she could hear the sound of some noisy kids' cartoon. The woman had brown hair tied back in a ponytail, discreet gold earrings, and beautifully (if not recently) applied make-up. She was wearing a light, loose blouse, a smart skirt and tights. Vanja got the impression she had picked up the kids on the way home from work, and had just got in.

'Ellinor Bergkvist?' Vanja asked as the woman looked enquiringly at her.

'Yes?'

'My name is Vanja Lithner.' She paused and waited for a reaction. Her surname was unusual; if this woman was involved in the business surrounding her father, she would find it difficult not to react at all. Vanja observed her closely; she was good at this. Spotting the little signs, the nuances: a blink, a shifting of the body weight. The woman facing her displayed nothing but genuine surprise.

'Valdemar Lithner is my father,' Vanja went on, then she paused again. Watched and waited.

'I'm sorry, but what is it you actually want?'

A roar came from inside the apartment, followed by a yell for mummy, the information that Hugo was fighting, then a flat denial and an assertion that Linnea was lying.

'I'm coming! Play nicely!' the woman shouted before turning back to Vanja.

'Have you had anything to do with Valdemar Lithner and a man called Trolle Hermansson?'

'No, I haven't. I don't know what you're talking about.'

Stress in the eyes and voice now, but that was probably because Linnea was loudly informing everyone how stupid Hugo was for changing channels. The first Ellinor was not the right Ellinor, Vanja was sure of it.

'I'm sorry, in that case I've got the wrong address. I do apologise,' she said, taking a step back.

The woman nodded and slammed the door shut. There was another shriek followed by the sound of crying as Ellinor Bergkvist also questioned her son's intelligence – did he really think hitting his sister on the head with the remote was the way to solve the argument?

Vanja set off down the stairs. Two more Ellinors in Stockholm. Twenty in the rest of the country. But she was in no hurry.

After all, she wasn't going to the USA.

Mehran took the blue line to Fridhemsplan; he didn't need to change. He knew the small shop was inside the underground station, but he wasn't sure which exit to take. He hadn't been there for ten years, and knew he couldn't rely on the memories from when he was a little boy. What had seemed an enormous distance to a five-year-old might be no more than a 100 metres in reality.

When he came up from the platform into the wide tunnels leading to the various escalators, he got a text from Levan confirming that the party was still on. Mehran deleted it; he had more important things to think about right now.

He knew that the shop wasn't in the passageways close to Fridhemsplan itself, where he had been many times, but in one of the smaller ones on the Stadshagen side. He followed the signs for Mariebergsgatan; he thought he recognised the name.

Mehran found the place sooner than he had expected. It was squeezed into a narrow pedestrian walkway with grey cement walls, at the foot of a staircase leading to the city up above. Three dirty barred windows displayed handwritten notices advertising special offers, and a reinforced steel door stood wide open to prove to the few passers by that the shop really was open. It looked different from the way he remembered; at first he couldn't work out what it was, but then he realised. The sign was different. In the past it had been saffron yellow, with bright-red writing. He didn't know what it had said, because he hadn't learned to read at the time, but he did remember the strong colours, probably because they reminded him of his homeland. Now it was black on white. Convenience store. Brief and functional: it evoked no memories whatsoever. He went inside. The smell was exactly the same: the faint whiff of the underground, mixed with dust and something sweet. They had moved the till closer to the door. Behind the counter sat a man in his fifties wearing a black pullover and reading a newspaper over a coffee. He had short, receding grey hair. Mehran didn't recognise him.

He went over, smiling politely. He started in Pashto, almost out of habit.

'Hi, is Rafi here?'

The man looked up, uncomprehending.

'What did you say?' he responded in heavily accented Swedish. Mehran guessed that his origins were Arabic, but switched to Swedish to be on the safe side.

'Rafi. Is Rafi here?'

'I don't know any Rafi.'

'He owns this shop.'

The man looked even more puzzled.

'My brother and I own this shop.'

Of course. That was why he had heard nothing about the shop for such a long time; they had sold it.

'We bought it from some Afghans,' the man went on. 'Is that who you mean?'

'I think so. Rafi and Turyalai?'

'I don't remember their names, but there were three of them, as far as I recall.'

Mehran nodded. Said would have been the third man.

'Was the other man called Said?' he asked, just to make sure.

The man shrugged. 'I've no idea. My brother took care of all that. Are they relatives of yours?'

'No. My father was a friend of Said's.'

The man took a sip of his coffee.

'It took my brother a long time to close the deal. He didn't like them at all. They were very difficult, arguing with us, arguing with one another.'

Mehran was taken aback. That wasn't how he remembered Said and the others at all.

'Do you know what they argued about?'

'They couldn't agree on whether to sell or not. They kept changing their minds, and we thought the whole thing was going to fall through, but then suddenly they called and everything was settled within twenty-four hours. We were amazed; we'd actually started looking for other premises.'

301

Mehran's mouth was suddenly dry. He couldn't marry the story the man was telling him with his memories of Said and the others. They had been good friends. They were family, after all; distant relatives on Melika's side admittedly, but even so. Surely they had got on well? He had always believed so, but perhaps there had been some conflict that had passed him by as a child? It wasn't impossible, but wouldn't Shibeka have mentioned it? She had hardly thought of anything else over the past few years. Something didn't add up.

'How long have you owned the business, if you don't mind me asking?'

The man smiled and leaned back on his shabby chair.

'Far too long, if you ask me. Nine years, I think, but my brother has all the details. I can give him a ring if you like.'

'Please, if that's OK?'

'Do I look as if I've got too much to do?' the man said drily, waving his hand at the empty shop. He picked up his phone, pressed a button, got to his feet and was soon speaking in Arabic. Mehran managed to pick out the odd word, but not enough to understand fully. He gazed around; how many times had he been here as a child? Ten, fifteen perhaps? Said was usually here, Rafi sometimes, Turyalai never. Mehran had met him occasionally at Melika's, but not often enough to have a clear memory of him. Turyalai was the biggest of the three, as far as he recalled. Not overweight, but both Said and Rafi were tall and slim – so compared with them he had seemed big. Round face. Short hair. Slightly bad-tempered. Mehran hadn't thought about them for a long time, and never as individuals. He had bundled them together as three friends, three relatives – Said and the other two. Now it turned out that they might not have been as close as he had always believed.

The man behind the counter had finished his conversation.

'We bought the place in September 2003 after negotiating with them for almost a year.'

Mehran nodded stiffly; he couldn't think of anything to say. His mind was whirling. The two cousins had sold the shop only a month after his father and Said had disappeared. He wasn't sure if that meant anything, but it was too soon. And they had argued about the sale; why had Melika never mentioned that? They were her cousins, after all; she should have said they'd sold the shop. Why hadn't he known? Once again, it didn't add up.

302

'Does your brother remember who didn't want to sell?' he heard himself ask.

'He thinks it was Said, but he's not sure. Anyway, Said wasn't around when the sale went through, so my brother assumed he wasn't happy with the arrangement.'

Said wasn't around at all, Mehran thought. He'd gone missing by then. Along with my father.

When he emerged from the shop he broke into a run, raced down the escalators. He didn't really know where he was going, but he knew that something was wrong.

There was only one person he could talk to.

One person he had to tell.

His mother.

The second Ellinor lived on Västmannagatan in the city centre. After spending almost twenty minutes looking for a parking space, Vanja gave up and abandoned the car much too close to a pedestrian crossing. She refused to use the multi-storey car parks; the cost was beyond ridiculous. She preferred to take her chances and just hope she wouldn't get a ticket during the half hour or so she needed.

There was no entry phone, just a keypad. Vanja hung around near the door; it was a comparatively large apartment block, and there was bound to be someone getting home from work or heading out early for a night on the town. After ten minutes two young men emerged and headed off towards Odenplan. Vanja slipped in before the door closed. Another stairwell, another list of names. Bergkvist, third floor. She set off up the stairs, rang the doorbell. Tried again. Nothing.

'Are you looking for Ellinor?'

Vanja turned around. An elderly lady in a coat that was far too big for her had just arrived on the landing. Beneath the wide-brimmed hat she could see pure white hair and a face that was so lined it made Vanja think of an Egyptian mummy rather than a raisin. At least raisins had some moisture left in them, whereas the woman approaching Vanja looked completely desiccated. However, her eyes were sparkling with life and curiosity.

'Yes.'

'If she's not in she's probably at work. Is there anything I can help you with? My name is Tyra Lindell; I live upstairs.'

She pointed at the ceiling with a thin finger. Everything about her seemed dry and brittle. Vanja wondered why she hadn't used the lift, but then she realised the woman wasn't even out of breath after walking up three flights of stairs.

'Thanks, but I really need to speak to Ellinor. Do you know where she works?'

'At Åhlén's – household goods or interiors or whatever it's called.'

'OK, thanks.'

Vanja smiled and headed for the stairs.

'They're open till nine some evenings.'

'Thanks,' Vanja said again over her shoulder.

'And if she's not there I expect she'll be with her gentleman friend,' Tyra Lindell went on as if she hadn't noticed that Vanja was no longer standing in front of her. Vanja stopped dead. Went back up the stairs.

'Do you happen to know where he lives?'

'I've no idea, but if Ellinor is to be believed, he can't be all that difficult to find.'

'Oh?'

Tyra leaned forward conspiratorially and lowered her voice.

'Apparently he's very well known – famous, in fact.' She rolled her eyes to show how much faith she put in Ellinor's nonsense. 'She told me all about him, and she got quite annoyed because I didn't know who he was. In the end I had to pretend.'

'Do you remember his name?'

'Oh yes – Sebastian, Sebastian Bergman. Apparently he's a psychologist.'

Vanja stared at the old lady. It was impossible. She must have misheard. That name couldn't pop up here. Not now. The feeling she had had in her apartment earlier came back; this couldn't be reality. It must be a practical joke, one of those TV shows with hidden cameras. Soon someone would jump out, laughing at how easily she had been fooled. Priceless! Vanja didn't know who that someone might be, but surely that had to be the explanation.

'Sebastian Bergman is Ellinor's gentleman friend,' she repeated, noticing to her surprise that her voice was steady. Tyra nodded.

'Yes. As I said, he's a psychologist, and between you and me,' Tyra leaned closer once again, and this time she placed her wrinkled hand on Vanja's arm, 'I think Ellinor needs some help in that department from time to time.'

'Are you sure?'

'No, but she is a bit odd.'

'I mean are you sure she was talking about a psychologist called Sebastian Bergman?'

'Absolutely. She's practically living with him. Or at least she was; she's been home quite a lot lately. Maybe he's come to his senses.'

Tyra smiled at her, but Vanja didn't even notice. It was as if two parallel universes had collided in the stairwell of an apartment block on Västmannagatan and created an alternative reality. If anyone was going to jump out and laugh at her blank expression, then now would be a good time. But no one did. Unfortunately.

Anitha had kept a low profile since her long lunch with Morgan Hansson. She had done what she was paid to do, she hadn't logged in under anyone else's name, she hadn't even posted on Flashback. No doubt she was being excessively cautious, but she felt it was best to take a break from any supplementary activities until she heard back from Morgan. He had promised to go down to the data room in the basement the following morning, but he still hadn't contacted her. How long could it take to search through a couple of backup tapes?

For a while Anitha was worried; what if he had gone to his line manager and told him everything, instead of helping her? Perhaps that was why it was so quiet. However, she calmed down when she remembered how close Morgan had stood before they parted yesterday, the looks he had given her. She had played him to perfection; he wouldn't let her down. In fact, she suspected that the real problem would be getting rid of him when this was all over.

By the afternoon she couldn't sit still any longer; she decided to go down and see him. She had to know. Should she call first, or just turn up and surprise him? The latter option was probably best; she wanted to look him in the eye while he was talking so that she could tell if he was lying or not. She walked quickly towards the main staircase, hurried down to the first floor and didn't slow down until she reached his office.

He wasn't there. She did a tour of the whole floor, trying to look as if she had important business. Eventually she spotted him over by the smaller staircase; he seemed to be on his way up, presumably to see her. His whole demeanour told her that he had done it. She increased her speed, wanted to break into a run, but controlled herself. It would look weird, and she definitely didn't want to attract anyone's attention.

She caught up with him just as he reached the heavy glass door.

'Morgan,' she said, as casually as she could manage.

He turned and gave her a neutral look that she couldn't interpret. It wasn't nervous or excited; it simply was.

'How did it go?' she went on.

He didn't reply, but indicated with a nod that they should go through the door. She followed him as he set off down the stairs, their footsteps echoing. He seemed to want to get to the bottom before he said anything, possibly to avoid the acoustics in the stairwell. His words would be amplified, and could be overheard by the wrong person. It was a sensible precaution, but Anitha was suffering. Eventually he stopped and waited for her. She tried to look unconcerned as she joined him, in spite of the fact that she wanted nothing more than to shake him, make him say something.

'I've done it,' he whispered at last.

'Thank you so much,' Anitha said warmly. 'I've been a bit worried about you . . .'

'It was a stupid thing to do, but I wanted to help you and Eva.'

'Eva?' Anitha heard herself say; a second later she realised who he meant. Morgan gazed at her sceptically.

'Eva. The police officer in Solna. The friend you told me about.'

'Right, yes, Eva Gransäter,' Anitha babbled, cursing her stupidity. How could she forget her own lies? 'I've been feeling quite stressed,' she added in an attempt to explain.

'Me too,' Morgan said disarmingly. 'I thought I was going to have a heart attack down there.'

'How did it go?'

'Well, Adam Cederkvist is the name your colleague is looking for. Do you know who he is?'

'I've no idea,' Anitha replied with total honesty as a wave of disappointment washed over her. She had been hoping for a name she would recognise, some big shot whose ruined reputation would taste sweeter than that of some anonymous civil servant, if this led anywhere.

'Nothing else?' she said, unable to hide her feelings.

'That was the reference you deleted by mistake. And now I've got a question for you,' Morgan said with a wry smile.

'No problem,' Anitha replied, although she suspected she might regret it. All of a sudden Morgan seemed rather too sure of himself for her taste.

'What's this really about?'

'Sorry?'

'Why did you log in under a false name and search classified Säpo files?'

Anitha tried to look blasé.

'I've already told you – it was a stupid attempt to help a colleague.'

There was a brief silence. Morgan nodded to himself as if he had just received confirmation of something he thought he knew. He leaned towards her.

'I checked her out. Eva Gransäter. She's no longer a police officer. She left in 2007.'

Anitha's cheeks flushed red. She didn't have an answer. It was an odd feeling; she always kept to the shadows, and now she was caught in the light.

'So, are you going to tell me what this is about,' Morgan went on calmly, 'or would you rather I passed it on to my boss?'

'No. I'll tell you.'

'Good. I want to know everything.'

Morgan looked at her again with his newly found confidence. Anitha realised she would never get rid of him. They would be dining together quite often from now on. The question was, who had played whom?

★ ★ ★

Shit, he had to think fast.

Less than a minute ago he had been standing in the kitchen frying burgers when the doorbell rang. He had removed the pan from the heat before he went into the hallway. Asked who it was, he reminded himself that he must get a spyhole fitted. It was Vanja. He had felt his heart give a little leap of joy, even though she sounded quite subdued, as far as he could tell from 'It's Vanja.' Sebastian had taken a deep breath; no doubt she had heard about the FBI programme and was devastated. She needed someone to console her. He had opened the door.

She wasn't devastated.

She was furious.

'Ellinor Bergkvist,' she had barked as soon as the door opened, arms folded.

'What about her?'

'You know her.'

It wasn't a question. Sebastian thanked his lucky stars that he hadn't said 'Who's that?' when he heard the name of the woman who had lived with him for a short time.

'Yes.'

Brief answers. No point in expanding until he knew more.

'She's the one who handed the material about my father to the police.'

Vanja had stared at him with an expression that was even worse than when she had disliked him intensely several months ago.

He had to think fast.

Shit, he had to think fast.

He stepped aside and she strode in. Stopped just inside the door. Made no attempt to take off her jacket or shoes.

'Tell me what's happened,' he said, playing for time.

'Your girlfriend handed the Economic Crime Authority the material that got my father arrested, so I think you're the one who's got some explaining to do.'

Arms still folded. A challenging look in her eyes. Sebastian opted for the truth, or at least a variation on the truth. As close as possible, but with the omission of certain details. He let out a deep sigh to show how troubled he was. He didn't even need to pretend; this could wreck everything they had built up over the past few days.

'I did wonder, but . . .' he broke off and shook his head. 'I hoped it wasn't true.'

'What are you talking about?'

He took a deep breath. He would have to play it by ear, take his chances. The worst thing would be to try to wriggle out of it.

'Trolle Hermansson turned up here a few months ago and gave me a bag containing case notes on Valdemar.'

'But why? Why did he give it to you?'

'I've no idea. I assumed he knew that we work together now and again, but that I wasn't formally attached to Riksmord any more.'

'I don't understand – why was Trolle investigating my father in the first place?'

Sebastian shrugged. He could stick to his modified version of the truth.

'From what I knew of Trolle, he took whatever work he could get.'

'Did you know him well?'

'We worked together, but he got kicked out before I left Riksmord. That must have been . . . maybe fifteen years ago?'

'But were you still in touch?'

'We saw one another now and again. He was pretty lonely – divorced, lost his family. He was a bit of an arsehole – not many people were prepared to put up with him.'

'Apart from another arsehole.'

'I guess so . . .'

Vanja took in what she had heard. Sebastian was pleased to see that her arms had dropped slightly; she was beginning to relax. This was good in one way, bad in another. Now that her initial fury had abated, she was becoming pensive and analytical, which was much more dangerous for Sebastian. Any further questions would be dictated by her intellect, not her emotions.

'But if someone asked Trolle to investigate my father, why did Trolle give the material to you rather than to that person?'

A difficult question with a simple answer, because of course it was Sebastian who had asked Trolle to dig up as much dirt as possible on Valdemar Lithner, and that was the one thing he could never tell Vanja. Time to abandon the truth altogether.

'I don't know, maybe they fell out over the payment, maybe Trolle got mad for some reason and decided to mess them about.'

'So he gave it all to you instead.'

'Yes.'

They kept coming back to the same point; even Sebastian could see how hollow the explanation was. There were many more credible scenarios.

Trolle could have gone to the police.

Destroyed everything he had found.

Left it lying in a drawer in his apartment.

Why had he given it to Sebastian? It was essential to stop Vanja thinking about that, strengthen the motivation.

'I don't know, maybe he was scared of having the stuff at home, or maybe he just wanted somebody to see what he'd achieved. Like I said, he was pretty lonely.'

'So what did you do with it?' Vanja asked; at least she seemed to have dropped the issue of why Sebastian had acquired the material – for the moment. Back to the half-truths.

'Nothing. I read through it and decided not to do anything. Then when Trolle died—'

'What was his connection with Edward Hinde and Ralph Svensson – did he say anything about that?'

They were rapidly approaching the next critical point. He had to come up with a sensible explanation as to why an old disgraced cop who had been under the radar for almost fifteen years suddenly turned up twice in the course of just a few months. The common denominator was Sebastian, of course, but he had to find something else.

Someone else.

Vanja.

'I've been wondering about that too,' he said, stroking his cheek. 'The only thing I can think of is that someone asked him to investigate your father, so he ended up close to you, discovered that you were involved in a major murder inquiry, and decided to get one over on Riksmord by solving the case himself, and then he . . . died.'

Sebastian held his breath.

Too much? Too smooth? Too carefully thought out?

Vanja nodded thoughtfully. Sebastian decided to keep going while he was ahead, make sure she didn't have too much time to ponder.

'Anyway, I decided to throw away the material Trolle had given me, but then I got hurt and I had to stay in hospital. I asked Ellinor to destroy it, but obviously she didn't.'

'So who is this Ellinor?'

Back to the truth.

'She's a . . . sick woman who lived here for a while. When women I'd slept with started being murdered, I warned her and she . . . moved in. And stayed, somehow or other.'

He couldn't even explain it to himself.

'We're not together any more. I kicked her out. She's crazy,' he added, just to underline the fact that he had nothing to do with what had happened.

Vanja stood there staring at him, processing the information, trying to decide whether she believed him or not. He stepped forward, placed a hand on her arm, waited until she met his sincere, sympathetic gaze.

'I'm so very sorry this has happened, and I really hope you don't think it was anything to do with me.'

Vanja looked deep into his eyes, searching for any sign that he was lying, searching for something that didn't add up. Trolle, Ellinor, the material – all linked to Sebastian. It could be a coincidence, a quirk of fate. What else could it be? she asked herself. She still wasn't completely happy with the explanation as to why Trolle had handed everything over to Sebastian, but she was inclined to believe him. Sometimes stuff just happened; people acted according to a logic that was all their own, and this seemed to be one of those situations. What reason could Sebastian Bergman have for wanting to see her father end up in prison?

None whatsoever.

He was her friend.

She nodded, and she could see how relieved he was. How happy.

But once the anger and the uncertainty ebbed away, Vanja couldn't hold back the tears. Suddenly she was looking down at the floor, weeping silently. Sebastian didn't know what to do; he seemed to want to give her a hug, but he hesitated. She took a step towards him to show that it was OK, and he put his arms around her.

'I didn't get onto the FBI programme,' she mumbled into his apron-clad chest as she let out all the disappointments of the past twenty-four hours. She was sobbing so hard she was shaking now, and he did his best to comfort her. Like a father. He needed her, that was why he had gone to Riddarstolpe, but she needed him too. It was best for both of them if she didn't go away, he told himself as he gently stroked her hair.

Valdemar was lying on his back on his bunk, staring up at the ceiling and trying to think of something other than the slowly receding pain in his back. Same bunk, same cell, same ceiling, but he was now the responsibility of the criminal justice system rather than the police. He had been formally charged this afternoon.

He had never been in a courtroom before, and had expected it to look like the ones he had seen in American TV series, which turned out not to be the case, at least not when it came to the room in Stockholm's district court into which he was led at 13.05, along with Karin Svärd, the solicitor he had finally engaged. There was a podium at the front, with the high backs of five very comfortable-looking green chairs sticking up behind it. Two of the chairs were occupied by court officials, the others were empty. In front of the podium there were two curved tables, arranged so that it was easy to see whoever was at the other table, and to speak to those on the podium. Two people were sitting at the table furthest away from the door: Valdemar was informed that one of them was Stig Wennberg, the prosecutor, and the other was some kind of assistant; Karin didn't know his name.

They sat down and Valdemar had glanced at the public area. Anna was there, of course; Vanja wasn't. Just the way he wanted it. He allowed his gaze to sweep over the others who were present before he met Anna's gaze; no one he recognised. No one from the office. Nosey people with too much time on their hands, presumably. Anna looked tired. He gave her a little smile and she smiled back, but her eyes didn't light up as they usually did, and she quickly turned her attention to the two court officials.

The proceedings began. After establishing the names of those present, the prosecutor was asked to read the charges. Stig Wennberg cleared his throat and began. It was a long list. Valdemar glanced at

Anna; her features seemed to grow more rigid with each accusation that was read out.

They hadn't spoken since the police picked him up. Did she believe he was innocent? They had enjoyed the good life, been able to treat themselves, but did she really think he earned that much? Perhaps she hadn't concerned herself with that side of things, or had she suspected that some of the money came from slightly more shady activities? He didn't know. They had never discussed it. Judging by her expression in the courtroom, this had come as a complete shock, and she didn't seem to doubt his guilt. There were no little shakes of the head to show how ridiculous the prosecutor's charges were, no sympathetic looks at Valdemar to convey how sorry she was that an innocent man had ended up in this position. In fact she seemed determined not to look at him at all. It hurt, but he had only himself to blame. This was a devastating blow for his wife and daughter and, unlike him, they were totally innocent. It was hardly surprising if they decided to distance themselves from him. He had a long road back if he was to regain their trust and love; too long, perhaps.

He didn't really understand how it had come to this. He couldn't blame ignorance; he had known that what Daktea were doing, what they had asked him to do, was illegal, but to be fair he hadn't appreciated the scope of the operation until it collapsed. However, he also knew that they were smart; with his help they had built up a solid structure riddled with dead ends and countless transactions that were nigh-on impossible to trace. As time went by he felt more and more secure. He was only a small cog in a huge machine. Why would anyone track him down?

Wennberg concluded his statement, and Valdemar was asked if he pleaded guilty or not guilty. He glanced at Karin, who gave an almost imperceptible nod. She had told him what to say, even if it was a lie.

'Not guilty.'

The proceedings had continued for another thirty minutes. Karin did her best to expose any weaknesses in the prosecution's case, but Valdemar didn't give much for her chances, and indeed the result was as he expected: he was charged with serious fraud. The prosecutor asked that all restrictions should remain in place, and his request was granted. It was over. Anna had got up and left the room before anyone else; Valdemar thought she was trying hard not to cry. That was the worst thing. Not the humiliation, not being locked up, not the punishment that would inevitably follow, but the damage he had done to those he loved. It was almost more than he could bear. He had hoped to be able to exchange a few words with Anna, but instead he instructed Karin to tell her that under no circumstances was she to inform Vanja that he had been charged.

Back in his cell he lay down on the bunk; there wasn't much else to do. After an hour or so his back had started aching again. It wasn't because he had been lying in the same position for too long, but he turned over anyway. It didn't help. He had asked for and been given painkillers. He hadn't felt like eating when dinner was served, but had asked for more painkillers. And now he was lying on his bunk, staring up at the ceiling and trying to think of something other than the slowly receding pain. He kept coming back to Anna and Vanja, which was even more painful in its own way. He got up with some difficulty and went over to the small toilet. He pulled down his pants and peed. Was the light playing tricks on him? He finished peeing and bent down to take a closer look. Turned his head slightly so that the ceiling light illuminated the toilet.

The contents of the bowl were red.

Blood red.

The meeting broke up.

Torkel had gathered them all in the room that was always known simply as the Room, for a final briefing before the weekend. Six chairs arranged around an oval conference table on top of a grey-green fitted carpet. On one wall was the whiteboard where Billy had recreated the timeline with the help of the information they had gathered in Storulvån. The Room was silent; they were supposed to be discussing the progress made over the past twenty-four hours, reporting back on what they had done and what results they had achieved or were expecting to achieve. Unfortunately there was depressingly little to discuss.

Torkel began by telling everyone that he had called Hedvig Hedman in Östersund to inform her that they had now been able to confirm the identity of the Dutch couple. It was common practice for Riksmord to report back on parts of an ongoing investigation to the local police who had requested their help, with the emphasis on *parts of*. It was important for the local force to feel involved, but it was even more important for Riksmord to be in control of the flow of information, which was why he said nothing about their theory that the Dutch couple just happened to be in the wrong place at the wrong time, nor about the camera or how the rest of the case was going.

Fortunately.

Torkel hadn't been particularly surprised to find a full-page spread in the online edition of *Expressen* that afternoon, with the headline 'THEY DIED ON THEIR DREAM HOLIDAY'. The introduction stated that Riksmord were now one 100 per cent certain of the identity of two of the six bodies in the mass grave in the mountains: Jan and Framke Bakker from Rotterdam. The article carried a picture of the couple, a fairly emotional piece about how much they had been looking forward to their week in the mountains of Jämtland, a brief interview with a friend who was grateful for some kind of closure, and a fact box about 'The Mountain Grave', as the paper had dubbed the case.

If Torkel had had any doubts, he was now quite sure: informing Hedman and the Östersund police was virtually the same as issuing a press release. He ended his summary by stressing how important it was that he and he alone dealt with the press.

The team merely nodded.

Same as always, in other words.

Jennifer was the next to report: lots of work with little to show for it more or less summed up her continued efforts, using every imaginable international database, to find more families who might fit the profile of the four unidentified bodies. Either the team already knew about those she came up with, or she was able to eliminate them more or less straight away, thanks to the fact that the forensics team in Umeå had given estimated ages and a pretty accurate assessment of the height of each person. Which took them to Ursula, who immediately handed over to Billy.

He had started the day by tackling the camera from the Dutch couple's rucksack. He managed to find a cable that fitted, but the camera refused to charge. Too long in the ground, he assumed. It was hardly surprising if being buried for nine years was more than it could cope with, even if it had been wrapped in plastic and tucked inside a rucksack. He concentrated on the memory card instead, but soon realised he wouldn't be able to remove it from the camera without damaging it. He had consulted Ursula, who was of the same opinion, so they sent the camera down to the National Forensics Lab in Linköping by courier, with a message to say that retrieving the pictures was a matter of the utmost urgency. Ursula had called her former colleagues during the afternoon, partly to check if the camera was there and partly to stress that urgent meant exactly that. She was told that they had prioritised the camera as soon as it arrived, and things looked promising. They should have the pictures on Monday.

Torkel nodded appreciatively. At least that was something to keep their hopes up over the weekend. Finally, Ursula added that she had been right about fingerprints on the rucksacks found at Harald Olofsson's place: it was impossible to lift any at all. They were still going through the clothes, and had found some strands of hair which they hoped to match with the bodies in Umeå.

Towards the end of the meeting they put the investigation to one side and stopped being police officers for a little while. It started with Jennifer asking what everyone was doing at the weekend; Billy and Maya were going mushrooming. It was Billy's first time; he was trying to go into it with an open mind, but he had a feeling it wasn't going to be his new hobby. Jennifer was going to visit her mother, but stressed that she could be reached on her mobile 24/7. She didn't say it, but she was convinced she would be longing for Monday morning as soon as she left.

Ursula said she was planning to visit Bella in Uppsala, which wasn't true. She didn't really know what she was going to do, but she thought there was a chance she might end up at Sebastian's place again.

Torkel was spending the weekend with his daughters, pleased that he had been able to keep his promise for once.

There was an unusual atmosphere in the Room. The topics of conversation in there were generally violent and sudden death, theories about crimes and criminals – focused discussion with details that everyone left behind when they went home, because otherwise they would pollute the atmosphere outside. But right now, for a moment, things were different. They were colleagues, almost friends, talking about life instead of death.

They got up and went home for the weekend.

Like normal people.

It was a strange feeling.

Her hand was just as warm as it always was. He had told his story, and now he was holding her hand as tightly as he could. She had reacted with both surprise and anxiety, pacing around the living room before sinking down in front of him. He thought back to when he was a little boy, when her hand was all he needed to comfort him. Back then his little paw had almost disappeared in her loving grip. It wasn't like that any more; these days his hand virtually covered hers. The tenderness was still there, but now she was the one who needed solace. They sat in silence for a moment; he could tell that she was struggling to work out the significance of what he had told her. Then Shibeka let go of Mehran's hand, got to her feet and slowly walked over to the photograph of Hamid, which had stood in the same place for as long as he could remember. She picked it up, caressed the glass covering the black and white mouth with her index finger. Mehran realised he was about the same age as his father in the picture. Young and tall, with their whole lives ahead of them.

'Hamid once said that Said regretted buying the shop, but that was the only negative thing I ever heard. Are you sure they quarrelled?'

'I don't know, but why would someone lie about it?'

Shibeka shook her head. She couldn't think of a reason either.

'Melika told me her cousins had sold the shop, but I thought it was only about a year ago.'

'They sold it a month after Hamid and Said disappeared; maybe Melika didn't want us to know.'

Shibeka gently replaced the photograph, gazing lovingly at the man who had been such a big part of her life. Even after his disappearance.

'My parents gave me this picture when I was thirteen years old, so that I would know what the man I was to marry looked like. I used to sit and stare at it, wondering what sort of person he was. Would he be a good husband? Would he be kind, harsh, gentle? I had no idea. I was very frightened – not that I dared say anything to anybody. I decided he was going to be a good man. I looked at his picture and told myself that his eyes were both curious and kind, that he looked wise. But you know what?'

Her eyes were soft as she contemplated her son.

'I was still surprised. When I met him he was even better than I could have hoped; kinder and wiser, more loving than I could possibly have imagined. That's why this picture means so much to me. It gives me hope.'

She went back to Mehran, her eyes shining with the memory.

'Hope that things can be better than you expect,' she went on. 'That sometimes our worries are unfounded. I am still hopeful.'

'But you know Melika lied, don't you? About Joseph.'

Shibeka nodded.

'In which case she might have lied about other things,' Mehran went on. 'Like this business with the shop.'

'Perhaps, but what can we do, Mehran?'

'I'll talk to her, and I won't let her get away with it this time.'

Mehran knew what he had to do. He would use his new voice to find out the truth. Presumably that was why Allah had given it to him; not to grow in front of Memel and the other men as he had thought, but to face up to something much more difficult.

Much more important.

Shibeka looked at him, and after a while she nodded.

So be it.

This time Vanja waited for over half an hour outside the apartment block on Västmannagatan before a middle-aged couple came strolling along arm in arm, entered the code and disappeared inside. Vanja quickly slipped in after them. They looked at her suspiciously as she walked past them while they were waiting for the lift; she almost expected to have to produce her ID, but neither of them said anything; they just watched her as if they were trying to memorise her appearance in case they were called as witnesses to something or other at a later date. Vanja quickly made her way up to the third floor. This was probably a stupid idea, but she had to know.

She hadn't stayed long at Sebastian's. She had cried, let it all out. He had held her, standing there in the hallway until the worst had passed; he had asked her to stay for something to eat – he was cooking burgers – but she had declined. She needed to be alone, think about what had happened, what she knew. She really wanted to believe him, but it wasn't that simple. He might be a new improved version, but he was still Sebastian. Smart, unscrupulous, with a liberal conscience – the very qualities she had valued just a few hours earlier now counted against him, which was why she was back in the apartment block on Västmannagatan. She had to know the truth before she could truly regard Sebastian as the friend she so desperately needed.

She rang Ellinor Bergkvist's doorbell. It was almost midnight, but she didn't care. She rang again, keeping her thumb on the bell. She could see movement behind the spyhole, then the lock clicked and the door opened as far as the security chain would allow.

'Hi, my name is Magdalena,' Vanja said. 'Could I have a word with you about Sebastian Bergman?'

'What about him?' Ellinor asked, her voice a mixture of scepticism, joy and anxiety.

'May I come in for a moment?'

'No.'

In order to put weight behind her response, Ellinor pushed the door shut so that only a tiny gap remained. She peered out with one eye.

'What about Sebastian?' she reiterated.

Vanja started by explaining that she was a police officer, keeping her fingers crossed that Ellinor wouldn't ask to see her ID. An ongoing investigation by the Economic Crime Unit had led to Sebastian, and things weren't looking too good. From the little she could see of Ellinor's face, she seemed distraught. Daktea, Trolle Hermansson's death, the fact that all this information had been handed in by someone with a connection to Sebastian, meant that the police had to dig deeper into Sebastian's role in the whole thing, Vanja clarified. It was a complex case, and when a colleague came up in an investigation, it was a matter of routine to dig a little deeper. Ellinor nodded. Vanja was impressed by what a good liar she had turned out to be.

Ellinor started talking; she appeared to be proud of what she had done, and equally determined that no shadow of blame should fall on Sebastian.

Yes, he had asked her to throw away the bag, but she had read the contents and decided to help him.

No, Sebastian had never said that Valdemar was a threat, or expressed any desire to harm him in any way; that had been Ellinor's own conclusion. She might have been mistaken.

Yes, she thought he had been give the material by someone called Trolle, but she wasn't sure.

Vanja could feel herself relaxing more and more each time Ellinor confirmed something Sebastian had said. Life had been enough of an emotional roller-coaster lately; she couldn't cope with finding out that Sebastian had been involved in bringing down her father, for some inexplicable reason. In fact it seemed as if the reverse was true.

He had wanted to protect her.

Save her. Again. Just as he had done from Edward Hinde.

He would have succeeded if it hadn't been for this woman with her face pressed against the door. Vanja felt a surge of rage, a pure, clear emotion – welcome after the mixture of sorrow, pain, suspicion and confusion she had endured over the past twenty-four hours.

'Is Sebastian back in town?' Ellinor asked, sounding hopeful.

'Why do you ask?'

'I want to see him.'

Under normal circumstances Vanja would have felt sorry for a woman in Ellinor's situation; she would have found Sebastian's actions in kicking her out and then refusing to talk to her both cowardly and insensitive. Bastard. She would have been completely on the side of the woman. Under normal circumstances.

'He said you weren't together any more,' she said bluntly.

'He's only saying that to protect me,' Ellinor insisted.

'From what?'

'Valdemar Lithner.'

Vanja's anger was overlaid with impatience. Ellinor was contradicting herself: she had just said that Sebastian didn't regard Valdemar as a threat. That was the final straw; Vanja felt a sudden urge to go on the attack. She had taken so much crap; it was time to give something back. This woman had destroyed so much, and besides, she would be doing Sebastian a favour, she told herself.

'He kicked you out because you're crazy. He never wants to see you again,' she said, fixing her gaze on the eye peering through the gap. Ellinor jerked back as if someone had slapped her.

'He didn't say that.'

'Yes, he did.' Vanja revelled in the knowledge that she had regained control. She might not be proud of herself tomorrow, but she would worry about that when the time came. Right now she decided to twist the knife a little more.

'He said you were sick; he let you stay with him for a while out of kindness, but he can't cope with you any more. Particularly after what you've done to Valdemar Lithner.'

The light in the stairwell went out, and in the compact darkness that followed, Vanja didn't see Ellinor's eye narrow and darken as it stared at her with an emotion that was unmistakable: hatred.

'Stay away from Sebastian,' Ellinor heard from out of the darkness, and then the figure outside her door was gone. She didn't switch on the light as she went down the stairs, presumably to make her departure more dramatic, Ellinor guessed as she closed the door.

She hurried into the bedroom, over to the window. If Magdalena crossed the street and turned left, Ellinor would be able to see her.

That was exactly what she did, and Ellinor watched her until she disappeared from view. Ellinor sank down on the unmade bed.

The woman had said such terrible things.

Terrible and true?

Valdemar Lithner had been arrested. He could no longer constitute a threat to anyone, and yet Sebastian hadn't been in touch, hadn't asked her to come back now the danger was over.

According to the woman, Sebastian had never been afraid of Valdemar. Had she misinterpreted the situation? If so . . .

She could hardly bear to formulate the thought. If so he had meant what he said on the note attached to her suitcase.

If so he hadn't said those hurtful things and thrown her out in order to protect her. He had grown tired of her. He really did see her as a home help he had sex with, and now it was over. That nurse he had told her about – he really had slept with her. With her and God knows how many others.

Ellinor had loved him.

He had just been toying with her.

He had spent Saturday alone with his music and his thoughts as they billowed back and forth, stopped then slipped away. However, he kept coming back to the same point, and by the evening he knew what he had to do. He had to confront Melika. She couldn't be allowed to hide the truth any longer. His mother would have wanted to come with him if she had known; he understood that, but it was better if he did this on his own. If it was just him, Memel and the others wouldn't be able to say much, and if it went wrong and caused problems, it would be better if they only had him to blame. Mehran would be able to explain, put his cards on the table, tell them about Melika's lies; they would have to listen. They didn't have to listen to Shibeka. That was the difference between men and women; he needed to take it on board and learn to exploit it.

This morning Shibeka had made him breakfast. He ate well, told her he was going out, but didn't say where. Now he was standing outside Melika's apartment block. Mehran wanted to take her by surprise, make sure she didn't have the opportunity to prepare herself in any way; he would strike suddenly, with no warning. He just didn't know how. Ringing the doorbell would surprise her, admittedly, but he couldn't force his way in, and he definitely didn't want to have this conversation on the landing.

Eventually he got his chance. He had seen her set off with a friend an hour or so earlier, and now her son Ali was coming down the street with a couple of friends. They parted company where the paths crossed, and Ali continued on his own. The other boys' voices faded away. Mehran was half-hidden behind a tree, watching Ali as he strolled along without a care in the world. He knew Ali, of course, but Eyer was closer to him in both age and interests, and it was a long time since they had spoken. He straightened up and walked quickly towards the other boy. Ali's face lit up when he saw him.

'Hi, Mehran!'

He seemed genuinely pleased to see Mehran. Good – that meant his mother hadn't said anything about her problems with the Khan family, which should make things easier.

'Hi, Ali, how's things?'

'Great.'

'Is it OK if I come up for a bit? I've forgotten my key and it's a bit cold; Mum won't be home for hours.'

He tried to look as frozen as possible in order to make his story credible; Ali bought it.

'Course you can, although I don't think Mum's home, so there won't be anything to eat.'

'No problem – we can watch TV.'

Mehran felt both nervous and excited as Ali unlocked the door of the apartment. He had no idea if this was going to work, but at least he would have a slight advantage when Melika got home and found him sitting on her sofa. If she came home alone . . . otherwise he would have to come up with another plan.

He and Ali spent an hour in front of the TV. They chatted about Eyer and school and friends before they ran out of things to say. Mehran had other matters on his mind. If Ali found the silence uncomfortable, he didn't show it; in fact he seemed delighted that someone so much older was sitting watching cartoons with him. Perhaps it wasn't so strange; all his friends had brothers and sisters. None of them was an only child, like him.

At last they heard a key in the door. 'Here she is!' Ali said happily.

'Good,' Mehran said, getting to his feet. He fixed Ali with a hard stare.

'Go to your room.'

Ali looked shocked. 'But why?'

'Go to your room, I said. Now!'

Ali stood up, his expression mutinous. This was his home; he wasn't going anywhere.

Mehran was annoyed; obviously he didn't carry enough authority. However, he didn't want to shout at Ali, who was no more than an innocent kid, just as he had once been. No doubt that was the problem; he was too sensitive.

'I need to speak to your mother,' he said in a more reasonable tone. 'Alone.'

Ali didn't have time to respond before Melika walked in with a carrier bag of food. She was shocked to see Mehran.

'What are you doing here?'

'I think you know the answer to that.'

He walked past Ali, who didn't seem to know how to react.

'What's happened, Ali?' Melika asked anxiously. Mehran answered for him.

'I've asked him to go to his room. I know you're lying. I didn't think he needed to hear this.'

Her face lost its colour and she dropped the bag on the floor.

'Get out of here, Mehran. Right now.'

He shook his head. He had no intention of giving up. Not until he got to the truth.

'You don't have to tell my mother, but you do have to tell me.'

'Tell you what? I don't know what you're talking about.'

'I went to Said's shop. Your husband's shop. Ali's father's shop. Do you know what they told me?'

For a second she had no idea what to say. Mehran could see that his words had hit home, got past the protective wall of lies. She stood there in silence, as if she was hoping that if she kept quiet for long enough, he would give up and go home. No chance. He felt more powerful than ever; his strength of will had driven out his nerves.

'I can pass it on to Memel if you like. I think he would be interested to hear that your cousins and Said fell out. That they sold the shop a month after he disappeared. Or does he already know? Does everyone know except us?'

'That's not true,' she whispered, sinking down onto the stool by the door.

'What's not true, Melika?'

She stared at the floor. At her feet. Then she looked up at her son.

'Do as Mehran says. Go to your room.'

Ali couldn't believe his ears. 'But, Mum—'

'Go to your room!' she yelled. Mehran could tell that her voice was on the point of breaking. He, on the other hand, had most definitely found his voice.

Ali slipped away to his room. He would probably never look at Mehran in the same way again. At last Melika met his gaze. Her expression was no longer hostile, merely sad.

'I don't know what happened, Mehran. Honestly I don't.'

'But you know more than you told us.'

She nodded almost imperceptibly.

'Who's Joseph?'

She went as white as a ghost. 'An evil man. It's all his fault.'

There was no longer sorrow in her eyes; instead he could see fear. A nagging anxiety, perhaps even terror.

Mehran held out his hand to her. He wanted to be gentle now; he thought that was what the truth required.

'Tell me,' he said.

Morgan Hansson had shown Anitha a number of new sides to his character over the weekend. He wasn't a troll at all.

He was something much worse.

A *bon vivant*.

A man who really knew how to handle the cards he had been dealt. After she had told him the truth about Lennart Stridh and the TV programme, Morgan had suggested they go out to dinner, just as she had feared. That would be nice, wouldn't it, now they knew each other so well and no longer had any secrets? Anitha couldn't say no. She was going to have to butter him up, agree to all his suggestions for the rest of her life, or at least as long as she stayed with the police.

They had eaten at his favourite place, Texas Longhorn on Sankt Paulsgatan on Friday night, and Anitha had learned the following:

1) He loved talking, particularly when he'd had a couple of drinks.
2) He loved large quantities of red meat, served with baked potato filled with sour cream and Cheddar cheese. She was surprised he wasn't fatter, given the amount he put away.
3) He liked ale and noisy pubs, preferably in the Söder district of the city. According to him that was the best way to finish off an evening, and he was often one of the last to leave.
4) He was obsessed with sparkling water. He had told her in detail about the joy his own carbonating machine brought him, and now there was one in her kitchen too. He had tried to come up and install it for her, but that was where she had drawn the line. On this occasion. It was only a question of time before he made himself at home, and was standing in her kitchen happily carbonating water.

5) He loved the Kista Galleria shopping centre. That was where they had bought the machine. He liked the fact that there were so many people there, different cultures from all over the world. It was so 'un-Swedish', he thought. She had to agree, even though she just wanted to scream with every fibre of her being.

This evening they were going to the cinema – Morgan's decision, of course. He always went to the cinema on Sundays, and presumably so did she, from now on. Some 3D film, apparently. She didn't dare tell him that she'd never seen anything in 3D, otherwise he would no doubt make her watch everything that had ever been produced in that format.

She tried to think of one positive aspect of her new 'friend'.

She couldn't come up with anything.

Nothing at all.

Something had to change. Anitha needed to feel that she was at least getting something out of the road to Golgotha that her life had become; even if it wasn't very much, her pride demanded some restitution, otherwise she might just as well lie down and die. She refused to do that; she had to keep control of something.

She decided to call Lennart Stridh; she might as well get some money out of this. It wouldn't be a great deal, she knew that, but right now it was better than nothing. The feeling of control was priceless; that was what she really needed.

She would give him the name.

It wasn't much, but he would pay a higher price than he had ever done before.

Ursula was sitting on the sofa watching TV.

On Sebastian's sofa, watching Sebastian's TV.

With Sebastian.

She had ended up there on Friday after work. Stayed the night. They hadn't had sex; to her surprise the question hadn't even come up. Without the slightest hint or innuendo, he had made up her bed in the guest room; the following day he had woken her when breakfast was ready. She went home on Saturday morning.

She had toyed with the idea of actually going to Uppsala to surprise Bella; didn't parents do that kind of thing? Little unannounced visits? A few pleasant hours together, lunch, then back home. It was a nice idea, but it didn't happen. She just didn't have the nerve. Instead she spent Saturday cleaning, shopping, doing the laundry: the chores a divorced woman had to tackle at the weekend.

This morning she had gone back to Sebastian's. He was pleased to see her; she had eaten a second breakfast with him, then they had gone for a long walk while a couple of workmen did a job for him. It cost more on a Sunday, of course, but on the other hand they came exactly when they had said. They were fitting a spyhole in the door. One thousand eight hundred and fifty kronor.

They talked about everything under the sun as they walked. Ursula found it relaxing to be with someone she could be open with, someone who knew all about her and Mikael. She didn't have to think before she spoke. They had touched on the investigation, but it was obvious that Sebastian wasn't interested and had no intention of getting involved. Not at this stage, anyway. Skeletons, rucksacks and passenger lists didn't appeal to him at all. The American woman – if she was American – who was somehow mixed up in the murders, now she was interesting. But she was also dead.

He needed people, living people. Damaged, twisted, sick. People whose perception of reality and view of the world challenged his own. Psyches that were complex, hard to understand. People others classified as evil in order to make it easy for themselves. If someone like that turned up he would be happy to contribute, but until then . . .

Eventually they had ended up at a pool hall in the Söder district, played some form of eight ball with made-up rules. Ursula won three out of four games. She offered to buy Sebastian a beer, but to her surprise he wanted a Coke. Back in the day when they had been together, he had drunk alcohol. Not alarmingly large quantities, but he was happy to have a drink when it was on offer. Once again she wondered what had happened to him.

'What did you dream about,' she said suddenly, 'when we were up in Jämtland?'

Sebastian was taken aback by the question. Her steady gaze revealed nothing of what was going on in her mind. He couldn't help smiling. If he had been surprised when she turned up on Thursday evening, he had been astonished when she came back the following day and stayed the night. And now Ursula was harking back to their conversation in Storulvån in an ordinary, chatty tone. Her eyes might not give away what she was thinking, but the question did. She thought their brief encounter in the hotel restaurant was worth returning to.

She was curious.

About him.

Put that together with the visits to his apartment: two evenings, no sex admittedly, but Sebastian still felt as if they were slowly, slowly finding their way back to something resembling what they had had all those years ago, before she found out he had been sleeping with her sister.

It felt good, but he wondered why.

Ursula had made it very clear that she would never forgive him, so what was she up to? The divorce must have messed with her head, but even so. Was she playing some kind of game? Was this part of a refined plan to get her revenge? Was she intending to hurt him? Whatever was going on, it was exciting, and the most interesting thing that had happened during this pointless investigation.

'Why do you want to know?'

'You said you'd tell me.'

'Yes, but why do you want to know?'

Ursula picked up her bottle of beer and took a swig. He studied her; he thought he knew what she was doing. Working out exactly what to say. If she simply said she was curious, she would get nowhere with him, and she knew it. She needed to be honest, challenge him, or come up with a theory he just had to disprove.

'Because when you came into the restaurant, when you didn't know I was watching you . . .'

'Yes?' Sebastian said almost expectantly when she paused. It seemed as if she had chosen the honesty option; he could see her choosing her words with care.

'You looked like a person who had lost everything. A man who had nothing left.'

Sebastian didn't answer immediately. She had done well. No real challenge, and certainly not something he could disprove. Honest, and unfortunately perfectly true.

'I will tell you one day,' he said quietly. 'Not here and probably not tonight, but I will tell you. I promise.'

Ursula nodded. She could tell from his voice and the look in his eyes that she couldn't have been far from the truth. It was perfectly understandable that he didn't want to sit on a bar stool with an old Eurythmics track in the background and tell his story, and she didn't really want to hear it in a place like this.

'Soon, I hope,' she said.

Neither of them had mentioned it again. When they got back the workmen had gone, and there was a spyhole in the middle of the door. They had rustled up an early dinner, then ended up on the sofa. Sebastian couldn't remember when he had last sat side by side with someone mindlessly watching TV with his feet up on the coffee table. It must have been with Lily.

'Can I stay over?' Ursula asked as she reached for the remote to silence the adverts.

'Of course.'

'Thanks.'

She flicked through the channels and found some kind of survival programme on Discovery. Sebastian glanced at her out of the corner of his eye as he wondered once again: what was she up to? Was it a game? Revenge?

He didn't know. More importantly, he didn't care.

Lennart was on his way to the stadium, standing with Benke and Stig in a carriage packed with other Hammarby supporters when Anitha called. They were playing Brage tonight, and he could hardly hear her over the racket the fans were making. He had to move to the far end of the carriage and press the phone right against his ear to have any chance of making out what she was saying. She spoke fast, and seemed to have found something. It wasn't much, but at least it was a start. A name. Adam Cederkvist. He was the Säpo officer who had taken over responsibility for the case of the two missing Afghan men in the autumn of 2003. That was all she knew. She spent the rest of the call telling him that she was going to send him a bill for lunch at the Lake Mälaren Pavilion, which she expected him to pay for, and that she also expected an additional payment. Lennart said he would see what he could do, and promised to call her back when things were quieter. That didn't satisfy her; she said he was going to have to come up with a decent amount of money, because she had had to go to considerable lengths to help him. Lennart wondered if she had got into difficulties, but she merely repeated that the money was important, and cut him off. His friends looked enquiringly at him; he said it was work, unfortunately. They seemed disappointed, and it didn't exactly improve matters when he said he was going to get off at Skanstull and go back home. They put all their efforts into changing his mind, particularly Benke, who had been in Spain for two weeks and had really been looking forward to hanging out and seeing the match together. Surely nothing was so important that it couldn't wait? They'd been talking about this game for such a long time. Eventually Lennart gave in. It was Sunday, after all, and there wasn't much he could do apart from an Internet search, and that could wait until he got home. He had missed the last two games, and the only time he saw his old friends these days was when the football was on. They had known each other since they were teenagers, but now they were all so preoccupied with their respective families, kids, girlfriends and work that they never had time to hook up. Lennart decided he would work for an hour or so after the match. It couldn't possibly make any difference; the whole Shibeka Khan case was virtually dead in the water anyway. He had already told Sture Liljedahl that the family had pulled out. The question was whether Anitha's information could bring the story back to life; if so he would have to dig up something more. One name wouldn't go far.

Their seats were right by the pitch. Benke had managed to get season tickets. He had been promising to do it for years, but this was the first time he'd actually managed it. The atmosphere was terrific and it was a good match, but Lennart couldn't stop thinking about what Anitha had told him. He had a name, a concrete individual to follow up. Maybe it was worth a shot. He would do a quick search as soon as he got home.

Sigurdsson scored a terrific goal with five minutes to go, and the whole stadium erupted. Hammarby won, and Lennart roared his approval along with everyone else. Stig persuaded him to come for a few beers. It was too late to work, he insisted, and Lennart agreed to a compromise: two beers, then he would have to go home.

After eight beers and several shots he was listening to the booze and his noisy friends instead of the call of duty. He joined them at a party somewhere near Zinken and managed to avoid smoking, against all the odds. Not that he could claim the credit; he was standing on a crowded balcony belonging to someone he barely knew with an unlit cigarette in his hand when Benke spotted him and wrestled him to the ground. It was a joke but they were both pissed, and Lennart cut his hand on a broken glass. Stig separated them and wrapped the hand in a wet handkerchief. Then they sat there for a while, weeping over how much they loved one another, even though they never said so when they were sober. At three somebody reported the party to the on-call noise and disturbance team, and everyone was thrown out. He got home at four thirty and fell into bed. The last thing he remembered was that there was something he had to do today.

He just wasn't sure what it was.

When the team gathered on Monday morning, they quickly established that nothing much had happened.

They had received preliminary results from the DNA samples taken from relatives of the missing families: the father of the mother from the Thorilsen family, who had disappeared up near Trondheim. The mother's sister from the Hagberg family from Gävle, and a brother of the father from the Cederkvist family, who were presumed drowned in the Indian Ocean. None of them matched any of the bodies in the mountain grave. It wasn't much of a surprise, and anything that could be ruled out freed up time for other lines of enquiry.

Billy was sitting at his desk when his computer pinged. The National Forensics Lab had sent the photographs they had managed to retrieve from the memory card, ninety-three of them. He downloaded the file and started to go through them. They seemed to date from early spring up to the deaths of the Dutch couple. A birthday party for someone who was presumably the daughter of a friend, as she didn't appear in any further pictures. Photos from cycling trips, more parties, outings to the beach, walks, football matches. Happy, smiling faces. The odd picture taken in what could only be the Bakkers' home. Everyday life.

The last thirty-seven were interesting. One had been taken at the airport in Trondheim: Framke with her rucksack outside the terminal building, smiling into the camera. Then they were up in the mountains; this time it was Jan's turn to stand pointing at the mountain tops, as if to show where they were going. Picnics, overnight stays, stunning views. Billy selected and printed all the pictures from the mountains, and as the printer did its job he jumped to the last few.

Framke taking down the tent.

A swirling stream.

Reindeer high up on a mountainside.

The entrance to a valley with Jan in the foreground, drinking from a small waterfall. The final picture: he looked happy, smiling at the camera and his wife. Billy checked the date: 30 October. The day they died. The valley extending behind him, a little house on the right-hand side and beyond it a plateau, blue sky, more mountains forming a backdrop. Billy recognised the skyline; he had been there. The plateau was where they had found the bodies. It was difficult to judge distance, but he estimated that Jan and Framke Bakker had about an hour's walking ahead of them before they reached the spot. An hour left to live, which of course the smiling man didn't know when the picture was taken. It added a mournful gravity to the frozen image. Billy was about to move on to something else when he was struck by one particular detail.

The house.

The little house in the valley, at the foot of the mountain. The team had searched for the scene of the crime, but failed to find it. There was no house now, but obviously on 30 October 2003 there had been. Billy enlarged that section of the photograph on his screen: a log cabin with a chimney, steps leading up to the door. Not very big. A hunting lodge.

He got up and went into the Room to study the map they had brought from the hotel. The grave was marked with a cross. They had all looked at the map, of course, but he wanted to double-check.

No house was marked where a house should have been, according to the Bakkers' photograph.

Billy picked up the phone on the conference table and glanced at the wall, where Mats and Klara's business card was pinned up. He dialled the number; Klara answered on the second ring.

Lennart was woken by the rays of the sun on his face. The light hurt his eyes, and he rolled over to pull down the blind, but instead managed to bring the whole contraption down on his bandaged hand. That got him out of bed with a yell.

Wide awake thanks to the pain, he staggered to the bathroom and swallowed two strong painkillers. He sluiced his face with cold water, thinking that he should have taken them before he went to bed; that usually helped when he had a hangover, but he hadn't been thinking straight last night. He hadn't been capable of thinking at all, to be honest. He contemplated the bandage on his left hand. What a night it had turned out to be – a lot crazier than he had expected. The man in the mirror was definitely going to be working from home today.

Work . . .

It was all coming back to him now. Anitha had called yesterday . . . she had found out the name of the guy from Säpo back in 2003. Adam . . . Adam . . . he stiffened. Surely he hadn't forgotten the fucking surname? He'd been thinking about it all evening – well, until the fifth or sixth beer anyway. Deep breaths. No point in getting stressed, otherwise the name on the tip of his tongue would be lost for ever. He definitely didn't want to contact Anitha; he would look like a complete idiot who didn't take his job seriously.

A complete idiot was exactly what he felt like.

Adam.

Adam.

'Adam C-something,' he said out loud. Or was it D? No, C. He had been thinking about the name all along, so it had to be in there somewhere. It had just gone missing. Temporarily, he hoped. He decided to have a cold shower, break his train of thought.

It worked.

Adam Cedergren or Cederkvist, one or the other. At least he had something to go on, and he knew the guy worked for Säpo. He sat down in his study and started making a few calls.

After an hour or so he knew there was no Adam Cedergren or Cederkvist working for either the security police or the regular police service. However, he did find an article in the news archive about an Adam Cederkvist who had gone missing with his wife and children off the coast of Africa during a sailing trip in 2004. They had never been found. Lennart called a friend at *Dagens Nyheter*, a researcher he had worked with many times, and asked for his help. He was putting together a story about long-distance sailors who disappeared, he said, and wondered if his colleague could take a look in the newspaper's archive, which was much more extensive than anything Lennart had access to. Was there anything about the Cederkvist family? Twenty minutes later he received an e-mail.

It wasn't much, but it brought him a step closer. Adam Cederkvist had been on a sabbatical from the police when he disappeared. Unfortunately it wasn't clear whether he had worked for Säpo. He had a brother, Charles Cederkvist, but no other relatives.

Lennart thought for a while. He really didn't want to call the security police and start asking questions about Adam Cederkvist. Someone had put a lot of effort into concealing his identity. If *Investigation Today* started poking around, it could destroy everything. He had very little to go on, so he had to be careful.

However, he liked what he did have. If Adam Cederkvist worked for Säpo, it was a good start to a conspiracy theory. Why would they need to hide the name of one of their own who had been dead since 2004? He didn't want to hear their explanation until he knew the answer himself.

He decided to contact the brother and see if he knew anything. There was a Charles Cederkvist in Oskarshamn; it must be him.

The man answered right away, sounding fresh and alert – the exact opposite of the way Lennart was feeling.

'Is that Charles Cederkvist?'

'Yes.'

'My name is Lennart Stridh; I work for Swedish Television on the *Investigation Today* programme.'

'Oh yes . . .'

340

Charles suddenly sounded less sure of himself, but then almost everyone did when Lennart said where he was calling from. *Investigation Today* was supposed to make people nervous; that was the whole point of the programme.

'I have a few questions about your brother Adam,' he went on.

'He's dead. He died a long time ago.' Charles sounded very surprised.

'I know that; he went missing during a sailing trip, I believe.'

'That's right. Why are you asking about him?'

Lennart thought the question was justified; he needed to allay Charles Cederkvist's fears.

'His name has come up in something I'm working on; I was wondering if we could meet up for a chat?'

'What's this about?'

'If we can meet up I'll explain everything,' Lennart insisted. He had no desire to go through the whole thing on the phone; his head-ache had come back. How much had he actually drunk last night?

'Not unless you tell me what this is about,' Charles said; it was obvious that he meant it. Lennart had only one option.

'It's to do with his role in Säpo and a missing persons case in 2003.'

'What missing persons case?'

'I'd rather not go into that over the phone.' The response was silence. 'I can assure you I have absolutely no intention of dragging your brother's name through the mud. I just want to find out the truth.'

'He never discussed his work with me,' Charles said, and Lennart felt as if he had broken through the other man's initial reluctance to co-operate.

'He might have said something you didn't attach any import-ance to at the time, but it might help me.'

There was another brief silence.

'OK, but I live in Oskarshamn.'

'I can get there.'

'All right. When?'

'Now?'

'Fine.'

Lennart couldn't help smiling. The conversation had gone better than he had dared hope. The story was back up and running.

Just over an hour after Billy had gone through the Bakkers' photographs, the team were gathered in the Room. Torkel had called Vanja and Sebastian; Vanja didn't answer so he had left a message, but he had spoken to Sebastian and more or less ordered him to come in. They were back in Stockholm, and if he regarded himself as a part of Riksmord, he needed to get his arse in gear. So now four of the six chairs around the oval table were occupied by Torkel, Ursula, Jennifer and Sebastian; they were looking at the whiteboard, where Billy had put the picture of Jan Bakker drinking from the waterfall, with an enlargement of the cabin in the background. He pointed at the slightly out-of-focus image as Sebastian reached for a bottle of mineral water.

'This is the building you can see in the background here,' he said. 'Just so you know where we are . . .'

He moved over to the map.

'This is where the picture was taken,' he said, indicating a spot about ten centimetres from the cross marking the grave. 'The bodies were found here, which means the cabin was about here,' he went on, pointing to a location only a centimetre from the grave.

The door opened and Billy broke off as Vanja walked in. Torkel's first thought was how tired she looked.

'Good to see you,' he said, sounding pleased and surprised.

Vanja nodded in response, pulled out a chair and flopped down.

'I left you a message,' Torkel said as she shrugged off her jacket. Was it his imagination, or had she lost weight?

'I know, that's why I'm here.'

'How's it all going?' Vanja didn't reply immediately. She looked over at Sebastian, who nodded encouragingly.

'I didn't get onto the FBI programme,' she stated in a voice devoid of emotion.

'What? Why not? What happened?'

Torkel seemed completely taken aback; clearly nobody had bothered to inform him, Sebastian thought.

'Håkan Persson Riddarstolpe happened,' Vanja said with shrug. 'He said I wasn't suitable.'

There was silence around the table, the kind of silence that arose when everyone knew they ought to say something reassuring and sympathetic, but nobody had a clue what that might be.

Torkel was finding it difficult to make sense of what she had said. Håkan Persson Riddarstolpe was a very competent individual. He might not be among the very best, but Torkel had never heard of him making a mistake like this. Not since that business in Sala all those years ago at any rate. What had happened? Nobody was more suitable than Vanja. This had to be sorted out before it was too late.

'Is there anything I can do?' he said, breaking the silence.

Vanja shook her head.

'There's no appeal.'

'He's an idiot, I've always said so,' Sebastian chipped in.

'It's obviously a mistake; I'll find out what's going on,' Torkel said.

Vanja gave him a faint, grateful smile. Sebastian wondered how much influence Torkel had; would his costly visit to Riddarstolpe be in vain? Jennifer slowly raised her hand.

'This might not be the right time, but if I'm supposed to be filling in for Vanja—'

'We'll consider your position later,' Torkel interrupted her.

'You might as well stay,' Vanja said. 'I'm going to need quite a bit of time off. My father's been charged . . .'

She saw Ursula, Billy and Jennifer give a start; they knew nothing about Valdemar's arrest.

'I want to look in detail at the preliminary investigation, so I'm going to be a bit . . . distracted.'

Sebastian took a swig of his mineral water. This was news to him, and it wasn't good. Vanja was intending to help Valdemar. Sebastian had to bring her back to him, make her think of her father as a criminal, someone who had let her down. He hadn't wanted to push himself forward after his successes with the FBI and Ellinor; he had assumed she would be in touch if she needed him, but it was obviously time to step things up again.

'Have you been to visit him again?' he asked in what he hoped was a neutral tone of voice.

Vanja shook her head.

That was something, at least.

'We can talk about that later,' Torkel said, bringing them back to the matter in hand. 'We have some new information about our family on the mountain.'

Billy took over once more. 'As I said, there was a cabin here in 2003, an old hunting lodge from the 1930s. It burnt down in January 2004.'

He went back to his seat and glanced at his laptop.

'It was privately owned until 1969, when it was donated to the armed forces. From 1970 it was available to rent by anyone who was employed by the forces, or who had a family member in the forces.'

Everyone was interested; this was good. This would give them what they really needed, something to work on. A name.

'Do we know who rented the place during that week in 2003?' Vanja wanted to know, drawn into the course of events, the tension, the chase, in spite of herself.

'First of all we had to find the right administrator, then we had to get her to dig out records from ten years ago—'

'We know you've been working hard,' Torkel said impatiently. 'Give us a name.'

'Adam Cederkvist rented the house in week forty-four in 2003,' Jennifer said. 'He had his family with him.'

'Lena, Ella and Simon Cederkvist,' Billy supplied.

The air seemed to go out of everyone in the room as a sense of anticlimax took over.

'But it can't be the Cederkvists in the grave.' Vanja said what they were all thinking. 'They set off on a round the world sailing trip in November. They sent postcards from Zanzibar in February.'

Ursula leafed through her notes, even though she knew exactly what she would find.

'Adam's brother Charles Cederkvist's DNA didn't match either the male or the children in the grave.'

'Oh, come on – it has to be them!'

Once again someone put into words what they were all thinking; this time it was Sebastian. He got up and started pacing around the room.

'Adam and his family rent a cabin in the same week that a family is murdered a hundred metres away; the place burns down a few months later, then Adam and his family vanish without a trace off the coast of Africa. Can't you hear what it sounds like?'

He stopped. Of course they could. Life was full of coincidences, they knew that, but this was too much.

'Did Adam work for the armed forces?' Vanja asked.

'No, but his brother did,' Jennifer replied. 'Still does – the military intelligence and security service. He lives in Oskarshamn.'

'So what did Adam do?' Torkel wanted to know.

'He was a colleague, in a way. Säpo.'

Military intelligence and the security police. The chances of the whole thing being a coincidence suddenly seemed even more remote.

'Let's say it is Adam Cederkvist – how do we prove it?' Billy wondered.

'The wife's relatives,' Vanja suggested.

'That will take a few days,' Ursula said.

Torkel made up his mind. 'Do it. There are too many question marks. Billy and Jennifer, find someone who saw the family after that week in the autumn of 2003 – colleagues, neighbours, anyone.' He turned to Vanja. 'Check with the school and nursery, find out if the kids came back at all after the autumn half-term holiday.'

Vanja nodded. She had been getting a little tired of these situations, the hours spent in various conference rooms, the whiteboards and theories, but when something like this happened, when they got a breakthrough, when the search turned into the chase, she had to admit the feeling was hard to beat.

'Ursula, contact the National Forensics Lab and ask them to double-check the results of Charles Cederkvist's DNA sample,' Torkel rounded off the barrage of orders. 'I'll speak to the police in Oskarshamn.'

'What shall I do?' Sebastian said.

'Nothing at the moment, but if the bodies in the grave are the Cederkvist family, I'd really like you to have a chat with the brother.'

★ ★ ★

Torkel went to his office and picked up the phone. He found the number for the Oskarshamn station on the computer and made

345

the call. The switchboard put him through to the officer who knew who had gone to collect the DNA sample; he was out, but could be reached on his mobile. Torkel rang the new number and waited. When 'Jörgen' answered, Torkel explained who he was and why he was calling. Apparently Jörgen had gone to see Charles Cederkvist at the end of the previous week as instructed; he had been invited in, and Charles had offered him coffee. Ursula came into the office at that point; Torkel waved her to a chair and switched to speaker-phone. This was her area, after all.

'And you took the DNA sample?' Torkel asked, even though the answer ought to be self-evident. That was the only thing Jörgen had been asked to do.

'Yes. Well, he took it himself.'

Torkel glanced over at Ursula, who was looking less than impressed.

'But you saw him do it?'

'Not as such – he went into another room to do it.'

Torkel felt a creeping weariness in his bones. He had an idea of what had happened, but he had to make sure.

'And where were you?'

'I was in the kitchen, drinking my coffee.'

Ursula sighed audibly and sank back into her chair; yet more evidence to support her theory that the level of competence among her fellow police officers fell on a rapidly diminishing scale the further you got from Kungsholmen. Obviously Oskarshamn was far enough away to approach the Keystone Kops model.

'Was anyone else in the house while you were there?'

'His partner, but she was asleep. She works nights.'

'I don't suppose he could have gone into the bedroom to take the swab?'

'Well, yes, he could – I don't know where he went.'

'I don't suppose he could have taken a sample of his partner's saliva instead of his own?'

Silence. Torkel thanked his colleague for the information, and ended the call.

'Wouldn't the lab check whether the sample came from a man or a woman?' he asked Ursula as he dialled another number.

'Not if we only ask them to compare it with another sample,' she said with a shrug, as if to apologise on their behalf.

'But the sample was labelled with Charles Cederkvist's name,' Torkel persisted. 'Shouldn't they have reacted to that?'

'There's no guarantee the technicians even saw the name. They were looking for evidence of a relationship.'

Torkel got through to Oskarshamn again, and asked to be put through to the officer he had just spoken to; he wanted them to bring in Charles Cederkvist.

While he was waiting, he met Ursula's gaze, but said nothing.

He didn't like this.

If it was Adam Cederkvist they had found, then someone had put a considerable amount of effort into authenticating the story of the round the world sailing trip. They also had a man who worked for the military intelligence service faking his own DNA sample, and a dead woman with two false identities who, in all probability, had carried out the highly professional execution of four people, one of whom worked for the Swedish security police.

This was too big.

Bigger than a mass murder.

Torkel didn't like it at all.

After Charles had given the man from the TV programme directions and put down the phone, he remained standing in his living room for a while. They were coming at him from all sides now, surrounding him, trying to corner him. He needed to take care of it, just as he had taken care of everything else. He had to keep going, rationally and methodically. For a moment he had allowed himself the luxury of thinking about his brother, about the children, but emotions got in the way. They slowed you down, made you stand still, made you vulnerable. Action was the only answer. He would close every door they opened for as long as he could. This wasn't about him, it was a matter of national security. Charles quickly packed a few essentials and went out to the car. Looked back at his house for what he presumed was the last time. He had been happy there. It had been a good house. A good life. It was a shame he would never get it back. Should he write a letter to Marianne? She would never understand. It would be better to call her. Later, when he had come up with a way to explain, to calm her down. She would be devastated.

He realised he had come back to emotions again. That was no good. They would destroy him. Nine years ago he had let them take over, and Patricia Wellton had died. This time he had to be proactive. He got in the car and drove off. He turned onto the main road, and after a short distance he saw a police car coming towards him. He slowed down, keeping well within the speed limit. The two cars passed, and in his rear-view mirror he saw the police car slow down and indicate right. He couldn't be sure, of course, but he had a feeling they were heading for his house. He had been right. He wouldn't be coming back. Not ever.

Vanja said thank you and put down the phone. She had been speaking to the headteacher at the Vallhamra school in Märsta; the woman had been in the post for only five and a half years, but she had fetched one of the lower-school teachers who had worked there for over fifteen years, and who remembered Ella and Simon Cederkvist very well. Everyone had been terribly upset when they died.

Vanja went along to Torkel's impersonal but functional office; Ursula was already occupying the visitors' sofa.

'Charles Cederkvist wasn't at home,' Torkel said before Vanja had the chance to say anything.

'At work?'

'Not according to his boss.'

'Are we putting out a call for him?'

'I don't know,' Torkel said hesitantly. 'We haven't got much to go on.'

'And I'm afraid I can't really help.'

Vanja perched on the arm of a chair.

'The children didn't return to school after the autumn half-term break, but they weren't supposed to.'

'Why not?' Ursula asked.

'Because of the round the world trip. They attended school up to the holiday, then they were going to be educated at home. Their mother was a teacher.'

'But nobody saw them after half term?' Torkel wanted confirmation.

'No, but as I said, that doesn't really mean anything.'

'Thanks. Let's hope Billy and Jennifer have more luck.'

Vanja nodded and got to her feet.

'Any idea where Sebastian went?'

'Down to the canteen, I think,' Ursula replied.

Vanja was about to leave the room when Torkel stopped her.

'Vanja . . .'

She turned around.

'I'm going to have a word with Harriet about this FBI business, and I'll go higher if necessary.'

'Thanks, but I don't think it will make any difference.'

Torkel watched her walk away, a troubled look on his face. Ursula stretched.

'Look on the bright side. You get to keep her.'

'That's not what she wants.'

'We don't always get what we want,' Ursula said laconically. Torkel nodded in agreement. As far as Ursula was concerned, he was painfully aware of that fact.

Mehran got off the green line in Vällingby. According to Melika, Joseph lived in an apartment on Härjedalsvägen. Or at least he used to; she didn't know if he was still there. She didn't want to know, she insisted. Mehran glanced at the GPS on his mobile and set off. He was in no hurry; he didn't even know what he would do if Joseph answered the door. Everything Melika had told him was spinning around in his head; he almost felt dizzy. It had been parts of a story, fragments of events from long ago that raised more questions than they answered. The main thing was that she was frightened. Terrified. He believed her; he had never seen that kind of fear before. It was as if it had been dammed up inside her, and came gushing out when she decided to open up to him. It made her story credible, even though Mehran couldn't get his head around the whole picture.

Said and Melika's cousins had borrowed money to set up the shop. They borrowed from family and friends, but were barely making ends meet, so the cousins wanted to sell – particularly as more and more of the lenders started asking for their money back. They even had prospective buyers – two brothers. Said was sure the shop would start doing well before too long, and wanted to hold on to it. However, he didn't have the money to buy out the other two. They had argued all the time, and it had taken its toll. Melika had been caught in the middle. She had to be loyal to her cousins, but at the same time she loved her husband, even if she sometimes thought he was naive.

The problems really started when Rafi, the younger cousin who always spent more than he earned, borrowed from a man called Joseph. In fact his real name was Mohammed Al something – Melika couldn't quite remember, but everyone knew him as Joseph. Nobody was happy when Rafi got involved with Joseph; there were plenty of rumours about him, about how he made his money.

It was said that he knew people. Not just good people. That it was dangerous to cross him.

To begin with he had been very nice and helpful, particularly towards Rafi, but soon he started turning up at the shop with increasing frequency. He had an opinion about everything, acted as if he owned the place. It drove Said crazy. Rafi tried to mediate, so did Turyalai, but it didn't do any good; Said continued to accuse Joseph of meddling in matters that were not his concern.

Joseph insisted that the loan to Rafi meant he was now joint owner.

Said insisted that the loan to Rafi had nothing to do with the shop.

Joseph said the shop was his security; he was simply looking after his investment.

The arguments continued. Eventually the cousins had intervened and asked Joseph to stop coming round. They promised to repay the loan, and Joseph agreed. He drew up an instalment plan, with interest that would become interest on the interest if the payments were late; he described in graphic detail what would happen if he didn't get his money. Rafi and Turyalai started stealing from the till in order to be able to pay him, and after a while Said caught them.

It had been terrible, Melika said. Said had accused her entire family. They had told him about Joseph, how afraid of him they were. Said was furious; he would show Joseph! Anyone who stole from the shop stole from Said, and no one stole from Said! No one!

He and Hamid had gone to Vällingby. They never revealed how they did it, but they came back with the money. They had allowed Joseph to keep the amount he had originally lent, but they had taken back the rest. They boasted about how scared Joseph had been. Said was the hero; he was unstoppable. He and the cousins became friends once more. They apologised, and he accepted their apology. They all promised to stick together from now on – no more arguments. Everything was going to be fine.

But it wasn't fine.

Melika had started to weep as she went on with her story.

A month later, Said and Hamid vanished without a trace. Shibeka had been the first to worry when they didn't come home. She had called everyone she could think of; Hamid wasn't the kind of person to disappear. They had searched everywhere, spoken to all their friends. But Said and Hamid were gone.

No one knew anything.

Rafi got the idea that Joseph was involved. He plucked up his courage and tried to get hold of him, but Joseph was in Egypt.

A few weeks later, Joseph had come into the shop. He had stood there and demanded his money back, now they could no longer hide behind Said.

Rafi persuaded his brother to sell up. They repaid Joseph, gave Said's share to Melika. They couldn't prove anything, but they always suspected that Joseph was somehow involved in Said's disappearance. Rafi was the one who felt most guilty. He had borrowed from Joseph, he had stolen money from the till. If he hadn't done that, perhaps Said would still be here. It almost killed him. He didn't want to see Melika any more, or his brother. He moved to Malmö, and soon after Turyalai followed him. Melika hadn't seen either of them since.

Mehran couldn't understand why no one had said anything. How could they just leave it, without finding out the truth? Said was her husband. The father of her children. And Hamid was his father.

It had been difficult to explain, but also very simple.

They were all scared. They didn't know anything for sure. They started off by keeping quiet, and it was easier just to carry on.

That was how her life had been since Said went missing. First of all she had been frightened of Joseph. Frightened that Shibeka and the others would find out about the loan.

She had been frightened all the time.

At first Mehran had expected to hate her, but he couldn't. He and Shibeka might have lived with uncertainty, but at least they hadn't lived with fear. He actually felt sorry for Melika.

However, Mehran had forced her to give him the address. He wasn't afraid. He needed to understand, for Shibeka's sake, but he hadn't said anything to her; she would never have let him go. She would only worry, so he had pretended to go off to school as usual.

He had reached Härjedalsgatan. It didn't look much; red apartment blocks, not as tall as the ones in Rinkeby. He counted three storeys. Older, but in better condition. There was a large patch of grass in front of the L-shaped building. Number 44 was in the long part of the L. He looked around, glanced down at the scrap of paper Melika had given him. Number 44, that was right. An elderly couple was walking along the pavement a short distance away, otherwise the place was deserted. He set off.

He just needed to know if Joseph was there, that was all. He wasn't going to do anything else. He would tell him he was Hamid's son, see how he reacted. If he was still there, of course. It was an old address.

Slowly, Mehran approached the door. This wasn't as easy as he had thought; the closer he got, the heavier his footsteps became. After a while he had to force himself to keep going. He could feel the sweat trickling down his back, even though it was a chilly day. However, he couldn't come all this way without trying. He would be careful, he promised himself. But he would also act like a man. He was Hamid's son. One day long ago his father had walked through this same door and met Joseph. Now it was his turn.

No entry code was required for the main door, and he stepped into the dark entrance hall. Didn't bother switching on the light. He looked at the list of residents; there was someone called M. Al Baasim, which was the only thing that even came close to the name Melika half-remembered. Silently he climbed the stairs to the first floor. Stood outside the door. He tried to picture his father; Hamid had stood here with his friend Said. He had rung the bell, forced the man inside to return the money Rafi had stolen from the shop. Mehran wondered what had happened; had Hamid been the strong one, or had he just gone along to support Said? Mehran decided that Hamid had been the hero.

Just like him. He was walking in his father's footsteps now.

A stocky, unshaven man opened the door.

'What do you want?'

Mehran didn't recognise the voice. He was unsure about a lot of things as far as Joseph was concerned, but he would recognise that rasping voice anywhere. He was absolutely sure of that; the man in front of him was not Joseph.

'I'm looking for Joseph,' he said, sounding as confident as he could.

The man stared at him. Mehran wasn't sure what that look meant.

'Joseph? He doesn't live here any more. He moved away a long time ago. Who wants to know?'

'My name is Mehran, Mehran Khan. I'm Hamid's son.'

'I don't know any Hamid.'

'But Joseph did. Can you tell me where he is?'

The man laughed, showing an array of yellow, uneven teeth.

'No, but if you see him, tell him he owes me money. He hadn't paid the water or electricity bills when I took over the apartment.'

Mehran didn't have time to answer before the door closed in his face. He stood there for a moment, then went back down the stairs. He didn't really know what to do now.

Inside the apartment the man with the yellow teeth was peering through the spyhole in the door, watching as the boy disappeared.

From the living room came a voice speaking Arabic. It sounded more like a croak than anything else.

'Who was that?'

'Problems, I think,' the man replied.

Vanja emerged from the lift on the ground floor, walked along the corridor to the left and went into the staff canteen through the open glass doors. On the right was the self-service section: four large gondolas with a selection of dishes for lunch. Meat, fish, vegetarian and salads. Two queues snaked past the tills and out into the main dining area, where drinks, bread and condiments were available from a long counter. There were some forty tables covered in white wax cloths, with a vase containing sprigs of lingon on each. The largest had room for sixteen people, the smallest for four. Lots of people, long queues, the constant hum of conversation, the clatter of cutlery on china.

Vanja stopped dead when she saw who had just paid and was making his way between the tables. Håkan Persson Riddarstolpe. She stared at him, wondered whether to catch him up, ask what had happened, what she had done wrong. She would have to find out some time; she wouldn't be able to put this behind her if those questions remained unanswered. But was this the right time, the right place? Why not, she thought, setting off after him.

Then she noticed Sebastian, sitting at a table by the window. Riddarstolpe was about to walk past him. Sebastian looked up at his former colleague. Vanja slowed down; she wanted to see whether Sebastian was going to speak to him. It would suit her very well if Sebastian had a go at Riddarstolpe in front of a packed canteen, told him he was an incompetent fool. Nearly there. If Sebastian was going to do something, it had to be now. And he did do something, but definitely not what Vanja had expected.

Sebastian closed his eyes for a second and nodded.

A nod.

Vanja couldn't believe what she had seen.

A nod – and it wasn't a greeting, it was more like an acknowledgement, a mutual agreement.

Crazy.

She was going crazy.

Sebastian didn't like Riddarstolpe. He hated him. Maybe he didn't want to make a scene, but a nod? Had it been a polite, reserved nod? With a hint of disdain, perhaps? Had she misinterpreted it? No, she knew what she had seen. It was a satisfied nod, eyes closed, the kind of nod you give to thank someone who has done you a favour.

But that was ridiculous.

What could Riddarstolpe possibly have done for Sebastian? Nothing. In fact Sebastian ought to dislike him even more after recent events. Ignore him. Glare at him. Treat him with arrogant contempt.

Anything but that nod.

The idea came from nowhere. Took her breath away. It was impossible. There was absolutely no reason to suspect such a thing. She really had lost her mind.

But recent events . . .

Nothing good. Valdemar, Trolle, Ellinor, the FBI. One common denominator.

Sebastian Bergman.

But why? What possible reason could there be? Now? None at all. It was insane, but the thought had taken root. The explanation as to why Trolle had handed the material over to Sebastian hadn't been completely convincing, and now that conspiratorial nod. Vanja backed out of the canteen. When she got in the lift, she pressed the button for the sixth floor.

★ ★ ★

She looked around; the whole floor seemed to be deserted, probably because it was lunchtime. She set off along the corridor. The first offices were empty. She heard the main door open, and turned around. A woman with short dark hair and brown eyes came in, carrying her lunch in a plastic bag.

'Can I help you?' she said as she went into the little kitchen next to the door. Vanja joined her.

'I'm not sure . . . My name is Vanja Lithner, and I'm with Riksmord. This might sound a bit weird, but I have a colleague called Sebastian—'

'Bergman?' the woman said, turning around with a smile.

'That's right – do you know him?'

'I do.'

The brief response and the accompanying smile told Vanja that she knew Sebastian in the biblical sense of the word. They had slept together, Vanja was sure of it. She couldn't suppress a sigh.

'He was here last Thursday,' the woman said, placing her meal in one of the two microwaves on the worktop. Vanja stiffened. She had come here to confirm how insane it was to imagine that Sebastian was involved in everything that had happened to her, to push those thoughts aside once and for all.

'Here?'

'Yes, he came to see Håkan,' the woman said as she closed the door and set the timer for one minute forty-five seconds.

Chaos. There was no other word to describe what was going on inside Vanja's head. Her mobile rang. She looked at the display. Anna. She couldn't cope with that right now. She rejected the call. The dark-haired woman was leaning against the worktop, looking at Vanja as if she was expecting their conversation to continue, but Vanja was in a world of her own. She didn't even know where to start. For some unknown reason she kept coming back to Sebastian's apartment. Dinner. The overnight stay. The evening when he gained her trust. Not because he wanted to sleep with her, he had said. So, why? Her phone rang: Anna again. This time she answered.

'I'm busy,' she snapped. 'Is it important?'

It was.

Lennart had gone straight to Swedish Television and taken out one of the production department's cars. He decided it was a good idea to use an official vehicle; it would serve as a business card for the man he was going to meet. He hadn't told anyone where he was going; he wanted to follow this lead first. If it was any use, he would tell Linda and possibly Sture when he got back; if not, he didn't need to say anything, and could avoid the humiliation of getting it wrong. What worried him most was that he still had too much alcohol in his bloodstream. It took something like twelve hours to leave the body, and he had had his last drink at half three, four in the morning. He was in the risk zone, but he would just have to drive with extra care. He had got away with it before.

It took a little while to escape from the city; Valhallavägen was busy with lorries from the Freeport, but once he got out into Essingeleden the traffic was flowing well. Charles Cederkvist called and suggested they should meet north of Söderköping instead; he was out on business. That suited Lennart very well; it was a shorter journey. He reprogrammed the sat nav: just over two hours. He felt as if fate was smiling on him. He had a lead to follow up, the traffic on the E4 wasn't too bad, and on the radio there was a fascinating programme about the repercussions of the Fukushima disaster. Lennart had always been interested in the issue of nuclear power, and he still proudly remembered one of his best reports, which was about inadequate safety procedures at the Forsmark nuclear power station. He had been nominated for an award; it had been a good story. Once upon a time he really had been capable of finding pure gold.

The sat nav beeped and interrupted his train of thought. Apparently he was supposed to turn off. Was he already there? Lennart pulled over and stopped. He looked more closely at the sat nav; it seemed the address Charles had given him was much further off the motorway than he had first thought. It was very close to the water at Bråviken.

He set off again, and took the next exit onto a minor road. He was in a good mood. This was the kind of road he loved, narrow and twisting; it required a certain amount of effort from the driver. That was probably one of the most boring aspects of living in Stockholm: there were no roads like this.

He was concentrating so hard on his driving that he didn't notice the black car that pulled out from a dirt track and settled in at a safe distance behind him.

The urology unit, Karolinska Hospital.

That was where they had taken her husband. The custody officer had called in the morning to tell her that Valdemar had been suffering such severe back pain that he had briefly lost consciousness when he tried to get up from his bunk. He had been taken to A & E, where the doctor had quickly referred him to urology. An hour ago Anna had arrived in A2. Valdemar was being examined, so she sat down to wait and called her daughter.

Vanja was here now. They had hugged when she arrived; Anna's first thought was that Vanja had a hunted look. Hunted and exhausted, as if she was keeping herself upright through sheer willpower.

Vanja asked if she knew what had happened; Anna had no idea.

They had sat down on one of the pale blue sofas in the relatives' room. Anna wondered whether to ask Vanja how long she had been back, and why she hadn't been in touch when she heard that Valdemar had been arrested, but decided against it. No good could come of it. The fact that Vanja and Valdemar had a special relationship was no secret; they were much closer than she and Anna had ever been, or ever would be. That was just the way things were. If she started asking questions, Vanja would say that the telephone worked both ways. Which was true. Anna hadn't called Vanja either.

'Did you know?' Vanja said suddenly.

'No.' Which was true, whatever Vanja was referring to.

'How is that possible?'

Anna turned to look at her daughter, who was staring straight ahead.

'You mean did I know he was ill?'

'No.'

'You're over thirty years old. You knew what kind of life we lived. Did you know?'

'No.'

Vanja met her gaze. There was desolation in her eyes; could such a depth of unhappiness really have come only from what had happened to her father?

'I'm sorry,' Vanja said, placing her hand on top of Anna's. Somewhat surprised, Anna patted it reassuringly.

A doctor came into the waiting room and they both got to their feet. He introduced himself as Omid Shahab, and suggested they should come along to his office for a chat. That wasn't a good sign, Anna thought.

'Do you mind going on your own? I'd rather wait here for Valdemar.'

Vanja shook her head. Anna watched her daughter walk away with the doctor. It might seem odd, staying in the relatives' room, but she just couldn't cope with hearing bad news about her husband. She'd had enough. No more.

★ ★ ★

Vanja sat down in Omid's office, and he rolled his chair close to hers. Not a good sign, she thought. A private room, close proximity and a grave, sympathetic expression. This was serious.

'We've carried out an ultrasound scan,' the doctor began.

'And?'

'We sent him straight up for a CT scan, just to make sure, but all the indications are that Valdemar has renal cancer.'

Not this. Not again, Vanja thought. He'd been given the all clear not long ago. Hadn't they suffered enough?

'He had lung cancer a little while ago,' she informed the doctor.

'Yes, we're aware of that. It seems likely that the cancer cells have metastasized and taken hold in the kidneys.'

'OK, so what happens now?'

'We need to find out what stage cancer we're looking at,' Omid explained, making sure she understood everything he was saying. 'We can operate, and in the best-case scenario it won't have spread beyond the kidneys.'

Vanja didn't need to ask about the worst-case scenario. The key word was 'spread'. Her father's body could be riddled with cancer; if so, he wouldn't be able to cope with that. Neither would she. But there was another word that bothered her: kidneys. Plural.

'Are both kidneys affected?' she asked, even though she thought she knew the answer. Omid's nod confirmed her fears.

'That's what the scan indicates, which means we can't operate until we have a donor.'

'I'll donate,' Vanja said immediately.

'I understand that's your first instinct, but this is a serious procedure for both the donor and the recipient,' Omid said, shaking his head. 'You need to think it over.'

'No, I don't. I want to donate a kidney.'

Omid looked at the young woman sitting in front of him. He had a feeling it wouldn't matter what he said; she had already made up her mind.

'I'll make you an appointment with the donor team,' he said after a moment.

'Lennart Stridh killed in car smash.'

The headline filled the screen of his iPad. It was big news. One of Sweden's best known investigative journalists had driven off the road into the bay at Bråviken, hit his head on the windscreen and drowned. 'Seatbelt could have saved him' read the caption under a picture of the car being lifted out of the water, the Swedish Television logo clearly visible on the side. That wasn't true. From the moment Lennart decided to call Charles Cederkvist, nothing could have saved him.

Charles quickly checked out the other evening paper. Same headline, but with the additional snippet that the police hadn't ruled out drink driving. Excellent. He carried on looking through online reports; there was no suggestion that foul play was suspected.

One door slammed shut, or at least partly closed. Had Lennart told anyone where he was going, who he was due to meet? If not, would they wonder what he was doing at Bråviken? Then there was Lennart's mobile. He had rung Charles; if someone decided to trace his final hours and found the call, they would see a name that already featured in another case.

Charles put down his iPad, started the car and drove on towards Stockholm. There were too many ifs and buts. He felt like a man standing next to a huge dam where small fissures were starting to appear. He was covering them as best he could, but there was every indication that the dam would soon burst, and everything would come gushing out. Charles wanted to be far away by then.

His phone rang. He glanced at the display: a name he hadn't seen for a very long time. He briefly considered letting it ring, but he needed all the information he could get in order to stay one step ahead for as long as possible.

'What do you want?'

'It's Joseph,' said the heavily accented, rasping voice on the other end of the line.

'I know. What do you want?'

'A boy came here. Hamid's son.'

Charles remained silent, which Joseph took to mean that he didn't remember who Hamid was.

'One of the men we gave to the Americans,' he clarified.

Charles could see them in his mind's eye. Lying on the floor, their hands and feet bound. At that point he hadn't known their names; they had already been picked up when he entered the frame. His job was merely to observe – to be the Swedish presence when American agents were operating on Swedish territory, to report back, maybe even to learn something.

'What did he want?'

'He was looking for me.'

Charles closed his eyes for a second. Another breach in the dam. He had to seal it as quickly as possible, before it got any bigger.

'Arrange a meeting, pick him up and call me as soon as you've got him.'

He ended the call before the man with the rasping voice had time to respond. He put his foot down and continued his journey north. Two things to do now: get hold of another car, and make sure he didn't have to fix this on his own.

Epic fail. Total disaster. Everything was in the process of blowing up in front of him. He had thought what he had done was against the rules, possibly illegal, but presumably not dangerous; it had turned out to be anything but.

It was fatal.

There was no other way of interpreting the front page of *Aftonbladet's* online edition. A journalist had died. Lennart Stridh.

The article said it was an accident, but Anitha's ashen face said something different. When she stammered that less than twenty-four hours ago she had given Stridh the name Morgan had found in the computer system, he understood. It was impossible to see the whole picture, it was too complicated, but there were too many coincidences. He couldn't explain it away as a mere quirk of fate, however hard he tried.

It was all connected.

He had to lean on Anitha's desk for support. He had blood on his hands. A man had probably been murdered because of information he had helped to track down.

All he had wanted was for Anitha to spend time with him. His intentions had been good. He had been looking for love, someone to share his everyday life with. Nothing else.

This was where it had led. To computer hacking and death.

He had known that what he was doing was wrong, but it was just a name. Nothing more.

Then he had exploited what he knew; that was his biggest sin. It had been stupid and unkind. You couldn't force someone to love you. That wasn't how it worked. But he had hoped that if Anitha spent some time with him, she would change her mind, see the positive aspects of his character. Perhaps she might even learn to like him, just a little bit; that would have been enough for him.

Now he was being punished. It might seem entirely dispropor-
tionate, but it was the only possible interpretation.

We reap what we sow.

With interest.

He had to make this right, even if it meant she would never speak to
him again. She had said it would be a disaster for both of them if anyone
found out what they had done. No doubt she was right, but he couldn't
keep quiet. Mistakes didn't go away just because you buried them and
moved on, particularly if someone had died. That was where he drew
the line. If he was a good person, it was time for him to prove it.

Tell the truth.

But who to?

Morgan had no idea. Firstly, the knowledge he had was clearly
dangerous, and secondly, there was the risk that no one would
believe him. He didn't even know where to start.

He ought to speak to someone who knew him, someone who
knew he wouldn't exaggerate or make things up – someone who
could pass on the information without dragging his name into it. A
police officer.

In spite of the fact that he had worked at Police HQ for such a
long time, he didn't know very many officers. His colleagues were
mainly civilian employees, and they wouldn't be able to help him.
The only person he could think of was a guy with Riksmord who
shared his interest in computers. They used to chat about hard
drives and networks occasionally, and he was always very pleasant.
Seemed conscientious. And surely Riksmord would be able to keep
the name of an informant quiet? Perhaps he could ask him what to
do. Billy Rosén would know.

He didn't tell Anitha what he was planning to do; there was no
point. Morgan realised this was the end of their relationship, or
whatever he should call the situation into which he had forced her,
but there was nothing he could do about that. The important thing
now was to save himself.

Riksmord was on the third floor.

The taste in his mouth was back, but this time it wasn't love; it
was fear.

He asked to speak to Billy in private.

★ ★ ★

367

Jennifer was sitting in the back of a car that had just left the car park beneath Police HQ at Kungsholmen and turned left; it struck her how fast things happened sometimes.

Just over half an hour ago, Billy had had a visit from a bearded, overweight man in an extremely unbecoming pale beige jacket. Billy had introduced him as Morgan Hansson, a colleague from the IT department. Morgan had barely managed to say hello before asking to speak to Billy in private.

Five minutes later she saw Billy running to Torkel's office, and shortly after that they were all gathered in the Room. Everyone except Vanja. No one knew where she was; she wasn't answering her mobile, but at the moment Sebastian seemed to be the only one who was concerned. The others were completely focused on Billy, who was writing on the whiteboard while explaining that Morgan had done a colleague a favour, searched through the backup tapes and found a name that had been removed from a report. He had passed this name on to his colleague, who in turn had passed it on to Lennart Stridh from *Investigation Today*.

'He's dead, did you know that?' Jennifer had said, slightly unsure of where this was going and whether or not they were up to date. 'He died in a car accident just a few hours ago.'

Everyone nodded. They knew. Billy went on:

'The report was about two men who went missing after they were refused asylum in the autumn of 2003: Hamid Khan and Said Balkhi. The Solna police were ordered to stop looking for them. Säpo took over the case, and the officer responsible was Adam Cederkvist.'

Silence. What they had just heard seemed so impossible that Ursula felt compelled to ask: 'Do you mean *our* Adam Cederkvist?'

Billy nodded.

'But how does that fit in with the family being murdered up in Jämtland?' Jennifer wondered.

'I've no idea, but Lennart Stridh was given the name yesterday, and today he's dead.'

'Why was *Investigation Today* interested?' Torkel asked.

'Morgan didn't know.'

'Who's the colleague he was helping?'

Less than five minutes later Anitha Lund was sitting in front of them, indignantly protesting that she knew her rights, and that she had absolutely no intention of saying anything. One minute and one quiet conversation with Torkel later, she changed her mind.

All she knew was that Hamid Khan's wife Shibeka had contacted Lennart. Anitha had been curious when she saw that the reference to the contact at Säpo had been removed from the original report.

'When was the name removed?'

She gave them the date – only a few days after the bodies had been found in the mountain grave. She also gave them the piece of paper Lennart had given her, and Shibeka Kahn's address, and now Billy was driving onto the roundabout at the end of Rålambshovsleden.

They would be in Rinkeby in less than fifteen minutes.

Mehran had got off at Fridhemsplan to change trains. He didn't feel like going straight home, so instead he went to the Västermalm shopping mall right next to the underground station. He wandered aimlessly around looking in the shop windows. He knew he really ought to go home and tell Shibeka what had happened, but he wanted to find out more before he did that. His mother needed to know the truth so that she could stop going round in circles, obsessing about Hamid's disappearance.

She needed a conclusion. A proper conclusion.

So did he. He went back out onto Fleminggatan; it was very crowded. He stood in the middle of all those people, hurrying about their business. Looked over at the tall yellow building on the hill a short distance away. Down at the bottom of the hill was the passageway where Said's shop had been. If only he had gone there in the first place, he would have found out about all this a long time ago. But he knew why he hadn't done it; there were places where he'd been with his father that he had chosen not to revisit. The shop was one of those places. So was the football pitch halfway to Tensta where Hamid had taught him to ride a bike. The play area outside Melika's apartment block.

He had always thought they would remind him too much of his father. He didn't want to feel that sense of loss; he wanted to lock it away, leave it alone. At least that was what Mehran had believed, but in fact it wasn't true. He needed the places, the memories. They didn't hurt; they could tell him things.

Because it turned out that some of his memories were inaccurate. People he had thought were friends were actually anything but. The shop where he had been given sweets had led to all this darkness. Melika wasn't always angry, she was just frightened.

But one thing was still the same.

He missed his father, both as a child and now as an adult. There was no doubt about that.

Life was very strange. Everyone he knew wanted to get so much out of it: possessions, success, respect. He was the same, but what he really wanted was a context. Things he could understand. Memories that didn't change. Friends he could trust. Parents who were still around. It sounded so simple, but he was coming to understand more and more that those things were hard to find.

His mobile rang, interrupting his train of thought.

He didn't recognise the number on the display, but he did recognise the voice.

'Mehran?' it rasped.

It took him a second to answer. Two. Maybe three.

'Yes.'

The man didn't wait; his voice was in Mehran's ear, demanding a response.

'It's Joseph. I heard you were looking for me.'

Mehran didn't say anything. He stood there watching the cars go by. The voice sounded so sure of itself that he glanced around to see if Joseph was standing somewhere nearby. There was no sign of him, but that didn't necessarily mean anything.

'I haven't seen you for a long time, Mehran. How have you been?'

'How did you get my number?'

'It was easy. I know a lot of people who can help me with all kinds of things.'

The threat wasn't even veiled. He wanted to show Mehran who could find whom. Mehran decided to stick up for himself; Joseph didn't scare him.

'I want to see you,' he said as calmly as he could.

'And why is that?'

'I want to speak to you. I think you want to speak to me too.'

The voice at the other end was silent for a moment.

'In that case you can come to me,' it said eventually.

'Fine. Tell me where you are.'

Sebastian followed Jennifer and Billy up the stairs in the apartment block on Stavbygränd. It was almost symbolic: the hungry youngsters rushing ahead, with intellect bringing up the rear. There wasn't really much point in his being here, but it was better to come along than to stay back at HQ worrying about Vanja. Besides, the case seemed to have taken an interesting turn. If Adam Cederkvist had been responsible for the case of the two missing Afghan men, and that had somehow led to him and his family ending up in a mountain grave, then the case was not only intriguing from a conspiracy point of view, it was also unique. Adam's brother Charles had tried to conceal Adam's identity from them, which suggested that he was involved. They might even be looking at fratricide. Very interesting indeed, if it was true. He was hoping to meet Charles in order to study all the repressions, rationalisations and projections he would probably employ.

Jennifer and Billy rang Shibeka Khan's doorbell. Sebastian hung back; the narrow stairwell seemed very crowded. The skinny thirteen-year-old boy who opened the door must have felt the same; he stared at them with huge eyes.

'Hi – we're looking for Shibeka Khan,' Billy said in a friendly tone.

'Police,' Jennifer added quickly, showing her ID. She loved saying that, Sebastian thought. It was obvious that she regarded herself as a police officer above all else. That was presumably why Torkel had chosen her, because her energy and commitment made up for her lack of experience.

'Has something happened?' the boy asked anxiously.

'We need to speak to your mum – is she home?' Sebastian asked, trying to sound less like a cop show. They were talking to a child, for pity's sake!

The boy nodded and went back inside. They heard him calling to someone in a different language. Jennifer turned to Billy.

'I assume they're a Muslim family; it could be that she's only prepared to talk to me.'

'OK.'

A woman of about thirty-five came to the door. She was beautiful, with dark intelligent eyes and well-defined features, stylishly framed by the black shawl covering her hair. Sebastian smiled when he saw her. It just happened. He realised he had never slept with a woman who wore the veil. No doubt it was very difficult to achieve, but then again he'd never tried.

'Shibeka Khan?' Jennifer asked. The woman nodded.

'Yes.'

'We're from the police; may we come in?' Sebastian said politely, moving in front of Jennifer, who looked surprised to say the least. He ignored her.

'Has something happened to Mehran?' Shibeka asked, looking suddenly anxious.

'No. Who's Mehran?'

'My son. My eldest son.'

'Nothing has happened to him; we're here because we believe you've been speaking to Lennart Stridh from *Investigation Today*—' Jennifer began, but Sebastian interrupted her in his warmest, most sympathetic voice.

'I don't know if it's appropriate for me to ask, given that I'm a man . . .' He placed particular emphasis on the word 'man'. 'But this won't take long.'

'It's fine,' Shibeka said, stepping aside to let them in.

The hallway was neat and tidy, and there was a wonderful aroma from the kitchen – saffron and some other spice. Shibeka took her son's hand, still looking worried.

Sebastian gave them both a reassuring smile.

'That's a fine young man you have there.'

Shibeka didn't reply, and before Sebastian could say anything else, Jennifer the police officer took over.

'I believe your husband, Hamid, went missing nine years ago?'

Shibeka nodded.

'Lennart was the only person who would listen to me. You've done nothing.'

Sebastian got there before Jennifer jumped in, probably to say something about Lennart; there was no reason why Shibeka should be told he was dead. Not before they were sure there was a connection.

'Did anyone come to see you after your husband's disappearance?'

Shibeka's reaction told him this was a question she had wanted the police to ask for a long time. A very long time.

'A man came a week or so after Hamid went missing. I've always thought he was from the police, but he never came back.'

'What was his name?'

'He didn't say.'

Sebastian turned to Billy and held out his hand. 'Have you got the picture?'

Billy opened his folder and handed a photograph to Sebastian.

'Is this the man?'

Shibeka stared at the picture. Sebastian knew the answer before she spoke.

Adam Cederkvist had been here.

There was definitely a connection.

After the brief meeting with Anitha Lund, Torkel contacted Britta Hanning at Säpo. They didn't really know one another, although they had met occasionally when their paths crossed. They were the same age, and had had a similar career path within the force, but that was unlikely to make things any easier. Britta Hanning was Säpo, after all and, just as he had expected, he got nowhere with his query about the case of two missing asylum seekers that had landed on their desk nine years ago. Torkel didn't get through until he said they had found one of her former colleagues, a man everyone thought had drowned during a round the world sailing trip, in a mass grave in the mountains.

'How sure are you that it's Adam you've found?'

'We're sure,' Torkel replied firmly, even though they had no forensic proof as yet. 'Didn't you miss him?'

'He was on leave from the autumn half term onwards; he was going to spend a year sailing round the world with the family.'

'Someone made it look as if he'd gone, but he died up in Jämtland in October.'

After a brief silence Britta had said she would get back to him. Ten minutes later she called and asked him to come over.

Now he was sitting in her corner office right at the top of Police HQ, in the section closest to Polhemsgatan – Kronoberg Park on one side, the green roofs of the buildings on Kungsholmsgatan on the other. He had declined the offer of coffee when he arrived, but was waiting for Britta's PA to bring hers before they started. Britta had no interest in small talk in the meantime; she explained apologetically that she had one or two emails to deal with, and focused on her computer. Torkel gazed out at the park. The wind had got up during the morning, and now the leaves from the trees opposite were swirling around seven floors up. There was still warmth in the sun, at least when you were indoors behind glass, but soon it would be nothing more than a source of light for a few short hours each day, a glowing promise of heat in a distant future.

There was a knock on the door and Britta's PA placed a green Höganäs cup of cappuccino on the desk in front of her; she smiled at Torkel on her way out. As the door closed, Britta turned to Torkel.

'Tell me.'

Torkel began with the call from Hedvig Hedman in Östersund, and ended with the events of the past few hours, and the fact that some members of his team were now in Rinkeby. The only thing he left out was the names of those involved in the hacking incident; he had no doubt that Britta would soon track them down now she knew where to look.

'Have you spoken to Charles Cederkvist?'

'We can't get hold of him.'

Britta sighed audibly as she picked up her cup and looked out of the window. Torkel remained silent, giving her time to think. To an outsider it was perhaps obvious that the different departments within the police should help one another, and in most cases that was what happened, but this was Säpo. It would take a lot to be given access to their material, certainly during a spur-of-the-moment visit without pressure from higher up within the organisation. Britta seemed to have reached a decision. She turned back to Torkel and put down her cup.

'OK.'

She pushed a dossier over to him. Just as Torkel was about to pick it up, Britta placed her hand on it. Torkel looked up enquiringly; her expression left no room for negotiation.

'It stays here,' she said, removing her hand. Torkel leaned back in his chair and opened the folder.

He had expected to spend some time reading intensively while Britta finished off her cappuccino, but when he saw the contents he realised this wasn't going to take very long at all. He skimmed through the brief notes, then closed the dossier and regarded Britta with ill-concealed distrust.

'Is this all you've got?'

'Yes.'

'But there's nothing here.'

It was no exaggeration. According to the dossier, Adam Cederkvist had been informed that Hamid Khan and Said Balkhi were suspected of terrorism, or at least of having contact with terrorists, and that it therefore seemed unlikely that they had disappeared because they were threatened with deportation, particularly in view of the fact that Said already had a permanent residence permit. Instead it was assumed that they had travelled overseas in order to carry out terrorist attacks, or to undergo training in preparation for such attacks. A case for Säpo, to put it simply. But apparently Adam Cederkvist hadn't accepted that theory, and had carried on looking. He had even visited the wives of the two men; for some reason he had then become even more convinced that this wasn't a voluntary disappearance – quite the reverse. A final note right at the bottom of the page was the only thing that could be useful, as far as Torkel could see.

'There's a mention of American agents at the end here . . .'

'Yes, I saw that. I checked it out before you arrived; we had no active overseas agents in the country during that period.'

'Officially.'

'We had no active overseas agents in the country during that period,' Britta repeated in a tone that made it very clear to Torkel that this would be a very short conversation unless he played by the rules. Her rules. He understood and moved on.

'Where did the suggestion that the two men were involved in terrorist activity come from?'

'I can't answer that.'

'I don't need a specific name.'

Britta looked him in the eye and said nothing. Torkel sighed to himself. He fully understood the issue of national security, but sometimes the secrecy between departments could be a little ridiculous.

'Let me put it this way. Does the military intelligence and security service sometimes share information received?'

'Sometimes.'

'Is that what happened in this case?'

'I don't know.'

Torkel contemplated the woman sitting opposite him. She looked sincere, but that was irrelevant. She wasn't going to tell him anything. He thought through a possible scenario. Military intelligence had found out that someone was preparing to carry out a terrorist attack on an American target, perhaps in the very near future. Hamid and Said were named. They were picked up and the Americans were allowed to . . . do what? If the two men had been taken out of the country, surely it would have hit the headlines? When it was revealed in 2004 that the CIA had removed two Egyptians from Sweden in 2001, there had been a hell of a row. If it had happened again two years later, it would definitely have come to light. Or had they learned their lesson? Managed to hide it this time? Did American agents take Hamid and Said out of the country?

There was no point in running his theory past Britta; even if she knew, she would never tell him. He tried a different tack; this was his last shot.

'If Adam thought American agents were operating in Sweden, why wasn't this followed up?'

'I wondered the same thing.'

Torkel was struck by the sudden honesty in her voice.

'You don't know?'

'No.'

'So what do you think?'

'I think someone made sure it didn't go any further.'

She pointed at the ceiling. As they were on the top floor, there was no physical presence above her, and it seemed unlikely that God had decided to intervene in a police matter. Therefore, the finger had to mean 'a higher power'.

But that wasn't all.

It also meant they had a big problem.

★ ★ ★

Torkel was on his way back to Riksmord when he decided to go for a walk, clear his head. The autumn afternoon had looked so beautiful from Britta's window, like a commercial with cheerful people in chunky jumpers playfully chasing children and dogs, ending up on the sofa in front of a crackling fire enjoying whatever product was being advertised. For a brief moment he pictured himself and Ursula as those cheerful people, but he quickly dismissed the thought. A stroll, some fresh air would do him good. As soon as he walked out of the main entrance he realised that the weather was much more pleasant through a pane of glass than it was in reality. The wind tore at his clothes as Torkel lowered his head and turned left. He bought a cup of coffee from the café on the corner, then walked back with the wind behind him and sat down on a bench in the park. It was in the shade and it certainly wasn't sheltered; he was freezing in no time, and the hot coffee didn't really help at all. However, having decided to sit outside for a while, he wasn't about to give up so easily.

He concentrated on the case.

So many question marks. He just couldn't make it add up.

If military intelligence had picked up Hamid and Said, why tip off Säpo? Why not just put it down as a disappearance following a refusal to grant asylum, and leave it at that?

Because that kind of disappearance wasn't conclusive. Relatives might be able to convince someone that the individuals in question hadn't vanished of their own free will, and if they shouted loud enough, the police would have to take up the case again. Start searching. Investigating. Someone wanted to avoid that at all costs.

As it was, the case was closed as far as the Solna police were concerned. Nobody was going to feature it on *Crimewatch*, *Most Wanted*, or in the tabloid press. The Säpo stamp was an unbreakable seal, which indirectly implied that the two Muslims had had something to hide. To most people, the fact that Säpo were interested in them meant that they must be guilty of something.

Lennart Stridh, Anitha Lund and Morgan Hansson had broken that seal, and one of them was dead.

Torkel got to his feet, considered a walk, but decided that he'd had enough of the great outdoors. He set off back to the office, still thinking about the case.

Charles Cederkvist receives a warning about terrorist activity. He has Hamid and Said brought in. Contacts the CIA. Hamid and Said vanish. Charles asks his brother to take over and shut down the case. So far so good. Torkel thought he could see the end of the labyrinth through which his thoughts were picking their way.

OK, but what next?

Adam didn't just do as he had been asked. He started digging. Linked the disappearances to the unofficial American presence in Sweden.

Was that why he died?

If so, who was behind it?

Surely Charles wouldn't have his own brother killed because he was getting close to an uncomfortable truth?

The end of the labyrinth receded into the distance, and as Torkel pulled open the door with a sigh, he realised that even if they were moving in the right direction, they still had a long way to go.

Alexander Söderling pushed open the door and said hello to Hanna on reception, who responded with: 'You have a visitor'.

Alexander quickly ran through his diary in his head. As far as he recalled, the meeting he had just left in Vasastan was the last for today.

'Who is it?'

Hanna nodded towards the stylish seating area, where Charles Cederkvist was just putting down the latest edition of *Industry Today*. He got up with some difficulty from the low, deep-pink leather sofa with its yellow and white irregularly shaped cushions and came towards Alexander with a smile.

The two men shook hands, and Alexander made a point of saying what a long time it had been and how pleased he was to see Charles before he showed his guest into his office.

'I need to get away. Far away, for a long time,' Charles said as soon as Alexander had closed the door.

'I don't understand how I can help you with that.'

Charles gave him a look, making it very clear that he didn't think he should need to explain. Alexander spread his arms wide, as if to indicate that their location should be enough to make Charles see how unreasonable his demand was.

'I run this business now; I can't help you.'

He met Charles's gaze and saw no sympathy. 'It would have been difficult when I was with military intelligence, but now it's impossible.'

'Nothing is impossible,' Charles said, walking over to the window. People were battling along Drottninggatan, leaning into the wind. 'You've got contacts and money, or at least contacts with money. Use them.'

Alexander went and sat down in his comfortable office chair. This was an unwelcome visit, reminding him of things he would prefer to forget, but there was no reason why it should be anything more than that.

'Let's not rush into things,' he said calmly. 'They've found the bodies, they're looking into the car accident, but—'

Charles interrupted him with a brief, joyless laugh as he turned to look at the man behind the desk. Ten years older, fifteen kilos heavier. Alexander really had lost his grip. The good years running a PR company had taken the edge off, transformed him from a vigilant panther to an indolent house cat. Back then, all those years ago, Alexander Söderling used to say that you could never have too much information. Now he didn't even seem to know the basics. Time for an update.

'Joseph called. Hamid's son came looking for him,' Charles said in a quiet, intense tone. 'The police are looking for me; they've identified Adam. *Investigation Today* have started digging, and as you know it's only a question of time before the CIA realise that Patricia Wellton was murdered, if they don't know already.' He kept his eyes on Alexander, making sure his message hit home. Alexander felt the colour drain from his face. This was bad, really bad. On every level. The worst aspect was probably *Investigation Today*; Lennart Stridh had been found dead in a car in Bråviken. For God's sake, what was Charles dragging him into?

'I'll see what I can do,' he said; he was pleased to hear that his voice was steady.

'No, you'll do it,' Charles said, moving over to the desk. 'I've sacrificed too much to go down because you're bone idle, and scared to upset your friends.' He leaned forward and picked up a pen. 'My new number,' he said, jotting it down on a piece of paper by Alexander's left arm. 'You've got until this evening.'

He straightened up and headed for the door.

'What are you going to do now?' Alexander asked, in spite of the fact that a part of him thought it was best to know as little as possible.

'I'm going to take care of Joseph and the boy.'

'Did you take care of Lennart Stridh too?' Alexander heard himself say, even though this time he was absolutely certain he didn't want to know the answer.

'You do what you have to do and let me do what I have to do.'

Then he was gone. The door closed behind him with a quiet click. Alexander stayed where he was. Let out a long breath. So many thoughts crowding into his head. The key question: how should he handle this? Charles was obviously desperate, and therefore unpredictable and dangerous. He wanted to run, which meant he was under pressure from so many directions that he didn't think he was going to get through this, and if Charles thought it was over, how was Alexander going to survive? He wasn't. Not without help.

He picked up his mobile and scrolled through to the number he wanted. She answered right away.

'You told me not to call unless we had a problem,' Alexander said without preamble. He assumed she knew who he was. He paused for a second. 'We have a problem.'

★ ★ ★

Veronica Ström ended the call and took a deep breath, trying to remain calm.

Yes, they had a problem.

At the worst possible moment.

She turned to the woman at the other end of the pale conference table. The man beside her was just lowering his camera; he had taken several shots while she was on the phone. For a moment Veronica thought they might have overheard what she was saying, then she remembered that her responses had mostly been monosyllabic, apart from a parting promise to take care of things.

The woman was Maria Stensson, and she was a journalist. Veronica didn't recall the photographer's name. He had introduced himself when they met, but it had gone in one ear and out the other.

'I'm sorry, but I have to make a call,' she said, smiling apologetically.

'No problem,' Maria Stensson said, returning the smile. Veronica could see that her colleague was about to protest; he wanted to take some pictures in her office and perhaps outdoors, down by the water behind the parliament building, before it got too dark.

'It won't take a moment,' she said, pre-empting him. She left the room and went out into the corridor that housed the majority of the Social Democrats' representatives in parliament. She was going to take care of things, just as she had promised Alexander Söderling. She dialled +1, then a number she knew by heart. A male voice answered on the second ring with a curt 'Yes?'

Veronica introduced herself and briefly told him why she was calling; she was sorry to disturb him, but one or two problems had arisen.

The man on the other end, with his southern drawl, asked how he could help.

Veronica began to explain.

Mehran had never been this far south. He and Levan had once been to Flemingsberg with a friend, but he had just passed that station and was heading towards Tullinge. He was to get off at the penultimate stop, which was called Södertälje Port.

Joseph would be waiting for him there.

Mehran was supposed to call him when the train left Östertälje. He was finding it hard to sit still, and kept going to look at the blue-and-white poster showing all the stations on this line. Seven to go. Six. He went back after every stop, as if the number of stations might suddenly change while he was sitting on the train. The metal in his pocket was warm, although it ought to be cold. He had sorted it through Levan: a drilled-out starter pistol. It looked a bit silly, copper-coloured with a slender barrel, but Levan's friend had assured him it would work. All Mehran had to do was take aim and fire. Six shots. He had been hoping for something better, but in spite of the fact that Levan was always talking about knowing the right people, that was the best he could come up with – at short notice, anyway. Mehran had no idea how to get his hands on a gun, so he was still pleased to have it.

He had picked it up from Sergels torg. Levan had had to vouch for him, and had come straight down when Mehran called. It cost 1500 kronor; Mehran managed to swap it for the new mobile phone his mother had bought. Levan had to lend him 200 for the cartridges. It annoyed Mehran that he had to pay for them separately, but Levan and the supplier said that was the way things worked. The pistol was like a car and the cartridges were the fuel, they insisted. Two totally different things. Mehran knew he was being conned, but he had no choice. He had no intention of going to meet the man who might well be behind his father's disappearance without being armed. It was out of the question. If anyone was going to be taken by surprise, it was Joseph, not him.

He fingered the gun. It felt warm, but nowhere near as reassuring as he had expected. Mehran glanced around the carriage; he felt as if everyone was looking at him. They probably were, because he kept getting up and going over to the route map between stations, but he couldn't shake off the feeling that they all knew he was armed. That he shouldn't be there. That he was about to make a serious mistake.

His mobile rang; the sound made him jump, and he started searching for it. He didn't really want to answer, but it might be Joseph. He couldn't find it; had he put it in the same pocket as the gun? That would be really stupid. What if he pulled the gun out along with his phone? It might fall on the floor, and everyone who already knew he was armed would see the evidence. Feverishly he groped in the narrow pocket; the gun which had seemed so small suddenly seemed huge and cumbersome. Eventually he realised the ringtone wasn't coming from that pocket, but from his jacket. Where he always kept his phone. Obviously. He grabbed it as it stopped ringing as abruptly as it had begun.

He took several deep breaths, tried to regain his composure before he checked the display.

It wasn't Joseph, it was his mother.

He really didn't want to talk to her right now. He didn't even want to think about her; it would merely serve to weaken his resolve. But she wanted to talk to him. She called again. He knew her; she wouldn't give up until he answered.

She sounded cheerful and enthusiastic, which didn't feel right at all. What had she got to be cheerful about?

'Mehran? Where are you?'

'In town.'

'Listen, the police were here. They believe me.'

Mehran couldn't understand what was going on.

'The police?'

'They were here. You have to come home.'

He had heard correctly, although he still didn't understand.

'I can't, Mum.'

'You have to, Mehran. There were three police officers here. They're taking it seriously this time.'

'Mum, I can't. I've found Joseph. I'm on my way to see him now.'

He heard her gasp for breath; it sounded as if someone had slapped her across the face.

'What are you talking about?'

'I've tracked him down. I'm going to find out the truth. I have to do this.'

'Come home, Mehran,' she begged. 'Please come home.'

'Afterwards. When I know. When I know what happened. I promise.'

'Mehran!' She was screaming now; he moved the phone away from his ear. He could still hear her pleading as he ended the call.

It was wrong, he knew that. We should always listen to our mothers. But he had no choice, regardless of what the police may or may not know.

For nine years Shibeka had waited for them to listen to her.

For nine years he had waited for Joseph.

Today both their wishes would be granted.

★ ★ ★

Eyer couldn't understand why his mother was yelling. He gave her a hug, tried to console her. She barely even noticed him. She was still clutching the telephone, ringing the same number over and over again, but Mehran seemed to be rejecting the call every single time. Eventually she slumped to the ground. Eyer tried to hug her even more tightly; all he knew was that he mustn't let go of her. Ever.

At last she calmed down slightly and looked at him. Her eyes were full of tears, but she wasn't sad in the way that she usually was. This was something different, a horror he had never seen before. He realised something awful was happening; his hugs seemed so ineffectual.

'What's happened, Mum?'

'It's Mehran. It's Mehran. He . . .'

She broke off and held him close, buried her face in his hair. She didn't know whether she should, or even could, tell him any more. How could she explain something she barely understood herself? How could she tell him about the name that had walked beside her like a ghost for so long, the shadow whose very existence she had doubted?

Joseph.

Mehran was on his way to see him, and it was going to happen again, just like the last time Joseph's name had come up. Mehran would disappear, just like his father. The man who had been nothing more than a name would hurt her family again. She knew it. And it was her fault. She was the one who had let him back in by refusing to forget. She had kept the monster alive, nurtured it, and now she had given it her firstborn. Shibeka clung to Eyer, wondering if she would ever be able to let go of him. She didn't think so. But she had to do something, she couldn't just give up.

She noticed the card the slightly overweight police officer had given her; he had looked at her in a way she didn't like at all. It was lying on the table next to the telephone.

The police might not have helped her in the past, but right now she had no one else. She had to make him understand.

'Charles Mikael Cederkvist, born 1966 in Hedemora. He's been living with his partner Marianne Fransson in Oskarshamn since 2006. No children. His brother Adam was two years younger.'

Billy was addressing the team in the Room, where everyone except Vanja had gathered. Sebastian had called her several times, but with no luck. He was starting to get seriously worried. She had gone off at lunchtime, and no one had heard from her since then. He decided to call round at her apartment later that evening, but right now he needed to focus on the man Billy had plastered all over one wall via the projector. The man who had probably killed his brother.

'The family moved to Södertälje when he was thirteen and his father got a job with Scania,' Billy went on. 'Charles did his military service there, applied for officer training, then went on to specialist training. He was recruited to the military intelligence and security service in '98, but that's all we know. They're not telling us anything; they weren't even prepared to confirm that Charles works for them. If we want more information, we have to go down the official route: a formal request from one authority to another.'

He looked at Torkel, who nodded to show that he understood. The official route also meant the slow and bureaucratic route, unfortunately. Billy brought up another image on his laptop and Jennifer took over.

'The head of military intelligence in 2003 was Major General Alexander Söderling. He left the army in 2008 and moved into business. He's the Managing Director of Nuntius, a PR company on Drottninggatan. We haven't tried to contact him yet.'

'There's no point,' Torkel said with a sigh. 'If military intelligence won't even confirm that Charles works for them, Söderling isn't going to say anything either.'

Sebastian's mobile rang. He grabbed it, hoping it would be Vanja, but it was a number he didn't recognise. He ignored the irritated glances of everyone else as he got up to answer it. Ten seconds later he had left the room.

'I've been in touch with *Investigation Today*,' Jennifer went on. 'Lennart Stridh's boss . . .' she looked down at her notes, 'Sture Liljedahl, said that as far as he was aware, Lennart had given up on Shibeka's story. He had no idea what Lennart was doing down by Bråviken, but he promised to go through his computer and let us know if he found anything.'

Before she could say any more, Sebastian flung open the door.

'That was Shibeka Khan. Her son is on the way to meet some-one called Joseph.'

'Who's Joseph?' Ursula wondered, not unreasonably.

'Shibeka didn't know, but he was associated with Hamid and Said. Shibeka thinks he had something to do with their disappear-ance, and her son is absolutely convinced he was involved.'

'Where are they meeting?' Torkel asked, ready to leave the Room immediately.

'He didn't say.'

'Could it be Charles?' Jennifer suggested. Torkel nodded. Possibly – probably, in fact.

'In which case, we have to find him fast. Billy?'

Billy was already at his computer. 'He called from a mobile; I can try and trace it.'

He looked up at Sebastian. 'What's his number?'

'How the hell should I know?'

'Could you try and find out?'

Sebastian called Shibeka, explained the situation and handed the phone to Billy.

'Hi, my name's Billy, I need . . .' He glanced enquiringly at Sebastian.

'Mehran,' Sebastian supplied.

'Mehran's phone number so that we can try and trace him.'

He made a note of the number, and asked Shibeka for a few more details. Soon he knew the operator (*3*), what kind of phone it was (*one of those with a screen you just have to touch*), and who the subscriber was (*Shibeka Khan*); he asked her to see if she could find the receipt. He thanked her for her help, gave the phone back to

Sebastian and picked up his own. He contacted 3 and gave them a three-digit number plus the password that proved he was calling from the police. After thirty seconds he had an IMEI number. Meanwhile, Shibeka had found the receipt. Billy checked that the IMEI number was correct, just to be on the safe side, then typed the fifteen digits into his computer.

'What's that?' Jennifer asked; she had come around the table and was standing behind him.

'Every mobile phone has a unique ID number. As long as it's switched on, I should be able . . .' He didn't finish the sentence; all his attention was on the screen.

'I'll get a car,' Torkel said, leaving the room.

'Bingo!' Billy leaned back on his chair, hands linked behind his head; he was obviously pleased with himself. Sebastian moved closer and saw a blue dot appear against a grey background.

'Where is he?' he said impatiently.

'Just wait,' Billy said, holding up his hand. Around the blue dot a map began to appear, bit by bit, and finally names and other reference points emerged. Billy studied the screen and ran his finger along a thick black line, which the blue dot appeared to be following.

'That's the railway. He's on a train, just outside Södertälje.'

'That's where Charles Cederkvist did his military service,' Jennifer informed them.

Billy closed his laptop and he and Jennifer ran out of the door.

Shibeka had called so many times that he had had to switch his phone to silent; now it kept on vibrating instead. He ignored it. He gave Joseph a quick call as the train reached Östertälje, as agreed. The rasping voice answered right away.

He would be waiting at the next station, in the car park just outside.

The voice didn't say any more.

Nor did Mehran.

It wasn't necessary.

He went and stood by the doors, one hand in his pocket. The metal no longer felt warm, and nor did he. The heat in his body had been replaced by a cold sweat that almost made him shiver.

It was normal to be afraid. There was nothing wrong with that.

Not having the courage to act, that would be wrong. Warriors were afraid, he understood that now. Bravery meant being able to act in spite of one's fear.

The train began to slow down: Södertälje Port. Mehran stepped down onto the platform, saw the red station building a short distance away; the exit must be over there. He felt better when he started walking; the anxiety was still there, but the movement made it easier to handle. He entered the large brick edifice, saw the big doors leading to the car park. He didn't know what he would do if Joseph really was standing there waiting for him. He was glad they had agreed to meet in a place where other people were around; it felt safer than in an apartment. Some of the other passengers were behind him, and he slowed down to allow them to pass. Mehran was in no hurry, and there was a certain security in having people in front of him. There were a dozen or so vehicles in the small car park. Two passengers were picked up in a red Ford just by the entrance, while some headed for the bus shelter a short distance away. The others went off in different directions, and soon Mehran was the only one left. He stood by the door, looking around.

A man got out of a black, highly polished BMW, his eyes fixed on Mehran. He looked Arabic, and was in his fifties; well built, with short grey hair, a few strands of black remaining in his beard. Mehran didn't recognise him. He was wearing a short black leather jacket, jeans and loafers; the combination of the car and the jacket made him look rich. Powerful. Or maybe that was just Mehran's mind playing tricks on him. The man nodded to Mehran, who nodded back. Slowly he began to walk towards Mehran. Perfect. Joseph could come to him. However, he didn't know what to do with his hands. He didn't dare touch the gun; the man might notice the movement and realise he was armed. He let his arms dangle by his sides; it didn't feel right, but he couldn't work out what else to do. He didn't want to seem nervous, didn't want to give Joseph (if it was Joseph) the upper hand in any way. The man was strolling towards him as if he didn't have a care in the world, as if he had come to pick up an old friend. Not a hint of unease in his body. That annoyed Mehran; he wanted Joseph to be afraid of him, rather than the reverse.

'You wanted to speak to me,' the man said when he was five metres away. It was him. There was something special about hearing that voice for real, so close, rather than on the telephone or as a memory. Mehran was even more confused about what to do with his hands.

'I have some questions about my father,' he said as clearly as possible. His voice was steady, which was something.

'Your father's name was Hamid, wasn't it?'

Mehran nodded.

'I hardly knew him. He was a friend of a friend.'

'Said wasn't your friend. I know you lent money to Rafi, his cousin.'

Joseph shrugged.

'I help many people. Many, many people.' He smiled. 'That's just the way I am.'

'My father disappeared. I'm trying to find out what happened.'

'You're asking the wrong person.'

Mehran met Joseph's gaze. It was as deep as a grave. In Joseph's eyes there was no hope, no future. He really wished the gun was in his hand right now, but he couldn't get it out, not here. There were too many people around. He took a step back; he couldn't help it.

'Am I?' he said, trying to sound confident. 'I think you know what happened to him.'

'I don't understand why you would say such a thing,' Joseph said, a fraction more gently. 'There must be some kind of misunderstanding.'

'I don't think so.'

'You're wrong. Shall we go somewhere, sort this out?'

'We can sort it out here.'

Joseph laughed.

'No. Either you come with me, or we forget it.'

He turned away and walked back to his car. 'You won't get another chance,' he added.

Mehran wasn't sure what to do. He hadn't planned beyond actually meeting Joseph, but now he realised he had to act. Give this arrogant man something to think about. Take him by surprise. Perhaps he should take out the gun, press it against Joseph's forehead.

But not here; he needed to get him on his own, but he really didn't want to get in the car. It was too risky. Joseph had reached the BMW and turned around.

'Are you coming?' he said irritably.

Maybe he should give up, Mehran thought. Accept that he wasn't going to get any further. He hadn't made a fool of himself, he hadn't bottled it; he could walk away with his head held high. And it didn't mean it was over; he now knew that Joseph existed, and he would be able to plan their next meeting more carefully.

But that wasn't what he had promised himself.

He had promised himself that he would find out the truth.

For Shibeka's sake.

He slipped his hand into his pocket; the metal felt warm again. It was ready, and so was he. He set off towards the car, gripping the butt of the pistol.

'Wait!' he shouted. He looked around; the car park was empty. It could work. It had to work. If he could just get Joseph into the car with a gun to his head before someone came along, it might work. The metal in his hand gave him strength. He increased his speed while trying to look as relaxed as possible, as if he had changed his

393

mind, but perhaps hadn't quite decided. He wanted the threat to remain invisible, in his pocket rather than in his body language.

Joseph went round to open the passenger door. Mehran tightened his grip on the pistol, got ready to whip it out. He was almost smiling to himself. Joseph was going to get one hell of a surprise.

With only a metre to go, he heard the sound of voices. Two girls appeared from behind the bus shelter. They were in their twenties, laughing and joking as they walked towards the station. Instinctively Mehran let go of the gun and slowed down so that they could go past. However, if he lingered for too long he would give himself away; Joseph would wonder why he was reluctant to approach the car while the girls were still in sight. He had to keep going. Joseph was smiling now.

'You come here and accuse me,' he said softly, felling Mehran with a single well-aimed blow. Mehran crashed to the ground behind the car and landed on the gravel. Joseph kept an eye on the girls as he kicked the boy hard in the head. Twice. The faint groaning ceased after the second kick. The girls didn't appear to have noticed anything; they were still chatting and giggling. Joseph waited until they had gone inside, then dumped the unconscious boy in the boot of his car. Mehran weighed less than he had expected, which was good. Bodies that were too heavy were always a problem. He took out his phone and called Charles, who answered immediately.

As usual.

They had the blue lights on; Jennifer was driving. They had just reached Essingeleden and their speed was approaching 140 kilometres per hour. Torkel was clutching the handle above the door out of habit; it made him feel safer. He would have preferred Billy to drive; he was the best in the team when it came to high speed, but he was in the back seat bent over his laptop, following the signal from Mehran Khan's mobile. Torkel had just finished speaking to Britta Hanning at Säpo; she had been slightly more co-operative this time. He turned to Billy.

'They know of someone called Joseph. Britta wasn't prepared to give me his real name, but apparently he's a so-called friend of theirs.'

'A friend?' Jennifer was curious.

'An informant. Someone who tips off the security services about extremists and other groups.'

Billy leaned forward; he couldn't believe his ears.

'So we're going after one of our "friends"?'

'It looks that way.'

The car swerved as they raced past a Polish articulated lorry. Torkel tightened his grip on the handle, but Jennifer seemed totally unmoved.

'But if he's helped Säpo, perhaps he's helped other organisations, like military intelligence for example,' she said as she switched lanes again.

Torkel nodded. That wasn't out of the question. By this stage nothing was out of the question when it came to this case. Times had changed, and these days the fight against terrorism and extremism set the agenda for those charged with defending the country. They were suddenly battling an invisible enemy who didn't wear a uniform, and the rules of engagement had changed. The secrets were bigger, the methods less refined. The open society became a casualty, and eventually the poison generated by those secrets seeped through. He thought about the fifteen-year-old boy who had somehow ended up in the middle of this mess, a boy who had lost his father. This was where the secrets led: to family tragedies. He turned back to Billy.

'Are you still picking up the signal from Mehran's phone?'

Billy shook his head.

'No, I lost the connection to the server for a while. The last position was just outside the station at Södertälje Port. I'll ask the local police to send a car down there.'

Torkel could hear Billy's fingers flying over the keyboard. I'm getting old, he thought. He remembered when you had to pick up the phone to speak to colleagues, when you had to use dogs to search for people. Now Billy was sitting in the back of the car taking care of the whole thing. As long as he was connected to the server.

'We should be there in fifteen minutes,' Jennifer said. Torkel's stomach really wasn't enjoying this.

'He's not there any more,' Billy announced. 'He's heading towards the E20.'

'Put your foot down,' Torkel said to Jennifer.

Back again. Almnäs. Södertälje.

He had done his compulsory military service here. Thought of it as a necessary evil at first, but quickly came to love it. He wasn't sure why; there was something about the routines, the discipline, the rigour that he could embrace if he allowed himself to do so, unlike most of his fellow recruits who treated the whole thing like a game. The physical side of the training appealed to him right away, but as time went on he became increasingly fascinated by the strategies, the way of thinking used to outwit and defeat the enemy. He discovered two things about himself: a predilection for military life and a competitive instinct, which came as a complete surprise. He and his brother had engaged in various sports while they were growing up, but he had never been hell-bent on winning. Not until he ended up in the army. It was as if he couldn't fully commit until it was a matter of life and death. He started training like a madman. Looking after his body. Loving it, like an elite sportsman who had to be able to rely on it in order to achieve. Weapons were the tools of his trade; he learned to use them all, single-mindedly and with respect. Halfway through his compulsory service he had applied for officer training, and had of course been accepted. He had good, life-changing memories of this place.

But they weren't all good.

The second time he had been here was in August 2003. The regiment had been disbanded six years earlier. Swedint, the Swedish Armed Forces, still operated here, but most of the square, impersonal buildings from the Seventies stood empty and had been allowed to fall into disrepair.

Alexander had ordered him to go to Almnäs; Joseph had tipped them off about two Afghan men, and the Americans wanted to talk to them. Any activity on Swedish soil required a Swedish presence.

anonymous Volvo had been parked outside the storage depot when he arrived. The man standing by the car threw his cigarette on the ground and came to meet Charles. They shook hands; Charles said his name, the other man didn't. Charles was struck by how young the American looked. Well built, the way Charles pictured a college student whose special talent was for American football. Red hair. Irish origins, perhaps.

The other American was inside; he didn't give his name either. Slightly older, slimmer, more muscular. A long face, nose slightly too large, side parting, a fringe hanging over one lens of the aviator sunglasses he never took off.

Two men were lying on the floor on their backs, their hands and feet chained to metal posts screwed into the floor, arms stretched as far as possible above their heads. They were twisting and turning, trying to free themselves as they talked non-stop, begging to be released, insisting this was a mistake, screaming, demanding answers.

They didn't get any.

The men were naked apart from their underpants. Charles couldn't see their faces; they were covered with towels. Without exchanging a single word the man in sunglasses picked up a bucket of water and began to pour it onto the thick fabric covering the face of one of the men on the floor. His body jerked in a powerful gag reflex, and he immediately fell silent. His companion seemed to sense that something had happened, and shouted out a name.

Hamid!

The American carried on pouring water onto the towel. The man who was apparently called Hamid pulled at his chains, trying to escape. Charles saw the skin tear around the metal cuffs and Hamid's wrists began to bleed. The flow of water stopped. The red-haired man crouched down and pulled back the towel. Hamid gasped for air; he was almost hyperventilating, and fear shone in his eyes. His gaze fastened on Charles, and he started begging for help. The red-haired man hit him across the face, and he stopped talking. Then the questions began.

Where was it going to happen?

When was it going to happen?

Who else was involved?

Hamid clearly didn't understand. He simply shook his head, managed to get out something that sounded like 'wrong' and 'please' before the towel was replaced. He screamed, and his companion joined in.

This time both Americans picked up a bucket and poured water over both men at the same time. Unmoved, implacable.

Charles was ordered to refill the other buckets. He did as he was told. Gave them the full buckets when theirs were empty. Refilled them again.

Crouch down. Towel off.

Where? When? Who else?

They got no answers.

At one point Hamid made a panic-stricken attempt to break free, and Charles heard the bones in his wrist break as he flung himself as far as he could to the right in order to try to escape the inexorable flow of water.

Where? When? Who else?

Charles had no idea how long it had been going on when he joined in. He positioned himself above the head of one of the men, legs wide apart, and tilted the bucket. The water flowed onto the fabric in a slow but steady stream, effectively stopping any air from getting through.

'When you think they can't take any more,' the man in the aviators said, 'you carry on for another twenty seconds, and then another ten.'

Over and over again.

Both men were bleeding heavily from their wrists and ankles, and Hamid's left hand was dangling at a very odd angle. They had stopped screaming. They weren't talking. No more pleading. They didn't even have the strength to whisper. They just stared with eyes that were already dead each time the towels were removed and the questions were asked. Their breathing became shallower and shallower; soon it was just a series of gasps.

When? Where? Who else?

Over and over again.

They took a break. Went outside for a smoke. None of them said very much. They went back inside and carried on.

Said died first; he simply stopped breathing. Dry drowning, the red-haired man stated before attempting to revive him with mouth to mouth resuscitation. Without success. The other man bent over the lifeless body and began heart massage, while his colleague continued to breathe oxygen into the damaged lungs. Without success. Charles was beginning to feel a sense of revulsion. This was bad. Really bad. Neither of the two Afghans were Swedish citizens, but one of them, the one who had died, had a permanent residence permit. The extreme interrogation methods were bad enough, but at least they could be justified; the open society was under attack. Democracy had to be protected, and the situation these days required a harsh approach. But this? How the fuck were they going to fix this?

The Americans gave up their attempts to revive Said, and returned to Hamid. Charles assumed they were going to let him go, stop the interrogation; it seemed obvious to him that the two men knew nothing. But no. The Americans pulled away the towel and turned Hamid's head to the left so that he could see his friend. A faint whimper was all he could manage before they replaced the towel and began again.

He lasted another thirty minutes.

The red-haired man and the man in the aviators left the country. Charles reported back to Alexander that Hamid and Said would never be found. If they could just shut down the missing persons investigation that the Solna police had embarked upon, everything would be fine.

Charles knew exactly the right man for the job, or so he thought. But Adam had let him down. Didn't understand. Didn't want to understand.

Instead of simply taking on the case and burying it, he had started investigating. He had visited the families, dug around for Foreign Office gossip. Alexander could make sure that Adam got nowhere, of course, but Adam was still a problem.

Charles was surprised. Admittedly his brother had always had a strong sense of right and wrong – that was why he had joined the police – but Charles had thought he would let it go when national security was at stake. There was a constant threat to the open society. For God's sake, the Foreign Minister had been murdered in a department store that autumn!

They had had long conversations. Adam wanted to know more, wanted to know everything. Charles gave him bits and pieces, but Adam wasn't satisfied. He told Charles he intended to get to the bottom of this, and if what he thought had happened turned out to be the truth, he wouldn't be able to turn a blind eye. Even if they were brothers. Charles had asked him to wait, let it go for a while. Think it over. Give it a week.

He had booked a mountain retreat, a log cabin in Jämtland. Couldn't Adam go up there, think things through? If he felt the same when he came back, then he could go ahead and do what he felt was right. A week. Putting some distance between himself and the situation might be a good thing – after all, he loved the mountains, didn't he?

Adam had gone.

Someone had called in Patricia Wellton. Charles didn't know whether Alexander or someone at the Foreign Office was responsible for making that kind of contact, but in the chaos following the murder of Anna Lindh, he assumed it wasn't the acting Foreign Secretary.

Charles had gone up to meet Patricia after the event so that she could report back. When she finally arrived, several hours late, she was furious. Nobody had said anything about a woman and two kids. How the fuck was she expected to do her job when the information about the target was inaccurate?

Adam. Stupid, stupid Adam, who loved his family so much. Charles had understood at once: Adam had taken the family with him. Lena, Ella and Simon.

Lena had been in the same class as Charles at the high school in Södertälje. They were good friends. Or she was his friend, at least; he was in love with her. He never told her; he was afraid of losing her completely if he gave the slightest hint of the feelings he had for her. She spent a lot of time at their house. She was two years older than Adam; at that age girls are supposed to think that younger boys are childish, immature and uninteresting, but Lena wasn't like other girls. She got together with Adam during her final year at school. He was seventeen, she was nineteen. Charles had to watch them curled up on the sofa together, kissing and cuddling and watching TV. He could hear them through the wall of his room at night, but he stayed strong; it was a teenage crush. Nobody expected it to last. But it did.

Year after year after year.

They got married in 1990, when Adam was twenty-two. They had Ella five years later, and Simon two years after that. A happy little family. They moved to Stockholm, Charles to Oskarshamn.

They met up often, enjoyed spending time together. Charles was Simon's godfather; he loved his nephew and niece, but he never got over the feeling that Adam had taken something that belonged to him. Wrong and totally irrational, of course; if Adam had known how he felt about Lena he would never have gone there, Charles was sure of it.

Adam was a fine, good man.

Patricia Wellton.

Everything had gone black when he realised she had killed Lena and the children. They weren't supposed to die. They were supposed to live. Who knew what might have happened in the future? Possibly nothing, that wasn't why he wanted Adam to go up to Jämtland. It was because he had no choice; it was a matter of national security, a sacrifice he had to make in order to protect a fragile democracy.

Lena and the children were never meant to die.

But they did.

Patricia had killed them, and therefore he had killed Patricia.

Charles gave a start. A car was approaching. The beam of the headlights swept across the deserted buildings as it turned in. How long had he been standing here, lost in his thoughts?

It was this place.

He should have chosen somewhere else. Too many memories. He looked at his watch, then peered out. Joseph had arrived. Time for yet another conclusion.

The old sentry post had been abandoned long ago. The windows were broken and someone had scrawled 'Armed struggle', appropriately enough, on the rotting walls. Joseph drove slowly through the raised barrier and carried on up the hill. Even the tarmac was neglected, with great big potholes and weeds growing through the cracks. When he reached the top of the hill he could see the barracks spread before him. He turned in and parked as far away as possible. He looked around, but couldn't see anyone. If the buildings were well past their best, that was nothing compared to this area. There was rubbish and broken glass everywhere, every surface was covered in graffiti, and there were even a number of burnt-out cars. It really was the perfect place to bury old sins. Once upon a time young men had trained here in order to defend their country; now it was just a ghost town. Joseph switched off the engine, and there was total silence.

Not a sound from the boot. Good. It would have been difficult if the kid had started kicking and yelling. It had happened to him once in Jordan when he was young, and it had been far from easy, driving around with that going on. He had enough of a headache as it was, particularly with the boy tracking him down after all these years. It would have made more sense if someone had started asking questions just after the two men had gone missing. Joseph had been quite worried at the time, but as the years went by he felt increasingly safe, and eventually he had more or less forgotten about it. Life went on. His misgivings dwindled day by day, until they were so small they no longer made their presence felt.

But he realised now that the children who are left behind do not forget. In fact, the desire to understand probably grew stronger as they got older, until one day there they were, asking questions. At least if they had a name to search for.

Which the boy evidently had.

Someone must have talked.

2003 had been a crazy time for him. Everyone was desperate for information: the Americans, the British, the Swedes, the Egyptians. They wanted more and more. It was as if they thought little Sweden was full of potential terrorists, and that belief made them throw money and resources in all directions. He had found himself right in the middle of the madness, and had quickly and willingly discovered his role. Important people started listening to him. His whispers gave him power and money. It was an intoxicating feeling, holding the lives of others in his hands simply by pointing them out.

But with the money came the demands. They wanted names. All the time. More and more. They were insatiable and paranoid. Why was this person travelling to that place? Who was that person meeting there? What was that imam doing in Sweden? Who invited him? Could he try to get closer to this particular group?

He had kept them happy while filling his pockets with money.

Things were different now. They no longer relied on individual informants in the same way. They had refined their methods; the information came from a range of sources and was checked more carefully. Coordinated. The rules had changed, and there was less money available. They used their own agents to infiltrate their opponents, while both sides tried to come up with new ways of fighting one another. The Americans used unmanned drones to deliver bombs and missiles while the enemy slept, and the extremists found new countries in which to operate. It was like a circus, constantly travelling from one poor country to the next.

Joseph had long ago realised that his glory days were over. He would need to find something else soon. The worst thing was that many of his potential employers had disappeared in recent years. Gaddafi was gone, so was Mubarak. The Libyans had been the best, better than all the western powers put together. They were totally paranoid, and willing to pay for information that was so easy to come by.

Ali was meeting exiled Libyans.

Tarek had shown an interest in this group or that group.

Mahmed had spoken about Gaddafi's sons in negative terms.

He had been able to exchange such banal nonsense for cash. He used to think that once upon a time he had had his very own sea, where he fished for people and information and sold them in his very own fish market.

Most of those he sold were guilty.

Hamid and Said were not.

They had been sold because he needed to deliver, and because they had humiliated him. He had been struggling; it had been difficult to come up with new names. Charles already knew about everyone he mentioned. The money dried up. He needed someone to sell, preferably someone really dangerous.

It had seemed like the perfect solution.

He told Charles that Hamid and Said were involved in the planning of a fresh attack on American soil. Charles had never heard of them. He had new names to work on, and Joseph had his revenge.

Hamid and Said had come to his home and humiliated him. Stolen from him. They didn't seem to understand who he was, what kind of contacts he had. But he had shown them.

Afterwards he realised it had been a stupid thing to do. Those who paid him began to doubt him. Hamid and Said led nowhere. Of course. But he learned from his mistake; he didn't do it again. He had thought it was forgotten, until the boy turned up.

Another mistake to correct, he thought. He got out of the car and walked round to the boot. Perhaps he should leave the boy where he was until Charles arrived. Just hand him over and drive away. That was how it worked; he never got blood on his hands. He simply delivered.

He lit a cigarette and looked over towards what had once been a firing range. Now it was an overgrown field, but the rusty metal stands to which the targets had once been attached were still there.

The boy should have come round by now. He moved closer and listened. Nothing. Joseph was a little concerned; he didn't want to deliver a dead body. He opened the boot to see if the boy was all right.

The bullet hit his right shoulder just below the collarbone, and he fell backwards, completely taken by surprise. It didn't hurt as much as he expected it to, but he could feel the blood soaking through his shirt. The boy jumped out and stood over him, waving something that looked like a toy gun. He fired another shot, but

Joseph threw himself to one side and it missed. He hurled himself forward and grabbed hold of the boy with his left hand; his right hand didn't seem to be working. He wrenched the gun from his grasp and it fell to the ground. The boy managed to kick Joseph's wounded shoulder. It was incredibly painful, and he collapsed, screaming. With the last of his strength he grabbed the gun and pulled it towards him. He heard the sound of running feet, and when he managed to get to his knees, he saw the boy racing across the field towards the firing range.

'I'll get you, you little bastard!' Joseph bellowed. 'Just like I got your father!'

He pulled himself to his feet. The pain in his shoulder was much worse now, and he was finding it difficult to move his right hand at all. He picked up the little gun with his left hand; it didn't look like much, but it would have to do. Suddenly he heard footsteps in the gravel and broken glass behind him. He raised the gun and turned around. It was Charles. He lowered the gun and pointed in the direction of the field.

'He ran away.'

'I saw him.'

Charles didn't move. Joseph couldn't understand it.

'He's getting away.' He pointed to his bleeding shoulder. 'You have to help me.'

Charles nodded and took a large black automatic pistol out of his waistband. It looked considerably more useful than the one Joseph was holding.

'Of course I'll help you,' he said as he slipped off the safety catch. He set off towards the field, and Joseph let out a grateful sigh. Just as Charles was walking past, he paused.

'But just so you know – this is the last time.'

He pressed the pistol against Mohammed Al Baasim's head and fired. Twice.

The body had barely hit the ground before Charles was on his way, following Mehran.

He couldn't have got very far.

They got stuck in traffic just before the Södertälje bridge. Roadworks had reduced the carriageway to one lane, and it took Jennifer several minutes to zigzag between the cars and get through. However, that wasn't their biggest problem. Billy had lost the signal from Mehran's mobile. Torkel was starting to get stressed.

'Where did you last see it?' he snapped.

'On the E20, but either someone's switched off the phone, or they're in an area with poor coverage. I don't know.'

'Fuck!'

Torkel knew it wasn't Billy's fault, but it was a disaster; they were so close, and they had lost the trail. Jennifer was able to pick up speed again, and she glanced at him uncertainly.

'Where am I going?'

'Carry on towards the E20.' He turned to Billy. 'Show me the map; where was he when you lost him?'

Billy turned the screen around and pointed.

'If the mobile's dead and they've stayed on the E20, we've had it. Let's hope they've turned off,' Torkel said.

Billy understood his reasoning.

'OK, so do we just guess where they've come off?'

'Almnäs is around here somewhere,' Jennifer said without taking her eyes off the road. 'Where Charles did his military service,' she clarified.

Torkel nodded and looked at the map again. Forest, lakes, and the odd place name. Almnäs. Just a few kilometres from the spot Billy had just indicated.

'Worth a try,' Billy said. 'It's the best we've got.'

'Send for the helicopter,' Torkel said. 'It's a big area; we're going to need some help.'

'I'm on it,' Billy said, still focusing on the screen. No blue dot. They could only hope they had guessed right, and that they would get there in time.

Mehran heard the two shots and threw himself into a muddy ditch. At first he thought someone was firing at him, but when he cautiously raised his head to look, he saw another man striding towards him through the undergrowth in the fading twilight. He was wearing dark clothes and had cropped blond hair; he looked fit and muscular. A Swede, presumably. Mehran had never seen him before. He seemed to be carrying something – a gun? Mehran knew it couldn't be anything else when he caught sight of Joseph's motionless, contorted body lying next to the black car.

He slid back down into the ditch in a panic. The cold from the earth and mud quickly penetrated his clothes, but he had more important things to think about. He had to get out of there. Fast. There was a clump of trees a short distance away, and the forest took over perhaps fifty metres beyond that. It was his only chance; he had to get away from this open area and in among the trees, where there would be a lot more places to hide. He didn't dare check to see how far the man had got; he simply started crawling, hoping he would be able to get close to the trees before he had to leave the protection of the ditch. The water was slimy and it stank, and the parts of the ground that weren't wet were overgrown with long grass that was as sharp as a blade, making it difficult for him to make progress. He couldn't get a grip; his feet kept slipping in the mud, and the struggle was exhausting. Suddenly he realised it wouldn't be a good idea to move quickly anyway, because the long grass would sway, showing the man exactly where he was. Trapped. The man was bound to reach the ditch before Mehran reached the trees. He would be lying there among all the crap, and the man would find him. He had to take a bigger risk if he was going to make it. He had to get up and run, hoping it would take a while for the man to spot him in the semi-darkness. He straightened up a fraction, got ready to go. Then he heard the man calling, much closer than Mehran had expected. And what was worse, he knew Mehran's name.

'Come on out, Mehran!' he shouted, so loud that it echoed across the field. 'I'm from the police!'

Mehran flattened himself, made himself as small as he possibly could.

'It's OK, Mehran. I want to help you.'

Mehran's head was spinning. He didn't understand this at all. How come the man knew who he was? Was that what Shibeka had meant when she mentioned the police? Had they come to help him? But how could they have found him here, in the middle of a field? Even he didn't know where he was.

It couldn't be true.

It was impossible.

Besides which, why would a police officer shoot Joseph twice?

He started crawling again, trying to use his legs to push himself forward. It was incredibly difficult. The mud sank down, giving him no purchase. His body was aching and his head was throbbing. The man was still shouting, getting closer and closer. Mehran tried to ignore the voice, block it out. Use it to gauge how far he was from the man, nothing more. He kept on going, but it was getting harder and harder. He hadn't really recovered from the blow Joseph had delivered, and he felt dizzy, weak and sick. But he couldn't give up; he had to find the strength, the adrenaline. The survival instinct.

Suddenly the shouting grew fainter; the man was moving away. It gave him a fresh burst of energy. Mehran went on, crawling, creeping; using his fingers and nails to drag himself along, pushing with his legs, his whole body screaming with pain. He was making progress, metre by metre. He hadn't heard the man for a while; hopefully he was still moving in the other direction. He didn't even have the strength to listen any more.

At last he saw the clump of trees straight in front of him. Just a little bit further. He decided to run the last few metres, in among the trees then on to the safety of the forest. He would run and run and never stop, away from this stinking ditch, from the grass that had torn his body to shreds. Just a little bit further, he said to himself. Just a tiny, tiny bit further.

You can do it, Mehran. You can do it.

He leapt out of the ditch; his legs didn't give way, which surprised him. However, he was still feeling dizzy, and he soon lost his balance. Fell, got back up again. Kept on going. Gained control of his body. At least he didn't need to use his aching arms any more, and as he picked up speed he felt as if there was more power in his legs than he had first thought. He heard the man shouting at him to stop, but Mehran didn't turn around. He just ran and ran, as he had promised himself. He passed the clump of trees and kept on going, crossing the field beyond them, not far now. The forest was perhaps thirty metres away.

Still no sound of gunfire.

He might just make it.

He might just make it.

He didn't see the hole until it was too late. Some kind of military defence, a trench or a rampart perhaps. He tried to jump over it, but lost his balance again on the other side and fell in. He landed awkwardly on one foot, and screamed in pain as it bent and snapped with a horrible noise. He collapsed in the bottom of the trench, trying not to cry out again. He didn't want to make a sound, but he couldn't help it. He was crying even though he didn't want to, whimpering with pain even though he knew he mustn't.

★ ★ ★

Charles saw the boy go down. He had been out here on exercises many times, and knew how difficult it was to see the trench when you were running; in the dark it was virtually impossible. Which was the whole idea, really; the enemy weren't supposed to see it. One of his men had once made the same mistake when he was leading a platoon; those days felt like a different life, when the worst that could happen was someone getting injured during training.

He increased his speed; he could hear the boy crying. He seemed to be hurt, and would probably still be down there when Charles reached the ditch, but there were no guarantees. The boy seemed to be made of stern stuff. Just like his father.

★ ★ ★

He felt as if he was already lying in a grave. The rough moss-covered cement walls of the trench formed a rectangle, and up above he could see the black sky, dotted with the odd star now the sun had gone. Mehran almost felt the man's shadow fall on him as he silently stepped forward. He could just make out a silhouette, a denser patch of darkness, standing up there looking down on him. Mehran watched as he slowly raised his gun.

This was his opportunity to find out the truth. Not all the details, perhaps, but the key points. His father's death was linked to things he didn't understand at all, but there was a connection. The inexplicable had been logical all along; it was just that he and Shibeka hadn't had access to all the pieces of the puzzle. Now he had the most important piece. His father had died; he had been murdered for some reason. He hadn't walked away from his family; he hadn't stopped loving them and disappeared.

Mehran almost felt contented. That was the strange thing about death, he thought. You expected to be afraid of it, but instead it brought the knowledge of how things really were.

It would be very difficult for his mother. She would blame herself. He had the easy option. That was another truth: being left behind was the hardest thing of all. He knew that already.

He would be following in his father's footsteps earlier than he had hoped. They would soon be reunited, he and Hamid. He wanted that and yet he didn't, but it was no longer his choice.

However, Mehran had no intention of dying in tears. He didn't want to give the man the satisfaction, but no matter how hard he tried to hold back those tears, he just couldn't do it. He was sobbing with fear, but he wasn't ashamed. Courage meant acting even though you were afraid.

'What happened to my father?' he yelled up into the darkness. The man didn't answer.

He didn't want to.

He couldn't.

Charles looked down at the boy, lying amongst the stones and branches. It looked as if he had broken his leg, but still he refused to give up. He was crying, yet at the same time he was staring up at Charles with undisguised hostility. Strength. It always impressed him. The boy was so young, no more than a child really, and yet he was showing such fighting spirit.

He took aim, but suddenly hesitated.

Was he going to kill a child? Was that really where he had ended up?

This boy had been six years old when his father disappeared. And Simon had been six when he died.

Had Patricia Wellton hesitated before she shot him? Probably not; professionals like her never hesitated.

He was also a professional, but this time he wasn't sure.

He was no common killer, he was just trying to close doors. Protect secrets. The boy asked about his father again; he deserved to know.

'I'm afraid he's dead. But you already knew that.'

The boy nodded, his expression even more hostile, if that were possible.

It could just as easily be Simon down there, Charles thought. He would be about the same age now as this boy. Fifteen, almost sixteen. Simon's birthday was in November, 18 November. He wondered when Mehran's birthday was.

Perhaps it wasn't a coincidence that they were the same age. Perhaps that was what this was all about.

Seeing the consequences of one's actions.

Realising at last that it was impossible to close any more doors. That the price was too high.

Suddenly Charles heard the sound of a helicopter, approaching fast. He could tell it was a Eurocopter EC135, a police chopper. It would be right above him in less than two minutes.

It was over. They were going to catch him, so what did it matter if the boy was dead or alive? It mattered to him.

Killing a child when everything was already lost.

That didn't make him a protector.

That didn't make him a soldier.

That made him a monster.

He lowered the gun, jumped over the trench and ran towards the forest. He would follow it back to the car in a wide circle, remaining outside the police's sphere of operations with a bit of luck. There was a chance. But if they caught him . . . if they talked about him afterwards they would say how evil he was, what a terrible person. They would call him a psychopath. Charles didn't care. He had done what he had done for the things he believed in. War was war; sacrifices were necessary. Everyone wanted a good, free society, but no one was prepared to pay for it.

Would they remember that he had let the boy live? Would they see a spark of goodness in that? Probably not.

But it didn't matter.

He would know that he wasn't a monster.

★ ★ ★

Torkel, Billy and Jennifer jumped out of the car and drew their guns. It was Jennifer's first time. She gripped it with two hands and kept it pointed at the ground. Between the barracks, in the far corner of the yard, they could see uniformed officers examining the body of a man who couldn't possibly be Charles Cederkvist, judging by his appearance. There was no trace of Charles or the boy. They started searching the area around the nearest buildings, but soon realised they would have to call for backup. The helicopter was circling, its powerful searchlights constantly sweeping across the ground.

'Spread out,' Torkel instructed Billy and Jennifer. They started to move along the dark, dilapidated buildings on the right, with the forest on their left. Jennifer could see Billy up ahead, then he turned left and disappeared. She kept going; the darkness seemed somehow thicker in front of her. More buildings – old ammunition stores, if she remembered rightly from the map. The beam of her torch lit the way as she crept along the stony track, listening hard. She could hear the voices of the uniformed officers behind her, growing fainter as she got closer to the stores. Then she heard something else, from the forest on her right. She stopped and swung around, shining her torch among the trees. The sound came again, slightly further away this time; definitely someone or something on the move. Jennifer followed the line of the trees with the light and picked out a figure dressed in black just metres away.

'Don't move!' she yelled, but her instruction had the opposite effect. The man started to run. Jennifer lost sight of him, but set off at speed, shining her torch among the trees. After a few seconds she saw him again; he had increased the distance between them. She kept going, doing her best to train the beam on him all the time.

He was about ten metres ahead of her when he ran out onto the road and increased his speed even more. Jennifer was running as fast as she was able, while calling for backup via the two-way radio clipped to her shoulder. Now she could see where the fleeing figure was heading; there was a car down by the ammunition stores. The torchlight was reflected in the glass of its headlamps.

'Stop!' she yelled, without much hope of being obeyed this time either. He didn't even slow down. Jennifer could feel the adrenaline giving her that extra power; this was what she had longed for. Action. Instant decisions. The chase, the excitement. This was why she had become a police officer.

When the man, who she assumed was Charles Cederkvist, had almost reached the car, there was a flash and the locks opened with a click. He was fast. She didn't slow down, in spite of her slightly laboured breathing. He reached the car and opened the driver's door. Then something weird happened. He stopped. Stood there behind the door as if he was posing for a photograph. Jennifer stopped too and took aim.

'Raise your hands and step away from the car,' she said, edging forward. Charles didn't move. She couldn't see his hands. She repeated her instruction. Where were the others? Charles still didn't move.

'Raise your hands and step away from the car,' she said for the third time. Why didn't he just give up? This was like her dream. The hunt was over. She was armed. He was supposed to feel beaten, outmanoeuvred, finished. He was supposed to give up. Jennifer lowered her gaze. There was a chance she might be able to hit his feet under the door, or his left shoulder above it. Maybe. But she didn't really want to shoot; the best thing would be if she could get him to surrender.

She realised that definitely wasn't his intention when he suddenly raised one hand, rested it on the door and fired two shots. Jennifer threw herself to one side; Cederkvist leapt into the car and sped away with a screech of tyres. Jennifer had to roll out of the way to avoid being run over.

She saw the red rear-lights disappear, then she saw Billy illuminated by the headlights for a second before he broke into a run, shouting and swearing.

He jumped into their car, started the engine, backed out and gave chase while calling the patrol car on the radio. He put his foot to the floor; he could just see the red lights of Charles's car up ahead on the narrow, winding track from time to time. Billy changed down; he wasn't good at everything, but not many people could beat him when it came to driving. He raced through the night, all his senses on full alert. The headlights illuminated trees, bushes, signs flashing by and vanishing in the darkness behind him. He was getting closer; his success spurred him on even more. The helicopter's searchlight fastened on Charles's car and Billy pushed even harder; he wanted to end it here where there was no traffic, rather than taking the pursuit out onto the main roads.

He was getting closer and closer, and seconds later he caught up. It was impossible to overtake; the track was too narrow. Billy was only about a metre behind, slightly worried in case Charles slammed on the brakes. If he did that, Billy would end up in the back seat of Charles' car, but at the moment his quarry was showing no sign of slowing down.

Suddenly the lights of the car ahead picked out a road sign warning of a sharp bend to the left, and Billy saw his chance. He moved a fraction closer, and when Charles braked to take the bend, Billy changed down again, wrenched the wheel to the left and accelerated. He caught Charles's car by the back wheel. The rear of the car swung outwards, and Billy thought he could see Charles trying to regain control. In vain. Billy stamped on the brake and watched as the other car left the road and turned over on the field below. He quickly undid his seatbelt and got out.

★ ★ ★

Charles quickly realised two things.

He wasn't unconscious.

The car was upside down.

A third realisation hit him as soon as he tried to move.

He was in pain and he was bleeding.

He tried to orientate himself. The helicopter was still circling, holding the car in the beam of its searchlight, which made it easier for him. He could see his gun lying over by the passenger window, and reached for it.

It was over now.

The business of the two Afghan men had grown into a hydra. Every time he chopped off one head, two more grew in its place. He couldn't carry on. It was over. He tightened his grip on the gun and managed to push open one of the doors. Laboriously he started crawling out.

Billy was on his way down the slope when he saw movement from the car, which had ended up about ten metres away from the track. He drew his gun, undid the safety catch and kept it pointing downwards.

Charles emerged; he was bleeding heavily and his clothes were badly torn.

Billy edged closer.

As Charles grabbed hold of the car to get to his feet, Billy saw the gun in his hand and raised his own weapon.

'Drop the gun!' he yelled above the noise of the hovering helicopter. Charles was still trying to stand up straight, giving no indication of whether he had heard or not.

'Drop the gun!' Billy roared as loud as he could. Charles was on his feet; he wobbled, then slowly turned to face Billy. The scene was suddenly lit up even more brightly as the patrol car arrived, its headlights picking out Charles Cederkvist as he deliberately raised his gun and pointed it straight at Billy.

Billy fired two shots.

Both penetrated the heart.

Charles's dead body fell to the ground.

Night, darkness.

The desk lamp facing the wall was the only source of light in the room; Sebastian and Torkel were sitting in the gloom, their bodies casting long shadows on the walls. The wind was rattling the windows.

If Sebastian had been a drinker he would have had a glass of whisky in his hand to complete the picture; Torkel was drinking beer straight out of the bottle. He was on his second or third.

'It's a long time since we sat like this,' Torkel said, breaking the silence.

'We've never sat like this,' Sebastian replied, 'and if you're going to start being revoltingly nostalgic, I'm going home.'

Torkel smiled and took a swig of his beer. He thought Sebastian had had a different attitude to the job and the team this time, but perhaps he hadn't changed too much.

'Why haven't you gone home already?' he asked.

'Why haven't you?'

'I'm lonely,' Torkel said honestly. 'I don't like being at home these days.'

He fell silent, and Sebastian realised he was expected to react in some way. He had no interest whatsoever in hearing about Torkel's emotional life, so he chose to answer the original question, divert the focus from anything personal.

'I'm angry. Charles Cederkvist wasn't behind the disappearance of Hamid Khan and Said Balkhi, or the execution of Adam and his family.'

Torkel nodded in agreement.

'But he was involved.'

Sebastian grunted. 'So what do you think happened?'

Torkel leaned back, had another drink, and thought about the question in silence for a few seconds.

'I think,' he said slowly, 'that the CIA were here, and they either took the two men with them, or killed them. I think military intelligence knew about it, and Charles asked his brother to shut down the investigation, but Adam found out too much and was murdered up in Jämtland.'

'By Patricia Wellton?'

'Yes. But why someone then killed her . . . I don't know.'

'Charles is dead. Do you think he's the only one we're going to be able to link to this?' There was no mistaking the displeasure in Sebastian's voice.

Torkel leaned forward, resting his elbows on his knees, and studied the man opposite, the man he still wanted to call his friend.

'I thought you didn't care about all that conviction/punishment stuff. The destination is nothing, the road is everything. Isn't that what you usually say?'

'That doesn't mean I want them to get away with it,' Sebastian said acidly.

'But sometimes they do,' Torkel said in a matter-of-fact tone, leaning back on the sofa.

'Besides, the road was so fucking boring this time,' Sebastian went on in an attempt to explain his smouldering irritation. 'Billy shot the only person who was remotely interesting.'

'You might have enjoyed it more if you'd been around all the time,' Torkel replied with a teasing smile.

'I had other fish to fry.'

Torkel sat up straight.

'How is Vanja – have you heard from her?'

Sebastian shook his head. 'She hasn't answered her phone all day.'

'She took the FBI rejection very hard,' Torkel said pensively.

'She's a strong person.'

'She's certainly very good at giving that impression, but I think on top of the business with her father, this could almost break her.'

Sebastian's irritation was tempered with a sense of unease, and perhaps something he couldn't recall having felt for a very long time: guilt. It was definitely time to change the subject.

'We know a lot,' he said, going back to the original topic of conversation and hoping Torkel would follow him. 'Lennart Stridh must have colleagues; I could leak the story to them.'

Torkel shook his head and leaned forward yet again as if to confide in his colleague. Sebastian didn't like it at all.

'Do you know why I'm where I am, and why I hang on in there, year after year?'

'No – it's never crossed my mind,' Sebastian said candidly.

'It's because I know when to step back. Choose your battles, Sebastian. Fight the ones you can win.'

'That's not really my style.'

'It makes life easier.'

'And more boring. Speaking of boring . . .'

He raised his arm in an exaggerated gesture, looked at his watch and got to his feet. Torkel smiled and stood up as well.

'I'm leaving too; there's something I need to do.'

In spite of everything that had happened, it was obviously impossible to wind Torkel up today. Perhaps that was his way of dealing with the frustration: with a smile. Sebastian picked up his jacket and headed for the door; Torkel switched off the lamp.

'How high up do you think it goes?'

'I'm not interested. We'll never know.'

'And you can live with that?'

'Yes, and so can you.'

They went down in the lift in silence. Torkel was right, of course. Sebastian could live with it, just as he had to live with everything else.

The police officer had just left. Shibeka hadn't recognised him; his name was Torkel Höglund, and apparently he was in charge of something called Riksmord. He had been warm and engaging and had asked how Mehran was getting on, what the doctors had said; he had seemed genuinely interested. However, when they got to what had happened and what they actually knew, the words were depressingly familiar.

They didn't know much. They didn't dare speculate.

They were good at words. But not at the truth.

Or perhaps they realised the price was far too high. Maybe it was that simple, and they were wiser than her. In spite of what everyone said about freedom and openness, maybe there were things that were best left undisturbed. She had almost lost her son because she had failed to understand that; was it worth it?

Never.

But could she really keep quiet? Right now, sitting by a hospital bed with her son in plaster, the choice was very straightforward. But in three months? Six months? When the questions came back to haunt her?

She didn't know if she could do it.

She took Mehran's hand. The colour was beginning to return to his face, probably thanks to the strong analgesics he had been given. His eyes were more beautiful than ever. Hamid's eyes.

'Mum?' he said quietly.

'Yes?'

'They know more than they're saying. They must do.'

'Don't think about that now. I thought I was never going to see you again.'

She leaned forward, wanting to hold him tight, never let him go, but she knew it would hurt his bruised and battered body. She squeezed his hand more tightly instead. Mehran looked at her sadly.

'I'm sorry I didn't tell you what I was going to do.'

'You don't ever need to apologise,' she whispered. 'If anyone should say sorry, it's me.'

'For what?'

'For dragging you into all this.'

'You don't ever need to apologise either. Never again.'

Those lovely eyes filled with tears.

'He's dead, Mum. He was murdered.'

'I know. I think I've always known.'

'But we don't know how. Or why.'

'We can talk about it later – whether the how and the why are really important.'

They fell silent. Mehran gazed at his mother, and a thought came into his head. Simple. Self-evident. But he couldn't remember ever putting it into words. No doubt he had assumed that she knew, that it didn't need saying.

'I love you, Mum.'

She couldn't stop herself this time. She stood up and gave him a big hug, which he loved even though it hurt.

'Can you tell me about him?' he said softly when she had sat down again.

'About Hamid?'

'There's so much I don't know. I didn't want to know until now; I always thought it would be too painful.'

'I understood that, Mehran.'

He took a deep breath and went on: 'But I was wrong, I realised that today. He lives on through our memories, gives us strength. Those of us who are left.'

Shibeka smiled at him. Memories. There were so many. So many. At last she had someone to share them with.

Alexander Söderling had had a good morning. He had allowed himself a lie-in and had breakfast with the family. When they had gone off to school and work, he had settled down with his iPad and glanced through the newspapers. No link between the events out at Almnäs and the bodies on the mountain, or two missing Afghan men. Nor between Charles and the car accident that ended Lennart Stridh's life. The boy had survived with a broken leg, but Alexander assumed that someone had been smart enough to make it clear that under certain circumstances it was best to keep one's mouth shut. It looked as if they were going to be OK. Veronica Ström had kept her promise when she said she was going to take care of everything.

Alexander left the house at 9.15 and went to the car. He usually left early so that he could beat the rush hour; today it would take him at least an hour to get to work, but that was fine. He unlocked the Audi as he was walking down the path. He glanced over at the extensive lawns, which were covered in leaves. Bloody neighbours – couldn't they get rid of those huge maples? It was bad enough that they stole the sun from his garden in the summer, but in the autumn 90 per cent of their leaves ended up on his side of the fence. More than once he had toyed with the idea of going round there one night and hammering a few copper nails into the trunks, but how long would it take before the fuckers died? Years, probably. If it worked at all. Maybe it was just a myth. A chainsaw would work, he knew that for sure. It was tempting. What would the consequences be? A fine? Having to pay compensation? The odd article in the press? It might be worth it; the neighbours wouldn't be able to resurrect the fuckers if he chopped them down.

He opened the car door, tossed in his briefcase and sat down. He felt a sharp pain in his lower back, like a wasp sting or . . . He slid his hand behind him, pricked himself again. A pin. How the hell had a pin got into the upholstery? Where had it come from? He was just about to get out and see if he could remove it when he noticed something was wrong.

His heart was racing.

Not beating faster, not starting to pick up speed. Racing. He slumped back and tried to gain control of his breathing. He had to relax. Deep breaths. But it was no good; his body was running on autopilot. The beating of his heart was pounding in his ears, and he had a pain in his chest. He realised he was about to have a heart attack. There was no way his heart could cope with this level of strain for very long. He pressed both hands against the horn, hoping to alert someone. It didn't work. He thumped the button. Not a sound. The cramp in his chest got worse. The veins in his neck were throbbing. He had to get help, and fast. But from whom? The quiet residential area was more or less deserted at this time of day.

Across the road, about twenty metres away, there were two men sitting in a car. A dark-red Volkswagen Alexander had never seen before. He tried to attract their attention. Waved his hands, tapped the windscreen. That was the best he could do; he wouldn't be able to get out even if he managed to open the door.

Was it his imagination, or were the two men watching him? The one with red hair definitely was. It was difficult to decide about the other one, because he was wearing sunglasses. Aviators. Why weren't they doing anything? As his heart threatened to burst out of his chest, he suddenly understood.

His final thought, just after his heart had stopped beating, wasn't about Annika or the children, strangely enough. It was about Veronica Ström and the fact that he now knew exactly what she meant when she said she would take care of everything.

Billy popped two slices of bread in the toaster. Went over to the fridge and took out butter, cheese and marmalade, which he placed on the tray on the kitchen island. Switched on the kettle. Folded the omelette in half and left it on the warming plate. Got two mugs out of the cupboard above the sink. There was no rush; he was suspended from duty again, for the second time in just a few months. It didn't look good, of course. The press would go to town if they found out, but so far he had been lucky. There had been surprisingly little publicity about what had happened out at Almnäs.

Billy couldn't stop thinking about it, however.

Charles getting out of the car. A gun pointing straight at Billy. Could he have done anything differently? Aimed for the shoulder or leg, for example? Put him out of action? His memories of the incident weren't 100 per cent crystal clear, but one thing he did remember with painful clarity: the feeling of anticipation as he made his way down the slope and approached the car.

Torkel would speak up for him, of course. Charles Cederkvist was a highly trained intelligence officer who had drawn a gun on Billy at a distance of only a few metres. Even though he was injured, it was highly likely that he represented a lethal threat. There were plenty of witnesses. No, he wasn't particularly worried about the internal investigation. Not at all, in fact. What was eating away at him was that even if he didn't recall everything that had led up to the shot, he did remember the feeling immediately afterwards. A wave of warmth had flooded his body when he saw Charles go down. More endorphins than adrenaline, he was sure of it. A sense of well-being. It was crazy, but the only thing he could compare it with was the way he felt after sex. Really good sex.

The kettle switched itself off and he poured water into the two mugs, dropped a teabag in each. Flipped the omelette onto a plate and added it to the tray along with the runny honey. He contemplated the tray with satisfaction; he hadn't forgotten anything. Yes he had – the toast. He wrapped it in a clean tea towel. Maya's influence on him extended to all areas of his life, but she might well have had the greatest effect on his diet and what he could do in a kitchen, he thought. He went into the hallway, got a key out of his jacket pocket, placed it next to the butter knife, then picked up the tray and went into the bedroom.

Maya was sleeping on her left side. A little dribble of saliva ran from the corner of her mouth onto the pillow; Billy even found that adorable. She was good for him. Right now she was really good for him. At first it had been a bit difficult; he had believed she would think less of him if he was the kind of person who was perfectly satisfied with the way things were at work, while she had believed he wanted her to help him change his life. That was why he had clashed with Vanja. He had sorted it out now, with both of them. More with Maya than with Vanja, he had to admit.

He woke her gently; she was wide awake at once as always. It was as if she had an on/off switch: bright as a button first thing in the morning, fast asleep in two seconds at night. She sat up, discreetly wiping her mouth. Billy carefully put down the tray and joined her.

'You're a star,' she said, giving him a kiss before she started her breakfast.

As she picked up the butter knife, she stopped mid-movement. Put it down and picked up the key.

'What's this?'

'It's a key.'

'I thought you didn't want to.'

'I thought so too.'

Cautiously, to avoid upsetting the tray, she leaned over and gave him a hug. He hugged her back, for a long time. When he was here, he was the person he wanted to be. Maya didn't know the other Billy, the one who felt good after he had killed someone. Only Jennifer knew that Billy. Could he move in with Maya without telling her? What would happen if he did tell her? Jennifer hadn't reacted particularly strongly, but then she was a police officer herself, and she wasn't going to move in with him.

' . . . in the spring.'

Billy realised Maya had murmured something in his ear. He broke away.

'Sorry? What??'

'Now we can get married in the spring.'

Billy couldn't say a word; he couldn't even manage a smile. Maya, however, was grinning.

'I was just joking! I was joking, darling!'

She put her hands on his cheeks and kissed him on the mouth. His phone rang; he slid out of bed and picked it up. It was Vanja.

She was pleased to see him.

He was concerned about her; she could see that when he walked into the room. In spite of the fact that she was dressed and sitting up in bed, this was a hospital and she was a patient. She reassured him; she was only there for tests and a discussion about a kidney transplant. She was the donor, so there was nothing to worry about.

He pulled a chair over to the bed and started to fill her in on what had happened since she left them. He told her he had moved in with Maya, but spent most of the time updating her on the case.

'You had no choice,' Vanja said when he reached the part about shooting Charles Cederkvist dead.

'I know,' he lied.

She took his hand; she could see that the gesture surprised him. Sebastian had said she couldn't do anything about their disagreement, that the ball was in Billy's court, but she had to try. Besides, her opinion of Sebastian as a trustworthy mentor had dropped considerably of late.

'I shouldn't have said I was a better cop than you.'

'You are,' Billy said with a shrug.

'I really need a friend, and you're the best I've ever had,' she said with such candour that Billy felt himself blush.

'It's cool, I am your friend, forget about that other stuff.'

Vanja smiled at him with so much warmth and relief that he had to make a real effort not to look away. Her phone started vibrating on the bedside table. Billy picked it up, grateful for the diversion, and glanced at the display.

'Sebastian.'

'Ignore it,' she said. Billy put it down, wondering what was going on.

Sebastian. Vanja realised she needed to share with someone. If she kept it bottled up inside, it would consume her. She had to confide in a friend.

'I think Sebastian . . .'

She hesitated, knowing how ridiculous it would sound when she said it out loud. Billy would think she'd gone mad. There was no doubt about it; she placed heavy demands on her friends.

'This business with my dad, and the fact that I didn't get onto the FBI programme,' she began, speaking slowly and choosing her words with care.

'Yes?'

'I think Sebastian had something to do with both of those things.'

Billy's expression told her that she sounded just as crazy as she had feared.

'Why on earth would Sebastian be involved?' he asked her, with every justification.

'I don't know. I've thought about it, and the best I can come up with is that he's sick. He wants to ruin my life, for some strange reason.'

Billy nodded to hide his confusion. It was hard to reconcile what Vanja was saying with his own speculation about Sebastian. Why would he want to hurt Vanja if he was her father?

'That sounds a bit . . . crazy.'

'That's why he's getting away with it,' she said as calmly and sincerely as she could. 'It's so crazy that nobody could possibly believe he's done it. I think he's a psychopath.'

What could he say? The door opened and a doctor came in, much to Billy's relief.

'You can go home,' Dr Shahab said to Vanja.

'OK – when shall I come back?'

'You don't need to come back. We can't proceed with you as a donor; your kidney isn't a match.'

Vanja didn't understand a thing; it was as if he had suddenly started speaking a foreign language.

'Of course it is. I'm his daughter.'

'I'm sorry.' The doctor spread his hands apologetically. 'Unfortunately this kind of thing happens sometimes.'

'What's her blood group?' she heard Billy ask.

'A lot of things have to match up, not just the blood group.'
Which wasn't an answer at all. 'In our professional opinion, the risk
of rejection is too great.'

'I'm group O,' Vanja told Billy.

'And what about your dad?'

'I don't know.'

She turned to Dr Shahab, whose eyes slid away. He scratched his
chin. Vanja's instinct as a police officer kicked in. He was hiding
something.

'What's my father's blood group?' she demanded.

'I can't tell you that; it's confidential.'

'He's my father. I'll find out one way or the other within the
next fifteen minutes, so you might as well tell me now.'

Omid Shahab hesitated. He wasn't supposed to give this kind of
information to anyone, whether they were a relative or not. At the
same time, he had no doubt that Vanja would find out in considerably less than fifteen minutes.

'He's AB,' he said quietly.

Vanja understood the implications immediately.

Even if she didn't remember the genetic crossing scheme from
school, her knowledge had been regularly updated thanks to years
of working with Ursula and her analysis of crime scenes.

A parent with blood group AB couldn't produce a child with
group O.

She couldn't process the implications of what she had just heard.
It was too big. Too much. Billy leaned over and gave her a hug. She
clung to him, afraid that she might fall apart.

Billy didn't say anything, but his mind was racing.

He wondered what Sebastian Bergman's blood group was.

He was pretty sure it wasn't AB.

Ellinor took off her name badge and placed it in one of the small metal cupboards lining the wall in the staff room at Åhlén's. She picked up her bag and coat and closed the door. The bag was heavier than usual, or was she just imagining it? Eight hundred and seventy-four grams wasn't very much, but she thought she could feel the difference. Perhaps it was psychological, like when people thought they were on medication and felt better, even though they were actually taking a placebo. She slipped her bag over her shoulder – it was definitely heavier – and walked towards the staff exit. Said goodbye to three of her colleagues on the way; they were going out for a drink and had asked if Ellinor would like to join them, but she had declined.

She had other plans.

She emerged onto Mäster Samuelsgatan and fastened her coat. Looked around. First of all she would go and get something to eat. Jensens Bøfhus was handy, just a few hundred metres away. Holding the lapels of her coat together against the wind, she set off. There were quite a few people around, but no one took any notice of her.

No one knew she was a sick home-help that Sebastian had sex with.

No one knew her bag was a little heavier today.

No one knew. Yet.

There was no hurry. She would take her time over a nice cut of meat, have a glass of wine, maybe two. Finish off with a coffee and one of those little truffles, if they had any. She had plenty of time, and the metro station was nearby if she decided not to walk to Sebastian's apartment afterwards.

The place was spotless.

Torkel usually tried to make a bit more effort with the apartment when he wasn't actively involved in a case. It wasn't a lost cause this time, but he had decided to do a big clean, partly to pass the time, give him something to do.

He tidied things away, vacuumed, dusted, took the rugs and seat cushions outside and beat them, changed the beds, shook out the duvets. He opened the wardrobe and considered giving everything a good airing, but decided that was a step too far.

It was eight o'clock by the time Torkel finished. He had a shower, sat down on his dust-free sofa and switched on the TV, then realised he couldn't be bothered, and switched it off again. He went into the kitchen and opened the fridge; he wasn't hungry. He got himself a beer and sat down with the morning paper. Fifteen minutes later, the phone rang.

'Evening – it's Axel Weber from *Expressen*.'

'Evening.'

'Sorry to call so late, but I was wondering if you've got anywhere with those bodies on the mountain?'

At first the question surprised Torkel, but then he remembered that only he and the team knew whom they had found; the official version was that they had been unable to identify the bodies.

Choose your battles.

He gave Weber the official version and hung up.

With regard to the shooting in Södertälje, there wasn't even an official version. Military intelligence had embargoed the whole thing, still refusing to confirm or deny that Charles Cederkvist had been a part of the organisation. If Torkel had interpreted the documents in front of him correctly, the story would be leaked in a day or so, then completely disappear. No trial to follow, no grieving relatives to speak out, no suggestion that the incident was gang related. Without those ingredients, a fatal shooting in the Södertälje area wouldn't be news for very long.

After he had ended the call with Weber, he sat there for a few moments with the phone in his hand.

Axel Weber, crime correspondent.

Could be a pain in the arse, but he was good at his job.

If he found out the identity of the bodies in the grave, he would immediately make the link with Charles Cederkvist. He might even connect them with the dead man who had been found at Almnäs, who was apparently known as Joseph, and that could lead him to the case of the two missing Afghan men, Hamid and Said.

He had met Hamid's widow and son today. Lied to them. Fudged the truth. Made them understand that with both Charles and Joseph dead, they weren't going to get anywhere. No one was going to get anywhere.

But then Weber called.

Choose your battles. Or get someone else to fight them for you, he thought as he dialled a number.

'Good evening, it's Torkel Höglund from Riksmord . . .'

Five minutes later he ended the call. He had followed the correct procedure and informed the local police who had originally sought their help of the final outcome of the investigation. No one could object to that. They had identified the four remaining bodies, and the case was now closed. He assumed that Hedvig Hedman and her team wouldn't pass on that kind of important information . . .

Satisfied, with a feeling of having done something illicit that he hadn't experienced since he was a teenager, he got up and wandered around the apartment. The evening was still comparatively young; he wanted to go out.

He called his daughters; did they fancy going to the cinema? They could choose the film. They were pleased to hear from him, but they were doing something else. Another time. Torkel toyed with the idea of calling Ursula, but couldn't come up with a spurious yet convincing reason, so instead he poured himself a whisky and switched on the TV again. Drinking alone wasn't a good idea, but if he didn't do that, when the hell was he supposed to have a drink? He knocked back the first glass and poured himself another.

★ ★ ★

Ursula was sitting in the kitchen with a glass of wine as Sebastian served up the food he had just been out to buy. If anyone who knew about her history with Sebastian had seen her now, they would have wondered what the hell she was doing. The fourth time in a week. Sometimes Ursula wondered too, but she had found the word that summed up the time she spent with Sebastian: undemanding.

That was what she needed at the moment: an escape, a diversion, silliness – she didn't know what it was, but she enjoyed Sebastian's company. She could relax. He would never get the idea that it could turn into something more, and nor would she. He would never say 'I love you' – or at least he wouldn't mean it. It was better than being alone, but it was on her terms. She was going in with her eyes wide open. He wasn't monogamous, and neither was she. She had loved him once upon a time, and he had let her down, but that was because she had had unreasonable expectations.

About togetherness. Fidelity. Life.

Besides which, he was good company. Apart from the fact that they had a lot to talk about, something happened to him when he was alone with a woman. He became more sensitive, seemed more open, more interested. She was under no illusions that this had anything to do with her; no doubt he was the same whichever woman was sitting at his table. Operating purely on autopilot. He had been compulsively seducing women for so long that his brain automatically disconnected the bastard aspect of his character when he was on his own with a member of the opposite sex. Anything to get them into bed. He hadn't succeeded with Ursula this time. Not yet, she added to herself as he brought the plates over and smiled at her.

'Dinner is served,' he said.

The TV programme was still on but the bottle was more or less empty, Torkel noticed when he poured himself another glass. It hadn't been full when he started, but he had put away a fair amount. Enough to feel tipsy. On the sofa, alone in front of the TV. Pathetic. He sat up straight, feeling slightly dizzy and with a burning pain in his stomach. He ought to eat something, but there it was again: the loneliness. It was sad, cooking for one. And going out to eat alone was even sadder. His daughters had other plans for the evening, and that wasn't going to change over the next few years. He reminded himself that he must make sure he met this boyfriend – at least while he was still around; such things tended to be short-lived at that age. Wishful thinking? Yvonne had Kristoffer; what did he have? Who did he have? No one.

He thought about Sebastian.

Sebastian always had someone, whenever he wanted. If Torkel had had only a fraction of Sebastian's success with women, he would have been a happy man.

With one woman.

With Ursula.

Because that was the problem. Even if he'd been comfortable with going out and trying to meet someone, or registering with an online dating website, there was no one out there that he wanted. He knew he wanted Ursula.

Was this really a war he couldn't win? She was married, but that hadn't stopped her in the past. This business of her and Mikael finding their way back to one another was bound to be a passing phase. Mikael wasn't what Ursula wanted or needed, and she knew it. Perhaps she just needed a clearer sign from Torkel so that she would have the courage to let go, certain that he would be there to catch her. It was a bad turn of phrase; Ursula didn't need someone to catch her. She had more integrity than anyone else he could think of, but the fact remained: she didn't know how he felt about her. He could never win if he didn't enter the fray. Torkel picked up the phone and called her. He got to his feet before she answered and started pacing around the room, which made his head spin even more. How much whisky had he actually got through?'

'Ursula.'

'Hi, it's me,' he said brightly. 'Torkel,' he added, to be on the safe side.

'I can see that. How are you?'

'I'm fine. Absolutely fine.' He took a deep breath, which almost turned into a belch, but he managed to convert it into a hiccup. 'How are you?'

'I'm fine too, thanks.'

'Good.'

'Was there something you wanted?' Ursula asked after a few seconds of silence.

Torkel stopped by the window and scratched his head. He couldn't come up with anything convincing, so he told her the truth.

'No, I just wanted to talk to you.'

'OK, but things are a bit . . .'

She glanced at Sebastian, who got up and took their plates over to the dishwasher.

'I love you.'

Ursula was glad Sebastian had his back to her. She didn't quite know how she reacted, but given that she almost dropped the phone, surprised was probably an understatement. What was she supposed to say? That was definitely the last thing she had expected to hear from her boss.

'I know you've got Mikael and everything,' Torkel went on, saving her from having to respond to his declaration, 'but if you ever break up . . . I'm waiting. I love you.'

Ursula still couldn't think of anything to say. She could feel Sebastian looking at her, but didn't want to meet his gaze.

'That's nice,' she managed eventually; she had to say something. There was silence on the other end of the phone; she wanted to break it, but had no idea how. Torkel cleared his throat as if he had realised he had put her in an impossible position.

'It was stupid of me to call, but I wanted you to know.'

'I knew already.'

Torkel seemed to be in a hurry to bring the conversation to an end; she didn't think he had heard her response.

'Anyway, sorry,' he said. 'See you tomorrow.'

'See you.'

Then he was gone. Ursula slowly put down her phone as she tried to regain control of her facial expression, her thoughts and her voice. After a few seconds she looked up at Sebastian.

'That was Torkel.'

'What did he want?'

'Nothing. Work. He'd had a few drinks, I think . . .'

Sebastian obviously didn't need to know any more. He pointed to the espresso machine.

'Coffee in the living room?'

Ursula nodded and got to her feet. It would be a while before she forgot that particular conversation.

Ellinor keyed in the code, and when the door buzzed she pushed it open and walked in. She switched on the light and looked around the familiar entrance hall. No doubt he thought she was stupid. He expected her to turn up when he was on his guard. Ring the doorbell and make a scene. Bombard him with calls and text messages. But she had kept her distance. She hadn't called, hadn't sent a text, hadn't come round. She had bided her time. If Ellinor knew Sebastian, and unfortunately she thought she did, he had probably forgotten her by now. He would have congratulated himself on getting rid of her so easily, and once he had kicked her out and humiliated her, he wouldn't have given her another thought. But she was about to change that. Show him that he couldn't treat her that way. Men had tried it before.

Göran, for example.

The local defence volunteer in Aspudden.

That was how he introduced himself: Göran Jönsson, local defence volunteer. For most people the activity fell between a necessary evil and a pleasant hobby, but for Göran it was nothing less than a vocation. He really did take his duties seriously; he might well be able to save Sweden single-handed if the Russians came. It would be the Russians, Ellinor had learned. It was always the Russians.

But Göran had had to leave his beloved defence group. It was his own fault. If he hadn't threatened to hit her, she would never have felt the need to arm herself. Never taken an interest in his Glock, which weighed exactly 874 grams.

She set off up the stairs. She had run up here so many times, eager to see her darling Sebastian. It was as if she started living only when she came home to him; the rest of her days, when they were not together, were drab and colourless. She had been sure he felt

438

the same. He didn't. He never had. She reached the right floor and walked up to his door.

A spyhole. Because of her? Well, at least she had left some trace of herself in his apartment. Soon she would leave another. She had just decided how.

★ ★ ★

Sebastian poured two cups of coffee while Ursula settled down on the sofa, puffing up the cushions behind her.

'I'll stay over, if that's OK with you.'

'You don't need to ask, the bed's made up.'

'Do I have to sleep in the guest room?'

Sebastian carefully put down the coffee pot on the table, as if any sudden movement might make Ursula realise what she had just said and change her mind.

'No . . .'

Ursula nodded with satisfaction and tucked her feet up on the sofa. 'So tell me,' she said with an expectant little smile.

'Tell you what?'

'About the dream.'

Sebastian sighed deeply as he sat down in the armchair opposite her. He really had hoped this wouldn't come up again, particularly not right now, when he was already visualising what was going to happen in the bedroom in the not too distant future.

'Why do you keep on about it?'

'Why do you keep ducking and diving? If you don't tell me, I'll be spending the night in the guest room. Or I'll go home.'

Sebastian looked at her; she was still smiling, but he knew she was serious.

'You want me to confess in exchange for sex?'

'Exactly.'

'And you think this is going to work?'

'Absolutely.'

He sighed again. She knew him so well. But he didn't necessarily have to run the race in order to win the prize; Sebastian Bergman was no stranger to a little subterfuge.

'And I'll know straight away if you're lying,' Ursula said as if she had read his mind. Once again, she knew him well. Too well.

'I need a pee first.'

Ursula leaned forward and peered into her cup.

'Have you got any milk?'

'In the fridge – you know where it is.'

She raised one eyebrow, got up and went back into the kitchen.

★ ★ ★

Ellinor stood motionless on the landing, waiting. The light went out. It took a few seconds for her eyes to grow accustomed to the darkness, but then she could see the light from inside the apartment through the spyhole. She would easily be able to tell when Sebastian was looking out. He would be so surprised. If he had time.

She rang the doorbell and reached into her bag.

★ ★ ★

Sebastian was in the toilet when the doorbell rang.

'I'll get it,' Ursula called on her way back from the kitchen.

She went over to the door, and out of habit put her eye to the spyhole. Stupid, of course; whoever was out there hadn't come to see her, and she didn't know any of Sebastian's friends. To be honest, she was surprised he had friends.

It was pitch-dark in the stairwell. Whoever was out there didn't seem to have switched on the light.

★ ★ ★

Ellinor saw the pinprick of light from the hallway disappear as an eye was pressed against the spyhole on the inside. She placed the Glock against the convex lens and pulled the trigger.

Acknowledgements

As always, thanks to everyone at Norstedts: Eva, Linda, Catherine, Sara, Tulle, Zandra, Loveina and everyone else who works so hard to make sure our books are read. We really appreciate all the effort you put in.

Once again special thanks to Susanna Romanus and Peter Karlsson for your unshakeable optimism and constant support. It means a great deal to us.

Thanks to our overseas publishers for believing in us, and for your commitment to getting Sebastian out there all over the world.

Thanks once again to Rolf Lassgård for everything you have given us when it comes to the creation of Sebastian Bergman. You are a joy to exchange ideas with, and a true inspiration.

HANS:
I would particularly like to thank all the fantastic staff at St Erik's eye hospital in Stockholm, above all Dr Manoj Kakar, whose skill and vast professional expertise mean that I won't have to read Braille for the rest of my life.

Camilla Ahlgren, who has been my dear friend for the past twenty years, and who makes my life easier by taking on so much responsibility for the projects on which we work.

And of course to my family: Lotta, Sixten, Alice and Ebba. Thank you for all the love and all the laughter.

MICHAEL:
I would like to thank all my colleagues at Tre Vänner, with Jonas, Mikael, Tomas, Johan and Fredrik leading the way. My warmest thanks go, as always, to my wonderful family. You are my backbone through thick and thin. Caesar, William, Vanessa and my darling Astrid, I love you all. You are amazing, and you are the most important part of my life. A million hugs. And then some more.